Seduced by Promises

KATE S. BURNS

WARRINGTON

Danbury, Connecticut

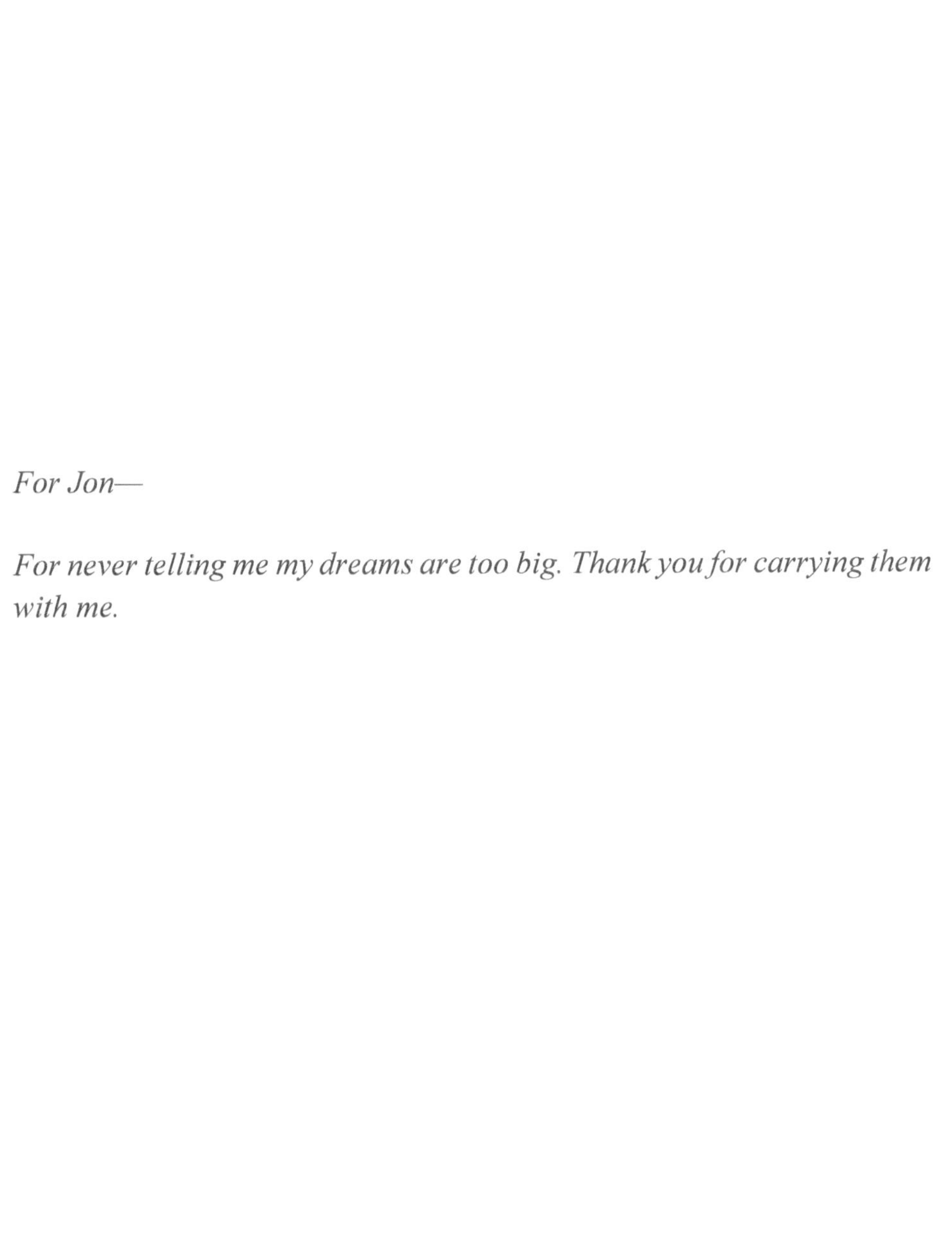

For Jon—

For never telling me my dreams are too big. Thank you for carrying them with me.

Part One:

Family

Celeste's Office

The leather of the therapist's couch creaked beneath me as I shifted, seeking comfort and finding none. I sat on the edge of the cushion, prepared to make a quick getaway. The last few years, after all, had been full of them.

Celeste Nixon's office was meant to be a sanctuary with soft lighting and muted tones, located in a quiet corner off Boylston Street. A single flickering candle sat on Celeste's desk, beside neutral wooden bookshelves and sage green walls. The smell of vanilla permeated the small office as Vivaldi's *Four Seasons* quietly announced "Spring" from the overhead speakers. It was designed to feel like a sanctuary. I wondered if I'd ever be able to trust the feeling of sanctuary again.

Celeste sat across from me, her posture relaxed. Her brown hair was streaked gray at the temples. Her gold-rimmed glasses framed eyes that were warm and patient. Her style was simple and elegant—a cream-colored blouse sat atop olive-green slacks, with matching cream-colored pumps. Her ankles were crossed and tucked to the left of the wheels on her desk chair.

Silence stretched between us with an uncomfortable void. I twisted the gold charm that hung around my neck, and I wrapped the chain around my fingers; my nervous habit I no longer realized I was doing until my fingers ached.

"Starting this process can be intimidating, Macy," Celeste said patiently. "But the hardest step was the one you took through my door today."

I offered a small nod, my copper curls bouncing and coming to rest at my collarbone. "I'll be honest. It doesn't feel like the hardest part."

"What feels like the hardest part to you?"

I sighed so deeply that it almost triggered a yawn. "I don't know how to tell my story without sounding pathetic."

Celeste didn't push the silence. Somewhere, a clock ticked away my hour as "Spring" came to an end.

"I used to think I had the world at my feet," I finally started. "For a while, I thought I was happy. But lately, my mind replays the choices I've made, the ones that led me here."

"Can you tell me more about what you mean by that?" Celeste spoke in a calm and truly curious tone—not patronizing or bored. She truly wanted to hear what I had to say.

"Um," I stuttered, and a dry laugh escaped. "I made the choices that I thought were right. The ones I thought were going to lead me to the life I wanted. Isn't that worse, sometimes?" I raked my hands through my curls and finally rested against the back of the couch. "I did this to myself."

Celeste cocked her head, and her pen paused above her notepad. "Why do you believe you did this to yourself?"

I stared at the flickering flame of the candle on Celeste's desk. "Did you ever want to believe in something so badly that you looked the other way when something was waving at you to say, 'this isn't right?'"

A slow smile stretched across Celeste's face. "I'm pretty sure we all have. On your intake form, you said you've been dealing with a lot of anxiety and—" She glanced at her notes. "—feeling haunted by your past. Can you tell me more about that?"

"Haunted is the only word I can use for it," I replied. I shrugged, a ghost of a smile playing at my lips. "It's seeing ghosts in the ordinary things. Familiar songs I used to love, the smell of a cologne hanging in the air, and random phrases. They all drag me back. I wonder sometimes if I'll ever be able to feel like I'm free."

Celeste gave me a small nod. "You will. That's what I'm here for. But in order to fully understand why you feel haunted, we will have to go back to where it all started."

I traced the lines on my jeans with my finger. Everything started the day everything ended.

Chapter One

ENDINGS

Outside Macy Walker's office window, birds chirped in the soft afternoon air. One of the first warm days of spring had settled over Manhattan, and the city shimmered with the promise of new life: buds on the trees, sunlight on the pavement, and the fresh breath of springtime that made even the most jaded New Yorker take notice.

As Friday afternoon stretched toward evening, Macy decided to take a mini-break from her end-of-week reporting. She grabbed her purse and wandered to the break area, already anticipating the teasing message she knew would be waiting from Catherine Phelps, her roommate, best friend, and relentless instigator.

Sure enough, Macy's phone lit up with a familiar taunt:

Catherine
Heyyyyy Red. Do I need my earplugs tonight?

Macy
Hey yourself. Very funny!

I think we are planning to go to a movie. Stay tuned!

But we will see who's laughing and who needs earplugs when Shane gets back from overseas, ma'am.

Catherine

Damn right you will. I'll make myself scarce then. See ya later!

Macy smiled, shaking her head. Then she saw the message from Jack.

Jack

Hey, pretty lady. Any reason we can't just stay in at your place tonight? There's something I want to talk about.

Her fingers hovered over the screen.

Macy

Sure, I don't see why not! Is everything okay?

Jack

It's fine, but it's important. I'll come over right after work, okay?

Macy

> *Oh, okayyy. I'll have something prepared for dinner then.*

Jack
Isn't that just like you :) See you then.

Macy frowned slightly. "'Isn't that just like you?' I'm not sure how to take that." She stared at the screen. "Is that meant to be cute or...?"

She wandered back to her desk with a fresh cup of coffee, trying to shake off the unease. But before she could refocus, her manager's voice called from behind her cubicle.

"Hey, Mace? Can I see you for a minute?"

Her heart jumped. "Of course, Nancy."

She stepped into the office of Nancy Chen, the woman who had been her manager for nearly seven years.

"Please close the door."

Uh oh. No conversation that began like this on a Friday afternoon ever ended well.

Nancy smiled, but it didn't reach her eyes. There was a heaviness in her expression—regret, maybe even guilt.

"Macy, I...I don't know how to tell you this, but—"

Macy held up a hand. "Nancy, are you firing me?"

"Well, not exactly," Nancy said gently. "This wasn't my decision. You know VitalSync's been expanding, and with the acquisition by OptiHealth, they're reorganizing. That means cost control and workforce reduction. I'm very sorry to tell you that your position came up for elimination."

Macy's throat began to tighten, and her heart raced as the implications of Nancy's words sank in.

"This isn't about your performance," Nancy continued. "You've always been exemplary. I fought for you. But their decision was final. I'm so sorry."

Macy stared, numb. The fear of being unemployed in New York City—with student loans and rent and no safety net—wrapped its icy grip around her chest.

"You'll have thirty days to explore your options," Nancy said. "There's a generous severance if you don't find something by then. I know this is a terrible way to end the week, but I wanted you to have the weekend to process."

Macy tried to speak, but her voice failed her.

"If there's anything I can do—recommendations, leads—I'm here. Brett in HR can help with your resume and interview prep."

Macy nodded, wiping the first tears from her eyes. "I'll be all right," she whispered, though she didn't believe it.

"You can take the rest of the day off, with pay," Nancy offered. "Beat the rush hour. Start making your plan."

Macy was already halfway to her desk, barely hearing the words. She grabbed her purse and walked out, her face blank with shock.

By the time she reached the subway tunnel, the wheels were already turning. Shock was giving way to panic. Thirty days. Thirty days to find a new job in one of the most competitive cities in the world.

And Jack wanted to talk tonight. Could it be something good? A vacation? A trip to meet his family? They'd been steady for six months. Surely, it wasn't bad news.

She tried not to dwell during the ride home. The job hunt could wait until tomorrow.

As Macy approached the stoop of their brownstone, Catherine was just stepping outside, dressed to kill in a sleek black dress with a rhinestone belt. Her auburn bob framed her freckled face, and her blue eyes sparkled with mischief.

"Hey! I'm glad I caught you," she said. "You won't believe it. Shane's deployment is ending early. He'll be back in time for Christmas!"

Macy forced a smile and hugged her friend. "That's amazing. I'm so happy for you."

"You have no idea." Catherine's forehead furrowed as she studied Macy's face. "Wait...what's wrong?"

"I'm fine!" Macy said too quickly.

"Mace, it's me. The only people who've known you longer are your family. I can tell when your smile doesn't reach your eyes. Spill it."

"It's just work stuff," Macy admitted. "I don't want to rain on your parade."

Catherine hesitated, then relented. "Okay. But call me if you need me. I'm not going anywhere fancy. Just maybe meeting up with Nina for a movie."

Macy watched her go, the warmth of spring brushing her skin, the city alive with possibility. But inside, everything was shifting.

Jack was coming over.

He had something important to say.

And Macy wasn't sure if she was ready to hear it.

Macy smiled in spite of herself. "Red, you're the only person I know who could turn visiting a friend into a fashion event."

Catherine returned the grin, already halfway down the stoop. "Don't do anything tonight that I wouldn't do...Or that Nina wouldn't!"

"That doesn't leave much if we're talking about Nina!" Macy called after her, laughing. Then she turned and climbed the stairs to their little apartment, ready to distract herself with dinner prep and the promise of a quiet night with Jack.

Cooking and cleaning had always been Macy's way of de-stressing. They were skills honed on the farm, where rhythm and routine were survival. It had made her indispensable in college. Tonight, it was her lifeline. She needed something to anchor her, something to drown out the storm of uncertainty swirling in her head.

She chose her specialty: stuffed chicken breasts and risotto. Ambitious for a Friday night, but she needed to keep her hands busy. Garlic and sage filled the air, the familiarity of the process easing the tension between her shoulders. The chicken was just coming out of the oven when Jack buzzed from downstairs.

She pressed the button to let him in, set the plates on the table, and smoothed her apron. A quiet evening. That's all she wanted.

"Something smells amazing," he said, stepping in and setting his bag down. "You didn't have to—"

"I wanted to." Macy smiled, untied her apron, pulled the pin out of her long curtain of red curls, and stepped toward him. He didn't reach for her. She let her arms hang awkwardly in the air for just a second too long before dropping them.

Her gut tightened. "What's going on? You said you had something to talk about."

Jack looked down at his shoes. "Yeah...Can we sit?"

Macy didn't move, but folded her arms in front of her chest. Her pulse pounded in her ears as she waited for him to speak.

He sighed. "Okay, we'll do this here. This is hard. You're...incredible. Kind. Thoughtful. And you've made me feel really cared for."

His words sounded mechanical and rehearsed.

"Jack," Macy said slowly, deja vu washing over her. "Are you breaking up with me?"

He winced. "I didn't want to do it like this. But yeah."

A beat passed as she let the words sink in. This couldn't be happening, not after she just lost her job, too. "You said you loved me. Just yesterday."

"I thought I did. But lately...something is different. Like we're stuck in a routine. It's too comfortable."

Macy blanched as she reached up to twist the chain around her neck. "Too comfortable?"

Jack rubbed the back of his neck and paced the small kitchen. "Look, I know how this sounds. I'm not trying to be cruel. But attraction matters. And you—well—there's something else. Some ONE else."

"*Excuse* me?"

He gestured toward her body. "Well," he stuttered. "This is harder than I thought. But, look. You used to turn heads. You had that sharp city style, you looked like you could model for a tech campaign. And now..."

Macy stared at him, hardly believing the words she was hearing.

"You've gotten...comfortable. Soft. I don't know. Then I met Amanda and...nothing's happened yet but—"

"So, you're dumping me for another woman, because I gained weight."

He recoiled as she said the words. "It's not just the weight. But yeah. I miss the spark. The fireworks."

Once again, Macy found herself too stunned to speak. The words would come later. She knew that. They always did. In bed, staring at the ceiling, turning over every moment like stones in her palm. But right now, all she could do was try not to cry.

"Get out," was all she managed.

Jack flinched at the venom in her voice. "Wait, Macy—"

She turned away, unwilling to let him see her cry. But his hand caught her elbow.

"Wait!"

"Get your miserable hands off me."

She yanked herself free and stormed into her bedroom. She tried to slam the door, but Jack shoved it open and followed her in.

"Wait, Macy!"

She spun around, green eyes blazing. "WHAT, Jack? What could you possibly have to say to me?"

He didn't flinch. Didn't apologize. "Um...my hoodie. I left it here."

Macy stared at him, slack-jawed. For once, she wished the words would come *now*. She pulled the hoodie from the drawer she'd once reserved for his things, threw it in his face, and shoved past him into the kitchen.

She heard his footsteps behind her, heard him heading toward the door. Her eyes landed on the untouched plates she'd set out so carefully. The wheels turned.

"Hey, Jack?" Her voice was suddenly sweet. Too sweet.

He turned, hand on the doorknob. Macy's face had turned to stone.

"Don't forget your dinner," she spat icily.

Before she could think better of it, before he could step fully into the hallway, she launched a chicken breast at his head. It hit its mark: between his eyes. He gasped, stumbling back.

A spoonful of risotto followed before he could duck out of the way.

"Can't let a gentleman go hungry. Right, Jack?" She couldn't stop the fury flowing out of her. "Oh, and you look thirsty. Can I offer you a bottle of wine, sir?"

She reached behind her for the Chardonnay she'd used for the risotto. Jack turned and raced down the stairs.

Macy slammed the door and leaned against it, clutching the bottle to her chest. "That was a close call," she muttered. "Throwing this would've been a horrible waste of wine."

The apartment rang with emptiness.

Despair for everything she lost today burned in her chest. Hot. Bright. She didn't want a glass. Only the bottle would do. She wanted to stop feeling, just for a while.

Maybe she wouldn't find peace at the bottom of the Chardonnay, but she intended to look.

With every swig, the anger dulled into a void. Macy stared at the mess by the door, the ruined dinner, considering the words Jack had left behind.

It's gotten too comfortable...You used to turn heads...There's someone else.

Even worse than his cruelty was her silence. She'd had no comeback. No defense. She envied people like Ethan. Her brother was always quick with a retort. The bullies at school, who never left a conversation without the last word. Macy never had that gift. Her perfect responses always came hours too late.

Tonight was no different.

Though maybe, this time, her dinner service counted for something.

"Well fed," she muttered. "Don't worry, Jack. My fridge will feel relieved it no longer has to carry your weight along with mine."

She laughed, bitter and breathless, feeling the wine take hold.

"I'll give you fireworks, Jack. You couldn't light a spark with a flamethrower. Not that there's ever a grand finale when there are fireworks with you."

The responses were coming now. It was too late, but they came.

"My sympathies to Amanda."

So did the tears.

Her mind replayed the breakup. Then the meeting with Nancy. Two blows in one day. Two people confirming what she already feared: that she wasn't enough.

Not for Jack.

Not for VitalSync.

Not for the life she thought she was building.

Her phone buzzed on the table, pulling her from the fog. It was Catherine.

Catherine

Hey, just heading out from Nina's. Brian was working late, so we just had a drink. How's your movie with Mr. Redford?

Macy stared at the screen, thumbs hovering. She couldn't face it. Not yet. She set the phone down without replying. It wasn't like her to leave Catherine on read, but explaining what had happened tonight, she didn't have the words. Not even in text.

Instead, she cleaned up the mess by the door, the remnants of her fury still scattered across the floor. Once the kitchen was spotless, she took the bottle of wine to the living room, curled up on the couch, and pulled her favorite fleece blanket to her chin.

Catherine, tenacious as ever, refused to be ignored.

Catherine
Okay, what's wrong?

Macy chuckled softly. No one read her like Catherine. She flipped aimlessly through streaming services, trying to distract herself. But the ache in her chest wouldn't quit, and doom-scrolling through Netflix wasn't helping.

Half an hour later, the lock turned in the door.

Catherine walked in with a carton of Ben & Jerry's Churray for Churros! and two spoons. She didn't bother with hello. She simply dropped her bag and sat beside Macy.

"Okay, spill. What happened?"

Macy blinked; the words stuck in her throat. "Jack happened. How did you know?"

"You never leave me on read. Out with it. What did that piece of shit do?"

Macy gestured toward the kitchen. "I made dinner like the perfect girlfriend. He told me that's 'just like me'—that he loves how taken care of he feels. Then he broke up with me. Said I've gained weight. Said the sparks are gone."

Catherine's eyes darkened, her cheeks flushed with fury. "He said fucking *what*?"

Her mouth opened and closed, speechless. Macy couldn't help but laugh. Catherine's reaction mirrored her own.

Macy tore the lid off the ice cream and dug in. "And there's more. He's met someone he likes better. Now here I sit, making it worse. He's not attracted to me because I'm boring and predictable, and I got chubby. Yet, I'm stuffing my face with ice cream."

Catherine snatched Macy's spoon, swatted her hand with it, then dug in herself. "You stop that. I hope you told him off."

Macy gave a wobbly smile. "Well, I threw a chicken breast at him. And risotto."

Catherine choked on her spoonful. "Seriously? Mace, that's hilarious."

"I had the wine in hand, too, ready to go. But the coward ran before I could follow through."

"Good," Catherine muttered. "What a waste of wine that would've been. He deserved it, though. And whatever else you could've grabbed."

Macy stared at the floor. "Why do my thoughts always freeze up when it matters? It's always hours later when I think of all the things I should've said."

Catherine tilted her head, the mischievous twinkle returning. "Macy. You assaulted him with chicken. If that's not standing up for yourself, I don't know what is."

Macy smiled, but a tear still leaked from her eyes. "I suppose. But that's not even all. I got laid off today."

Catherine's mouth fell open. "Wait, what?"

"Yeah. VitalSync's merging with OptiHealth. Cost cuts. I'm one of them. Now I have thirty days to figure out what's next."

"Oh, Macy..." Catherine's voice softened. She placed a warm hand on Macy's.

"I just...don't know how to move forward," Macy whispered. "I thought I was finally getting somewhere since I left my parents' farm. But now, in one day, it's all gone. And I feel like I've just been treading water this whole time."

"You're not treading water," Catherine said firmly. "Look at what you've built. You're resourceful. Capable. You've got a degree from Columbia, for Christ's sake, seven years of experience, and a hell of a lot of grit. You'll land on your feet. And you won't be doing it alone."

"I'm supposed to go home next week," Macy said, flat. "My parents never wanted me to come to New York at all. It wasn't until I got the scholarship offer at Columbia that they started treating me like a member of the family again. Now I've got to go home with my tail between my legs and explain to them what I'm going to do about a job. I've also got no Jack to use as an excuse not to stay there in Iowa."

Catherine took a deep breath, her smile sympathetic. "Mace. You don't owe them any explanation."

"Somewhere deep down, I think I know that." She twirled the remote on the tabletop. "Just every time I see them, I'm that obedient little mouse they want me to be. I think I used up the only time I could stand up to them when I fought for my choice to come here at all."

"You could always bring Nina with you. You know she'd love a weekend away from Brian, and you can throw her in front of your parents as a buffer."

Macy laughed and rolled her eyes. "Imagine my perfect cousin mucking stalls with me on the old farm in her stilettos and silk blouse!"

After a pause, Catherine nudged her. "Okay then, Red. Here's the plan. Tomorrow, we get bagels—the everything kind you love—and the tallest lattes they make. Then we sit down with your resume and fix this."

Macy gave her a wan smile. "Bagels and job hunting. Sounds thrilling."

"Hey, it's got to beat throwing food at your ex."

Macy giggled, the sound fragile but real. "Maybe a little."

They sat in silence, the flicker of Macy's comfort episode of *Doctor Who* casting soft light across the room. The familiar dialogue washed over her, a balm for the chaos of the day.

The ending credits rolled, and Catherine grabbed the half-empty bottle of Chardonnay while Macy scraped the last bite of ice cream from the carton. Catherine raised the bottle with a wry smile.

"Here's to chicken breasts and fresh starts."

Macy clinked her spoon against the glass. "And here's to the women smart enough to throw the chicken at the man, but not the wine."

Catherine laughed, and Macy joined her. It was Macy's first real laugh since her meeting with Nancy, and it lingered in the air like a promise.

Catherine disappeared down the hall, and Macy turned off the TV, tidied the living room, and made her way to her bedroom. She didn't bother changing. Utterly drained, she collapsed onto the bed, fully clothed.

She had lived in the city for nearly ten years, and for the first time since she got here, she was starting over. She stared at the ceiling for a moment, then closed her eyes, fighting for sleep that didn't want to come.

Chapter Two

HOMECOMING

Outside the window of the Uber, South Dakota rolled past in a rush of color and motion—fields rippling with spring flowers, flashes of white picket fences, tiny villages tucked into green creases of land. Macy leaned her cheek against the glass, letting the hum of tires fill the silence inside her head.

Jack was supposed to have the seat beside her on the flight home. Instead, she found comfort in the empty row and the solitude that went with it. A short layover in Chicago gave her just enough time to try deep-dish pizza and contemplate her life over melted cheese and regret. By the time her plane touched down in Sioux Falls, the exhaustion had settled into her bones.

The final leg, this Uber ride across endless farmland, was the quietest stretch yet. Despite its speed, it dragged along. The scenery offered a stark contrast to the chaos she'd left behind: rolling fields, animals grazing in early dusk, wind turbines spinning like patient watchers.

Macy had brought her laptop, hoping to attack job listings during flights and layovers. But the Wi-Fi had been fickle, and her focus had been even worse. Still, she'd fired off a few applications. Nancy and Brett had assured her the door to OptiHealth hadn't fully closed. Seven of her thirty days were already gone. Macy could feel the countdown ticking with every passing billboard.

Truthfully, she would've preferred to stay curled up in the apartment with Catherine and Nina, buried under blankets and ice cream and love. But she knew this visit home was overdue, even if she wasn't looking forward to the questions. Or, for that matter, the expectations.

Her parents, George and Rebecca Walker, didn't quite understand her connection to Manhattan—to the noise, rhythm, and struggle. To them, New York was a chapter she'd outgrow. With every call, every visit, there was an underlying wishfulness for the prodigal daughter to wake up and come home.

She hated disappointing them.

And she dreaded explaining Jack's absence, already hearing the grinding of her mother's teeth and her father's irritated groan that she hadn't settled down yet.

The Uber turned onto the half-mile drive leading to the Walker farm in the one-stoplight town of Springwater, Iowa. The yellow colonial house rose ahead, tall and familiar, wrapped in white trim and weathered porches. Macy stared out at the cattle pens, the grazing horses, the crop fields swaying in a warm breeze. The soil had grown her once, and now it greeted her without judgment.

Everything looked exactly as it always had.

Except Macy didn't feel like the girl who used to belong there.

"Here goes nothing," Macy whispered, tightening her grip on the duffel as she stepped out into the familiar dust of the Walker driveway. The trunk clicked shut behind her, and the Uber pulled away, kicking up a soft trail of gravel.

Joy, her brother's wife, stood on the porch, beaming. One hand shielded her eyes from the sun while the other waved in broad arcs above her head. "Ethan!" she called, grinning wide enough to crinkle the freckles at her cheeks. Her light brown braid trailed over one shoulder, a few rebellious strands framing her heart-shaped face like soft parentheses. It was the kind of welcome Macy used to run toward.

Now, she hesitated.

Ethan popped his head through the screen door, blond curls flying, and barreled down the steps two at a time. He swept Macy into a rib-cracking hug. "Welcome home, little Red," he said, ruffling her curls in the same way he had since they were kids.

"Ethan, no!" Macy protested, squirming out of his grasp.

"Oh, come on. It's better than travel hair, right?"

Joy and Macy exchanged a practiced look: two sets of eyebrows arched in perfect unison.

Ethan groaned dramatically. "Oh no, the stereo glare. I've awakened the hive. What have I done?"

Joy tousled his hair with mock tenderness. "Make yourself useful, Walker, and get your sister's bags before we revoke your porch privileges."

"I've got it," Macy said quickly, adjusting her laptop strap. "Just the essentials. One duffel and my laptop—city survival gear."

"You always did travel lighter than the rest of us," Ethan teased, grabbing her bag anyway.

His words echoed, so like Jack's: "Isn't that just like you?"

Macy forced a laugh. "Well, I'm nothing if not consistent."

Joy lingered, eyeing the space beside Macy. Her voice softened. "Weren't we finally supposed to meet Jack this weekend?"

The question hit Macy like a sudden crosswind. Her smile flickered. Her hand tightened around the laptop strap.

"Oh, I'm sorry, honey," Joy rushed. "If it's a sore subject, we don't have to—"

"No, it's fine." Macy slipped a smile back on like armor. "We just decided we're better off as friends."

She stepped up onto the porch, the wood groaning beneath her feet as if it recognized her. The front door was cracked open, the sound of her mother humming and the sizzle of the kitchen stove greeting her. The nostalgia of home made her knees wobble.

God, everything looked the same. Even that dent in the porch rail from when Ethan tried to skateboard off it.

She could hear Joy's voice behind her, still chatting with Ethan, and the slam of the screen door bouncing on its hinges. The house loomed, warm and inviting and suffocating all at once.

She looked up at the second-story window of her old bedroom. The curtains were still floral. The walls still probably housed a poster or two she never took down.

"Okay, well, that's a shame," Ethan said, giving her a playful bump with his elbow. "In that case, let's get you settled. Mom and Dad are going to be thrilled to see you."

Before Macy could protest, Ethan snatched her duffel and hoisted it over his head, grinning like a mischievous schoolboy.

"Just let me, would you?" he said, stepping backward with exaggerated caution, as if she might lunge again.

Macy huffed a laugh but didn't chase it. Her energy wasn't quite up to the game. She wasn't looking forward to the inevitable conversation with her parents…not about Jack, and not about the messy state of her professional life.

Ethan tore through the front door like a herald at a royal court, calling out to the back of the house. A makeshift trumpet noise burst from his lips as Macy followed, startled by the fanfare.

Why the performance? It's just me. It's always been just me.

"Come on, come on, little sister!" he hollered over his shoulder. "Mom's got lunch almost ready!"

Macy hung back in the doorway, self-conscious. The scent of rosemary and roasted vegetables tugged at old memories—weekends home from college, surprise dinners after long shifts, the comfort of knowing there was a place where someone still cooked for you.

"Hi, Mom," she said softly, stepping into the kitchen like someone tiptoeing into a church. Her voice was pitched toward cheerfulness, but it came out thin, like a bell rung underwater. The weight of everything she hadn't said—about Jack, about the layoff, about her bruised plans—pressed tightly against her chest.

From behind, the back door swung open, and George entered, shedding the scent of hay and sun. Without missing a beat, he headed to the sink, sleeves rolled, and boots dusted. He looked like he'd been carved from the land itself: broad-shouldered, sandy-haired, with the same curls Ethan and Macy wore.

He leaned in and placed a peck on Macy's cheek before rinsing his hands.

"Sorry, I can't give you a proper hug," he said with a wink. "Just finished with the pigs. Figured you might want to take a rain check."

Macy laughed despite herself, warm and instinctive. "That's a safe assumption. It's great to see you, Dad."

Her smile lingered just long enough to be convincing. But inside, a question buzzed low: *How long can I keep this version of myself stitched together?*

Rebecca was just placing plates around the table, her blue eyes shining with confident warmth. Tall and poised, she wore her honey-brown hair cropped neatly at her chin, with a wide blue headband sweeping it from her face. The kitchen bore the essence of home, rich with butter and fresh cornbread, warmth, and memories.

"Sweetheart, welcome home!" she said, eyes softening as she took Macy in. She crossed the room and folded her daughter into a hug. Macy let herself melt into her mother's arms.

"I know real food's hard to come by during travel," Rebecca added. "So, I made fried chicken. Your favorite."

"That sounds great, Mom. Thanks," Macy said, easing down into her seat.

"I want to hear everything," Rebecca declared, already piling Macy's plate high with chicken and collard greens. She turned back to the stove and dropped a generous spoonful of butter into the mashed potatoes, humming to herself like it was just another Sunday.

"Ma, we talk a few times every week. There isn't that much to catch you up on," Macy said, trying to keep her tone light. "And this, this is too much. You didn't need to go all out."

Rebecca paused, her back half-turned. "You look different, Mace. Weary." She pivoted fully, concern seeping into her voice. "There's something you're not telling us. Wait…where's Jack?"

There it was. The moment Macy had been dreading since she left her apartment that morning.

She inhaled once, quiet and shallow, trying to compose the words she hadn't quite rehearsed. Something honest but digestible. She didn't want pity. Or worse, advice.

But before she could answer, the front door slammed open with a force that rattled the silverware.

"Aunt Erin?" Macy blinked.

Erin burst into the kitchen like a gust of late summer wind, her canvas bag swinging wildly, sunglasses sitting high on her head like goggles on a mad scientist. Her eyes scanned the room like she was on a mission.

"There you are!" she cried, pointing at Macy.

Macy blinked again, fork still poised mid-air. Rebecca's eyes widened in silent alarm.

Nina's mother, Rebecca's sister, had long earned her reputation as Springwater's reigning gossip queen. Not malicious, exactly, just relentless. She noticed everything, forgot nothing, and believed tact was optional if her intentions were "loving." As the proprietor of the town's only beauty salon, she had become the unofficial gatekeeper of local scandal. Between bleach treatments and perm rollers, secrets flowed like conditioner.

Her tightly coiled black hair was always lacquered into a perfect helmet. Her body, full-figured and formidable, had a strut that reminded Macy of the hens in the coop: loud, busy, and always watching.

"Oh, Macy Lynn! You're home!" Aunt Erin swept into the kitchen faster than a gust of hairspray, arms open wide. "Would you just let me look at you?"

Macy barely had time to stand from the lunch table before she was engulfed in a hug that felt more like an anaconda wrapping itself around its evening meal than a warm welcome. When Aunt Erin finally released her, it was only to hold her at arm's length and scrutinize her from head to toe.

"Well, Macy. I can't help but notice, you're looking...filled out. City life must be treating you well."

Macy pulled back, wincing at the hidden meaning behind Aunt Erin's words. "I guess," she said tightly, forcing a smile.

Aunt Erin chuckled. Not unkindly, but not kindly either. "You should walk more! New York's great for that. I swear, when I lived there back in the day, I stayed two sizes smaller just walking rather than taking the subway."

Rebecca's voice sliced through the awkward air. "Erin."

"What? I'm just being helpful!" Aunt Erin lifted her glass.

Macy busied herself with finishing her plate and scraping the chicken bones into the garbage, not wanting to meet Aunt Erin's critical eyes.

Eyes darting between Macy and Aunt Erin, Ethan jumped up and nudged Macy. "So, did you still need to go to the store, kiddo?"

Macy hastily threw her plate and glass into the dishwasher, grateful for the save. "Yes, thanks!" she shouted as she raced for her purse. "I can't believe I forgot to pack a charger for my cell phone."

Aunt Erin called after her, "Couldn't you just borrow your mother's?" But they were already out the door.

"Thank you!" Macy whispered to Ethan as soon as they were out of earshot.

"I know she never wastes a second. It looked like she was giving you a hard time," Ethan said sympathetically.

"You know Aunt Erin." Macy shrugged.

"Yeah, I know," Ethan agreed. "So, do you actually want to go shopping? The lie might look more convincing if we actually go somewhere."

Macy laughed in agreement. "Yeah, I definitely didn't forget my charger, but I'm sure I can find something once we get there."

They drove into town in companionable silence. "It really is good to have you home, Macy," Ethan said as they approached the town grocery store. "We do miss you around here, and not just for the extra hands."

"I miss you all too," Macy admitted. "But New York is home now. This life was never for me."

"I know. Maybe we'll just have to visit you next time."

Macy beamed at Ethan. "I would love to have you. Any time!"

They had barely walked into the store before a too-familiar voice rang out: "Well, if it isn't Macy Walker."

Macy turned slowly. Jenna Price, prom queen and Macy's biggest bully, had a perfectly manicured hand wrapped around a shopping cart. In front of the cart sat an equally perfectly looking little girl with blond pigtails.

A slow, wide smile stretched across Jenna's flawless skin. Her long blond hair was clipped into a perfectly messy bun at the top of her head. Behind her stood Jeremy Harding, their school's star quarterback, a toddler strapped into a carrier on his chest.

"I thought you'd left the cows behind for good," Jenna said sweetly. "Then again, I guess New York's not for everyone."

Before Macy could reply, Ethan stepped forward. "Hey, Jenna. Still confusing smugness with charm, I see."

Jenna's smile faltered. "Oh, Ethan. Always so protective. I was just saying hello."

"Sure, you were." He turned to Macy. "Come on, Red. Let's go."

Macy started to follow, grasping for words. Lining the nearby registers was a cluster of balloons, including a large clown with a bright red nose and white hair. Inspiration struck, and Macy spun back towards Jenna.

"Enjoy the circus, Jenna," she said. "But next time, try being the ringmaster instead of the sideshow."

Jenna flinched and cocked her head, caught off guard by Macy's calm delivery.

Jeremy, still at a distance, hadn't moved toward them. His expression was unreadable, caught between embarrassment and apathy. The little blond boy babbled in baby talk, oblivious to the tension.

Ethan looked at Macy, head tipped to the side, a smile playing at his lips. "Well, damn. That was more satisfying than punching her."

Macy laughed under her breath, though her hands still trembled. "I couldn't do it in front of her kids. Come on, let's grab some wine. I need something stronger than coffee."

When they arrived back at the farmhouse, Ethan went to clean up, and Macy set about helping Joy and Rebecca prepare dinner. Aunt Erin was still there and showed no signs of leaving, much to Macy's chagrin.

"So!" Rebecca started as they all sat down at the table. "Macy, tell us about your job? Are things going well for you there?"

In a flash, Macy wanted to get lost in the cornstalks. She was a terrible liar, so she knew it was best to just be out with it.

"Well..."

Aunt Erin cut in before she could speak. "And what about this young man I heard was supposed to come with you, Jake?"

Macy opened her mouth to speak, but the words tangled with the lump rising in her throat. Her fork hovered above the plate, unmoving. She inhaled slowly, counting to three, willing her voice not to betray the swirl of embarrassment and heartache churning beneath the surface.

"We broke up," she said at last, the quiet finality of it slicing through the room like a gust through still air. "It was mutual…and it's still pretty fresh."

Rebecca's face fell, softening into concern. "Oh, honey…"

Aunt Erin clicked her tongue dramatically and reached for her iced tea. "Well, I can't say I'm surprised. City men always seem charming until they aren't."

Macy ignored the jab. It wasn't worth the breath.

Ethan, now clean and changed, reentered the room and caught the mood midair. He slid into his seat beside Macy and gave her a subtle nod of support.

Rebecca shifted the conversation like only a mother could. "Well, you're here now. And I know things at work have been shaky. Wasn't VitalSync in the news?"

Macy dabbed her napkin across her lips, buying herself two seconds.

"Yes, they merged with OptiHealth," she said slowly, hoping they wouldn't ask any more questions.

"That's got to be good news for you, right, sweetheart?" Aunt Erin asked.

Swallowing the lump in her throat, Macy coughed. "I was laid off."

The words tumbled out in a hurried mumble. Aunt Erin gaped at her, fork paused halfway to her mouth. "Oh, well, I'm sure you—"

"I have thirty days' notice, and they've offered a severance package if I don't find something," Macy interrupted, not wanting to hear how that phrase was going to end.

"Macy, I have something to say." George waited for everybody's attention. "I am sorry that these things happened to you. But maybe they were divine interventions. Maybe you should consider that this was God's way of telling you it was time to come back to us."

Macy opened her mouth to argue, but George put his hand up, silencing her.

"Think about it. All within a week, you lost your job, your boyfriend, and came home for a visit. Listen. Do you think that was all just coincidences?"

Without waiting for her to answer, Aunt Erin had to insert her opinion. "Now, Macy, your dad might be right. Maybe coming back and working on the farm is the best thing that could ever happen to you.

There's nothing like some good and proper manual work, you know! It could even help you with those extra pounds. You can find someone else, someone here. I've seen all those jealous stares you've been making at Joy and Ethan today, and I'm sure we can find someone for you if you would just let me—"

"Please, everybody, stop!"

Joy's voice, firm and clear, cut through the din like a clap of thunder on a still afternoon.

"Aunt Erin, I know you want to help, but what Macy needs isn't a lecture or matchmaking. She needs support. She needs time. She needs grace."

A stunned silence fell over the table.

Macy stared at her sister-in-law, gratitude flickering behind her teary eyes. Joy, normally the mediator, had become the shield she hadn't known she needed.

Erin blinked, momentarily deflated. George cleared his throat and leaned back in his chair. Rebecca looked between her daughter and Joy, a hint of realization dawning in her expression.

Ethan, sensing the fragility of the moment, stood up and grabbed his empty glass. "Anybody want some iced tea?" he asked, trying to break the tension. "Or maybe something stronger?"

A few chuckles rippled cautiously around the table. It wasn't a resolution, but it was a breath.

Rebecca reached out and gently touched Macy's hand. "You don't have to have everything figured out right now, sweetheart. But please just think about it."

Macy took a breath, the kind meant to center rather than calm. Every eye at the table was fixed on her—not hostile, but heavy with expectation.

"New York is my home now. I'm figuring things out—a new job, a new direction." Her voice didn't waver, though her stomach did. "I'm an adult. I will decide what happens next."

George sighed with a hint of resignation, his forehead settling into a "V" of frustration. "You are that, but we're still your parents, and we still know what's best for you."

Macy's shoulders rounded, and her eyes dropped to her plate. Deflated, she muttered, "I'll think about it."

Ethan tapped his fork against his glass. He looked toward Joy, who gave him a small nod and reached for his hand.

"Well, I think the tone in this room could do with a little changing," Ethan said, smiling. "Joy and I have a little news."

"Oh, God!" Aunt Erin clapped her hands. "Are you saying…?"

George and Rebecca leaned in, eyes wide.

"We're having a baby," Ethan said proudly. "Due just after Thanksgiving."

The room erupted in shouts and hugs, laughter, and clinking glasses. Macy smiled, wide enough to be seen and measured, her arms looped dutifully around Joy and Ethan, but inside, a quiet ache bloomed.

After plates were cleared and voices had mellowed, Macy excused herself. Upstairs, her room greeted her like a still photograph—crisp linen, lemon-scented dust, corners untouched by time.

She collapsed onto the bed, her bones heavy. The walls didn't hold her story anymore, but they still remembered it.

Her phone buzzed and lit up with a FaceTime call. Catherine.

Macy answered, heart tugging toward familiarity.

"Finally!" Catherine shouted. "I haven't heard from you in two days. I was about to send out a search party. I will track down this cornfield cult."

Macy groaned, pressing the pillow over her face with a grin. "Please. I'd probably be the only person ever kicked out of a cult."

Face turning red, Catherine slammed a fist on her desk top. "Who said it, and what did they say?"

"Down, girl," Macy replied with a dry edge, knowing full well Catherine was two syllables away from going full scorched-earth. "Good old Aunt Erin just couldn't help herself. And then Jenna…same cruelty, different day."

Catherine winced. "Please tell me you put them both in their place."

Macy sighed, eyes drifting toward the ceiling. "I did finally get a good one-liner on Jenna. But with Erin, I just…froze."

"One of these days," Catherine muttered, wagging a finger at the screen. "One of these days, you're going to summon that redheaded fire I know is in you."

"Maybe." Macy's shoulders sagged. "What can you do? At least I won't be seeing either of them again this weekend."

Catherine tilted her head with mock innocence. "So...you gonna trawl Tinder now that you're officially back in cow country?"

"Catherine!" Macy half-laughed, half-groaned.

"Oh, come on, Mace. Screw chicken boy. You're young. Gorgeous. You deserve some fun."

Macy shook her head, fingers clutching the edge of her pillow. She knew her body had changed, but it hadn't dented her confidence until Jack used it as an excuse. She had, in fact, sized out of her favorite jeans twice over. And now her job would soon be gone. What did she have left to offer anyone?

"I'm not looking for fun," she said quietly. "If I'm going to meet someone, I want it to be real. I want someone who sees me fully. And right now…I don't see myself like that."

Catherine sighed, the playfulness fading into something gentler. "All right. Spoilsport. But you're worth more than you know. You think about it. Call me later."

"I will. Bye."

The screen went dark, leaving Macy alone in the familiar echo of her childhood room.

She flopped onto her back and stared at the ceiling fan spinning lazily overhead.

She'd hoped this trip would be grounding. Something to soften the raw edges. But instead of comfort, she felt displaced. She longed for the clatter of subway doors. For anonymous coffee shops, where no one asked about Jack or told her what her body should look like.

She missed disappearing into a crowd.

Here, in Springwater, she wasn't anonymous.

She knew she couldn't stay. New York was home. Still, her father's words echoed over the laughter that continued below.

Part Two

The Shadow Jack Made

Celeste's Office

"That sounds like a lot to happen to one person all at once," Celeste said as I came to the end of my story. "Do you want to talk to me about what you were feeling during that visit?"

A barking laugh escaped before I could stop myself. I leaned forward and rested my elbows on my knees, my chin resting in my right hand. "Have you got a listing for all of the negative emotions that one can feel at a particular time?"

I sighed, picking at the skin on my lip. "Well, I was scared about losing my job. How was I going to make it in one of the most expensive and competitive cities in the country? I was depressed, wondering if my dad was right, that I should move back to Springwater. I was shocked and sad over Jack—I really thought we had something good. I never questioned my self-image until he made remarks about my body. I was comfortable with myself the way I was, but he and my aunt made me start questioning everything.

"My feelings about my brother having a baby are a bit more complicated. I was so happy for them! But it carried unexpected bitterness with it, too. My aunt accused me of being jealous, and I can't say she's wrong. Ethan was always the golden child. Popular at school, excelled in sports, and it was always known he was going to take over the farm one day. I didn't resent him for that. I knew I didn't want that life for myself. But sometimes I felt like I never had much of anything that made me stand out…to my family, or to anyone. Other than the bullies, that is.

"I always liked Joy. Right from day one, she treated me like a little sister. So, I knew they would be great parents, and I truly was happy for them. But with all the things I was going through in that moment, it made me feel very small."

"That's a complicated dynamic," Celeste said. "I want to talk more about these feelings. I think there's more here to uncover."

I nodded and collected my thoughts. "All the way home to New York, my dad's thoughts ran through my ears. I wondered if he was right, if I should go home. What was left for me in New York? I had Catherine, though she was about to have her other half back. I had my cousin, Nina, and while I always wondered if she had settled when it came to her husband, she had a lavish lifestyle in her Fifth Avenue penthouse. They were making it, and my life was suddenly in rewind. I was starting over."

Celeste didn't interrupt. She nodded in all the right places and took down notes, but did not appear to be bored. "That sounds incredibly lonely."

"Yes!" I all but shouted. "I don't think I'd ever put a word to the emotion before. It was more than just the relationship with Jack; it was the fact that everybody else seemed to know their place, where they belonged. But I never did.

"Time was ticking away in every facet of my life. I had thirty days to find a new job, or the countdown would start until I couldn't afford my share of the apartment. Shane was coming home from deployment—which was a great thing; I always liked Shane—but I knew everything would change between Catherine and me when he did. I was also just about to turn twenty-eight, and while I wasn't in a big hurry to have kids, I knew the clock was ticking there, too.

"I didn't even realize until I started talking it out just how much pressure I was under. And a lot of it was self-imposed. Do you see that?"

Celeste nodded, her eyes warm, with an easy smile. "I do see that, and it's a big step that you can see it, too. That's what I'm here for: to help you figure these emotions out."

"I knew I didn't want to go back to Iowa, though. I never really had a place where I fit in at home. I knew I had to find my way in Manhattan.

"After a long weekend at home, I went back to New York with fresh determination to prove them all wrong."

Chapter Three

WHERE SHE BELONGS

Macy closed her eyes as she reached the final stretch of her journey home from her parents' farm. She stepped out of the subway tunnel and let the sounds of the city wash over her. People shouted, dogs barked, someone on a saxophone played half a jazz riff, and then gave up. She was back in Manhattan, and the noise in her chest softened to a pulse of relief.

Her mind drifted to that first day at eighteen, stepping into the city with a heart packed full of ambition and hunger. She and Nina had stood arm in arm, the world at their feet. Catherine had grown up in Springwater before her father's job took them to Long Island, so when Macy had gotten accepted at Columbia, it was an easy decision for the three of them to share a place.

Nina had gone to Manhattan with plans of being on the stage. She had charmed her way onto some production crews, but didn't make it as a performer. She had met wealthy architect Brian Simpson and traded the stage for a penthouse.

Back then, Macy had arrived in New York young and fearless. She'd carried her dreams like armor, hoping they would shield her from the weight of expectation. And now, battered though she was, she still stood.

She smiled as the sun broke through the clouds and warm sunlight washed over her. Ethan's voice rang in her mind: Welcome home, Mace.

Dragging her suitcase through the Upper East Side toward her building and up the final flight of stairs, she reached her apartment on the fourth floor. The hall smelled of curry, lemon-scented bleach, and the reliable, faint undertone of mildew. New York's signature blend.

It wasn't glamorous. But it was home.

Her fingers fumbled with the keys as she balanced her laptop bag and duffel, already anticipating the quiet waiting inside. She had missed her family more than she'd expected. But even that familiarity had come tied to old baggage. Her aunt's criticisms. Jenna's bullying. That constant reminder that the past still had claws. And always the feeling that she wasn't good enough.

Just as she found the right key, the sound of footsteps echoed up the stairwell. Quick, hurried, and growing closer.

She paused. She half-turned toward the noise, and her breath caught as the shape rounded the corner.

"Hey there, neighbor! Need a hand?" a familiar voice called out behind her.

Macy turned, a little startled, to find Theo Martinez, her long-time friend and fellow fourth-floor dweller, grinning in the hallway. A bag of takeout dangled from one hand, his hoodie speckled in paint, black hair pulled into a messy bun. A vivid smudge of green streaked across his cheek like a misplaced brushstroke.

"I'm good, Theo, but thank you," Macy replied, offering a tired smile. "What's with the paint, though? Renovating?"

Theo chuckled, that dimpled grin tugging him younger than his thirty years. "Hardly. More like a failed attempt to be the next Picasso. I was staring at a blank wall and got inspired. Either that or distracted. I'm not sure which."

He glanced at her overloaded arms and gestured at her duffel bag. "You look like you just came back from a war."

Macy let out a weary laugh. "Close. A weekend at the Walker family farm. Overbearing aunt, childhood bully, four flights, two Ubers, one ridiculously long subway ride…stopped just shy of a partridge in a pear tree. I'm ready to sleep until Tuesday."

Theo gave a knowing grin. "Okay, let me guess: Your mom tried to love you to death with fried chicken and guilt trips, your dad warned you about New York like it's the seventh circle of Hell, and your brother reminded you that he's everyone's favorite child?"

She narrowed her eyes. "Are you spying on Springwater now? Because that's disturbingly accurate."

He held up his free hand in mock surrender. "You're not the only city kid with country roots. It's basically the universal script. That, and you're clearly hauling more emotional baggage than that duffel."

Macy laughed, a real one this time, letting the knot of tension untie a little. "Yeah...that's fair. It was a lot."

Theo's expression softened, voice lowering into something more genuine. "You know, we've been neighbors for almost five years. And for all the hallway chats and stolen cups of sugar, I feel like I barely know the real Macy. Springwater Macy. All of it."

He lifted the takeout bag with a sheepish smile. "Want to change that over some lunch? General Tso's chicken and emotionally fraught storytelling. Best cure for a rough trip—scientifically proven."

Macy hesitated, keys still in hand, the door still unopened. The idea of talking sounded exhausting when all she wanted to do was get to work on finding a new job. But then she looked at Theo again, at the paint on his cheek, the warmth in his voice, and the comfort of someone offering to actually listen.

She nodded slowly. "Only if you throw in an egg roll."

His grin spread wide. "Deal."

She gave him a skeptical look but unlocked the door and held it open. "All right, Professor Chicken. You bring the takeout; I'll bring the wine. It'll be nice to actually drink it instead of hurling it across a room."

Theo blinked, pausing at the threshold. "I feel like I'm missing context."

Macy snorted. "Long story. Let's just say wine and emotional repression don't mix well."

He stepped in, grinning. "Sounds like an abstract painting waiting to happen."

Macy chuckled as she fetched a bottle of Riesling and two wine glasses. Theo made himself comfortable at the kitchen table, unpacking the food like he was hosting a dinner party for two.

Neither of them heard the footsteps until Catherine appeared in the doorway, arms crossed, and smile widened to full mischief.

"Well, this is a surprise."

Macy jumped, nearly dropping the glasses. Theo greeted her with his signature megawatt grin.

"Emergency Chinese delivery for your emotionally compromised roommate," he announced. "There's wine involved and stories with minor trauma. I'm just the guy who brought General Tso and listening skills."

Catherine reached for a glass, eyes glinting. "Chinese and wine? Mmm...sounds suspiciously like foreplay. Is this spilling the tea or a date?"

"Catherine!" Macy groaned, cheeks instantly flaming.

Catherine widened her eyes in mock innocence. "What? I'm just observing."

Macy felt herself floundering. "Theo's just being nice. I mean, come on. I'm definitely not his type," she said, gesturing vaguely to herself.

Theo leaned back, clearly intrigued. "Who's the professor now? Please feel free to explain what my type is." He popped a chopstick into his mouth and pretended to puff contemplatively, channeling Sherlock Holmes with a playful glint.

Macy blinked. "I...I don't know. Someone polished. Confident. The kind of woman who wears heels to brunch and actually knows what contouring is. Not the queen of frump who loses it as soon as my dad gives me 'the tone of Dad talk.'"

Theo chuckled, eyes warm. "Pretty sure confidence isn't about brunch wear and face paint. But I do appreciate emotional fluency. Very underrated."

Catherine rolled her eyes and jabbed Macy with her chopstick. "Girl, you need to rewrite your script. You're smart, gorgeous, and emotionally fluent. And if you're frumpy, then I'm a raccoon in heels."

Macy poured the wine with a little too much focus, hoping the clinking glasses and splash of Riesling would distract from the warmth blooming across her cheeks. She snatched her chopstick back from Catherine and tried to act casually, but the red creeping up her neck said otherwise.

Theo leaned back, tapping his own chopstick against his lip like a professor calling class to order. "So, Cath. What's the latest in PR disasters? I feel like you thrive in the land of headline damage control."

Catherine smirked, folding a dumpling between her chopsticks. "Oh, it's a circus. Some fledgling CEO let loose on a podcast about how empathy is overrated. Now the shareholders are clutching pearls, and I'm tasked with spinning his Neanderthal comments into punchlines. We're calling it satire. Internally, it's just code for panic faster."

Macy laughed. "I don't know how you do it. When the data fights back in my job, I just twist the lens until I find a version of the truth that behaves."

Catherine winked. "Well, that's the beauty of billing hourly. People pay you to tell them how wrong they are, slowly."

She turned to Theo. "And you? Still knee-deep in urban chaos? I bet the boroughs are throwing zoning curveballs like rice at a wedding."

Theo shook his head with a rueful smile. "Rice, confetti, flaming hoops. Take your pick. Brooklyn's heating up again. Lots of developers are sniffing around those abandoned warehouses. I'll be buried in permits till retirement."

He dipped a piece of chicken into the sauce, then added with mock solemnity, "It won't make me rich, but it funds my art habit and my search for obscure soul records. A man's gotta have passion."

Macy put a hand to her heart in shock. "And here I thought takeout was your deepest love."

He shrugged and gave a small giggle. "Art needs fuel. Chicken and dumplings are as close to divine inspiration as I'll get."

Catherine leaned in, eyes twinkling. "So, this masterpiece of yours. Are we ever going to see it? Or is the gallery opening permanently postponed due to perfectionism?"

Theo waggled his chopsticks in her direction. "It's not perfectionism. It's suspense. I'm building anticipation. Like Banksy, but with worse lighting."

Macy laughed into her wine glass, the conversation revitalizing the weariness her soul had carried back from Iowa. For the first time in days, she didn't feel like she had to perform for anyone. She could just be. "Think you could let us in on the secret?"

He hesitated for a beat, then smiled. "For you two? Anytime. It's good therapy. It keeps my hands busy when my brain gets too loud."

Macy tilted her head, recognizing the weight behind his words. "Yeah. After a while, this city starts to echo."

Theo let out a low hum of agreement. "I've been here eight years, and it still feels like I just arrived. Like I'm still trying to find my footing."

"Constantly," Macy said, her voice barely above a whisper.

"I think that's why we all get each other," Catherine added, swirling the last of her wine. "Nobody here has it all figured out. We're just trying to make everyone else think that we do."

The words settled over them like a soft blanket. The tension that had followed Macy home from her weekend away—the guilt, the frustration, the ache of old wounds—began to dissolve into the hum of shared understanding. She found herself retelling the weekend's chaos, starting with the infamous airborne chicken, and for the first time in days, her thoughts didn't feel like they were trying to drown her.

As the wine dwindled and the takeout containers emptied, Theo stood and gathered the plates, moving to the sink with practiced ease.

"That hardly seems fair," Macy protested. "You brought the food, shared it with both of us, and now you're cleaning up?"

"You had a rough weekend," he said simply. "It's the least I can do."

Catherine shot Macy a knowing look. Macy shook her head and pressed a finger to her lips, silencing the commentary before it could begin.

"Thanks again for lunch, Theo," she said, her voice softer now. "I actually do feel a lot better."

"See?" he said with a grin. "General Tso. It's the cure for anything."

He hugged them both, warm and brief, then headed for the door. "Until next time, ladies."

The door clicked shut behind him.

Catherine turned immediately, eyes gleaming. "Not his type, huh?"

Macy groaned. "You never stop, do you?"

Catherine threw her head back and laughed, then drew a halo in the air above herself with her finger. "He sure seemed invested in your emotional well-being."

Macy scoffed, though her cheeks betrayed her. "Please. He's just being nice."

But even as she said it, the words didn't hold the punch they had before. The city still echoed—but tonight, it echoed with laughter, with warmth.

"Uh-huh. And I just keep wine stocked for health reasons."

Macy smiled but looked away, swirling the last sip in her glass. "It's stupid, but...it felt good. That someone saw I wasn't okay and didn't treat it like a burden."

Catherine leaned against the counter, watching her. "You know, it's okay to admit it hurts."

"What does?"

"All of it. Jack, the job, going home, feeling stuck. You don't have to brush it off every time."

Macy let her elbows drop onto the counter and rubbed her temples. The weight behind Catherine's words settled over her shoulders like the familiar ache of a long day. "I know. But if I admit it to myself just how not okay I actually am, I think I might break."

"Well," Catherine said, refilling her glass with the last splash of wine, "that's what friends are for. To help you hold the pieces until you're ready to fit them back together."

Macy's gaze flicked toward the door, as if Theo's presence still lingered in its frame. She chewed on the edge of her lip, weighing the ache inside her chest against the comfort of shared space.

"You don't need to be throwing me at every available man in Manhattan, though. I'm nowhere near ready yet after what happened with Jack. I need some time to heal."

Catherine scoffed at her. "Girl, maybe a rebound would do you some good."

Macy muttered under her breath but smiled despite herself. "Anyway!" she said, forcing brightness into her tone, "Enough about Macy's drama. Tell me what you're doing at home."

"Oh, stop spoiling all my fun. Can't a lady decide to work remotely once in a while?"

"Of course she can," Macy said, crossing her arms in front of herself. "But you usually don't. So, why today?"

Catherine sighed, her playfulness slipping. "I didn't want you to be upset."

"Why would I be?"

"Because I know things have been rough lately, and I didn't want to drop more weight on your shoulders."

Macy crossed her arms and started tapping her foot. Their signal. Time to spill.

"Okay, okay," Catherine relented, lifting both hands. "I took the afternoon off because I've got a major interview tomorrow, for the director of PR at a startup in the Wall Street district. I figured I'd hide out here and prep."

Macy raised her glass toward her. "See, now that wasn't so hard, was it? We'll call Nina and Brian and celebrate this weekend."

"But we don't even know that I'm going to get it," Catherine said.

Macy grinned. "*Now* who needs the self-esteem boost?"

She stepped back toward her bedroom. "Well, you get yourself ready. I need to scrub the Iowa off me before my skin starts absorbing corn-based nostalgia."

As she dug through her dresser for a clean change of clothes, her phone pinged. A new email lit up the screen: Brett from HR at VitalSync.

She clicked it open, eyes scanning the message quickly. Though Brett knew it wasn't in her preferred wheelhouse, there was an opening: Amara MacNash, director of product development, needed a new personal assistant. It wasn't guaranteed, but Brett was offering a favor—he could personally secure her an interview.

Macy stared at the screen for a moment longer.

She hadn't asked for this lifeline, but maybe it was time to stop waiting for doors she actually wanted to open and start considering the ones that did.

Feeling a flicker of hope, Macy replied to Brett without hesitation. The position was far from perfect. A manager outside her field needed an assistant, at a company she wasn't sure she fit into, and it would come with a pay cut, but it was a paycheck. And right now, a foot back in the door was more valuable than certainty. She typed out her availability for the following week to meet with Amara and hit send before she could second-guess herself.

It was something. A step. And lately, steps had been hard to come by.

She pulled a change of clothes from the dresser and walked toward the bathroom, pausing at the door. Her fingers rested on the handle, but she didn't turn it right away.

Instead, she looked out at the apartment. Wine glasses were drying on the counter, the scent of ginger and sesame still lingering in the air, Catherine humming quietly from the living room as she reviewed her notes.

It didn't feel so heavy anymore. The apartment hadn't changed, but something inside her had. Maybe it was the wine. Maybe it was Theo and the warmth he'd brought with him. Or maybe it was just that she'd allowed herself to believe, even for a moment, that things were going to work themselves out.

She opened the door and stepped into the steam, letting the city peel off her skin, one drop at a time.

Chapter Four

CLUB ECHELON

When Friday evening finally arrived, Macy was resolute. She needed to shed the remnants of the past week. Not just the mud and memory of Iowa, but how she shrank into the shadow of her childhood. Tonight, she wasn't Macy Walker, the cautious girl from Springwater who knew how to herd cattle and sidestep family expectations. Tonight, she wanted to be someone else. Or at least, the version of herself she wasn't afraid to see.

Brian had bowed out, swamped with work, but gave Nina the green light to enjoy a well-earned girls' night out. That left her with Macy and Catherine to take the city by storm.

The transformation began slowly. Macy had spent over an hour painstakingly straightening each ringlet, flattening her curls into a shimmering curtain of copper silk. Her hair was once a practical choice—cropped short and restrained to survive barns and feed lots—but since Ethan and Joy's wedding, she'd let it grow. Now, when straightened, it flowed nearly to her waist like a quiet rebellion.

Makeup was a rare detour. Macy dabbed concealer over her freckles to start fresh. They dotted her cheekbones in faint constellations, familiar and harmless, but tonight, she wanted boldness, not comfort.

She admired the result in the mirror with a cautious nod of approval. Still, the outfit eluded her. She wanted something daring without feeling like a costume.

Naturally, Catherine took charge.

To Macy's dismay, the choice was bold: a deep emerald-green minidress, shimmering like crushed glass under light. It clung to curves Macy often tried to hide, with an open back that was barely disguised by a single inch-wide strap. The neckline plunged with unapologetic drama.

"CATHERINE!" Macy yelled. "Are you kidding me with this scrap of fabric? What exactly do you expect this to cover?"

Catherine entered like the queen of New York nightlife: black dress, royal blue stilettos, and completely unbothered. "Put it on. The green makes your hair look like firelight…and the cut? Chef's kiss. Though I'd pin up that blanket of hair. It's begging for an updo."

Macy groaned. "Do you know how long I spent straightening this blanket? This is borderline abuse."

"Everyone's going to be staring at you," Catherine said with a smirk. "And not because it's scandalous, but because you look like you could start a fire just by walking past."

Macy rolled her eyes, but couldn't stop her smile from flickering in the mirror. As much as she resisted, the idea thrilled her. Self-doubt had taken hold the day Jack broke up with her, and a spark of boldness was just what she didn't know she needed.

She slipped into the dress, drew her shoulders back, and stared herself down in the mirror.

Just as Macy was about to turn tail and dive headfirst back into her closet, the front door flung open.

"I'm here, bitches!" Nina declared, her voice a cocktail of confidence and delight. "Manhattan's not ready for what's about to hit it."

She strutted into view, platinum blond hair sculpted into a flawless updo, her hot pink velvet dress hugging every curve with unapologetic glamor. Her presence didn't just enter the room – it stole it.

Macy, meanwhile, fidgeted with the hem of her own dress, unsure whether to pull the neckline higher or the skirt lower. Standing next to Nina, who was long-limbed and radiant, Macy felt stubby and exposed. Jack's cruel remarks surfaced uninvited. That familiar chorus of criticism echoed in the back of her mind.

"Stop fidgeting," Catherine said, eyes gleaming with mischief.

"Yeah, Mace," Nina added, her grin wide. "You've got the girl-next-door-meets-stripper vibe. It's working for you."

"Stripper? Are you kidding me?" Macy spun around, tugging at the straps as if retreating were still an option.

Nina broke into hysterical laughter. "Not actual stripping, drama queen! I meant you look hot. You're gonna turn every head in that club."

"That's what I'm afraid of," Macy muttered, reaching for her heels and purse with a theatrical sigh of defeat.

"Tonight isn't for overthinking," Catherine announced, looping her arm through Macy's with ceremonial flair. "I nailed that interview. You've got yours next week. Tonight is for celebrating. Big nights call for big looks."

Nina swooped in on Macy's other arm like a wingman with glitter and attitude. Macy laughed, half-embarrassed, half-energized. She was clearly outnumbered, so she finally gave in.

"Okay, fine. You bad influences win," she said. "Let's go celebrate our 'maybe' jobs and definite insanity."

Macy grabbed her purse from the dresser. As she slid her phone inside, the screen lit up with a new message.

Jack

I know I'm probably the last
person you want to hear from
right now, but can we talk?

Stomach clenching, she looked at the phone as if it might burn her if she responded. Heartbeat ringing in her ears, she pulled it out anyway. She typed her reply fast, before she could think about what she was doing.

Macy
No. I'm leaving now with the girls, and I have nothing to say to you anyway.

Jack
Echelon?

For a moment, she was tempted. That had been their place where they spent too many Friday nights. Birthday toasts, when he had been promoted, and a couple of drunken karaoke nights. If he was going to look for her on a Friday night, that would be the first place he would think to try.

Nina bumped her hip and peered over her shoulder to read the text. "Earth calling Macy! *What?* Give me that phone."

Nina grabbed the phone from Macy and typed a quick "No" in response, then slipped the phone back into Macy's clutch. "He is not going to ruin one more night for you. Now, are we going, or am I drinking your share tonight?"

The club was a jungle of strobe lights and pulsing heat. Music thumped hard enough to vibrate in her ribcage, distorting reality into rhythm. The crowd surged and parted like waves around her, bodies moving in sync with bass and bravado.

Catherine and Nina took to the dance floor like they'd been born in sequins. Macy, however, clung to the barstool as if it were a life raft. Her dress projected louder than she wanted to, and every shadow in the room put her in a spotlight.

"C'mon, Mace!" Catherine yelled over the music, grabbing her hand. "This was your idea, remember? Let's do this!"

Macy hesitated, thoughts still swirling around the text from Jack.

What could he have to say? Maybe I should hear him out?

Eyes still distant, she let herself be pulled into the sea of bodies. The music swallowed her doubts, one beat at a time. She moved stiffly at first, trying to remember how to be bold. But Nina laughed, spun her in a circle. Catherine raised both arms and threw herself into the rhythm.

And slowly, Macy began to move, not like someone trying to hide, but like someone daring to be seen.

She couldn't say when it happened. Somewhere between the third song and the fourth, the self-consciousness melted. Her dress stopped feeling like a mistake. Her body stopped feeling like a battleground.

Just for one night, she belonged to the beat. To her twenties. To the version of herself who wasn't afraid to take up space. Tonight, she wasn't hiding.

She was alive.

Just as Macy turned from the dance floor toward the bar—skin flushed, adrenaline buzzing—another voice cut through the music.

"I knew you'd be here!" Jack materialized out of the crowd, breathless, dressed in tattered jeans and a plain black t-shirt. His hair, brown and wavy, was slicked away from his face tonight. With her stiletto heels on, she stood nearly to his chin.

"I'm so glad I found you. Please, can we talk?"

"What?" Macy shouted over the music. "No!"

She turned away, scanning the crowd for Nina and Catherine. They had disappeared into the sea of bodies. "*This* is why we always travel in packs," she muttered. "I think I made myself pretty clear in how I feel about you right now, Jack."

"I know," he said, rubbing the back of his neck. "The things I said to you...I hate myself for it. I swear I didn't mean any of it. I just..." He hesitated, swallowing. "I panicked. Talking about meeting your parents, making plans, it scared the hell out of me."

Macy folded her arms in front of her chest, pursing her lips. "And Amber?"

Jack's mouth flipped open and closed, no sound coming out. "There is no Amanda."

"So, instead of telling me the truth, you humiliated me, *insulted me*, and made up this other woman?"

"I thought if I made it a clean break, I wouldn't want to go back." He gave a weak laugh. "But I missed you."

"Oh?" Macy said flatly.

He took a step closer, reaching for her. "Please, give me another chance. We can just start fresh like we're brand new again."

Her voice was calm, but firm. "Do you really think that would fix it? That I'd ever be able to trust you again?"

She shook her head and tried to push past him to the bar. His hand shot out, catching her arm. "Mace, please. I can't stop thinking about you."

"Jack, let me go."

"What if we just—"

"I believe the lady said no," came a voice from behind him.

Macy spun to find the source of the voice. Standing just behind Jack was a man dressed in dark jeans and a simple white button-down. He wasn't much taller than Jack, but had an imposing presence with broad shoulders, dark, curly hair that he had slicked out of his face, revealing eyes as blue as a summer storm. His posture carried a quiet air of authority.

"Are you going to remove your hand, or am I going to do it for you?" he asked, eyes not leaving Jack's face.

"This doesn't concern you!" Jack shouted and turned back to Macy. "Are you seriously going to throw away what we had over one stupid mistake?"

"We're done, Jack," she answered simply, and he finally released his grip. He turned and walked away, turning back once, but continued out the door after a brief pause.

Blushing, she mouthed a quiet "Thank you" in the direction of the mysterious stranger. He nodded, gazing softly, unmoving, unreadable. Macy looked down at the counter with a shy smile she didn't try to hide.

"Cade Donovan," the man said. "Macy. Macy Walker," she answered, shaking his offered hand.

"Thank you for that."

"Don't mention it," he said, flashing an easy smile and revealing a small dimple near his chin. "It looked like he was giving you a hard time."

"A bit, yeah. Ex-boyfriend. He broke up with me last week and decided he wanted to take it back." Macy didn't know why she was telling him all of this, but she couldn't stop herself.

"Well, he's a fool." His eyes studied her face, her hair, her dress. "What are you having?"

"Oh!" She gestured at the bar, remembering why she was there. "I'm on a run for my girlfriends that I'm here with and me."

Cade's mouth curved. "Let's not keep them waiting."

He signaled the bartender. "Whatever she's having, plus a gin and tonic."

"Two Cosmos and a Jack and Coke, please."

Cade slid a card across the counter.

"Thank you, two times!" Macy said. "You really don't have to do that."

"I know," he said. "Consider it a congratulations on not taking your ex- back gift."

Macy giggled into her hand, unable to stop the heat rising in her cheeks. "Is that a thing now?"

"It could be," he said. "We'll start the movement."

The bartender lined the cocktails up on the bar, and Cade leaned his elbow near where his gin and tonic appeared. "So, Macy Walker, what do you do when you're not dodging ex-boyfriends and playing fetch for your girl friends with the drinks?"

She hesitated, biting her lower lip. "I'm a data analyst. Or I was...my company is downsizing, and I got a notice. I guess at least they were kind enough to give me notice, but I've got three weeks to find something new. What do you do?"

"Marketing," he answered, offering no further detail. "And occasionally a bouncer, apparently."

Macy laughed as the bartender pushed the drinks their way. Cade helped her steady the glasses before taking his own.

"Do you dance?"

He stirred his gin and tonic and took a sip. "Not really. The DJ is an old friend of mine, so I come in to bother him sometimes. You go on, save your friends from their thirst."

"Thank you," she said a third time.

"Anytime, Macy."

She turned back into the crowd with the three glasses balanced precariously in her hands, searching for Catherine and Nina.

"Did you get lost looking for the bar?" Nina called over the music, taking her Jack and Coke.

"I ran into...someone...and got delayed."

Catherine's eyes flicked from Macy to the bar and back again. Cade had stayed at the bar, eyes on them. "I see," she said, her grin wicked. "We're definitely going to circle back to that one later."

When last call came, and the club began to unravel into goodbyes and cab rides, Cade gave Macy one last confident smile before slipping into the night.

In the Uber, Macy leaned her head against the window, her thoughts flickering like streetlights through the glass. The way Cade looked at her…like she was the only one in the crowd. She hadn't felt that in a long time.

The conversation with him had flowed naturally. Unforced. She wondered, with a quiet ache, why he hadn't asked for her number.

Not that she would've had the courage to give it. Or, to use his, if he had given it to her.

Beside her, Catherine and Nina were in full post-party gossip mode—the wine and laughter rendering their speech gleefully tangled. The cab smelled faintly of cheap cologne and candy wrappers, and Macy's emotions were slipping somewhere between tipsy and tender.

By the time the Uber pulled up to the Simpsons' building and they tumbled out into the elevator, she wasn't thinking about the dress or the club anymore.

She was thinking about the way he looked at her, and actually saw her. "Hi, ladies, did you have fun?" Brian greeted them with his usual warm smile. His sandy blond hair was neatly trimmed, and his soft brown eyes held a kindness that had always made Macy feel at ease. He wasn't exactly Nina's idea of "exciting," but no one could deny that he adored her. And he had never been anything but generous to Macy and Catherine.

"We did!" Macy said, returning his smile. "Thanks for letting us steal your bride."

Nina offered a brisk "hi" and breezed past him toward their room, stripping off her earrings as she went. She didn't glance back.

Brian's smile faltered. "Welcome home, honey!" he called, voice tinged with sarcasm. "I'm glad you're home, honey!" He turned to Macy and Catherine, running a hand through his hair and forcing the warmth back into his voice. "It's late, and the crazies are coming out. Why don't you both bunk in the spare rooms? I'm sure Nina's got pajamas for you somewhere."

"Thanks, Brian. We appreciate you," Macy said gently.

He smiled, more subdued this time. "I'm glad somebody does. Sleep well, ladies." He gave each of them a soft pat on the shoulder, then followed Nina down the hall. Moments later, she reemerged. Velvet had been traded for satin, looking both polished and impassive.

Catherine stretched out on the couch, toying with a throw pillow. "So," she said, eyes bright. "You going to tell us more about your new friend at the bar?"

Macy feigned confusion, scanning the room. "Friend? What friend?"

Nina narrowed her eyes like a cat tracking prey. "Oh, I think she means the guy who couldn't stop staring at you, even when you weren't looking at him."

Macy busied herself pouring another round of wine. "I have no idea what you're talking about."

"Oh, come on, Red," Catherine groaned. "Don't play dumb. I saw the way he looked at you. He was already mentally undressing you."

Macy gave her a withering look as she handed over the glass. "Did you see what you made me wear tonight? There wasn't much left to imagine."

Nina shrieked with laughter. "Still! You couldn't bring him over to meet us? Haven't even told us his name!"

"Cade," Macy said, rolling her eyes but unable to hold back a laugh. "His name is Cade."

"He looked like fun," Nina said with a wink. "You should've gotten his number. Maybe even taken him home to start your villain origin story."

Macy smacked her with a pillow. "We're talking about me, not you. I tried to get him to dance, but he said he doesn't."

Nina sighed dramatically. "It's like I taught you nothing."

Catherine burst out laughing. "Nina, you're such a romantic. It's like you run on chaos and pickup lines."

Macy sat back, her gaze drifting as the wine softened the edges of her thoughts. "He saved me from Jack."

"Say *what*?" Catherine shouted. "And we didn't lead with this because...?"

"Because Jack doesn't matter! He wanted to talk. I told him to buzz off. He grabbed my arm, Cade swept in, and told him to get his hands off me."

"Very interesting," Catherine said, swirling her drink.

Macy nodded, her thoughts flickering to Cade again. The way he'd watched her like she wasn't a movie extra. Like she was something worth seeing.

And for the first time in a long time…she wasn't sure if that scared her or thrilled her.

"You got some PJs that Catherine and I can bum?" Macy asked, tugging at the hem of her dress again. "Not trying to sleep in this sparkly napkin."

"Wait, you're staying?" Nina perked up, instantly reinvigorated. "Should we raid the liquor cabinet again?"

"I've hit my limit," Macy said, waving her off.

Nina groaned and disappeared into the master bedroom, emerging a minute later with two spare sets of satin pajamas.

"He's just so...clingy," she muttered, tossing the clothes Macy's way.

Catherine, now comfortably sprawled across the armchair, caught her own set of pajamas and dropped them into her lap. "Why are you so cold to him?"

Nina sighed, her posture deflating. "He's a good guy, he really is. But he's just...boring. This isn't the life I pictured."

Macy scoffed softly. "Preaching to the choir there, cousin."

They all changed, each slipping into the silky comfort of borrowed pajamas and the quiet that followed a night too full of sound. Macy had just pulled her blanket up when Catherine crashed into her room like a gleeful hurricane and flopped beside her.

"So, Red," she said, tugging on the end of the comforter, "are you going to tell me about your new friend?"

"It's nothing!" Macy replied too fast. The warmth that crept across her cheeks wasn't subtle.

"'Nothing' doesn't stare at you like he's reading your soul," Catherine teased.

And it was true. There was something unspoken but clear in Cade's eyes. Not assessment. Not flirtation. Just…recognition. He'd looked at her like she wasn't background noise. Like she existed in vivid detail.

"I mean…he didn't even ask for my number," Macy murmured. "So, it's not like anything will come of it."

Catherine bounced on the mattress with a giggle. "You got a name, didn't you? Facebook exists for a reason."

"I suppose I could," Macy said, rolling her eyes. "Now will you stop bouncing on my bed? You're making me seasick."

"Not until you promise to look him up."

Macy groaned and pulled a pillow over her face. "What difference would it make? If he wanted to see me again, he would've asked. As if."

"Oh-ho-ho! Look at you! You did like him."

Macy rolled onto her side and shoved her friend playfully. "Go back to your room, Catherine."

Catherine left laughing, her glee echoing down the hall.

Chapter Five

CHANGES

The hallway went quiet before Macy even saw her. A pair of stilettos clicked in a steady, unhurried rhythm, and people straightened in their chairs like kids caught passing notes. A dark bob appeared first, sharp and deliberate, then Amara MacNash herself: burgundy pantsuit, phone in one hand, eyes scanning the floor like she was hunting for weakness. She didn't slow until she reached Macy's cubicle.

Macy's stomach tightened as Amara swept into her space and perched on the edge of Macy's desk. "Miss Walker."

Macy withered under Amara's deliberate stare. She tugged at the fabric sticking under her arms and scrambled for words. "Ms. MacNash! I–uh–thank you for taking the time to speak with me yesterday. What can I do for you?"

Amara narrowed her eyes and surprised Macy with a faint smile. "I'm not your teacher, Macy. You can call me Amara." Macy returned her smile with a nervous one and shifted uncomfortably in her chair. "I wondered if you have a minute."

"Oh, of course, Ms. Mac–I mean, Amara."

"I wanted to talk to you about your interview yesterday," Amara began. She smiled again as Macy blanched. "Your face just turned the color of a sheet of paper, dear. The first thing we will be working on is your confidence."

Some of the tension drifted out of Macy's shoulders. "The first thing?"

"Yes," Amara answered simply. "I've heard nothing but good things about you and your work from Nancy and Brett. You're obviously very bright, and the fact that you're willing to consider alternative positions to the one you currently hold shows your dedication to the business. I like that. So, I would like to have you join me."

Unable to stop herself, Macy jumped up out of her chair and reached out to shake Amara's hand. "I accept, Ms.— Amara! Thank you!" Realizing her eagerness, she tucked her head down and sat back in her chair.

Amara crossed one leg over the other, still settled on Macy's desk. "Look, I know this isn't your dream job." She flicked her fingers toward Macy's computer screen. "You've got the background for bigger things. Nancy and Brett said you can actually think, which is rarer than you'd expect around here."

Macy gave a nervous laugh. "That's…good to hear?"

"It is. Which is why I don't want you treating this like a coffee-fetching gig. Sure, you'll manage my calendar and book my travel — that's the baseline. But when you see something that's broken, I want to hear how you'd fix it. Eventually, I want you to just fix it."

Macy nodded slowly, processing.

Amara leaned in a little, lowering her voice. "If you can do that, you'll have the right people noticing you. This…" She gestured between them. "…will be a stepping stone, not a cage. So, drop the scared-of-me thing, and start using that brain of yours."

Blushing again, Macy said, "I hoped it wasn't that obvious."

Amara let out a short but melodic laugh. "Let's add self-awareness to your opportunities. It was glaringly obvious."

Macy nodded and allowed herself to smile. "I promise I'll work on it. I appreciate this chance, Amara."

"I don't give chances, Macy. I offer opportunities." Amara stood, smoothing her pants and blazer. "What you do with them is up to you."

She strode out with the same commanding rhythm that had ushered her in.

As the rhythm of Amara's stilettos faded down the hallway, Macy barely registered her voice calling back, "I'll see you in two weeks, Macy!"

Macy stared at her screen for a moment, then smiled.

Her footing might still be shaky, but now, at least, she was standing on something solid.

Feeling deserving of a break for once, Macy decided to treat herself to lunch. Instead of the standard café in the building, she texted Catherine to meet her at their favorite spot: Eataly Downtown. Ever since Catherine had started her new job, they'd both worked within walking distance of Wall Street, a fact that never lost its shine.

"All right, Red," Catherine chirped as soon as they were seated, barely letting Macy open her menu. "Let's hear all the details!"

"Well, Amara came right to my desk and—"

"I meant your date, not your job," Catherine interrupted with a smirk that could slice through concrete.

Macy groaned and buried her face in her hands.

Catherine leaned in gleefully, watching Macy's face turn the same shade as her auburn hair. "That good, huh?"

Macy gave her a playful glare, cheeks still burning. "It was fine, honestly. We met at that pub in Chelsea, which was nice, but it was super loud. Had to shout just to hear each other. The conversation was okay, and he bought me a couple of drinks. We clicked a little, I think."

Catherine leaned in and circled her finger in the air, impatiently.

"He walked me to the subway," Macy added. "And…yeah. He kissed me. A really good kiss."

"Aha!" Catherine exclaimed, triumphant. "So, what's the problem?"

Macy shrugged. "I haven't heard anything from him today. We were texting nonstop before the date, and now? Radio silence."

"You texted him?"

"Just a good morning, nothing clingy!" Macy defended, shrinking as Catherine dropped her fork in horror.

"Macy!" Catherine groaned. "That's like an invitation to be ghosted. You gave him the opening. Men today are like squirrels in traffic. They freeze at the first sign of sincerity."

Macy covered her face again, groaning. "I swear, I don't know how to do this."

"Stop blaming yourself. Dating now is just digital roulette," Catherine said, tossing a piece of breadstick at her.

And then, a voice came from behind her.

"Date? Dang, I guess I missed my chance."

Macy turned, eyes wide.

Cade Donovan stood there with a crooked, dimpled smile, somehow effortless in a navy button-down shirt and tailored slacks. Her heart skipped a beat.

"Oh! Cade—uh, what are you doing here?"

"Well," he said, leaning against the table with boyish charm, "someone ran off from the club last weekend without giving me her number. I had to activate the spy network."

Out of the corner of her eye, Macy saw Catherine nearly vibrating with satisfaction, her grin positively predatory. A pit twisted in Macy's belly. *How could he possibly have found me in a city this massive?*

"I'm teasing!" Cade said, raising a hand. "Relax! You look like you've seen a ghost. I had a client meeting nearby and stopped in for lunch. May I join you ladies?"

Macy opened her mouth to decline, but Catherine pounced before she could. "Please do!"

Cade pulled out a chair and sat just as the server came to take their orders. Macy's phone buzzed, and her breath hitched.

"Oh! Maybe that's Gary texting me back," she said, eyes widening. Her face instantly fell.

The message was short. Polite. And unmistakably final.

Gary

Thanks for last night. Sorry, but I didn't feel any connection. Best of luck.

She locked her phone, trying not to let her disappointment surface.

"What is it?" Catherine asked, contorting her neck to glimpse Macy's messages.

"The curse of the Macy strikes again," Macy said with a shrug. It was only one date, but the conversations up to that point had been very enjoyable. "I told you I blew it somehow."

Cade peered over, trying to get a look at the phone. "Do you mind if I...?"

Macy hesitated for a moment but showed them both the message.

Catherine's temper started to flare. "I'm gonna string him up by his—"

"Catherine!"

Cade put up his hand in an effort to calm Catherine down. "If I could offer my opinion as a man?"

Macy shrugged again, noncommittally. "Might as well."

Cade leaned back in his chair, taking a sip from his drink. "That's guy code for 'I was hoping to get some, and when that didn't happen, I lost interest.'"

Macy frowned. "But I put it out there right in front that that's not who I am!"

Cade smirked and shook his head. "I hate to tell you this, but putting that in your dating profile is like putting a target on your back. Most guys see that as an excuse to make you their conquest. They'll go out with you and promise you the world just to see if they can get you." He studied her reaction and added, "It's all a game to them."

The server returned with Cade's drink order and placed their plates in front of them, lingering just a moment too long before departing.

Macy hung her head, stabbing at her ravioli with her fork. "I thought trying out these sites would be better than just a random meeting. I thought, if I put it out there that I'm looking for something real, someone I can build a future with, it would be better and not waste my time with people who don't want the same thing. Gary seemed so nice. I thought he wasn't like everyone else."

Cade's expression gave nothing away. "It's easy to pretend to be nice until you get what you want."

Catherine put her hand on Macy's. "Seriously, Red, screw that guy. Wait, no, I'm glad you *didn't* screw that guy."

That earned a light chuckle from Macy. But her face fell again as she looked back at her phone. "It's just another reminder that everybody else is moving forward, and I'm not. That I'm not good enough, and I'm forever swimming backward."

Cade leaned in slightly to catch Macy's eye. "I understand that."

For a moment, she didn't wonder about Gary, or her job, or even the kiss last night. She wondered what Cade really wanted to say.

Catherine scoffed, but her smile softened. "You say that like you've lived it."

Cade tilted his glass toward her in mock salute. "Let's just say I've spent a few years staring at the target, wondering if I even brought the right bow."

Macy chuckled under her breath, the sound tentative but real. She toyed with her fork, watching the sauce smear across her plate. "Do you ever stop feeling like you're behind?"

"No," Cade admitted. "But you get better at ignoring the scoreboard. Eventually, you realize the real race isn't with anyone else. It's with the version of yourself you're brave enough to become."

Catherine pointed her fork at him. "Damn. That's good. You should write that down."

Macy shook her head, a half-laugh escaping her. "You're either weirdly philosophical or secretly a therapist moonlighting as a barista."

"Guilty of neither," Cade said. "But I know what it feels like to have your confidence kicked in the teeth. Doesn't mean you stop showing up."

Something in the silence that followed felt steadier than the moment before. Macy glanced at her phone again, but this time didn't pick it up.

"Thanks," she said quietly.

Cade gave a modest nod. "Anytime."

Catherine leaned back in her seat, watching the two of them with an unreadable expression. "All I'm saying is, maybe the curse of the Macy isn't a curse at all. Maybe it's a filter."

"A very aggressive one," Macy muttered.

"But one that leaves room for someone who actually sees you," Catherine said.

Macy blinked, her gaze drifting to Cade, who looked back without flinching.

Cade offered a sympathetic smile. "Life isn't a straight line. Sometimes, you've got to pull the arrow back to be able to fire it forward."

Macy was caught off guard by his sincerity; her fork paused midair. Catherine, however, rolled her eyes as she lifted her wine glass. "That was deep," she teased, offering a mock toast. "Are you about to hit us with 'everything happens for a reason?'"

Cade chuckled, the sound low and self-deprecating. "Nah. I'm just saying, sometimes you think you're moving in the right direction, and then life throws a curveball. I told you at the club I'd had some upheaval. I didn't mention my fiancée, Hannah."

"Wait," Catherine interrupted. "You're engaged?"

"Easy," Cade said, both palms raised. "She passed away."

"What?" Catherine and Macy echoed, startled into silence.

He glanced down at his glass, his voice steady but quieter now. "I'll tell you the whole story another time if you want, but we had been together a while. I wanted to buckle down and start making plans, but she always had an excuse as to why we couldn't pin down a date. We were visiting with her family when the crash happened."

Taken aback by the sudden turn in the conversation and how easy it was for Cade to talk about it, Macy couldn't hide her shock. "I'm so sorry, Cade. That must have been—"

"Rough? You have no idea. It was a hard several months." He swirled the ice in his glass and finished his Coke. "I thought I knew her a lot better than I did, but one day, everything changed."

Macy's pulse raced, eyes wide. "What happened to her?"

"We'll never have all the details, I suppose, but she was out with a bunch of friends one night. She swore I could trust them. They were driving too fast and lost control of the car. It was when I was moving her things out that I found out she had another guy on the side and was planning on breaking up with me."

Macy's breath caught. She'd expected vulnerability, maybe some bitterness, but not this quiet, unflinching honesty. "I'm...I'm so sorry, Cade. That must've been a shock."

He offered half a shrug. "Yeah. A mess. And lonely."

Catherine's fire cooled, her expression softening with a rare flicker of compassion. "That's really heavy. I'm sorry."

Cade gave a thin smile. "As I said, life's not a straight line." He looked at Macy, his gaze gentler now. "Sometimes when you think you're stuck, you're just being redirected."

Macy didn't answer—she couldn't. Something was disconcerting about how calmly he described such painful unraveling, something she didn't quite trust. Had he processed it, or buried it too neatly?

Before the mood could anchor deeper, Catherine swooped in with perfect timing. She plucked Macy's phone from the table with a triumphant smirk. "Okay! Enough with the tragedy. We're here to celebrate, remember?"

Macy reached across the table, fumbling for the phone. "Give me that!"

"Nope." Catherine slipped it into her purse with the speed of a thief on a bank heist. "No more obsessing over texts from guys who aren't worth the data they burned to ghost you. Now—spill. You still haven't told us about this new job."

Macy narrowed her eyes and launched a breadstick at her, which Catherine caught with theatrical flair. "I tried to lead with that," Macy huffed. "But someone was way more interested in dissecting my dating life!"

Catherine popped the breadstick in her mouth and winked at her. "Come on, you know you're too good for him."

"But—"

"Nope. Be honest, Mace. Six months from now, will you even remember anything you talked about? Was he really that unforgettable?"

Macy sighed, the truth weighing heavier than the disappointment. "I guess not. He came off as nice at first, but we only texted for what, a week and a half? I'm not going to waste my energy mourning a fantasy."

"That's my girl." Catherine gave a satisfied nod, reaching for her wine glass.

Macy tried a tentative smile. Partly to appease her friend, partly because Cade was still watching her with quiet interest. Something was grounding about his presence, as if he saw through the act without intruding on it.

"Well," Macy said, steering the conversation deliberately, "my new boss thinks I'm overqualified for the job she hired me for."

Catherine's eyes widened. "Say what? I mean, obviously true, but spill."

Macy launched into a retelling of her meeting with Amara, the discussion about OptiHealth, and the strange mix of pressure and possibility that came with the new role. Catherine bounced in her seat with excitement, while Cade listened intently, his expression contemplative.

"I'm telling you," Catherine said, slapping the table lightly, "this isn't a moonwalk. It's a cha-cha. One step backward to take another step forward."

Macy twisted the stem of her water glass, her voice more cautious. "If you throw in one more corny platitude, you'll be wearing this water."

Cade chuckled, and Catherine shrugged. "I'm just saying!"

Macy rolled her eyes. "It's still a pay cut. And I'm nervous. She is...severe. She told me not to be afraid of her, but it felt more like a warning."

"Listen," Catherine said, now riffling through her purse to pay her part of the check. "You're a redhead. There's fire in your DNA. You need to act like it. Don't let Amara, or Gary the Ghost Texter, or anyone bulldoze you."

Macy chuckled, the edge of her doubt softening. "I'll try."

"No, Mace," Catherine said, locking eyes with her. "You show her the badass I know is in there. And trust me, once she sees it? The whole C-suite will be rearranging their schedules to follow your lead."

Cade raised his glass with a faint smile. "Quietly bold," he said.

Macy glanced between them, the tension of uncertainty shifting just slightly toward belief. Macy smiled warmly at her friend. "Thank you, Catherine. Really. You always know what to say. Now give me back my damn phone."

Laughing, Catherine fished it out of her purse and handed it over. Macy reached for her wallet, but Cade waved her off before she could open it.

"It's on me today, ladies."

"Oh! That's very kind of you," Catherine said, flashing her feline grin once more.

"Don't mention it," Cade replied easily, settling back as the two women gathered their things and headed for the door.

Outside, Catherine linked her arm through Macy's as they strolled down the sunlit sidewalk toward their offices.

"So!" Catherine said, her tone unmistakably mischievous.

Macy groaned. "Don't even start."

"What? If you're looking for rebound material, you could do a lot worse. And he's clearly ready to be molded into whatever your little heart desires."

Macy rolled her eyes, but the reluctant smile tugged at her lips. She shook her head at her, lost for words.

Still, Cade lingered in her mind. The conversation about Hannah had blindsided her. Not because he'd shared something heavy, but because he'd done it so plainly. It was too intimate, too exposed, for a second encounter. And yet...There he was. Calm. Composed. Watching.

After parting ways with Catherine, Macy pulled out her phone to check the time, but paused when she saw a notification.

One friend request. *Cade Donovan.*

Her breath hitched before she caught herself. Don't be ridiculous. It's just Facebook. And isn't this what you want—someone who's interested enough to follow up?

Still, the coincidence nagged at her. Cade had shown up at lunch as if by chance. But was it? Did he know she'd be there? Was it truly luck— or something more deliberate?

Pushing the thought aside, she tapped "Confirm," locked her phone, and tucked it away. She had enough on her plate today. No need to spiral over a social media ping.

Yet as she climbed the steps back into work, a strange chill pricked her spine. The feeling wasn't fear, exactly. But something sat heavy beneath her skin.

A quiet instinct whispered: This wouldn't be the last time Cade Donovan showed up somewhere unexpected.

Part Three

Cade

Celeste's Office

I arrived early for my second appointment with Celeste, needing time to settle before I stepped inside. The chair outside Celeste's office was surprisingly plush—inviting in a way that made me wish she used that one during our sessions. I sank into it, legs crossed neatly in my khaki slacks and forest green blouse, still dressed from work. I'd straightened my hair this morning, now kept at a shoulder length when natural, then pulled it into a bun high on my head.

I crossed and recrossed my legs, my foot tapping a jittery rhythm against the polished wood floor. I was less nervous than last time, but the unease hadn't vanished—it had only shifted shape.

Celeste greeted me with her signature warmth, dressed sharply in a cream-colored pantsuit that made her look more like a power CEO than a therapist. "Come on in, Macy. Welcome back."

The leather couch, previously a fortress of discomfort, was a little less unforgiving today. I folded my legs under myself and got ready to once again bare my soul. Celeste took her seat across from me, patient and composed.

"How are you feeling about our conversation last week?" she asked gently. "I know it must have been hard to start reliving those memories."

I let out a nervous laugh, eyes darting toward the flickering candle. "Hard doesn't even begin to cover it. I spent so long trying not to remember. Now I'm supposed to tear open everything I worked to forget. It's like deliberately walking back into a storm."

Celeste nodded slowly, grounding the moment with a clinical kind of compassion. "It's painful, I know. But I often compare it to resetting a bone that didn't heal right. We have to break it open, examine it, and set it properly. It hurts, but it's how you begin to heal."

I considered that. A broken bone. A clean break. A reset.

I pulled the throw blanket from the back of the couch, folding it over my lap like a buffer to hide my vulnerability. "It's exhausting," I murmured. "Wanting. Watching. Pretending not to care."

Celeste nodded. "That's the cost of silence. Of holding everything inside for so long. The healing begins when you give yourself permission to want without shame. When you stop apologizing for being hungry for something better."

A slow tear slipped down my cheek. Not from pain, exactly, but from the unexpected relief of being understood.

Celeste didn't rush me. She waited.

And for the first time in years, I didn't feel like I had to defend the ache in my heart.

Celeste folded one leg over the other, her expression warm but steady. "I'd like to shift gears today and focus on those feelings in the first weeks after you met Cade. You mentioned he pursued you heavily, though he didn't ask for your number that night?"

I shifted in my seat and reached instinctively toward my bun, searching for the curl I usually tug when nervous—another habit I didn't know I had until Cade pointed it out. My fingers met only smooth strands pinned tight, and I paused.

"Yeah," I said, fidgeting instead with the gold pendant at my collarbone. "First, he just…happened to be on the same side of one of the largest cities in the country. Same restaurant. Same exact moment as Catherine and me. Then, he found me on Facebook and sent me a friend request. It unsettled me. I couldn't name why exactly, but…I also liked the attention."

Celeste nodded with a small smile, gently urging me to keep going.

"That wasn't the only time he showed up unexpectedly," I continued. "I decided I wanted to do something about the weight I'd gained, so I went to this gym near the office. He walked in just as I was on my way out. Asked me how long I'd been a member. I told him it was new—told him I was trying to lose about forty pounds. He said he'd lost eighty himself and offered to help me."

I glanced out the window behind her, searching the skyline as if the memories were waiting there. "I said I'd see how the first couple of weeks went. But I couldn't shake the feeling. In a city this big…how did he keep showing up? How does someone just 'run into' you that many times?"

Celeste didn't speak, just waited. She nodded softly, head tipped in an expression of sympathetic understanding.

"I remember Catherine telling me Shane was coming home from deployment soon. She promised things wouldn't change—that we'd still have our girl time. So, I started trying again on the dating apps. I had a lot of conversations—some promising, some forgettable—plenty of first dates. Through all of it, Cade was texting me. Calling. Always trying to hold my attention."

I pulled the throw blanket tighter around my waist. "He told me about his career in marketing. Said he'd wanted to go into computer science at first, like me, and still liked building systems. We found overlap—same favorite authors, same old Nintendo games, even the same weird candy. It felt silly, but he kept calling it 'serendipity.' Like it meant something. Like we were destined, or something."

Celeste's pen moved slowly across the page, but her focus never wavered.

"His persistence eventually paid off. A couple of months after we met, he caught me on the right day—one of those days when the guard is down, and you're just tired of being disappointed. The date I'd been on the night before had gone especially poorly, one of those awkward dinners where silence says more than anyone means to.

"So, when Cade asked again about helping me at the gym, I said yes.

"He showed up when he said he would. He helped me with form, offered tips on routines, and encouraged me when the scale started to budge. We messaged often, sometimes joking, sometimes getting into deeper conversations. At first, he was a safe place. Attention that was given willingly, that I didn't have to fight for.

"At first, things seemed perfectly normal."

Chapter Six

BREAKING WALLS

The workout hadn't even started yet, and Macy was sweating. Mostly from her palms, but she could feel the trickle of heat gathering along her spine. *What am I so nervous about?* she wondered. *We've met before. It's not a date. He's just coaching me. It's only a workout.*

Still, as Cade approached with that familiar, easy smile, something tightened in her gut. She couldn't tell if the feeling was excitement or dread.

"Where do you want to start today?" she asked, reaching for her water bottle with more enthusiasm than she felt.

"Hi, by the way!" Cade said with mock indignation. "Nice to see you on purpose this time. I like my conversations with a proper hello."

Macy's fingers flew to her gold cross, her usual nervous tic. "Oh! Sorry. Hi, Cade. And thank you for helping me."

His smile didn't waver, though he tilted his head slightly. "Are you always this sensitive? I'm just giving you a hard time," he said lightly. "Let's warm up, hit the elliptical, and start focusing on calories out. You've got to watch calories in, too."

"Right." Macy nodded. "I know, I've gotten a little too attached to easy meals and a full plate."

"And that's fine, sometimes," Cade replied. He began guiding her through a series of stretches with practiced ease. "When I lost weight, I didn't give up what I liked. I just ate way less of it. And in my case? A lot less."

Macy glanced at his frame: lean, muscular, almost intimidatingly controlled. "It's hard to believe you had issues with weight. You look so...well, disciplined."

"Oh, make no mistake," he said, stretching out his arms. "I'm in control now. But back then? I was a total fatty. Soda was my weakness. Ever heard of Green River?"

"Green River?" Macy echoed.

He guided her into a seated V stretch and stepped behind her, gently pressing at her lower back. Her muscles resisted, but her body obeyed. "I'm going to pretend I didn't hear that," he teased. "It's pop. Lime flavored, total sugar bomb. If you've ever lived in Illinois, you'd know. It was all I drank. That, plus pizza and burgers…and those powdery candy bottle caps. Before I knew it, I was pushing three hundred."

Macy blinked, picturing him in that other body, trying to square it with the person behind her now.

"One day," he said, leaning back, "I just didn't want to be that guy anymore. Came to this gym. Swapped the Green River for water. Never looked back."

"I had my aha moment during my last visit home," Macy said, her voice tight but steady. "My aunt had some pretty unpleasant things to say. Then I ran into my old high school bully—still thin, blond, and flawless, of course. Perfect husband. Perfect kids. Living the perfect life. And me? I'd just been dumped. That night at the club, he was feeding me some line about how he panicked about getting serious, when on the day we broke up, he said it was my weight and another woman. So, yeah…now here I am."

Cade nodded like he'd heard this story before. "I get that. I was bullied too. No one wants the smart kid around. Makes them nervous."

Macy offered a bright smile, warmth sparking in her chest. "Right? I threw myself into dance, sports, and arts, and was never great at any of them. But I was smart, and that made me stand out in all the wrong ways."

She was starting to relax, at least enough for small talk. After finishing their stretches, they headed toward the elliptical machines and climbed on side by side.

Macy glanced over just in time to see Cade wince as he shifted his stance.

"You okay?" she asked.

He straightened and gave a short laugh. "Yeah. It's my knees reminding me they hate me. Old injury from high school. Football messed them up and did a number on my back, too. Most days I work through it, but cardio likes to remind me I'm not invincible anymore."

"And yet you still come to the gym," she said, impressed.

"Keeps me moving," he replied with a shrug. "A little pain's better than letting everything lock up. I've got a whole arsenal of tricks to manage it."

He didn't elaborate, and Macy didn't press, but the way he shifted his weight made her curious. She turned her attention toward the TVs set up near the cardio station, watching the highlights from the World Series game the night before.

"You into baseball?" Cade asked.

"I wasn't until I moved here."

He chuckled. "Yeah, this city worships its teams. Still, I'm a Cubs guy. Can't let that go."

Macy smiled back, cautious but trying to keep it light. "Makes sense. I'm a New Yorker now, so I guess that comes with the territory."

"Wait, do they even have baseball in South Dakota?"

"I'm from Iowa," she corrected gently. "Near South Dakota. We've got rec leagues, college teams…"

Cade threw her a grin laced with sarcasm. "I know, honey. I'm teasing. I know exactly where you're from."

Macy blinked, her fingers brushing the machine's handles as her chest tightened slightly. She looked down at the timer. "So…how long do we go on this thing?"

"You ready to be rid of me already?" Cade asked with a playful pout.

"Gotcha," Macy shot back, matching his sarcasm with a smile of her own.

They settled into a rhythm: easy conversation, steady movement. After five miles, Cade slowed his pace and announced they were done for the day. He led her through a cool-down stretch, his tone light again, almost rehearsed.

Macy took a long drink from her water bottle, her eyes scanning the gym without landing anywhere. She risked a glance in Cade's direction and caught him watching her, his stare deliberate, unreadable.

"What?" she asked, trying to keep her voice casual.

"Nothing," he said, smiling shyly. "You sure I can't take you for a drink?"

Macy laughed, the irony not lost on her. "We just finished a workout, and now you want booze?"

"Balance," Cade replied with an easy shrug.

She smiled, but it lacked enthusiasm. "I appreciate it, Cade. But if I'm really going to do this, I have to commit. All in."

Cade's expression shifted. "Macy, let me ask you something." His voice dropped, gaze flicking toward the exit. "How are those dating apps treating you?"

"Uhm—" Macy blinked, caught off guard by the sudden shift. The question felt loaded, like a trap disguised as concern.

"Sorry," Cade said quickly. Too quickly. "None of my business. I'll see you in two days." He nodded curtly and pursed his lips, then turned and walked out without another word.

Macy watched him go, a strange mix of disappointment and unease curling in her stomach. *Why do I feel let down when I was the one who said no?*

She gathered her things from the locker room, still replaying the moment. *Should I text him? Explain?* But how could she explain feelings she didn't fully understand?

She had a few conversations on the apps. Some promising, some not. But did she really believe any of them would end differently from the ones before?

Why does he unsettle me so much? Is it his intensity?

We have so much in common. We want the same things.

And he wants to date me.

So, why do I feel just a little bit intimidated by him?

How do we keep ending up in the same places? Was he teasing about spying on me?

Come on, get real. He was kidding.

She walked the seven blocks back to her apartment, the city buzzing around her, her thoughts louder still. By the time she reached the stairs to her building, she was exhausted from the mental tug-of-war.

Just as she started up, Theo stepped out, smiling warmly and waving to catch her attention.

"Earth calling to Macy!"

She blinked, startled out of her spiral. "Oh, hey, Theo."

"Sweet girl, who's winning that epic argument you've got going with your inner monologue?" Theo's teasing voice cut through Macy's fog like sunlight.

With a belly laugh, Macy finally came back to herself. "Thank you, Theo. I really needed that. How's the artwork?"

"It's another masterpiece, of course." He winked, then softened. "Seriously, though. You all right?"

"I'm okay. Just...lost in thought," Macy said, forcing a smile. "Honest."

Theo didn't respond right away, just studied her with a tilt of his head.

She smirked. "I'm fine, I promise. It's nothing a little General Tso chicken wouldn't fix."

"Touché," Theo replied, his grin returning as he rubbed her arm with quiet warmth. "I'm willing to share if you need a pick-me-up."

Macy summoned her brightest smile. "I'm headed up for the night. Catherine's home, and I might call Nina or my parents. I'm good."

"Okay, I'll believe you," Theo said, eyes still searching hers. "But I'm just down the hall if you change your mind. Well, after I grab my takeout. You know what I mean."

Laughing now, Macy gave him a playful shove. "Go get your dinner. I know where to find you if I need to talk."

By the time she reached the third flight of stairs, her legs were already reminding her that she and the elliptical had spent an hour together. She was eager to run things past Catherine and Nina. Maybe they could help her sort the tangle of thoughts Cade had left behind.

She hadn't meant to feel so thrown. But there it was: embarrassment, uncertainty, a reluctance she couldn't name or shake.

Inside the apartment, laughter floated in from the kitchen, glasses clinking like wind chimes. Before she could even scan the room, Nina threw an arm around her shoulder, and Catherine handed her a wine glass.

"Did I miss something?" Macy asked. "What's the celebration?"

"We've been waiting for you, my Macy Lynn!" Nina declared, hugging her tightly.

"Have you, now?" Macy raised an eyebrow, head cocked quizzically. "And exactly how many bottles of Cabernet have you helped yourselves to while you waited?"

Nina burst into laughter and flopped into her usual seat at the kitchen table. Catherine smirked and turned to Macy with a sparkle in her eyes.

"You are now looking at the new director of public relations for Beacon AI. Found out today."

"Why didn't you say so sooner? Pour that wine!" Macy exclaimed, throwing her arms around her friend. "Congratulations!"

"Thank you, thank you." Catherine offered a theatrical bow before joining Nina at the table. "Looks like things are finally turning for the

Red Roses. I will give notice tomorrow and start right after Thanksgiving. It's not a big raise, but the profit sharing is excellent, and the benefits? Outstanding!"

"That's amazing. I'm so happy for you," Macy beamed.

Catherine paused, her eyes narrowing just slightly. "All right, enough about me. You had the world riding on your shoulders when you walked in. How was your date with Cade?"

"Well..." Macy hesitated. "It wasn't a date. We met at the gym. He's helping to train me."

"Train you for what?" Catherine asked, her tone light but pointed. "Got an event coming up?"

"Funny," Macy muttered with a smirk. "You know how sensitive I've been about the weight. He lost a lot himself, so he offered to help me lose mine."

"Good," Catherine said simply. "You deserve some sparkle."

She narrowed her eyes at Macy, still smirking. "But if he ever dims it, he will lose his—"

"Catherine!" Macy and Nina shouted in unison.

"What? I have tools."

Nina threw a couch pillow at Catherine. "Oh, come on, Mace. He hasn't left you alone since that night at The Echelon Club," Nina slurred, swirling the last inch of Cabernet in her glass. "He was engaged once, so you know he's not afraid of commitment. He's got a decent job in marketing; he's rocking the tall-dark-and-mysterious thing, and looking fine while doing it. Why are you still holding out for one of those app guys when this one's basically ripe for the picking?"

Macy paused, staring into her own glass as she slowly rotated it. The wine caught the light in soft waves, giving her an excuse not to meet Nina's expectant stare, or Catherine's quieter one. The question wasn't easy. The answer, even less so.

"I feel...something," she said finally. "Intimidated, maybe. Cade's passionate, and—I don't know—it kind of scares me."

"That's fair," Nina murmured, her voice low and careful. "But have you ever wondered if maybe you're so used to things going wrong that it feels strange when things go right?"

"I hadn't thought about that. But you might be right. You should've seen the look he gave me when I said no to a drink tonight, as if I'd slapped him. I told him I wanted to stay focused on the gym, but on my walk home, I rehashed every word we said. I keep wondering if I chased him off."

"Well," Catherine said with an easy shrug, "why not just call him and talk about it?"

"Why do you always have to be so reasonable?" Macy teased, keeping her tone dry even as a smile tugged at her lips.

As the bottle finally emptied, Macy picked up her phone to order Nina an Uber. "You should just call Brian to come get you. And maybe be a little nicer to him?"

"Nah," Nina groaned. "He's just so...boring."

"I'll never understand you," Macy said, shaking her head as she tapped the screen. *Some people don't know how good they have it.*

After a pause, she asked, "Do you really think I should call Cade? It's getting kind of late."

"Yes!" Nina and Catherine shouted in unison.

Laughing, Macy hugged them both goodnight and slipped into her room. She sent Cade a quick text.

> *Macy*
> *Hey. Sorry if I was short earlier.*
> *Just a lot on my mind.*

Less than five minutes later, her phone lit up.

"Well, that was fast," Macy said as she answered. "Were you waiting on me?"

Cade chuckled softly. "Wouldn't say waiting, but I wondered if you would get in touch."

Macy settled back against her pillows. "Listen, I just wanted to say I didn't mean to be aloof earlier. I'm figuring some things out, and it's not about you—not really. I didn't mean to brush you off."

"Okay," Cade replied, cautious but listening.

She took a breath, slow and deliberate. "So…maybe I could say yes. If you still wanted to ask me out again."

"I have to admit, that's not what I was expecting to hear," Cade said, his voice low and measured. "That's a pretty sudden shift from earlier tonight. What happened?"

"I thought about our conversation all the way home," Macy replied. "Then I talked to my girlfriends, and they made me wonder…maybe I'm scared. Scared of something actually working out for once. And maybe they're right."

Cade exhaled slowly, almost as if trying to weigh the words. "Let me get this straight. You were putting me off because you were afraid it might actually work? Am I hearing that right?"

"It doesn't make sense when you say it out loud," Macy admitted, heat prickling her cheeks. "But yeah…that's their theory. Because 'things going wrong' has become familiar. Comfortable, in a way. And maybe I need to step outside that comfort zone."

He was quiet for a beat longer than she expected. "Still trying to wrap my head around it," he said softly. "So…you changed your mind because your friends talked you into it? What do *you* want, Macy?"

Her stomach clenched. That wasn't the response she'd anticipated.

"I want what you want," she said, voice tentative. "A stable future. A family."

"And you're saying maybe you want that with me?"

Macy hesitated, searching for footing. "I mean, it's a bit early to talk about that yet. But maybe we could try…"

Her words faded. A silence stretched between them, awkward and heavy. She suddenly wished she'd never made the call.

"Macy," Cade said finally, his tone unreadable, "you know, you're not the only one in this city using the apps."

"I'm…sorry?" Macy blinked. "What do you mean?"

"I've been talking to a few people, too. One of them, Natalie, asked me out tomorrow night. I said yes."

"Oh," Macy said, the word catching in her throat. "I understand. Enjoy yourself. I'll see you at the gym, like we planned."

They ended the call. Macy stood still for a moment before walking into the living room.

"I blew it," she said as Catherine looked up from the couch. "I told you I blew it."

"What happened?"

"He has a date tomorrow night. Gave up waiting for me."

Catherine offered a soft "It's okay," before her eyes sparkled with mischief. "We could always crash it. A little sabotage never hurt."

Macy gave a weak smile and shook her head. "No. I made my bed."

"Damn it," Catherine muttered. "I don't even have anything nearby to swat you with. It's just a date, right? Not a proposal. He didn't say anything about being exclusive."

"I guess not," Macy said. "I think I need to sleep on it."

But just as she turned away, her phone rang again.

"It's Cade," she said, breath hitching.

"Well, answer it!" Catherine said, already jumping off the couch, eager for intel.

Before Macy could get the phone to her ear, Cade's voice burst through: "I canceled my date. I'll call you tomorrow."

Macy froze. "Oh!" was all she could manage before the line went dead.

She and Catherine stared at each other, wide-eyed.

"Well," Catherine said slowly, "that was certainly… unexpected."

Chapter Seven

HONESTY

Macy sat at her desk that Friday afternoon, acutely aware that it was her final day with her current team before transitioning to Amara MacNash's office. The bittersweet hum of change hovered in the air.

"Ah!" Macy squealed, nearly leaping out of her chair as Nancy clapped her on the back.

She spun around just in time to see Brett stepping forward with a cake that read *Good luck, Macy!* in slightly smudged blue icing. Behind him stood Nancy, Libby, Randy, and Wayne—all familiar faces from her department.

"Surprise!" they called out in unison.

Macy blinked back sudden tears, smiling as warmth flooded her chest. She wasn't leaving the company, but everything else was about to shift. A new building. A new boss. A new rhythm.

She glanced around at her team, cataloging the moments she'd miss. Weekly status meetings with Nancy that came with coffee, donuts, and *Dancing with the Stars* gossip. The miniature York Peppermint Pattie Randy always left on her chair, without fail. Libby, her mentor since her internship. Wayne would be heading to Brett's team to develop training tools.

It was a small, tight-knit group. She knew their habits, their quirks, and they knew hers. The thought of her new office on the fifty-second floor of a glass-and-steel skyscraper in the Financial District made her stomach flutter. Amara was brilliant and intimidating, even when she insisted she wasn't. But Macy was ready to rise to the challenge.

"Try not to make us look bad over at the corporate office," Nancy teased, grinning.

"As if I could," Macy said with a laugh. "Amara's not exactly one for idle gossip. I'll be lucky to remember my lunch break."

"Oh, she'll keep you busy," Brett said, lowering the cake onto the table and carving out the first slice. "But she chose you for a reason. She doesn't waste her time unless she sees serious potential."

"That's equal parts comforting and terrifying," Macy replied, accepting the slice as he handed it to her.

Brett smirked. "Give it six months. You'll be running the place and telling Amara where to be."

Macy nearly choked on her bite, sputtering through a laugh. "If by 'running the place,' you mean memorizing her coffee order and managing her calendar, then sure!"

"No," Brett said, settling into a seat with his own slice. "You don't realize how capable you are. You know you're smart. But mark my words, there's a fire in you that hasn't been sparked yet. Amara might be just the one to strike the match."

Macy flushed, both flattered and unsure. "Thanks, Brett. I guess we'll see."

As the afternoon waned, she packed up the last of her things, shut down her computer, and turned off her desk lamp for the final time. At 4:58, her phone buzzed.

Cade
How's the last day going?

Macy

Just wrapped up. How was yours?

Cade

It's fine. I'm headed for the subway now.

Cade

Why don't you call me once you're settled in? We can talk about things.

Macy

I can do that! Safe travels.

Cade

You too.

Here goes nothing, Macy thought. This step of her career had come to a close, and she was about to take a leap in both her professional and personal life. She grabbed her purse and ducked into Nancy's office one last time.

Nancy pulled her into a hug that surprised her with its intensity. "Don't be a stranger, okay?" she whispered.

"I won't," Macy promised, her voice catching as the first tears slipped down her cheeks. She made a slow final round through the cubicles, letting the moment linger. At Brett's desk, she paused.

He smiled and gave her hand a gentle squeeze. "Leave your box, Macy. You're leaving the building, not the business. I'll have it sent to your new space Monday."

"Oh!" She blinked. "That's incredibly helpful. Thank you."

"No need to juggle a cardboard box on the subway," Brett replied with a wink. "We'll miss you around here. Now go—you've got bigger and better ahead."

"I hope you're right," Macy murmured, *in more ways than one.*

Macy hated phone calls. Always had. Texting was safer, cleaner. Email, even better. A phone call meant vulnerability. It meant immediate presence, no time to hide behind draft folders or rephrased emojis. That was part of why she chose computers and data: They didn't require nerves of steel or eloquence under pressure.

She spent her entire subway ride home rehearsing what to say. The words, the tone, and even how to breathe between sentences. By the time she emerged onto the sidewalk, the evening breeze kissed her cheeks, and her thoughts were still humming like a script on loop.

She didn't see Theo passing in the opposite direction. He clocked the intense focus fixed on her face and chuckled under his breath. "She's in the zone," he muttered to himself, deciding not to interrupt.

Macy reached her apartment door and took a deep breath.

"All right," she whispered. "You can do this. He's expecting the call. No backing out now."

She pulled up Cade's contact, hesitated for half a second, then pressed Send.

He answered on the second ring.

"Well, hello there," Cade said cheerfully. "How was the ride?"

"It was good! How was yours?" Macy asked. She placed her purse on the counter and settled on the edge of her bed, phone pressed lightly to her ear.

"Nothing exciting or out of the ordinary," Cade replied.

A pause stretched between them. Maybe thirty seconds, maybe less. But to Macy, it felt like the ocean had opened between them. She cast around for something, anything, that didn't involve the weather or subway delays.

"So," she said carefully, "I guess you want to ask me questions about last night."

Cade gave a quiet snicker, uneasy. "You could say that. I know you've had a rough time lately. And I get it; you're scared of getting hurt again. Hell, same here. But I need to ask you to be fair to me. Because I haven't done anything wrong. And I need to know your choices are yours. Not just what your friends think is best."

"That's reasonable," Macy said softly. "And you're right. I am afraid. But it wasn't about them. They were just the ones who helped me see I was letting that fear lead me."

"Well, I'm glad it's about me and not them," Cade said. "But could you elaborate on that a little?"

"Honestly?" Macy took a breath. "It was when you left the gym yesterday. I saw how hurt you were by my hesitation, and the feeling didn't go away. Even after we talked, I felt unsettled. Like I might've messed something up. That sense of dread made me wonder if I was making a mistake. Catherine and Nina helped me realize that I've been holding back because I'm terrified of getting hurt again."

"That makes sense," Cade said, his voice quieter now.

Another pause. Not quite as awkward this time.

"So," Macy ventured, "after tomorrow's workout...?"

She heard the smile creep back into Cade's voice. "Everyone does dinner and a movie, but I think that's backward. A movie first, then dinner. Gives you something to talk about if the chemistry doesn't kick in right away. What do you think?"

"I think..." she said playfully, "do you prefer popcorn or candy with your movie?"

"Why choose?" he teased.

With a shy laugh, Macy said, "Make it a box of those bottle caps we both like, and you've got yourself a date."

Cade groaned in surrender. "What is it about those things? They're just so irresistible."

"It's kind of a nostalgia thing," Macy explained. "The summer Catherine moved to New York, I had a hard time adjusting. No cell phones back then. We didn't even have dial-up yet at the farm. Only long-distance calling cards. Ethan, my older brother, took me on a two-day road trip to nowhere. We just drove around, camped, and stopped wherever it looked cool. At one gas station, he gave me twenty bucks and said, 'Get whatever junk food you want.'"

Cade laughed. "Classic big brother move."

"He was always good to me," Macy said, smiling at the memory. "I came out with a bag of bottle caps bigger than his face. We ate them until we were sick to our stomachs. And somehow, I still love them. They remind me of being looked after."

"I wish I had memories like that with my brother," Cade said, the humor fading a little.

"You haven't told me much about your family," Macy noted.

Cade let out a dry chuckle. "You know how you have the perfectly traditional, *Better Homes and Gardens* kind of family?"

Macy laughed at the idea. *My family? Perfect?* "We're a long way from that, but go ahead."

"Well, that's not mine."

They both laughed, though Macy's smile dimmed at the edges.

"We look good from the outside, but we have issues like any other," she admitted.

"My family is more like an episode of *Jerry Springer*," Cade said with a snort. "My parents were never married. They went out a handful of times, and I was the result of their one-night union. My dad didn't want anything serious, which crushed my mom. Then she found out she was pregnant. She tried to use it to get him to stay, but he'd already fallen for someone else."

"Wow," Macy said softly. "So, after sleeping with your mom and telling her he wasn't ready for anything serious, he just…fell in love with someone else?"

"You see the drama," Cade chuckled, though his laugh held a note of discomfort. "Sheryl's actually a great woman. They got married just after I was born. A year later, they had my brother, Sean, and four years later, my sister, Talia. My mom never got over it, though. She always assumed he picked Sheryl because she came from money. They're friendly now, but back then? It was pretty messy."

"I'm not going to lie," Macy said, eyes wide. "That's not the story I was expecting."

Cade sighed. "My brother and I are close. He's my buddy. Now that I'm older and have a little more perspective, I get along a lot better with my dad and Sheryl, too. As for my mom...I don't dislike her. But she went through a dark period. Fell into a depression. Drinking became her coping mechanism, and things got rough for a while. I ended up moving in with my dad."

"And Talia?" Macy asked gently.

"She's another story," Cade said, with a small huff of breath. "She's the youngest and the only girl, so there was always this cushion around her. When I moved in, she was six. I was a stranger. She didn't understand why she suddenly had this half-brother living there. I love her, don't get me wrong, she's got a good heart. But she can be pretty self-righteous. She never liked Hannah, either. That caused a lot of tension."

Macy hesitated before continuing, choosing her words carefully. "How have things been since her...you know?"

Cade chuckled. "It's okay, Macy. You can say it…since her death. Things have been…better, a little. Talia's been with the same guy since she was a junior in high school, and now she's twenty-one. I think she's a little annoyed they're not engaged yet, but they're still so young."

"Ha, tell me about it," Macy replied. "My parents married at twenty, my brother at twenty-two, and Nina, of course, was twenty herself.

Catherine's practically married already. As soon as Shane gets back from deployment, it'll be official. And here I am, almost twenty-eight, single again, starting over in my career with an entry-level job."

She let out a sigh, the weight of it settling into her chest. "I feel like I'm so far behind. Like one day I'm going to look back, still single and childless, and wonder where my life went."

"You're not alone," Cade said. "I always thought I'd be done having kids by thirty. Now I'll be lucky just to start."

"Yes!" Macy laughed, a spark of relief in her voice. She was beginning to feel more at ease. Like maybe, just maybe, they were on the same page. *Maybe I can let my guard down a little*, she thought.

"How many do you think you want?" she asked.

Cade paused, his tone shifting slightly. "Honestly? It was hard being an only child for a long time. I loved spending more time with Sean and Talia. So, I know I don't want to do this solo. I've never pinned down a number, especially now that I'm not getting any younger, but...a couple feels right."

"Yeah," Macy said. "Me too. It's just so much easier for a man. You don't have to think about whether your body's still up for the challenge."

"No, we just have to worry if we're still, uh..." He hesitated, then chuckled. "'*Up*' to the task."

Macy roared with laughter. "Well, it won't happen if you can't *rise* to the occasion!"

"Ha! There it is," Cade said. "I wasn't sure if I should toss in a joke. I didn't want to cross any lines."

"Cade, I'm no prude. I've got a solid sense of humor. I just take the act seriously."

"That's fair," he agreed. "So...I hope I haven't talked your ear off already. I'll try to leave something to talk about over dinner tomorrow. Worst case, we've got the movie. Or that new Stephen King novel!"

Macy smiled, her comfort deepening. "We'll be fine. I think I'll do my workout at home, so I don't show up smelling like gym funk."

Cade hummed thoughtfully. "I suppose I'll allow it. The movie's at 4:30. I'll meet you there a little early and grab the tickets?"

"I'll be there."

As Macy ended the call, she stared at the phone still cradled in her hand. A quiet, surprised smile found its way to her lips. That had gone...well. Better than expected. She wasn't sure what she thought might happen—awkwardness, regret, maybe even second thoughts. But instead?

A ghost of excitement tugged at her.

She opened her bedroom door to find Catherine standing just outside.

"If you're looking for a bedtime story," Macy said, amused, "you could've just asked."

Catherine gave an innocent shrug and gestured toward the kitchen. "I was checking to see if you're hungry. I cooked dinner!" Her expression shifted from playful to triumphant, flashing a wide, toothy grin.

Macy narrowed her eyes in mock irritation, but couldn't suppress her smile. She laughed, shook her head, wandered into the kitchen, and poured herself a glass of ice water. "So, what culinary masterpiece do we have tonight? Mac and cheese? Maybe a grilled cheese with flair?"

"You're glowing," Catherine said, not even looking up as she plated roasted sweet potatoes. "So, I'm guessing the call went well?"

Macy sank into her chair, finally able to exhale. "It actually did."

Catherine nodded and handed over a plate. "Did he apologize? Get dramatic? Propose elopement?"

Macy groaned at her and rolled her eyes, then recounted their conversation. They ate in comfortable silence for a few moments, the air easy now, the weight of the day beginning to lift. Then Macy looked up again. "It's strange. After everything that happened last year, I didn't think I'd trust anyone again. But Cade...he's different. He doesn't feel like he's performing."

"That's probably because he's not," Catherine said, pointing her fork. "He might actually be being real. Don't talk yourself out of that."

Macy smiled, half sheepish, half hopeful. "Do I ever not overthink something?"

Catherine gave her a look. "I've known you since fifth grade. So, no. But tonight? Maybe just enjoy the fact that he made you laugh...and didn't screw it up."

Macy raised her sparkling water. "To not screwing it up."

Catherine clinked her glass against hers. "To emotionally available gym boys."

They both laughed, and for the first time in days, some of the tension Macy carried in her shoulders started to unfurl.

After dinner, they loaded plates into the dishwasher and settled on the couch. Macy let out a long, dramatic groan.

"What's it gonna be tonight?" she asked. "Trash reality shows or trash documentaries?"

They looked at each other and said in unison: "Reality shows!"

With a laugh, Catherine queued up *The Bachelorette*. As the recap from the previous week played, she nudged Macy's arm.

"If it doesn't work out with Cade, I'm nominating you for this show."

Macy swatted her hand, grinning. "Don't even think about it."

Catherine wiggled her eyebrows. "Too late."

They fell into easy laughter and watched in companionable silence.

"Popcorn?" Macy asked, already shifting toward the kitchen.

Without tearing her eyes from the screen, Catherine answered, "Thought you'd never ask."

Chapter Eight

THE WAY FORWARD

Saturday afternoon was a whirlwind of frustration and flying fabric. Macy cycled through every conceivable outfit in her closet—most twice—and grew more irritated with each one. Shirts, dresses, and pants landed in messy piles across the room, none feeling quite right. Catherine sat cross-legged on the bed, sipping wine like a judge presiding over an unhinged fashion show.

Just as Macy reached the edge of total collapse, Catherine called for backup.

Nina breezed through the door with a garment bag in one hand and a bottle of Pinot Noir in the other.

"*Give me that*!" Macy shouted, lunging for the bag.

"The garment bag or the wine?" Nina teased, holding the bottle just out of reach.

"Both, obviously," Macy groaned, snatching the bag and hugging it like a life raft. "But mostly the outfit. I do not need more sugar right now. Are you sure this even fits me?"

Her voice wavered slightly, and she held out the bag as if it might bite.

"Relax!" Nina flopped onto the bed and popped open the wine. "Didn't you say you were working out with him first? He'll already see you sweaty. You should be more worried about smelling like gym socks at the theater."

"I worked out this morning, and I already showered, you bitch," Macy snapped, rolling her eyes.

She opened the bag and pulled out a royal blue wrap blouse and a sleek black pencil skirt. She buckled the clasp at her waist, stepped into the skirt, and added simple black pumps.

"See?" Nina said, gesturing like a proud stylist. "Perfect."

Catherine squinted, snatching up Nina's wine bottle. "Nina, he's taking her to a movie, not the Met Gala. Don't you think this is a little over the top?"

"You're no help," Macy grumbled.

"I'm plenty of help," Catherine retorted, refilling her glass. "Two hours in a theater, and last I checked, he's not whisking you off to a five-course tasting menu. Wear something comfortable. What about that cream sweater dress with the black leggings? Keep the pumps if you want. Just ditch the red-carpet vibes."

She paused, tilting her head. "And besides, he already asked you out. That's the hard part."

Macy hesitated. "I know you're right, but this feels different. He canceled with someone else to see me. I feel like...I need to impress him tonight."

Catherine smirked. "Red, if you don't pick something soon, I'm picking for you. And trust me, there will be sequins."

"You wouldn't."

"If she doesn't," Nina chimed in, "I will."

"With friends like you..." Macy muttered, grabbing the wine and taking a long drink.

She stripped off the pencil skirt and blouse and slid into the outfit Catherine had suggested. The sweater dress clung in all the right places, and the leggings gave just enough comfort to keep her grounded. She added a wide black belt, then turned toward the mirror.

For the first time in days, she saw herself again.

The outfit was soft and flattering. The pumps gave Macy height without sacrifice, and her curls framed her face with a curtain of fringe. Nina stepped in and gently pinned a wispy strand behind Macy's ear.

"Now you're ready to get it."

"Don't do anything Nina wouldn't do," Catherine quipped.

"That doesn't leave much," Macy replied with a crooked grin.

"Bitches, I'm right here," Nina huffed.

Laughing, Macy took another sip and handed the bottle back. "Are we wrong, though?"

Nina narrowed her eyes at her but didn't argue.

"Exactly." Macy gave herself one last glance in the mirror, then turned to her friends, a deep breath anchoring her. "I do appreciate you two. Whatever nonsense I say sometimes."

"We know," Catherine said, grinning as she shoved Macy toward the door. "Now go. Before we drag out the sequins."

Macy hugged them both goodnight and stepped outside. It was still light, with summer stretching the day toward evening. The city buzzed around her, alive and vibrant, but she kept one hand tucked inside her purse, her fingers curled around the cool metal of her pepper spray.

She caught the 4 train at Grand Central, then walked toward Rockefeller Center, weaving through sidewalk vendors and tourists holding ice cream cones like flags. Cade was waiting near the gate, watching a group of travelers marvel at the park.

He turned when he saw her and smiled. "You look pretty tonight."

He offered her a single white rose.

Macy's smile flickered shyly as she accepted it. "Thank you."

They began walking toward the AMC theater, arm in arm. As she let Cade guide her, Macy realized how little she still knew about him. But that could be something to unpack over dinner.

"I'm assuming you're good with scary movies?" Cade asked, his tone playful.

"Would I be any kind of Stephen King fan if I wasn't?" Macy replied with a smirk. It was one of the first things they'd found they had in common, along with a shared love of '80s music and classic Nintendo games.

"The scarier, the better, if you ask me," she added. "Though you really have to work to find one that actually scares me."

They walked in comfortable silence toward the theater, the quiet humming between them not awkward, just filled with possibility. When they reached their seats, Cade grinned and pulled a bag of bottle caps from one pocket and a chilled can of Coca-Cola from the other, complete with two straws.

"I'm nothing if not a man of my word," he declared.

Macy laughed, surprised and genuinely touched. The tension that had gripped her earlier began to ease, unraveling with each small, thoughtful gesture. She settled into her seat, her shoulder brushing his as the lights dimmed.

Halfway through the movie, Cade reached over and took her hand. Macy hesitated only a moment before letting him, leaning slightly in his direction.

After the credits rolled and the theater emptied, Cade turned to her. "You hungry? I was thinking Greek food."

"I can't say I've ever had it," Macy admitted.

"Well," he said with a slight smile, "it's my favorite. I know a great place on 46th if you're okay with a little walk."

"I could use the steps," she agreed. "Especially if I'm going to indulge. Though I did go to the gym again this morning."

"Nice!" Cade said, taking her hand again. "How's your nutrition going?"

Macy gave him a look and burst into laughter. "You're asking about my nutrition while taking me out for Greek food?"

He smiled, one dimple creasing his cheek, adding an unexpectedly mischievous charm to his otherwise composed demeanor. "It's all about balance. Follow my lead. Half goes in the to-go box before you take a bite. Save the rest for tomorrow."

"That's actually smart," Macy said, nodding.

They walked the remaining blocks mostly in silence, but it was an easy silence. Macy had questions she didn't quite know how to phrase yet, and Cade seemed content to let the evening unfold naturally. She tucked the rose he'd given her into her purse, careful to leave the bloom exposed so it wouldn't get crushed.

Inside the restaurant, Macy scanned the menu, eyes darting across unfamiliar dishes and ingredients. She'd planned to play it safe with beef with broccoli, a Coke, and maybe a spring roll to share. But before she could say anything, the server arrived, and Cade ordered for both of them.

"We'll each have the gyro platter with tzatziki," he said. "Water with lemon, and could we get two to-go boxes with that?"

"Oh!" Macy blinked, startled. "I was thinking of a chicken salad for something familiar."

Cade gave her a gentle smile. "Let's get out of your comfort zone a little. Trust me on this. You'll like it."

A bit surprised by his insistence—and having never been to a Greek restaurant—she relented. "I suppose you do know better than I do." She turned to the server. "I'll have what he's having."

With the decision made, the server walked away, and the two turned back to each other. Macy had so many questions, but she didn't want to make him feel like he was in an interrogation room. So instead, she asked his opinion about the movie just as the server reappeared with their waters.

Cade squeezed his lemon into the glass and took a sip, considering. "It's always hard with the level of depth and detail Stephen King puts into his books. It's impossible to get it all in there without making the movie three months long."

Chuckling, Macy nodded in agreement. "That's true, for sure. I think that's what I enjoy most about his books, though. The level of detail gives me such an accurate picture in my mind."

"You said before the movie that it's very rare for one to scare you. Which one got to you the most?"

Macy stirred the lemon into her water and tilted her head. "You promise you won't laugh?"

He gave her a wicked grin. "Oh, this has to be good. I'll do my best!"

Hesitantly, she said, "It was *Paranormal Activity*. The original one. My brother took me to see it when I was only fifteen. I didn't know anything about it going in, but I screamed so loudly at the climax that he thought I was actually going to faint. I couldn't sleep for days. My parents wanted to kill him."

"Not what I was expecting you to say! What scared you so badly?"

"It was the fact that they didn't show you anything. I feel like, as soon as they give the demon, or whatever it is, a face, it gets campy. But as long as my brain can do the work, there's no end to what it can come up with. And I always sleep with a foot sticking out from under the blanket, so I was terrified something was going to grab me and drag me down the hall!"

At that, Cade finally broke and started to laugh. "I'm sorry. I'm not laughing at you; I'm laughing at the visual. I know what you mean, though. It's a lot less scary once you see what you're dealing with and give it a name."

"Yes!" Macy said, feeling validated. The conversation had broken the nervous tension she'd been carrying.

"So, you work in marketing? Anybody I've ever heard of?"

"Not likely," Cade replied. "I'm not with one of the Big Five. We're just a startup. I do a lot of work with websites and search engine optimization."

"Oh, SEO!"

"I forget you're a computer person too," Cade said, smiling warmly. "I really wanted to get into cybersecurity, but apparently, so does everyone else. Still, I'm solid with websites, and people say I've got a pretty decent eye for design. So, now my job's this weird hybrid of a little bit graphic design, the rest SEO." He paused, then added, "And you're with VitalSync, now OptiHealth, right?"

"Yes, that's right," Macy replied. "I definitely never imagined I'd be the personal coffee wench to the illustrious Amara MacNash, but hey, it's a job. I'm just glad I managed to avoid a gap in employment."

"'Coffee wench,' that's a good one," Cade chuckled. Then his expression shifted. "Actually, there's something I've been meaning to tell you."

Oh, God. Here it comes. Macy's spine stiffened, and her hands clenched in her lap. "Okay. I'm listening."

"I told you at the gym, I think, about all my old sports injuries."

Macy nodded, her eyes steady on him. *Is that it?* she wondered.

He continued, "Well, it's a little bit more than that. When Hannah died, I had to move her things out of my apartment. I lost my footing trying to get her dresser down the stairs, since you have to walk up a flight to get to the elevator, and I seriously screwed up my neck. Then I lost my balance and fell down the stairs, smashing my face on the back of the dresser and breaking my nose and collarbone. So, they had to put me on some extra medicines to help me recover. They had to start me on morphine."

The server arrived with their plates and takeout boxes.

"Okay," Cade said, brightening a little. "Pour at least half into the takeout container, and then dig in."

She followed his lead, spreading some tzatziki on the shredded lamb with a squeeze of lemon and taking a bite. The light and fresh creaminess of the tzatziki pulled a pleased sound from her. "Mmm. Okay, you were right about this."

Cade flashed that signature dimple. "Told you!"

They ate in easy rhythm for a moment before he continued. "Honestly, I was scared to take the meds. But it got too hard. My doctor talked me through it, and I gave in. I started having panic attacks shortly after, and they had to finally add in an anxiety pill, too."

"I can understand why that would be scary," Macy said softly. "But you've gotta take care of yourself."

"Exactly. And I assure you, I've got it under control," Cade said, his voice calm but earnest. "Honestly, I never even use the anxiety pills anymore, and the morphine's powerful stuff, so I've been working hard to taper off. You have to do it slowly. It can cause some really scary withdrawal symptoms if you go off it too fast."

He picked up his fork but didn't touch his food, watching her closely. "Anyways, I just...wanted you to know that upfront."

The vulnerability in Cade's face was unmistakable, his forehead knitted in a mask of concern. "I hope that's not a deal breaker."

Macy chewed her food and rolled over the information in her mind. She answered slowly. "Well, Cade, you've been through a lot. This is a lot for me to take in. But it sounds like you and your doctor are handling it."

Relief washed over his features, and his smile returned. "I'm so glad you trust me. Now that that conversation's over..."

"Yes, now that that's over," she echoed with a grin, easing back into her chair. "So, you said you grew up in Chicago? How'd you end up in New York? I imagine you could've found what you wanted back home."

"I needed to get away," he said, tension broken by the change in conversation. "I stayed close for college and went to Northwestern. I liked being on my own. Chicago could've worked, sure, but something about Manhattan just...pulled me in."

"Yeah, I know all about the call of Manhattan."

"I bet you do," he replied with a warm smile. "I'm guessing it's a huge difference from a farm in the Midwest?"

Laughing at the understatement, Macy nodded. "That's putting it mildly. But you know, it's just as easy to feel lost in a city of ten million as in ten acres of cornfields."

"I suppose it's not all that different, huh?"

"Not really," Macy said quietly. "I was always in my brother's shadow. Trying so hard to be good at something, anything. But besides my grades, I was mediocre, at best, at everything. And then the bullies came, and I started dreaming about escape pretty young."

She paused, then added more softly, "When Catherine's family moved away, it was just my parents and me. So, when Columbia accepted me and offered a scholarship, I didn't hesitate. I never looked back. Even in a city this big, I've felt more seen than I ever did in a place where everybody knows your name...and every piece of your business."

Cade held her gaze, steady and unwavering. "You're definitely seen tonight. By me."

Slightly taken aback by the intensity in his eyes, Macy looked away, her voice soft as she offered a shy smile. "Thank you." When she glanced back, he was still watching her, as if she were the only thing in the room worth noticing.

Just then, the server returned to ask if they wanted dessert. Cade answered for them both without shifting his focus. "Just the check, please."

Macy, the moment weighing on her shoulders, broke the silence by gathering her things. She adjusted her coat and reached for her purse, unsure what to say next.

"Can I walk you home?" Cade asked.

She hesitated. The offer was kind, but a flicker of caution tugged at her. She appreciated his concern, but wasn't sure how far that care would extend.

"I remember what you said at lunch," he added quickly, reading her hesitation. "Please don't worry. I won't push. I just want to make sure you get home safe."

It was uncanny, the way he tuned into her thoughts. Still, she exhaled deeply, the tension in her shoulders loosening. "Yes, in that case...I'd like that."

As Cade settled the bill, Macy shrugged into her coat. When they stepped outside, he reached for her hand once more, and she didn't pull away. "Well, then," he said with a smile, "lead the way."

The restaurant sat just a few blocks from Grand Central Station, and Macy instinctively turned toward the entrance for the number 4 train. "So, how long did it take you to get used to the subway?" she asked.

"Not long," Cade replied. "We have trains in Chicago, though nothing as big and sprawling as this system. I've got kind of an eidetic memory for some things, so I rarely get lost." He paused, then glanced over. "How about you?"

"Oh, it took me ages," Macy laughed. "I never got lost in Springwater, but that's kind of hard to do in a town without a stoplight. Catherine and I are still in the same apartment we got when I first landed here. So, I've got the hang of it now."

The platform was quiet at this hour, and they found seats side by side with ease. The car rocked gently as it sped beneath the city.

"I'm on 79th Street," Macy said as they approached the 77th Street stop.

"Swanky!" Cade teased, casually brushing the back of his hand against hers.

Macy laughed. "Hardly. It's a little hole in the wall. But it's clean, and it's safe enough."

As they reached her building, she dug through her purse for her keys. Cade stepped closer, gently cupping her cheek and tilting her face toward him. His lips met hers in a soft, brief kiss, and a butterfly's wings fluttered in the pit of Macy's stomach.

From the third-story window above them came loud whistles and a slurred cheer: "Yeah, MACY!"

Startled, Macy looked up to see Catherine and Nina grinning from behind the glass, each clutching a wine glass like spectators at a play. Flushed with embarrassment, she covered her face with one hand.

"I'm going to kill them," she muttered.

Cade chuckled. "I'll call you tomorrow." He pressed a quick kiss to her forehead before turning back toward the subway. Just before rounding the corner, he glanced over his shoulder and smiled. Macy waved him off, still red-faced.

"Now, about those friends of mine…" she muttered under her breath as she started inside.

She stormed up the stairs and threw open the apartment door. "How long have you two been lurking at that window?"

"A bag of wine and Pinot Grigio ago," Nina slurred, sprawled dramatically across the couch.

"Long enough that that doesn't even make sense," Macy groaned. "Should I text Brian and tell him you're staying here tonight?"

Catherine flashed a triumphant grin. "Already done, roomie!"

Macy pointed an accusatory finger at her. "Don't even get me started on you."

She stowed her leftovers in the fridge and placed her rose in a vase by the window. Laughter echoed faintly from the living room as she retreated to her bedroom, pulling the door shut behind her.

MORE THAN THE MET

Macy lingered in bed on Sunday morning longer than usual, dreading the inevitable teasing from Catherine and Nina. Instead, she stayed curled beneath the blankets, doom-scrolling social media with one hand and nursing the nervous quiver in her stomach from the night before.

At exactly 8:30, her phone buzzed with a message from Cade.

Cade
I hope I didn't scare you off too bad last night!

Macy smiled, tapping out a quick reply.

Macy
Of course not! Why would you think you had?

Cade
It's just...I've been called clingy before. I feel things

deeply, and I'm not afraid to show it. That can freak people out if they're not ready.

Macy

Not at all. Honestly, it's refreshing to meet someone who's direct and doesn't play games. It's nice not to have to wonder for a change.

Cade

Good to hear it. I'll call you later. I'd love to see you again tonight—if you'll let me!

Macy

I think that can be arranged. :)

Still smiling, Macy finally pushed back the covers. She slipped into her bathrobe and padded into the kitchen, bracing for round two of last night's commentary. But instead of Catherine or Nina, Brian looked up at her from the table, nursing a mug of coffee. Catherine busied herself at the stove, scrambling eggs with focused intensity.

Glad she'd opted for the robe, Macy poured her own coffee and took the seat beside Brian. "Good morning, Brian! What brings you to our side of the borough so early?"

Brian greeted her with a gentle smile, but something in his eyes looked dimmed. "Good morning to you, too, Macy. I know Nina stayed over last night, so I came by to have breakfast with her." He glanced over at the stove, then back at Macy. "Truthfully, I miss her. I think she's here with you two more often than she's home. Not that I mind. I'm glad she has you both, I really am. It's good for her to have friends she trusts."

He paused, cradling his cup.

"But I worry sometimes that there's something wrong...between her and me."

"I'm sorry, Brian. I think this one's on me," Macy said, wrapping her hands around her coffee mug. "I was so nervous about my date last night, I couldn't get myself together. Poor Catherine must've hit her limit and called in reinforcements."

Brian gave her hand a gentle squeeze. "No, Mace, it's not you. Lately, the harder I try to make Nina happy, the more she seems to look for ways to be somewhere else. If it hadn't been you, it would've been an audition or babysitting for Zoe downstairs, or God only knows what. Honestly, I'm glad it was you. I know she's safe with you and Catherine."

"You can trust us, Brian," Catherine chimed in as she set a plate of eggs and toast in front of him. "And believe me, we've tried talking to her. She's got it good with you. She needs to see that."

"Thanks, ladies. Really," Brian murmured, picking up his fork. "So…Macy, how'd the date go?"

"Yeah, Macy! How was the date?" came Nina's teasing voice from down the hall.

"You tell me!" Macy called back dryly. "You got a front-row seat from Catherine's window."

Catherine's eyes sparkled as she leaned on the counter. "Not even close. Eggs?"

Macy rolled her eyes. "Please. And that goes for both your question and your commentary.

"It was a good night," Macy said, settling into her seat with a satisfied sigh. "We saw the new Stephen King movie and grabbed Greek afterward. We talked for hours. Then he walked me home, didn't even try to get invited upstairs. Just kissed me goodnight and headed out."

"Sounds promising," Catherine said with a grin. "What's next?"

"Well…he texted this morning to make sure he hadn't scared me off. So, that's probably a good sign. He's supposed to call later about plans for tonight."

Brian looked up from his breakfast. "Why would he think he scared you off?"

Macy pulled out her phone and read the message aloud. Catherine and Nina exchanged a silent glance packed with meaning Macy couldn't quite decode. Butterflies or nerves? She wasn't sure which she was feeling anymore.

"Anyway!" she said, pivoting with a bit too much enthusiasm. "Nina, Brian came here to see you. I'm heading to get dressed for the gym. Catherine, want to help me figure out what counts as fashionable workout gear?"

Nina rolled her eyes. "Subtle, Macy!" she called after them as the two slipped out of the room.

"She's your cousin," Catherine reminded once they were out of earshot.

"And?"

"Maybe we should stop luring her here with wine and gossip. She might actually stay home with her husband."

Macy frowned thoughtfully. "You know…I never pictured Nina as the first of us to get married. Do you ever wonder if she said yes just because he asked?"

"I kind of do," Catherine admitted. "What can we do?"

"Not much. We can keep encouraging her. He's a good man. Support him for the same reason. And stay out of it the best we can."

They pressed their ears to the door where muted voices drifted through the walls. The clatter of dishes broke the moment. Then—

"You can stop listening at the door now; we're going home," Nina said, her voice slicing through the crack, making Macy and Catherine jump.

The door swung open, and they greeted Nina and Brian with their best guilty-smile charm as the couple departed.

By late morning, Macy had showered, slipped into fresh clothes, and was halfway through folding laundry when her phone lit up with a call from Cade.

"Hey, beautiful," came his warm voice. "I couldn't wait till tonight. When can I see you again? That smile of yours. It's kind of addictive."

Macy laughed. "Is that your go-to line for all the girls?"

"Only the ones who make me fight the urge to call before noon. How's your day going?"

"Productive so far. Cornered Nina with her husband so she couldn't dodge him, hit the gym, and then tackled some laundry."

"Oof. Sounds...layered. What's going on with your cousin?"

"Honestly? Your guess is as good as mine. She was the loud blond yelling from the window last night. No idea how much she drank. We all like Brian. We always have. But lately, she's been snippy with him, calling him boring and brushing him off."

"Sounds to me like there's something deeper bothering her," Cade said thoughtfully. "Is she the kind who starts spilling secrets after a couple of drinks?"

Macy let out a laugh that nearly edged into a cackle. "Hardly. If anything, she clams up tighter. She's like Fort freakin' Knox—unless it's someone else's gossip. Then she's got no self-control."

"Noted," Cade said with mock seriousness. "Keep Nina far, far away from anything I want to stay private."

He shifted gears with a warm note. "Anyway...I had an idea. Can I pick you up in an hour?"

Macy smiled into the phone, her fingers idly toying with the gold cross charm at her neck. "I think that could probably happen. What do you have in mind?"

"It's a surprise. A friend owes me a favor."

She put her neatly folded shirt into her laundry basket and rested in the kitchen chair. "You're sure I'm not hijacking your Sunday?"

"You are my Sunday," he said gently. "Besides, I like spending time with someone who actually knows what she wants in life. No games, no wasted time. That's rare."

She wasn't exactly swooning, but Macy felt a tug of appreciation. Cade's directness grounded her—no second-guessing, no wondering where she stood.

"Okay," she said with a smile. "But do I have to dress up? I just got comfortable."

"I suppose comfortable works, if you must. But if you fancy up even a little, it would sure bring a smile to my face!"

"Well, how could I refuse that?" she said, giggling.

With the last of the laundry folded, Macy stuffed the basket into her closet and searched for something comfortable, but feminine. She settled on a black bell-sleeve shirt with an asymmetrical neckline set atop a pair of burgundy palazzo pants. She twisted her hair into a simple braid down her back. She added a thick, gold chain to her usual cross necklace and applied a small amount of mascara and lip gloss. Nodding to herself in the mirror, she wandered out and into Catherine's room, where her friend was sorting a stack of freshly laundered gym clothes.

"What's up, Red?" Catherine asked, gesturing at Macy's outfit.

"Cade's coming over," Macy said softly. "He's taking me out again. Says he has a surprise."

Catherine froze, towel half-folded. "Well, he's not wasting any time, is he? What's this far-off stare you've got going on?"

"It's just...this feels different," Macy said, her voice soft. "It's so refreshing not having to decode someone's texts or tone of voice. He's a little intense, which he admits, but I like how upfront he is."

"Just be careful," Catherine cautioned, folding the last towel. "Don't let him move faster than you're ready for."

"I promise," Macy said, her smile warm and genuine.

When the doorbell rang, she grabbed her light denim jacket without a second thought. She pressed the button to allow him entry and opened the door when she heard his footsteps approach. The scent of his sandalwood cologne greeted her. His black, wavy hair was thick and messy today, missing the usual gloss of being slicked back.

"We're not going far," Cade said, extending his elbow for her to loop her arm through. "Just a short ride."

"You're not going to tell me where we're going?" She grabbed her purse and closed the door behind them. Raucous laughter echoed from the apartment next door, earning a raised eyebrow from Cade. Macy giggled to herself. "My neighbor, Theo. He's a fun guy; you'll love him!"

He smiled back, rueful. "I bet. And no, I'm going to let you wonder."

A cab waited for them at the doorstep. Cade held the door open and helped her in before joining her in the back seat. They arrived at a side entrance to the Metropolitan Museum of Art, to a quiet service doorway, where a security guard tipped his hat to Cade and greeted him like an old friend.

Macy's jaw dropped as he guided her through the door. "Are you kidding me right now?"

Cade shrugged casually, his expression satisfied. "I did some work with the marketing team, so they owed me one. We don't have long, but they closed off this one exhibit just for us."

He led her down a dimly lit hallway through a labyrinth of corridors. The air was cool and still, and the silence rang in Macy's ears. When they turned the final corner to the Egypt wing, the Temple of Dendur waited for them in the soft afternoon light.

Macy stopped in her tracks, breath catching in her throat. "Wow."

"It's something, isn't it?" Cade said quietly, almost reverently.

A black, reflective pool shimmered next to a wall of windows. Egyptian statues lined the walls on the opposite side of the pool. Macy peered through the temple front, where elaborate carvings depicted the Roman emperor and ancient deities, and she froze as if breathing wrongly would ruin the ancient art.

"I can't believe we have this all to ourselves," she whispered. "It's like I stepped back in time, to another world."

"You deserve the extraordinary," he said, casually. "And, I like things that don't change."

Macy stepped farther into the temple, her ballet flats shuffling as she went. "Ethan—my brother—and I used to love things like this. We used to go to the library all the time, and I would get lost in the books about Egypt and Rome. I would pretend I was Cleopatra so that every once in a while, I didn't feel completely out of place."

Cade tipped his head, not taking his eyes from her. "Why did you feel out of place?"

She gestured at herself. "Well, look at me. Smart kid, redhead, nerdy girl in a small town. I stood out for all the wrong reasons."

"Wrong according to who?"

She turned to look at him, gasping at the weight of his stare. He watched her with a curve to the corner of his lips, as though he was cataloging a precious memory. Suddenly shy and self-conscious about the way he looked at her, she turned and started walking again through the exhibit.

"Here," he said, reaching for her hand. "Check this one out."

Macy slipped her hand into his, and he guided her through the corridor to a carved relief of a couple making an offering at the feet of Anubis. The relief was flanked by ancient pottery and statues carved from jade and turquoise.

"I wonder what they're offering up," Macy mused.

"It's a devotion to earn his favor," Cade said softly. "People carved what matters most. Love, loyalty. They committed themselves to each other in front of their god, and sealed it with an offering."

"It's beautiful," Macy said, studying the relief and the jars.

"It is." Macy looked over and saw that he didn't mean the relief.

Heat crept up the back of her neck, roses blooming on her cheeks. She smiled and pretended to go back to studying the inscriptions under the exhibits. Her pulse raced, thundering in her ears.

They weaved peacefully through the rest of the exhibit, in comfortable silence. When she talked about the artifacts, he listened. Really listened. And when she laughed, he smiled as though he'd been waiting all day for the sound.

All too soon, the corridor led them back into reality, where other tours continued: couples, families, small guided groups. Cade reached for Macy's hand, and she accepted, smiling at him.

"I don't want this day to end," he said. "I feel like I've been waiting for you my whole life. I wonder if you feel that, too."

Macy's breath caught in her throat. She smiled, suddenly shy, and looked down at her feet as they shuffled down the corridor to the next exhibit. "I bet you say that to all the girls."

"Why do you do that?" He was curious, not accusatory, as he tipped her chin back up to look at him. "I can't tell if you're joking or trying to push me away. I know you've been hurt, but please be fair to me."

"Sorry," she answered quickly, cheeks growing hot again. "I guess I'm just nervous, and making jokes helps to ease that."

"A defense mechanism," he stated. He led her through the Great Hall, where new patrons were queuing to see the Egyptian wing they had just vacated. Cade nodded at the security guard, who smiled in return and opened the exhibit.

"Yeah, something like that. I'm not used to such grand gestures and expressions of emotion, so I'm not sure how to respond to them."

Cade continued leading her through the gallery and into the next wing. Columns from the Temple of Artemis welcomed them into ancient Greece and Rome. "Well," he said, escorting her past a display of terra cotta jugs, "better learn. Because this is me."

"I think..." Macy swallowed hard, her voice breaking. "I can try to learn."

Cade's answering smile was triumphant. "I can live with that."

They explored the rest of the gallery hand in hand. The buzz of weekend tour groups swelled around them as they navigated the rooms. By the time they stepped out onto Fifth Avenue, the afternoon sunlight was turning into the reddish gold of early sunset. The cab ride home was quiet, flecked with stolen glances that made Macy's heart skip.

When the cab pulled up to Macy's building, Cade quickly jumped out of his side to run and open the door for Macy. She laid her palm flat against his as he gently helped her out and onto the curb. He asked the driver to give him a moment and framed Macy's face with his hands, kissing her softly.

"Thank you for today," Macy said when the kiss ended. "This was...unexpected."

"In a good way, I hope?" he asked, taking both of her hands in his.

"Of course," she said, smiling.

He kissed her knuckles then released her hands. "I suppose I will let you get some rest so you can crush that first day tomorrow. Maybe I can bring you dinner after, and you can tell me all about it?"

Macy nodded, pressing her lips together but still smiling. "I will check if Catherine has any plans, but I think I would like that!"

"I'll be thinking of you. Probably too much." He turned and got back into the cab, asking the driver to take him to 94th and Amsterdam.

Macy spun, starry-eyed, and found Theo standing next to the stoop, smirking at her casually. He wiped paint from his hands with a yellow rag, his earbuds hanging around his neck. A fresh painting lay at his feet.

"Ah! How long have you been standing there?" She laid her hand on her heart, startled.

"Long enough to feel like a Peeping Theo!" He gestured at the painting. "I came out to let this dry a little. Swear I didn't mean to stay for the show."

She laughed, breathless, as her cheeks flamed. "Sorry, he was just dropping me off."

"No need to be sorry!" he said, his eyes following the direction the cab had gone. "He seems serious."

"Is that bad?"

Theo shrugged a shoulder, folding his paint-stained rag. "Not necessarily. How long have you been dating?"

"This was our second."

Theo's eyes widened. "Second week or second *date?*"

Macy blanched, ears growing hot. Theo hesitated, opening his mouth and closing it again, like he wasn't sure if he should push. "Be careful, okay, Mace? The city is full of charmers who want to put everything in fast-forward and let you think it was your idea."

Macy waved him off, hoping she looked more relaxed than she felt. "We've known each other a few months now, but I'd just been too chicken to say yes. So, it's not as rushed as it appears."

He met her eyes, searching. Finally, he opened the door for them to go inside. "All right, I'll trust your judgment. But if he starts making you uncomfortable..." He trailed off.

She smiled easily as they started up the stairs together. "I promise, I'm being careful. Okay?"

"I got your back, Mace. Any time. Now, I hope he won't have you distracted from this new job of yours tomorrow, no?"

Thankful for the change of subject, Macy took the opportunity to ask about his latest painting and working in Brooklyn. When they arrived at Macy's doorstep, he gently squeezed her hand in both of his. "Goodnight, Mace. And good luck tomorrow."

"Thanks, Theo. Good night." The lock clicked, and she swung the door open—and nearly yelped.

Catherine sat on the couch facing the door, arms crossed impatiently, a foot tapping on the side of the couch. "Well, well," she said, slowly. "You going to tell me where Romeo whisked you away to? Or am I going to have to play Twenty Questions?"

Macy rolled her eyes and put her purse down on the counter, and shrugged off her coat. "Mother, may I get my shoes off before you start the interrogation?"

Catherine held up two glasses of chilled white wine. "If you want one, you'd better start talking."

Laughing, Macy kicked off her shoes. "He took me to the Met. You know, I can't believe we've been living here ten years, and I've never gone!"

"Ironic that yesterday, I joked about him taking you to the Met Gala. So, why do you look like Cupid slapped you across the face with a glitter bow?"

Macy slid onto the couch next to Catherine and swiped a glass out of her hand. "Why do you seem so defensive? Weren't you one of the ones shoving me at him in the first place?"

"Someone has to give you the hard time you deserve." She stole the glass from Macy and took a long drink of the wine, skillfully dodging the pillow Macy threw at her in response.

"Give me that!" Macy shouted as Catherine, laughing, handed her the full glass. "He called in a favor to get private access to the Temple of Dendur exhibit."

Catherine froze, laughter dying on her lips. "That's...a lot. For a second date."

"It was so thoughtful, though, Cath! Nobody has ever done anything like that for me before."

"I just want to make sure you're not getting swept up too fast. Sometimes, grand gestures can cloud things."

"You sound like Theo," Macy muttered, cheeks heating.

Catherine choked on her wine. "What did Theo say?"

"Just to be careful of him going too fast." Macy shrugged, mouth drawing into a pout. "First, I get told to just forget the ones who don't do anything to stand out, and now someone does something to stand out, and I'm told to be careful it's not too much."

Catherine's voice softened. "I just want to see you happy." She nudged Macy playfully. "Besides, you start a new job tomorrow. We can't have you being kidnapped by a man who can have museums shut down."

Macy snorted, tension forgotten. "He doesn't shut them down; he just borrows them."

"Yes," Catherine deadpanned. "Nothing says stable like a man with museum connections."

"Hush." Macy drained the rest of her wine glass. "It was a perfect afternoon."

Catherine sighed deeply, but smiled. "Then I'm glad for you."

Macy slipped back into the kitchen to start rummaging for dinner. The flutter in her stomach had returned as she replayed the afternoon in her mind. She pulled out a tray of leftover lasagna and plated a slice. Then, after a moment's consideration, she cut it in half.

Catherine, watching from the couch, tilted her head. "Since when do you portion like that?"

Macy blinked. "Oh. Cade suggested this when we went to dinner last night. Says the portion sizes are out of control and that it'll help if I start halving my meals."

"Does he, now?" Catherine said quietly, eyes cool.

She didn't see Catherine continue to watch her with a thoughtful expression. And she didn't see Theo watching out the window as if he expected someone to still be there.

Chapter Ten

OPTIHEALTH

The sun was still a long way from cresting the New York City skyline, but Macy was already up. She armed herself with coffee, sorting through outfit options, and wrestling the nerves only a first day at a new job could summon.

Her new office was just three blocks from VitalSync, so she had a decent sense of timing for the subway. Still, she wanted to make a strong first impression: confident, polished, and unmistakably prepared.

Can't ever go wrong with basic black, she thought, pulling out a pair of tailored slacks and a crisp black button-down blouse. For a splash of color, she added a lavender belt and clipped a matching barrette into her long curls. Her old faithful black pumps completed the look. She decided less was more with makeup and settled on mascara and lip gloss. Into her duffel that had become her gym bag, she threw her sneakers, a pair of leggings, and a tank top.

"Okay," she said to the woman in the mirror. "Let's go show the new boss why she needs me."

The kitchen was still dark, but the horizon was beginning to blush with morning light. Macy packed her lunch bag with a hastily thrown-together ham sandwich and a snack-size bag of chips, then scanned the fridge for a breakfast that aligned with her new guidelines. She settled on Greek yogurt topped with almonds and berries and tucked an apple into her bag for an afternoon snack.

Catherine waded out of her room in a bathrobe, rubbing sleep from her eyes as Macy rinsed her breakfast dishes. "Go knock 'em dead," Catherine said, pouring herself a coffee.

They clinked mugs in a quiet toast. Macy chugged the rest of hers, grabbed her purse and duffel, and stepped out the door to greet the city just as the sun had done the same.

She shouldn't have been surprised to see a text from Cade already, but it still caught her off guard. It was nice, she admitted to herself, having someone so attentive. Someone who was actually interested in her.

Cade

Good luck today! I know you're going to crush it. Hope the day flies by so I can see you again.

Cade

Don't forget your gym bag!

Macy smiled and typed back:

Macy

Thank you! Just headed out the door with it. Looking forward to seeing you there. Have a good day. :)

It was a short walk from the Wall Street stop, and Macy arrived at the office fifteen minutes early. Her VitalSync ID still worked, granting her access to the OptiHealth floor, but she knew she'd need new credentials for her role under Amara MacNash in the corporate office.

Amara was already waiting with a tablet in hand, posture crisp, and expression unreadable. She was styled as impeccably as ever in a plum-colored jacket and matching knee-length skirt, her black hair falling sleek and smooth just past her chin.

Macy hoped Amara couldn't hear the nervous knock of her knees beneath her slacks.

"I like an employee who knows how to be early," Amara said, her gaze sharp but kind. "Let me show you to your room, so to speak."

Macy followed closely, trying to commit every turn and hallway to memory. The office spanned the entire 52nd floor of a building that stretched half a city block. As they walked, Amara pointed out departments and break areas and asked if Macy needed fridge space for her lunch. Macy barely registered the words. Her nerves were too loud.

Several mini-break zones dotted the floor, each surrounded by managers' offices and equipped with vending machines, refrigerators, microwaves, and small tables. When they reached the back corner of the building, Macy spotted a bright lime green wall and silently marked it as her landmark.

"I hate this wall," Amara said, as if reading her thoughts. "The color's awful, isn't it? But it makes it easier to find home base. Each department has its own color. Lucky us! We get to look like a bad '80s spandex ad."

Macy smiled, but her nerves still wouldn't let her laugh just yet. Amara gestured to a cubicle just outside her office. "Here's you. Brett already sent your things over, so go ahead and settle in. Then we'll meet the rest of the team."

The cubicle had a small locker door for her coat and purse. Most of Macy's personal items from her old desk were minimal: a few family photos and a desk calendar. She took a few minutes to arrange them, trying to breathe through the nerves.

No sooner had she finished than Amara reappeared, tablet still in hand.

"Now, Macy," Amara began, her tone brisk. "We talked when you accepted the position about expectations. I'm not a micromanager. It's your first day here, but not your first day in the business. I won't hold your hand. The team will help get you up to speed, and then I expect you to rise to the challenge. It's sink or swim at the corporate office. I hope you know how to swim. Ready?"

Macy nodded vigorously and stood to follow.

Just beyond her cubicle wall were three more workstations. One sat empty. Directly across from Macy was Sebrina Lawson, who turned as they approached. Her raven-black hair swept over her shoulder, and her hazel eyes held a quiet confidence Macy instantly admired. Sebrina smiled warmly. "Macy, welcome! Pull up the chair from the empty cubicle next door."

Amara nodded. "I'll leave you in her capable hands, Macy. You'll shadow her this morning. After lunch, we dive into your first assignment."

Without waiting for a reply, Amara turned and strode away.

"So!" Sebrina said brightly. "Has she scared you off yet?"

Macy hesitated, unsure if Amara might overhear. Her mouth opened, but no words came. Only a nervous grunt as she scrambled for a safe response.

Sebrina laughed, full and warm. "It's okay! She knows she's intimidating. Honestly, I think she leans into it sometimes. But don't worry. I've worked with Amara for fifteen years. She's tough, but fair. Once you've earned her trust, she's actually pretty loyal. And believe me, she wouldn't have offered you this job if she didn't believe in you. I'll help you navigate her."

Before Macy could reply, a head of blond curls popped up over the cubicle wall.

"Is that her? Macy's here?" said the man attached to the curls. Without waiting for confirmation, he rolled his chair into Sebrina's cubicle. "It is Macy! Look at this: a blond, a brunette, and a redhead. Someone, cue the punchlines! I'm Ryan Jackson, but everyone calls me RJ."

"And RJ has no sense of boundaries," Sebrina said, rolling her eyes.

RJ stuck out his tongue. "You'd be lost without me."

Macy's shoulders eased as they teased each other. The easy banter between Sebrina and RJ was infectious. They clearly enjoyed working together.

"RJ's been with us for eight years," Sebrina explained. "We're the project managers. There's a separate department for product development, but we oversee the coordination and resources. You'll be Amara's personal assistant, but don't worry, you're not here to fetch coffee. We saw your resume. You were a seasoned data analyst at VitalSync, which makes you a great fit for this team. It won't be the same work, but you'll get to flex your skills. Especially with presentations and marketing. Think of it as an extension of what you've done."

RJ wheeled himself back toward his cubicle. "Lunch at noon?" he called over his shoulder.

"As usual," Sebrina replied. Then she turned to Macy. "You'll join us, right? We'll tell you our favorite stories about surviving Amara."

Macy laughed, though a trace of nerves lingered in her voice. "I'm not sure whether to be intrigued or terrified. But yes, lunch at noon sounds great."

"She speaks, at last!" RJ quipped over the cubicle wall.

The morning passed quickly. Sebrina walked Macy through the product development team's structure and helped her get familiar with the software she'd be using. Between tasks, they traded personal stories. Macy learned Sebrina had two teenage kids and lived on Staten Island with her husband of twenty-three years, Flynn. In turn, Macy shared her Iowa upbringing, her city life with Catherine and Nina, and her new beginning with Cade.

At noon, Macy grabbed her purse and lunch bag and joined Sebrina and RJ at their table in the break area. As she settled in, she checked her phone and found a missed text from her mom, one from Catherine, and four from Cade on top of his good luck message from that morning.

Cade

*Hope you made it to the office
safe!*

Cade

How are things going so far?

Cade

Is everything okay??

Cade

Text me! Macy?

The last message had come in at 11:30. Smiling, she pulled out her sandwich and sent a quick reply.

Macy

*Sorry, sorry! All is well so far! It's
been a busy morning shadowing
the team and getting acclimated.
I've been leaving my phone in my
purse...trying to make a good first
impression on the boss. I'll tell
you all about it at the gym tonight!*

Almost immediately, Cade replied:

Cade
Don't make me nervous like that!

Macy
What, do you think I'd have changed my mind already?

Cade
I'd appreciate it if you don't joke about that.

Cade
Stranger things have happened!

Macy
Oh no, I'm sorry! I didn't mean anything by it, I just don't want to get in trouble.

Cade
No problem. Can't wait to see you tonight.

"Checking in with the other boss?" RJ teased, raising his head to peek over the top of Macy's phone.

"Oh, can it, RJ," Sebrina snapped playfully. "You don't know her nearly well enough to start teasing her about her love life. Unless that means you're finally going to tell us about yours."

"Sorry, can't hear you," RJ said, standing abruptly. "I have to go check the microwave."

Sebrina chuckled under her breath. "That's what I thought. Putz."

Macy giggled, slipping her phone back into her purse and pulling out her apple. The microwave dinged, and RJ returned triumphantly with two Hot Pockets and a Mountain Dew.

Feeling bold, Macy gestured at his plate. "So, do you always eat like you're still in college?"

Sebrina nearly choked on her salad, covering her mouth as she burst into laughter.

Immediately second-guessing herself, Macy added, "No offense intended, RJ! I'm just kidding."

RJ rolled his eyes, clearly amused. "Honey, you'll have to try a lot harder than that to offend us. Thick skin is a survival skill around here."

Sebrina nodded, still smiling. "Honestly, if you're comfortable enough to jump into the heckling, I think you're going to fit right in."

Macy's shoulders dropped, the tension she hadn't realized she'd been carrying finally easing. Maybe, just maybe, she was going to be okay here.

"So," she asked, curiosity piqued, "what happened to the last person who had my job?"

"Jamie Hawthorne," Sebrina replied. "She got a big promotion. Amara's kind of like the world's scariest personal trainer. She'll push you hard, and sometimes it'll feel like she's out to break you. But the reality is, she's polishing you. Strengthening you. RJ and I are where we want to be, but Amara's had a few PAs who came in from other departments and moved up fast. I know the merger and downsizing were rough, but if Amara hired you, and you work hard, you've got a bright future ahead."

"Thanks, Sebrina," Macy said warmly. "Now, about those survival stories?"

RJ and Sebrina exchanged a look. RJ, mid-bite, gestured for Sebrina to go first.

"Well," Sebrina began, leaning back in her chair, "like I said, I've been with Amara for fifteen years. I was already a seasoned developer when I joined her team. My last boss? He liked to throw staplers when things didn't go his way."

Macy's jaw dropped. "Seriously? Nobody put a stop to that?"

Sebrina smiled. "Would you have?"

Macy pursed her lips and nodded at her. "Fair enough."

Sebrina leaned in, her tone shifting to storytelling mode. "I thought I'd seen it all. But my very first project here? I was designing the interface for a new software system for the hospital network. I poured my heart into it—spent a month just building the presentation deck. I walked into Amara's office, and without even looking up from her screen, she said, 'Sebrina, show me what you've got.'"

"I set up my slides and started walking her through the interface. Before I even finished the first slide, she held up her hand and said, 'No.'"

Macy blinked. "No?"

"'This looks great, Sebrina. Very sleek and modern. Users are going to hate it.'"

Macy tilted her head, confused.

"I'm pretty sure I made that same face," Sebrina said with a laugh. "My heart sank. I thought I was about to be fired. I'd worked so hard, and she told me it was great, but completely wrong.

"Then she said, 'Sebrina, this is going to a hospital, not a tech company. They don't want sleek. They want functional. They don't have time to learn a new interface. They want something familiar and comforting.' That's when I learned: I'm not designing for what I think looks good. I have to understand the customer and give them what they need."

Macy nodded slowly. "That makes a lot of sense. I would've been terrified to hear that, too. But it sounds like a pretty solid lesson."

"Yeah, Sebrina got the learning experience," RJ chimed in. "I got the binder."

Macy laughed. "Okay, this ought to be good."

RJ leaned back dramatically. "So, I started here fresh out of grad school. Fresh haircut, shiny suit, shinier shoes. I thought I walked on water. Amara meets me at the door with a binder labeled RJ's Survival Guide. She tells me to sit down and study it. I thought she was joking. I laughed. She wasn't."

Sebrina chuckled into her salad.

"By week three," RJ continued, "I was convinced she could teleport. I'd email her a question, and seconds later, she'd appear at my desk: 'RJ, check your survival guide. Page 38.'"

He leaned forward, eyes wide. "Now, Amara has one sacred rule: Don't be late unless you're in the emergency room. So, it's Friday. Staff meeting day. My train's delayed. I'm sprinting from the elevator like I'm auditioning for Formula 1. The meeting room's in sight, clock ticking 7:59. I trip over my own shoe and skid to a halt. *Right* at Amara's feet."

Macy burst out laughing. "No way!"

"Oh, yes," RJ said, grinning. "She looked down at me, completely unfazed, and said, 'Page 12, RJ. Dress shoes with traction.'"

Macy laughed, half amused, half alarmed. "I'm not sure if I should be terrified or entertained by that story, RJ. Wait, am I going to get quizzed on this survival guide?"

"Nah," RJ said with a grin. "I think she was just hazing me. I came in way too confident and fresh-faced."

"I see," Macy said slowly, not entirely convinced.

As lunch hour wound down, Macy checked her purse one last time and spotted another new message.

Cade
Hope your afternoon goes
well.

She smiled and sent back a quick *You too.*

He's definitely not shy about making his interest known, she mused. Pretty thoughtful.

She knocked on Amara's office door, but a voice behind her made her jump.

"Right behind you, Macy," Amara said from Macy's desk. "Ready to dive in?"

Macy was assigned her first project: designing a new dashboard to track key performance indicators for the monthly meetings. Amara gave her full creative freedom, but Macy, remembering Sebrina's story, asked if there was a preferred style.

She thought she saw the ghost of a smile flicker across Amara's face. "Simple and straightforward," she replied. "Not flashy."

At 5:00 sharp, Sebrina and RJ called out their goodnights. Macy laughed and reached to shut down her computer, but paused. She glanced at the small locker door and considered keeping gym clothes there. It wasn't high school phys ed, though. She'd have to learn to pack a bag on gym days. Maybe keep a spare outfit, just in case.

She walked to Amara's door. "Do you need anything before I head out?"

Amara didn't look up. "Yes. I need you to go out and do whatever it is twenty-somethings do after work. It's 5:00, Macy. Go home."

Macy didn't hesitate. She grabbed her purse and duffel bag and made her way to the elevator. After a long first day, she was ready to unwind with a workout and time with Cade.

Her phone buzzed as she crossed the threshold into the late afternoon sunset.

Cade
How was your first day?

She smiled and typed back:

Macy

Well, I survived! I'm ready to unwind for a while.

Cade

Funny you should mention that. You want to meet me at Rockefeller? I've got another surprise.

Macy

What about the gym?

Cade sent back just a smiling emoji. She agreed, tucked her phone into her purse, and hurried toward the Fulton Street subway entrance that would take her toward Rockefeller.

When Macy stepped out of the D train in the middle of 6th Avenue and turned toward 49th, she saw him standing near the plaza entrance, holding a large bundle of sunflowers. Cade was dressed in a slick, long black overcoat, a blue scarf tucked in. His black waves were slicked back and tame, a hint of stubble shadowing his chin. His answering smile when he saw her added warmth to his storm blue eyes. He handed her the bouquet and tugged her gently toward him, pressing a long, lingering kiss to her lips.

Macy blushed, instinctively glancing around to see if anyone had noticed. No one appeared to be watching until a whistle rang out from somewhere nearby, followed by a woman's voice shouting, "Get a room!"

Cade laughed while Macy covered her face with one hand. "You're turning redder than your hair. How cute!"

She stuck her tongue out at him playfully. "Cut it out," she muttered, laughing despite herself.

"Never."

"So," she said, "are you going to tell me what this is all about?"

He gave her a wide smile and shook his head. "I just thought you deserve a nice dinner with a view after your hard work today. Come with me!"

Chapter Eleven

CARE AND CONTROL

Cade offered his elbow, and Macy looped her free hand through. He led her toward 7th Avenue and to a large building off 47th Street. The doorman tipped his hat at them, smiling, as Cade walked her through a lobby. A man in a tailored blue suit waited near a small elevator, which opened as he pressed the button. "Cade, right this way!"

Macy looked at the elevator door and back at Cade, slack-jawed. "Do you know everyone in this city?"

He gave her a knowing smile. They entered the elevator, and the man in the suit slid a key into the elevator door. Turning the key, he pressed a button marked "Rooftop," and the elevator carried them away.

The door slid open to a New York City sunset that had Macy gasp. Streaks of blue and purple clouds dotted an orange horizon. Nearby, a single table sat with two covered serving plates. Twinkle lights were strung along the rooftop ledges. "Thanks, Arlo," Cade said as he slipped a rolled bill to the man.

"What...?" Macy started, but words failed her. Cade smiled and took her hand, running her toward the table.

"An old friend." He pulled out her chair and whisked the cover away from her plate, revealing a sliced tenderloin steak, set atop mashed potatoes, and a side salad.

"I hardly know what to say," Macy said, taking her seat. "This is breathtaking."

"You deserve it, and more," Cade answered as he took his own seat. "I took a guess that you take your steak medium rare."

Macy cut the first slice into a bite-sized piece and skewered it onto her fork. The tenderloin melted in her mouth, flecked with hints of garlic and smoke from the grill.

Cade raised a glass of rich, red Cabernet. "To new beginnings."

"To new beginnings," Macy echoed, smiling as the warmth of the evening settled around them.

"So," she asked between bites, "you've seen my little hole-in-the-wall. What about you? What side of the city are you on?"

"It's nothing flashy," Cade replied. "My dad and stepmom helped put me through college, so instead of drowning in student loans, I saved up and bought a small co-op on the Upper West Side. Funny enough, I'm not far from Columbia. I'm off 95th Street."

Macy nearly dropped her wine glass. "Wait, what? How is that not flashy?"

Cade laughed. "Trust me, it's no mansion. The boutique under my building is flashy, sure, but my place? Four rooms, and it could fit inside my parents' living room. My stepmom inherited her parents' house, so they were able to help me out with college. Without loans, I saved enough to get approved. It does have a decent view of Central Park. Just on the opposite side from yours. I'd love to show it to you sometime."

Macy chuckled. "I'm on the third floor with another building five feet away. My view is brick and pigeons. How long have you lived there?"

"Moved in two years after college. So, about five years now."

"So, you were literally a few blocks away when I was graduating. Funny that we never ran into each other."

"It's a big city," Cade said, grinning. "But I would've remembered you."

Cade's smile lingered as he held her gaze. Warmth bloomed on her cheeks, her heart giving a foolish little flutter as she looked down at her plate with a shy smile.

"At least," Cade added lightly, "I'd have found a way to make sure our paths crossed if I had seen you."

Their eyes locked as the last of the daylight slipped below the Manhattan skyline.

"Speechless?"

"Words aren't really a strength of mine," Macy admitted.

"That's okay," he said with a quiet laugh, returning to his meal. "I do enough talking for both of us."

Before the week was out, Macy and Cade had gone out three more times. The only night they skipped was Thursday, when she'd already made plans with Catherine.

On Friday, just after lunch, a massive bouquet of roses was delivered to her desk.

"What is this?" RJ practically sang as he twirled into her cubicle, eyes wide with delight.

As he admired the flowers, Macy's phone buzzed with a new text from Cade:

Cade
*I missed you last night! Hope
you enjoy your delivery.*

She smiled, fingers flying over the screen.

Macy

*Okay, these are gorgeous. Thank
you! But how did you know they
just got delivered?*

His reply came quickly:

Cade

I always have my ways.

Before she could respond again, RJ was calling for Sebrina to come and see the surprise. Macy sent a quick, distracted "Thank you!" to Cade and looked up just in time to catch a subtle nod from Amara across the office. Barely a hint of a smile, but unmistakably approving.

RJ leaned against her desk, grinning. "So, should we start designing your wedding registry?"

Macy laughed. "Maybe after you finally spill some details about your love life."

Sebrina nudged RJ with a laugh. "She turned that one around fast. I knew we'd like you, Macy."

"I'm glad to hear it," Macy said. "I hope Amara agrees."

RJ gave her a warm smile. "Trust me, you'd know it if she didn't."

"Good to know. I imagine you've seen it go less than well for someone here?"

Sebrina and RJ exchanged a look. Sebrina pursed her lips and pointed at RJ. "I was on maternity leave when it happened. Actually, it was the temp they hired to cover for me. RJ's got the full story."

RJ nodded. "She wasn't terrible, just...uninspired. No urgency, no initiative. Amara kept nudging her about a project, and finally, on the Thursday of her second week, Amara snapped. It wasn't pretty. The girl never came back."

"Yikes," Macy said. "So, basically, the less I see Amara, the more she likes me?"

"Exactly," RJ said with a wink. "But you got a smile today. Nobody gets a smile from Amara in their first week. You're doing just fine."

As the afternoon wore on, Macy was wrapping up a report when Amara appeared at her cubicle. She leaned casually on the edge of the desk, her usual composed expression softened just slightly.

"How are you feeling after your first week, Macy?"

Macy looked up, surprised but pleased. "I've got a lot to learn," she said, "but I feel confident."

Amara nodded. "Good. That's exactly where you should be. Go ahead and start shutting down when you reach a good stopping point. Hopefully, we'll see you Monday."

Macy leaned back in her chair, letting out a shy chuckle. "Why does everyone think I'm going to be scared off? I don't scare so easily."

"Aha!" Amara hopped down from the desk, her eyes bright with approval. "There it is: the confidence I want to see. Hold onto that. Go on home. We'll see you next week."

After powering down her computer, Macy grabbed her purse and checked her phone. Sure enough, Cade had texted her ten minutes earlier:

Cade

I miss your face. Instead of the gym tonight, how about one of your fruity drinks and a walk in the park?

She smiled and typed back:

Macy

Don't have to ask me twice!

Macy

Are you grabbing drinks, or should I?

Cade

I think you texted me your go-to once, so I'll get it.

Cade

Meet you at the 72nd Street entrance? Maybe we can make another stop after.

Macy

Another stop sounds mysterious. I'll see you when the train gets me there.

When Macy arrived, Cade's face lit up instantly. He stood waiting with a pink refresher in one hand and an iced mocha in the other. She looked him up and down, amused.

"It takes a secure man to stand there holding a drink that pink."

"Or just a man completely smitten with his girl." He handed her the refresher and pulled her into a firm kiss, his free arm wrapping around her waist. "You are beautiful."

Macy blushed, eyes dropping to the ground. "Thank you. I'm still not used to hearing that…well, from anyone but my parents."

Cade brushed a strand of hair from her cheek. "Then I'll just have to keep saying it until you believe it."

After their walk, he invited her to see his apartment. "No strings attached," he promised with a gentle smile.

Walking in for the first time took Macy's breath away. The building didn't have a doorman, but each resident had their own entry code. Cade lived on the 14th floor, and the view alone made her pause. His apartment was modest but thoughtfully arranged: an open-concept living room and kitchen, one bedroom, and a full bathroom with a tub. The space was sparsely decorated but clean and modern, with a quiet sense of comfort.

In the living room, a plush black sofa was draped with blue throw blankets, and a matching recliner sat nearby. Cade gestured around. "Told you it's not much, but it's comfortable. Enough for me. It's a little empty, though. Nice not having a roommate. Maybe one day, I'll share the space again."

He gave her a knowing smile and motioned for her to make herself comfortable. They settled on a movie, and Cade ordered pizza, lamenting the lack of good Chicago-style options in the city.

"What's the pizza like back in Springwater?" he asked.

"We didn't order it much," Macy said. "My mom was big on home cooking. But once in a while, we'd get McDonald's or chain pizza as a treat. Nothing special, just crispy crust, cheese, and toppings. The first time I had New York-style? It was like I'd never had pizza before."

"Seriously?" Cade looked at her like she'd just confessed a crime. "I can't imagine what you grew up with if you think New York-style is the best. You haven't lived until you've had Chicago pizza."

Macy wrinkled her nose. "I tried it on layover earlier this year. It was not great."

"I'm going to pretend you didn't just say that," he said, laughing. "You're not getting real Chicago-style pizza at the airport. Real Chicago pizza is tavern-style—thin, crispy, light on toppings."

"No, thanks!" she laughed. "Give me a good foldy slice any day, loaded with everything."

"Did you just say 'foldy?'" Cade teased.

"It's not New York-style if you're not folding it," she replied with a shrug.

The buzzer rang, announcing the arrival of what Cade claimed was the best pizza in the area. As he headed to the door, he glanced back with a grin.

"This isn't over, you know."

After she teased Cade mercilessly for ordering a New York-style thin crust, and they argued over its supposed inferiority, they finally settled in for their movie. The evening passed in laughter and quiet comfort, and when it was time to head home, Cade insisted on riding the subway with Macy to make sure she got there safely.

On the ride, he turned to her with a mischievous grin. "What do you say I bring my Nintendo over tomorrow for a Mario Party battle at your place? It's about time I meet this roommate of yours!"

"I say, prepare to eat my dust."

He chuckled. "I could leave the system at your place if you want. I don't play it much anymore. It's no fun solo. I bet you and Catherine would get more use out of it. And maybe, hopefully, you'll invite me over to play sometimes?"

"That's very generous of you, thank you," Macy said, surprised. "And honestly, I've gotten pretty used to having you around. I think we can work something out."

She winked, and Cade lit up like she'd handed him a winning lottery ticket. "Really? That means a lot. I love being around you, Macy. I know I'm kind of a hopeless romantic, but I just…want to be near you."

Macy's heart started to race. "I like being around you, too. When I'm with you, it feels like I actually fit somewhere."

"You do fit. With me," he said softly. "It didn't feel right being apart last night. I know we've known each other only a few months, and we've only been dating a week, but…the world just feels better with you in it. I've never met anyone like you."

She beamed, but words escaped her. Cade looked at her expectantly.

"Nothing?" he asked.

"Sorry," she said with a shy smile. "I told you, words aren't my thing unless I'm putting them into code."

He pouted playfully, then squeezed her hand. "I just want to know I'm not alone in how I'm feeling. This feels…special."

"It is," she said gently. "You're not alone."

"Good." He leaned in and kissed her, slow and tender.

She rested her head on his shoulder until they reached her stop, and they held hands all the way to her door. As they reached it, Cade hesitated.

"You know, it's Friday night," he said. "We don't have to be up early tomorrow. Can I come in?"

Macy paused. "Hmm…It's getting kind of late. I should probably get some rest."

He leaned in, brushing his fingers up the side of her neck and nibbling softly at her ear. "Are you sure?" he asked, his voice low, his lips curving into a faint frown.

"Yeah," she said gently. "I'm sorry. It's just…this is too soon for me."

He nodded, pulling back slightly. "We don't have to do anything. I just wanted to be with you. Doesn't matter what we're doing…or not doing. Can I?"

She hesitated, and though it was only for a moment, it was long enough.

"If it's not a hell yes, it's a no," he said quietly, more to himself than to her. "Okay. I'll see you another time."

"I'm sorry," Macy said, her voice soft. "Please don't be mad."

"I'm not mad," Cade said, flashing a brief smile, but the sadness in his eyes lingered. He squeezed her hand gently. "I didn't mean anything by coming upstairs. I just wanted to spend more time with you. I thought you wanted that too. But I get it. I won't bother you so much."

Wait! Macy thought, watching him let go of her hand and turn away, without even a goodnight kiss. *Does he think I don't want to see him anymore?*

"Cade, wait! That wasn't what I meant!"

"It's okay, Mace," he called over his shoulder. "I'm too much for a lot of people. I'm used to it. Call me when you want."

It's not like we didn't just leave his place, she argued with herself. What's wrong with letting him come in?

But I'm tired. I haven't seen Catherine much lately. I want to catch up with her.

Still…it's Friday night. What's five more minutes?

Macy called out before he was out of earshot. "Wait, Cade. Come back. I want to get some rest and brag to Catherine about my beautiful delivery and how you spoiled me again. But I suppose there's no reason you can't be there while I do my bragging. It's about time you two met anyway."

He turned back, his smile blooming with relief. "Yeah?"

"Yeah." She tugged him gently toward her. "Just make sure you're home in time for curfew, young man."

He gave her a playful salute. "Yes, ma'am!"

As Macy unlocked the door, Cade wrapped his arm around her waist from behind, nuzzling her ear and making her laugh.

"I'm not going to be able to open this door if you keep distracting me," she warned, giggling.

He spun her around and dipped her into a kiss. "So, I should stop doing that, then. Yeah?"

She swatted his arm playfully. "Yes! Cut it out, or I'll send you home without dessert."

"Dessert?" he asked with a mischievous grin. "I thought this wasn't that kind of visit."

"Not what I meant!" she said, cheeks burning, but still laughing as they finally wrestled the door open and bounded up the stairs to her apartment.

Catherine looked up from the couch, eyes wide, tea cup in hand, when Macy walked in with Cade right behind her.

"Well, this is a surprise," she said. "I was about to start getting ready for bed, but my night just got more entertaining. This must be the mysterious Cade?"

"Entertaining, huh?" Cade replied, smirking. "That must make you, Catherine."

"He didn't bring me cookies, Cath," Macy said.

"What? No cookies? It's over," Catherine teased, grinning at him.

"I did get a beautiful delivery at work today," Macy added. "Just flowers. Not cookies, but they were gorgeous. And he made the whole team jealous. Even Amara."

"Nice one, Cade!" Catherine said, raising her teacup in approval.

Cade watched the exchange between Macy and Catherine with an amused expression, like he was trying to decode a language he didn't quite speak.

Catherine turned to him. "Next time, bring cookies, and you might just win me over."

Macy glanced at Cade, who clutched his chest dramatically, as if mortally wounded. She laughed. "All right, let me walk you out before Catherine decides to start grilling you about your intentions."

But Cade didn't move. "I wouldn't mind if she did," he said, his voice soft but steady. "I think she'd be happy with what she heard. Actually…I was hoping I could stay just a little longer. We only just came up, and I wanted a bit more time before heading home."

Catherine raised an eyebrow. Subtle, but Macy caught it behind Cade's back. "I'll leave you two alone," she said, turning toward her room. "I've got an email from Shane to answer."

"Pleasure meeting you, Catherine!" Cade called out with all his charm.

Once her bedroom door closed, Macy and Cade sank into the couch. The TV was still on, low and aimless, as he slid an arm around her shoulders.

"Thanks for letting me come up," Cade said quietly. "I really needed this tonight."

Macy smiled, leaning into him. "It's been a great week."

"I'll say it has."

He leaned in and brushed his lips over hers. The TV murmured in the background as the kiss deepened, his arms tightening around her. From the bedroom, Catherine's laughter broke the moment, and Macy pulled back, startled.

"Sorry," Cade said, his voice gentle. "I don't mean to overstay my welcome. I just didn't want tonight to end."

"It's okay," Macy said. "But I really should get some sleep."

He nodded and stood, tugging her hand as they walked to the door. "I'll call you tomorrow."

She nodded, and he kissed her once more—slow, lingering. Macy watched him disappear down the stairwell before she closed the door behind him.

When she turned around, Catherine was standing in the hallway with a fresh cup of tea in her hand. She didn't say anything at first. She simply looked at Macy.

"May I help you?" Macy asked. She grabbed a cup to pour tea for herself.

Catherine stirred her tea slowly. "Does he always get his way?"

"What do you mean?" Macy asked.

"I saw your hesitation," Catherine said. "What happens if you tell him no?"

"Nothing!" Macy replied quickly. Too quickly.

A long, uncomfortable silence settled between them.

"He just likes being around me," Macy said finally. "It's sweet. I've never had someone actually want to spend time with me like this. Not without games or mixed signals. It's a nice change."

Catherine studied her carefully. "I don't know, Mace. The museum, the rooftop dinner, now this. It's a lot for only dating a week."

Macy sighed, the weight of the conversation pressing down. "I know you're looking out for me, and I appreciate it. I really do. But I've been waiting a long time to feel this kind of connection with someone. You know what I've been through. I just want to enjoy it without worrying that you're going to be mad at me."

Catherine raised her hand in mock surrender. "I'm not mad at you, you haven't done anything! I'm just looking out for you."

"Good," Macy said, heading toward her room. "Now, I invited him back tomorrow with some Mario Party for us all. I gotta be at my top form."

Catherine grunted at her. "If he doesn't bring cookies, you're on your own."

Laughing, Macy disappeared into her room with the tension between them finally eased. The smile lingered on her lips as she closed the door behind her.

Part Four

Love Bomb

Celeste's Office

"Catherine saw what I didn't want to see. Things in the beginning burned so fast and bright, and to me, it felt romantic. Like something out of a movie."

Celeste gazed at me thoughtfully. "That must have been difficult."

"It was," I admitted. "I didn't want to fight with Catherine, and I didn't want her to hate him. So, I started keeping things to myself to keep her from worrying. I wanted peace. I wanted them to like each other. But deep down, I was afraid she wouldn't like the way things were going…the way I did."

I paused, the truth settling in as I spoke it aloud. "That should've been a giant red flag. The fact that I felt I had to hide anything from my best friend out of fear that she wouldn't understand. It makes me feel foolish for continuing the relationship."

Celeste's expression softened, but her voice remained steady. "Macy, I feel like we're on the edge of something important. To get there, I need to ask you a few hard questions. I need you to be honest with yourself. Can you tell me: Even though Catherine voiced her concerns, why did you move forward with Cade?"

I took a breath. "It was everything I thought I'd ever wanted. The most serious relationship I'd ever had ended because I wanted to talk about the future, and he didn't. So, when Cade came along, I was pushing thirty, and I swore I could hear my biological clock ticking. Here was someone who wanted all the same things I did. And he wanted them with me. He showered me with attention and met my emotional needs. It was thrilling."

Celeste leaned forward slightly. "How did that make you feel when he told you about his relationship style?"

"Honestly, it was a relief," I said. "After all the false starts and bad dates, it was refreshing to meet someone who didn't want to play games. I wanted someone who wanted me just as much as I wanted them. We had so much in common, and everything in the beginning went so smoothly. Emotionally, Cade was a bit further ahead than I was, but I assumed I would catch up. Again, it was a relief to know where I stood."

I leaned back into the couch, eyes scanning the ceiling as I fought tears. "Those early days of a relationship are so heady with endorphins. You just want more of it. And the only way to get it is with your person."

Celeste chuckled. "'Heady with endorphins.' You're starting to think like a therapist."

I laughed, the tension breaking for a moment. "Yeah, I guess your words are starting to rub off.

"Anyway, everything felt so right. I liked how he prioritized our relationship. He said all the things I wanted to hear, showered me with gifts and affection. So, why would I question it?"

Celeste nodded slowly. "Do you know what we call that, Macy?"

I tilted my head, curious.

"He love-bombed you."

I paused, waiting for her to explain.

"It's a phrase we use to describe a manipulative pattern often seen in narcissistic relationships," Celeste explained gently. "The person showers their target with affection, gifts, and flattery. Everything is designed to make you fall fast. They'll mirror your interests, act like you're soulmates, and wonder aloud how you hadn't met sooner. It's all meant to trigger that exact endorphin rush you mentioned."

She leaned in slightly. "They need to be needed. So, they say and do whatever they think will make you feel safe, seen, and adored. But it's not real. It's an idealized version of them, crafted to make you believe they're the only person for you. And once they have you, that's when the mask starts to slip. You begin to see the controlling behaviors, the guilt trips, the emotional manipulation. The way you described with Cade."

Her voice softened. "If you don't do what they want, when they want it, they'll use that deep affection to make you feel guilty. And if that doesn't work, they may turn to insults. In some cases, it can escalate to physical danger."

Her words hit hard. They described exactly what I'd been feeling and hadn't wanted to admit. How could I have been so blind? Tears welled in my eyes.

Celeste noticed. "What are you feeling right now, Macy?"

A single tear slipped down my cheek. "Shame."

"Why do you feel shame?"

I wiped the tear away, trying to hold back the rest. "Catherine and Theo both saw it. Why couldn't I see it too? I fell right into his trap."

Celeste tilted her head, her expression warm and steady. "You are not to blame for what happened to you, Macy. People like this are very good at what they do."

"Does that make me naive?"

She paused, choosing her words carefully. "No, Macy. I don't believe that. Love-bombing is a calculated tactic. The guilt lies with the abuser, not the abused. And it's incredibly difficult to distinguish between genuine affection and manipulation. Especially for someone who fears abandonment or craves connection."

I let her words settle in, then sighed deeply. "That makes sense. Looking back, it did seem too good to be true. He definitely pushed the relationship faster than I was comfortable with, but in the moment, it didn't occur to me to mind."

"Do you want to tell me more about that?"

"We'd been dating a few weeks, maybe a month. Our dates had shifted a lot: less extravagance and more quiet evenings at my place. We were together almost every day. We watched movies and cooked for each other. He even brought over his Nintendo system, and we had a lot of Mario battles."

I smiled faintly at the memory, then continued. "I'd taken a pay cut when I started my new job, so I was worried about money. I was actually relieved when we started spending more time in."

It was around that time, about a month in, when he pushed me into something I wasn't ready for…

Chapter Twelve

LOVE AND DOUBT

The first signs of October began to blossom in the city. The air had a hint of crispness, and the leaves were starting to blush gold and rust. After nearly a month of spending every evening with Cade, Macy welcomed the change of pace when Catherine called for a girls' night in.

Catherine uncorked a bottle of wine while Macy set the table for dinner.

"I was about two days away from putting your face on a milk carton," Catherine teased.

Macy laughed, letting the whirlwind of the past few weeks roll off her shoulders. "Do they even still do that?"

Catherine shrugged, then gave Macy her sternest "Mom" face. "I want you home right after school tomorrow, young lady, to help me with the chores."

"I know, I've been kind of a ghost," Macy admitted, her tone shifting. "Cade's been keeping me…busy."

"That's one way to put it," Catherine said with a smirk. "'Busy,'" she repeated, fingers making air quotes.

Macy shook her head, laughing. "Pervert."

"You wouldn't have me any other way," Catherine said, rolling her eyes.

They sat down to eat, chatting about end-of-summer plans. Catherine swirled the last of her wine before finishing it. Macy reached for a second helping of pot roast, then hesitated and returned half to the serving dish. Catherine noticed.

"Are you doing that because you want to? Or because you think you're supposed to?"

Macy hesitated. "Both, I guess? But hey, it's working."

"But are you happy?" Catherine asked, her voice gentle but direct.

"Yes! I mean…I'm still eating what I like. I'm just adjusting to smaller portions. It's taken some getting used to, but it's getting easier."

"I see," Catherine said, her skepticism subtle but present. She leaned back. "So, how serious are we with Mr. Muscles?"

Macy laughed. "Mr. Muscles, huh? Well, you've seen us together. We're here as much as we're at his place. So, yeah, I'd say we're getting serious."

"That didn't take long," Catherine said, her expression unreadable.

Macy shrugged. "It just…happened. I've been going with the flow."

Catherine tilted her head. "And how do you feel about that, honestly?"

Macy paused, fork halfway to her mouth. "I'm happy. It's nice to feel wanted like this. No one I've ever dated made me feel like I was worth pursuing. Not just at the beginning, but even after they had me."

Catherine's expression softened. "I wish you could see what a prize you are. But let me ask you something: How much control have you honestly had over this 'going with the flow'?"

Macy blinked. "What do you mean by that?"

"I honestly don't know how you convinced him to let us have tonight, without him here," Catherine said, pouring another splash of wine.

"You don't like him?" Macy asked, her tone cautious.

Catherine placed a gentle hand on Macy's. "I'm not saying that. He's clearly eager to be with you, and on its own, that's not necessarily a bad thing. But you've been through a lot, Mace. He's attentive, which I know you like, and I just hope he's not using that to his advantage."

Macy stiffened. "He's not controlling me."

"I didn't say that. I just don't want you to lose yourself," Catherine said softly.

Macy stared into her wine glass, letting the words settle. She knew Catherine meant well. *She's just being protective,* Macy told herself. *She doesn't know him like I do.*

"I hope you're not mad," Catherine added.

"Of course not," Macy said, her voice quiet. Still, she avoided making eye contact. "I know it's been fast and intense, but I think something real is happening here."

Catherine raised her hands in mock surrender. "Okay! I will stop asking. If you say so."

They finished dinner in a gentle silence, and the mood between them subtly shifted. Macy wasn't angry, but she was unsettled. *She's been with Shane so long,* Macy thought, *she probably just doesn't remember the thrill of something new. I'm sure it'll come back when he gets home from deployment.*

Catherine glanced up and gave Macy a soft, supportive smile. She didn't want to let a guy come between them, but neither was she prepared to let one hurt Macy. She would keep her mouth shut, for now, but keep her eyes open.

After clearing the dishes, Catherine settled on the couch for some TV. Macy excused herself to call Cade. He hadn't been thrilled about missing their usual evening together, but he'd agreed to a FaceTime.

As soon as the screen lit up, Cade beamed. "Well, there's my pretty girl! I was starting to forget what you look like. It's been two whole days!"

Macy giggled. "Funny, Catherine said almost exactly that over dinner."

"I hope you haven't been skipping your workouts, too! How's that going?"

"I've been finding little ways to keep up around the house," Macy replied. "I've lost a few pounds. Nothing super noticeable yet."

"That's a good start," Cade said, then paused. "You look tired."

"It's been a long day," Macy admitted. "I'm liking the job, but Amara doesn't mess around. She's keeping me on my toes, and I feel like if I'm not five steps ahead, I'm falling behind. And I was just looking at my budget…"

She sighed and dropped her eyes as she ran her fingers along her gold chain. "Joy's baby shower is coming up. They'd understand if I joined by Zoom, but this is my brother's first baby. I really want to be there. I haven't seen them in months. But I had to take a pay cut when I took the job with Amara, and I don't think I can afford the trip."

Cade leaned back, thoughtful. "That's right, you were last home right before we met, weren't you?"

Macy nodded miserably.

He smiled. "You know, I've got a steady income, too. What if I took you back to Iowa? And maybe we can plan a layover in Chicago so you can meet my family. It's about time we start meeting families, don't you think?"

Macy was startled at the idea of Cade meeting her family, her jaw slack with surprise. *Are we ready for this?* she wondered. *Am I?*

Cade's gaze sharpened, forehead creased with concern. "That's not a good face."

Pulled from her thoughts, Macy blinked and tried to refocus. "No, sorry. I was just thinking. I hadn't much considered it yet. But…that's a lot of money for you to spend on travel," she said, aiming for a light tone.

"You let me worry about that, baby girl," he said smoothly. "I want you to see your family, and I can make that happen. Won't you let me help you?"

"Are you sure? That's going to be, like, a thousand dollars."

"There's nothing I wouldn't do for you."

Macy smiled, overwhelmed by the gesture. "Okay. If you insist, let's start looking at flights and dates!"

"This is going to be great. I can't wait to meet your family," Cade said, his excitement bubbling over.

"That's so generous of you. Thank you."

He looked down at his hands, tracing a finger over his knuckles like he was working through nerves. "I told you, Mace. I'm in this all the way. I've never felt this way about someone before."

He hesitated, then glanced at her sideways. He looked up, his voice softer now. "Can I ask you something, though?"

"Of course," she said, though her chest tightened with unease.

"Is there…anything else on your mind? Something you've been meaning to say but haven't found the right moment for?"

Macy shifted, the sinking feeling from her first day at the gym suddenly slamming back into her chest. "Like what?"

"Oh, I don't know," Cade said lightly, though his tone hinted he had expectations. "You were pretty lost in thought for a minute there. Almost like you were thinking beyond just a visit home."

"I mean, I kind of was," Macy admitted cautiously. "I was thinking about the bigger picture."

His lips curled into that slow, knowing smile. The one that always made her feel like saying yes to anything. "The bigger picture, huh?" His voice dipped into a coaxing rhythm. "Like what, Bella? Something you maybe want to say, but you're too scared to?"

Macy's pulse quickened, her breath catching in her throat. *Whoa…is he talking about love? This is too sudden.*

She felt boxed in, unsure how she'd gotten there or how to get out. The air felt tight, heavy.

He leaned forward, voice barely above a whisper. "Now would be a perfect time to say it."

Her stomach twisted. "Say what?"

"You know what," he murmured, eyes locked on hers. His smirk faltered, losing some of its confident edge. "I know how I feel about you. I thought we were on the same page…but maybe I was wrong."

A pang of guilt stabbed through her. "That's not—"

"No, no, it's fine," Cade said quickly, forcing a small, brittle laugh. "I mean, we've been spending all this time together, talking every day. I thought I was taking pretty good care of you. I'm flying you home to see your family, for God's sake. I know what I want, and I know what I feel. But if you don't feel the same way…"

He trailed off, shrugging and shaking his head like he was bracing for disappointment.

Macy's heart pounded. She could feel him pulling away. That sliver of hurt in his voice, the tension in his jaw. She didn't want her fear to cost her something real, the way it almost had before.

"I…" She hesitated.

Cade's eyes softened as he looked up at her, but there was something expectant behind them. "It's okay, baby. Don't be scared. Just tell me."

Her chest tightened, breath shallow. *Isn't this what I wanted?* Someone who loved her, who saw her, who chose her without hesitation. So, why was she hesitating?

It's so fast. Does he mean it? Do I?

The wounded look in his eyes tugged at something deep inside her. Even if she didn't feel it yet, wasn't she on her way?

"I love you," she whispered. The words tasted foreign on her lips, like they didn't quite belong to her.

Cade's face lit up. "There it is. I knew it was in there."

He blew a kiss at the screen, sealing the moment like a deal. "You have no idea what it means to hear that, baby. You just made my whole year. I love you too, Macy."

But the weight on her chest didn't lift. If anything, it pressed harder.

"Now we're really on the same page," he said. "You'll see. This is going to be everything we've both been waiting for. Get some sleep, Bella. We'll talk tomorrow about those travel arrangements."

The call ended. Macy wandered into the kitchen, hoping to talk with Catherine, but the room was dark and empty. She glanced at the clock. Midnight. She considered peeking into Catherine's room, just to see if she was still awake, but thought better of it. *I don't want to give her another reason to think badly of him.*

When morning came, the unease hadn't faded. She couldn't shake the feeling that something about last night was…off. Things with Cade had moved so fast. *Was he right? Am I hiding from my feelings?* Everything had felt so natural between them—until now. *Maybe I'm just overthinking.*

She checked her phone. A text from Cade lit up the screen: *Good morning, beautiful.*

Macy stared at it, then decided to have a cup of coffee before replying. She threw on her bathrobe and padded into the kitchen, where she found a fresh pot already brewed. Catherine was on the phone with Nina, moving around the kitchen with practiced ease.

Macy gave her a small wave, then decided on a shower.

As the water streamed down, she let the conversation replay in her mind. They had a great connection. He'd been patient, letting her set the pace. And he wouldn't be spending that kind of money to take her home if he didn't care. *Look how well he treats me. So, what's the problem?*

By the time she stepped out and wrapped herself in her robe, she'd talked herself into the words she'd said the night before.

Back in the kitchen, Catherine looked up as Macy entered. She smiled and said into the phone, "Macy just came out. Do you want to talk to her?"

Macy heard Nina exclaim that she did, and Catherine handed her the phone. Before heading off to take her own shower, Catherine hugged Macy and whispered in her ear, "I hope we're okay?"

"Always," Macy replied, returning the hug. Then, into the phone, she said: "Nina, I'm actually glad you're on the line."

"Obviously! Everybody's morning is better with me in it," Nina said brightly. "Catherine told me you finally came up for air last night. And that you two butted heads over Cade. What's going on?"

Macy had felt better after her shower, but the mention of her conversation with Catherine brought the tension creeping back. "Catherine and I are fine. She's just worried about me with Cade. She wanted to make sure I'm okay."

"And are you?"

Macy laughed nervously. "Well…Cade told me he loves me last night."

There was a pause on the line.

"Well, that's something new. Nina Simpson, rendered speechless!"

"Hang on," Nina said. "Let me wrap my head around this. What did you say?"

"I said it back," Macy admitted quietly, glossing over how the words had come out. "I honestly don't know if I was ready, but I said it. Am I crazy?"

She heard Nina sigh. "Truth? No. Things have moved fast and furious between you two, but sometimes, things just click. You've been through a lot, and people have made you feel like you weren't enough. Which is total bullshit, by the way. You're amazing. And Cade sees that. He makes you feel desired. Valued. There's nothing wrong with that."

Macy poured herself a cup of coffee and sat at the table. "I felt like if I didn't say it, I was going to shatter him. You should've seen the look in his eyes when I hesitated."

"Did he push you?" Nina asked, her tone neutral.

"Not exactly," Macy said slowly. "But I thought if I didn't say it, he'd think I was just using him. Or taking advantage of his kindness."

Nina hummed thoughtfully. "Do you want my honest opinion?"

"I would expect nothing less," Macy replied, half-exasperated with herself.

Nina's voice softened. "Are you thinking with your head or with your heart?"

Macy didn't answer. Her silence said everything she couldn't quite put into words.

"That's what I thought," Nina said gently. "Listen, Columbia, you've got to stop overthinking and just feel. Relationships don't follow a schedule. You're still figuring things out, and that's okay. Just be honest with yourself, and you'll come out all right. And, for God's sake, stop hoarding. I can't believe you haven't brought him to meet me yet!"

Macy closed her eyes and gave her a small and tired giggle. Her mind finally began to clear after the storm of the night before. "Thanks, Nina. I'll see what I can do about the hoarding."

As she ended the call, a voice came from behind her, making her jump.

"So!"

"Oh, God," Macy groaned, rolling her eyes as Catherine reentered the room. "How much of that conversation did you hear?"

Catherine grinned mischievously. "Enough."

"I know you, and I know what that 'so' means."

Catherine gestured dramatically. "Well then, go ahead!"

"You want to know if I'm going to sleep with him now."

"I'm just saying, Red," Catherine teased, leaning against the counter. "It's been a month now that you two have been joined at the hip. You got the 'I love you' conversation out of the way. Shane's not back for another month, and we both know Nina's holding out on Brian. Someone around here's gotta be getting some so the rest of us can live vicariously!"

"Catherine!" Macy gasped, laughing, her cheeks growing hot.

Catherine joined in the laughter, and Macy felt a sudden, unexpected ache in her chest. One that had nothing to do with confusion. It was the quiet realization that their lives were about to turn a corner, one they couldn't turn back from. Everything was about to change. She and Cade were getting serious. Shane would be home soon. And Macy wasn't sure how that shift would affect the closeness she shared with Catherine.

As if sensing her thoughts, Catherine reached over and nudged her. "I'm still going to be a pain in your ass, no matter what happens with our men."

"I'm going to hold you to that," Macy said, finishing her coffee. She smiled, then wandered back to her bedroom to get dressed for the day.

Her phone lit up with three new texts and a missed call from Cade:

Cade

I hope you're not having second thoughts about what we said last night. Because I meant it.

Cade

Macy?

Cade

Shit. Call me, please!

Her stomach dropped. Cade thought she was ignoring him. She hadn't meant to disappear. She just needed time to think.

Before she could dial him back, her phone lit up again. Cade.

She answered quickly. "Hi! I'm so sorry. I meant to text you back, but I went to pour a coffee and got cornered by Nina and Catherine."

"I was worried you changed your mind," he said with a light laugh, but the tension in his voice was unmistakable. "You left me hanging, Mace."

"No, I'm sorry," she said, trying to soothe him. "I left my phone charging and wandered off. I didn't expect it to be so long. I just got caught up talking."

"About me?"

"About everything," she replied, keeping her tone casual. "It was a big night."

Cade hesitated. "You promise last night didn't freak you out?

"I'm okay," Macy said, gently but firmly. "I just needed a minute to stop overthinking and breathe."

He exhaled; the relief was audible. "Okay. I meant what I said last night. I just hope you did, too."

"I know you did," Macy said. "And I really appreciate you and how well you take care of me."

His voice lifted. "In that case, what are we up to tonight?"

Macy smiled, her tone light. "Why don't we see if Nina and Brian are free? They'd love to meet you."

"Maybe after, we can sneak off for a little time to ourselves?" Cade asked hopefully.

"Perhaps," Macy said with a smile. "I'll see you then."

After she ended the call, she sighed and muttered to herself, "I'd better call my parents…"

Chapter Thirteen

MORE THAN PLANNED

"Are you sure you don't want to come?" Macy asked. "It hasn't been the three of us since Cade's and my first date."

Catherine looked up with a sarcastic gleam in her eye. "It still won't be the three of us. Your men will be there."

"Oh, stop it. You know you're not the fifth wheel with us. Nina will be doing her best to ignore Brian, you and I will be trying to push her to stop being a frigid bitch, Cade will be watching our interaction like it's a tennis match, and Brian will give her puppy eyes and eventually retreat to playing host."

Catherine laughed and shook her head. "Sounds delightful, but you'll have to tell Nina to stop ignoring her husband without me. I've got plans to see my parents tonight."

"All right, I guess I'll allow it," Macy said with a playful pout, though she was genuinely disappointed. "You should take Theo with you. The man eats way too much takeout. I don't think he'd recognize a home-cooked meal unless you packed it in a box."

"Great idea!" Catherine said. "You're right, he doesn't get out enough. I'm sure my parents would get a kick out of him."

Catherine left to check in on Theo, and Macy headed to her room to get ready. The overhead light cast soft shadows across the floor as she ran her hand along the row of shirts and dresses hanging in the small alcove that served as her closet. It was just a casual night in with Brian and Nina, but tonight, there was something different in the air.

The last time she'd been in their penthouse, she and Cade had only just met. Now they were falling in love.

In love.

The words echoed in her mind. Was Nina right that she was overthinking? The gravity of their conversation settled over her. This could be the new rhythm of her life. They were planning to travel together soon, meeting each other's families. Somehow, without her noticing, things had gotten serious.

One of these nights, when Cade walked her home, he might stay.

She pulled out a few hangers and held them up in the mirror. The blue wrap dress felt too formal. Her button-down blouses were too stiff. She cringed at the sight of the green club dress that had started everything. It had looked good, sure, but she still couldn't believe she'd worn it out in public. Her jeans and tank top felt too casual.

Tonight was special. She wanted to dress like it.

Finally, she settled on a baby pink, sleeveless V-neck top and paired it with a pleated black mini-skirt. It showed off her recent progress at the gym and struck a balance between polished, playful, and just a little flirty. She slipped on a pair of strappy black stiletto sandals and decided it was the perfect night to brush on a little nail polish.

As her pink toenails dried, she sat at her vanity and began her makeup. A shimmering silver dusted her eyelids, lined slightly heavier than usual to make her green eyes pop. She brushed on mascara and finished with a cherry-tinted gloss.

"Relax," Macy told the woman in the mirror. "It's just Brian and Nina. And a man who loves you."

Her red curls hung long and loose down her back. The scent of vanilla and jasmine lingered in the air as she spritzed her favorite perfume on her wrists, then dabbed a touch at her neckline where her gold cross faithfully rested. The reflection staring back looked poised. Maybe even confident. But on the inside, she felt exposed, as if her usual armor had been peeled away, leaving only delicate lace behind.

She wondered, not for the first time: Is this what a normal relationship is supposed to feel like? Giddy. Nervous. Thrilling.

Slipping into her sandals, she checked her phone. Right on time, Cade buzzed his arrival.

Macy tapped at Theo's door, and he smiled brightly at her. "Hi! You look fancy tonight. Big date with that guy?"

"Something like that!" she said. "I was checking if Catherine was still here, so I don't lock her out of the apartment."

Theo opened the door wide to show Catherine sitting at his dining table. Catherine waved, smiling. "I'll lock up. You two kids have fun!"

Macy hugged them both briefly and walked downstairs to meet Cade. The evening air was still warm, but the breeze hinted at the coming chill.

"Hi there, beautiful," Cade said with a broad smile as she stepped through the door. He swept her into his arms and kissed her hard, murmuring against her ear, "I love you."

Still getting used to the words, Macy whispered back, "I love you, too."

"I couldn't wait to say and hear those words in person," he said, releasing her gently. "You look absolutely incredible."

Cade had dressed for the occasion in black pleated pants, a crisp white button-down, and his dark waves slicked back. He looked like he'd just stepped out of a boardroom.

"I do love a sharp-dressed man," Macy said, almost shy.

"Do you now?" Cade teased, beaming. "I'll remember that."

They stopped at the corner bakery to pick up a sampler box of Italian cookies for dessert. Macy looped her arm through Cade's offered elbow and smiled up at him. After nearly a month together, she was comfortable around him, but their conversation last night had stirred the butterflies again. Cade carried the cookies as they descended into the 68th Street station.

"I'm already regretting these shoes," Macy muttered as they stepped onto the train. It was surprisingly crowded for a Saturday afternoon, leaving no seats available.

Cade chuckled, glancing down at her strappy sandals. "I don't know why you ladies torture yourselves with those things."

"They're pretty," Macy said with a sassy tilt of her head. "And I feel like a hobbit around all of you. Even Nina towers over me!"

"Well, I can't argue with that. It does make kissing you easier from up here," he said, leaning down for a quick peck.

After a quick transfer at Grand Central, they stepped off at their 5th Avenue stop. The early autumn air had cooled with the setting sun, brushing Macy's bare shoulders as she and Cade walked the short distance to the Simpsons' building. Inside, they checked in with the doorman, who offered a polite nod before waving them through.

The elevator ride to the penthouse was smooth and silent, save for the faint hum of classical music playing overhead.

As the elevator doors slid open, Brian was waiting, grinning warmly. "There they are, just in time! Shame you couldn't talk Catherine into coming. Cade, it's a pleasure to meet you, finally."

The rich scent of garlic and fresh-baked bread spilled into the foyer, wrapping Macy in familiar comfort as she stepped inside. Brian greeted her with a hug, then shook Cade's hand before handing them each a glass of red wine. On the kitchen island, a tray of cheeses, crackers, and vibrant, sliced vegetables was arranged with practiced elegance.

"I tried," Macy said, accepting the wine. "But she's spending the night with her parents."

Nina popped her head out from behind the oven door. "Too bad for her! She's missing Dad's famous baked ziti."

Cade pulled out a stool at the breakfast nook and handed Macy her glass before settling in beside her. "You know my step-mom is Italian, right? She taught me well. Pressure's on, Nina."

"You do know *my* dad is second generation off the boat, right?" Nina shot back, eyes sparkling. "Challenge accepted."

Brian chuckled, leaning against the counter as he watched the verbal sparring. "Now that's a cook-off I'd pay to see."

"I could take her," Cade said with a confident shrug.

Macy placed the bakery box of cookies on the counter and swirled her wine thoughtfully. "You haven't lived until you've had Nina's dad's cooking. His Nonna brought everything over from Italy. No recipes, just instinct. If there's a challenge happening, Brian and I are the lucky taste testers."

Brian poured another round of the wine, and Nina called them to the dining room. The table was set with simple white China and heavy silver cutlery. Overhead, a crystal chandelier scattered warm light across the table, glinting off the polished cherry China cabinet in the corner. A framed print of Monet's *Water Lilies* hung on the far wall, adding a serene touch to the stately room. Nina had scooped a pile of pasta onto each plate and placed a basket of freshly baked bread at the center of the table.

The baked ziti was rich and layered with flavor, and the bread practically melted in Macy's mouth. As Brian and Cade slipped into easy sports talk, Macy found herself tucked easily into Cade's side, his knee warm against hers beneath the edge of the table. He leaned in now and then to murmur things only she could hear, low and affectionate.

Across the table, Nina watched them over the rim of her wineglass. Brian was talking, animated and hopeful, but she only gave him half her attention. Instead, she caught Macy's eye and leaned in.

"So," Nina said quietly, "how are you feeling about…the talk this morning?"

Macy hesitated. "Better, I think. It's still a lot. After everything, I'm scared to let my guard down. But Cade…he makes it easy. No one's ever made me feel this wanted before. It's overwhelming, but in a good way."

"Don't ever apologize for being loved like that," Nina said, lifting her glass. She eyed Brian with just an ounce of disdain, then turned back to Macy. "The magic doesn't always last, so enjoy it when it shows up."

The men continued debating quarterbacks, and Macy reached instinctively for the bread basket. Cade's hand brushed her wrist casually and angled the basket closer to his place setting.

"Careful," he murmured lightly, barely audible over the TV.

As the cookie tray made its rounds and Nina cleared the dishes, Brian flipped on the TV and pulled out the Switch. "Anyone up for Mario Kart?"

Cade grinned. "As long as I get to be Yoshi, you're on. Fair warning: I don't lose."

"Except to me," Macy teased, nudging him with her shoulder.

Cade shot her a smirk. "Let's see if you can back that up."

The game quickly devolved into laughter and playful taunts. Even Nina cracked a smile as Brian spun out on a banana peel for the third time in a row. Eventually, the clock crept past ten, and the mood mellowed. Macy stretched, pressing her shoulder against Cade's, leaning into his warmth.

"We should probably head out," Cade said as the last of the wine glasses went dry. "We've got travel plans to map out."

"Travel plans?" Nina perked up. "What's this?"

Macy's eyes softened. "Joy's baby shower is coming up in a couple of weeks. I was struggling to figure out the finances, so Cade offered to take me home. We figured it'd be a good time to start meeting the parents before the holiday season kicks in. After Iowa, we're stopping in Chicago to see his family, too."

Brian's eyes flashed wide. "That's a big step."

"I don't shy away from big steps," Cade replied, resting a warm hand on Macy's knee.

She smiled up at him, letting herself live in the moment without worrying about what it all meant. Her gaze drifted to Nina, who was clearing wine glasses and returning them to the kitchen, very deliberately avoiding their interaction.

But when Nina glanced back, she offered Macy a quiet, knowing smile. No teasing. Just gentle understanding.

Macy squeezed Cade's hand to signal she was getting up and followed Nina into the kitchen to help load the dishwasher. Brian and Cade joined them shortly after, gathering their things. The men exchanged handshakes and goodnights. Brian pulled Macy into a hug and kissed her cheek, while Cade did the same with Nina.

Macy eyed her sandals, dreading the thought of putting them back on. She seriously considered carrying them home and asking Cade to give her a piggyback ride through the subway. Groaning, she pulled the straps up and around her ankles.

Nina laughed at Macy's pained expression and handed her a pair of ballet flats. "Don't be a martyr. Just take them."

Gratefully, Macy slipped them on. "Thank you. And thanks for having us tonight. Next time, we'll give you a little more notice."

"Yeah, this was great!" Cade echoed. "And Nina, I've got to admit, I'm impressed you threw together that ziti so fast. Next time, it's on me. Maybe one day…us." He looked pointedly at Macy, who blushed and smiled.

Nina pulled her into a final hug as they reached the elevator. "Remember our talk earlier. You're a grown woman. Don't overthink."

On the train ride home, Macy leaned against Cade, the familiar sway of the car lulling her into a calm haze. Streetlights flashed by outside, casting momentary glows across his face. She watched him in quiet contentment, grounded by the feel of his shoulder beneath her cheek and the steady rhythm of his breath.

She let herself imagine what it might be like to fall asleep like this every night.

Cade walked Macy up to her apartment, where she immediately kicked off her borrowed flats and discarded her sandals in favor of cozy slippers. She flipped on the kitchen light, revealing a quiet and empty apartment.

A note sat on the table in Catherine's handwriting. Theo had declined the invitation, having already made plans for the evening, but hoped to get together again soon. Catherine added that, depending on the trains, she might spend the night with her parents and come home in the morning.

"So…it's after eleven," Cade said, scanning the note. "I'd say it's safe to assume she won't be back tonight. You've got the place to yourself."

"I…" Macy started, but her voice trailed off when she saw the fire in his eyes.

He stepped closer, tucking a loose curl behind her ear, letting his fingers linger just behind it. "You're so beautiful," he murmured, brushing his lips gently over hers.

Any attempt Macy might have made to shift the mood dissolved beneath the intensity of his gaze. He kissed her again—softly at first, teasing—then deepened the kiss until she was breathless. His heart pounded against hers as he pulled her close, her cheek pressed to his chest. In his arms, she felt safe. Wanted. Loved.

"Let me stay tonight," he whispered, his breath warm against her ear, sending goosebumps down her neck.

Her heart pounded with nervous anticipation. She hesitated, thoughts racing out of control. *Am I ready?* She couldn't form a coherent answer as he trailed slow, tender kisses down the curve of her neck. He gently pushed aside the neckline of her shirt, exposing the sensitive skin at its base.

"Um…" she murmured, still unable to think clearly. It's so quick…but he loves me…he's taking me home to meet my family…

His fingers traced a deliberate path down her spine, making her shiver. He nibbled playfully at her shoulder and collarbone, exploring, teasing. *I'm not used to moving this fast.*

She was still adjusting to the weight of hearing *I love you*. Was tonight the night to push the boundary of more?

"Aaahh…" she tried again, but the words wouldn't come.

"Let me stay with you," he whispered once more, on the edge of demanding, as he nipped at her ear.

Her body responded faster than her mind could keep up. Need consumed her and clouded her hesitation. She remembered Nina's words: *You're a grown woman. Don't overthink.*

Stop thinking. Just feel.

The evening held a passion she hadn't quite prepared for, and at last, she surrendered to it.

When Cade touched her cheek and brushed his lips against hers, the noise, the lights, the bustle of the world outside faded away. Her hesitation melted into the quiet understanding between them. Tonight, she wouldn't ask him to leave.

As they walked down the hallway, Macy paused outside her bedroom door, her hand resting lightly on the knob. She turned to Cade. His eyes met hers—hopeful, soft, unhurried.

She opened the door and let him in.

He held her with gentle intent. In touches and whispers, they exchanged quiet, unspoken promises beneath the soft light of her bedroom. For once, she didn't try to name every feeling or dissect every breath. She simply let it be.

And in his arms, she dozed peacefully.

Chapter Fourteen

FAMILY TIES

Catherine had taken the early train back to Manhattan from Elmont and was unlocking the apartment door by 9:00. As she set about brewing coffee, she heard Macy's bedroom door creak open.

"How was Brian and Nina's last night, Red?" she called out casually, nearly dropping the coffee pot at the sight that met her eyes.

"Good morning, Catherine!" Cade said brightly, saluting with a grin, wearing nothing but a pair of blue boxers. "Got enough coffee for one more?"

Catherine stared, jaw slack. "Y-yes? We have coffee. But—"

Before she could finish, Macy emerged from her room in a bathrobe, her face nearly as red as her hair. Cade leaned in to kiss her forehead, then disappeared into the bathroom with a polite "Excuse me."

Catherine turned to Macy, eyes wide. She practically spat at Macy, "*Details!*"

Macy groaned, burying her face in her hands.

"Oh, no, you don't," Catherine said, trying to pry Macy's hands away. "There's no walk of shame in this house. Girl code demands full disclosure!"

"He walked me home from Nina's last night," Macy muttered. "Asked if he could stay. So…he stayed."

Catherine waved her hands in a rapid circle, silently shouting for her to continue. Macy gave her a sheepish, conspiratorial look.

"Well?" Catherine prompted.

"He's…quite capable."

"Capable?" Catherine scoffed. "You're going to have to give me more than that."

"For God's sake, Catherine, he's right over there!"

"Then talk fast. And quietly. I want all the juicy details!"

Macy groaned again and reached for a coffee mug, clearly desperate for a distraction. "He's going to help me get home for Joy's baby shower. Did I tell you that?"

Catherine pouted. "You're not getting off that easy."

Macy grinned behind her mug and gave a barely perceptible wink. "I wouldn't say that. But you're on the right track."

"That's my girl!" Catherine said, grabbing her own mug. "Now, back to this baby shower?"

"Took you long enough to catch that," Macy teased.

"Oh, I caught it," Catherine said, lips curved up into a playful smirk. "I just have priorities."

They laughed easily as Macy explained the plan. "He mentioned scheduling a long layover in Chicago to see his family before we head back, but it's not going to work out this time. We talked about going for Christmas instead, since my parents are coming for Thanksgiving."

"It's a shame the baby will be too young for Joy and Ethan to travel with him," Catherine said wistfully. "I'm going to want to meet the little nugget!"

Macy's face softened into a dreamy smile as she imagined holding her niece or nephew for the first time. "You'll just have to come with us next time. You know they'd love to see you, too."

"They wouldn't put me to work mucking stalls, would they?"

Macy shrugged thoughtfully. "Nah. We'll just send the men."

Cade strolled into the room, grabbed a coffee mug, and kissed Macy's cheek. "Where are you sending the men now?"

Catherine gave him an angelic smile. "To form a shirtless calendar called Men of the Manure Pile."

Macy, deadpan, added, "Oh, definitely. April will be Cade holding a shovel, looking confused."

Catherine burst into laughter. "June is Brian running from a chicken in gym shorts."

"November is Ethan in flannel, romantically holding a pitchfork like it's a rom-com poster," Macy said, now howling with laughter.

"Wait. Shane needs in on this, too," Catherine chimed in. "He gets February. He's gazing at a basket of fruit with an egg in his hand. Tagline: He came for the harvest, but stayed for the heartbreak."

Cade sipped his coffee, grinning. "Do I get creative control over my month?"

"Only if you pass the goat-milking challenge," Catherine replied. "Eye contact mandatory."

"It's a trust exercise," Macy added. "For the goat."

She and Catherine dissolved into laughter, tears streaming down their faces, as Cade muttered, "What have I gotten myself into?"

Macy suddenly turned serious, locking eyes with him. "Oh, sweetheart. We're just getting warmed up."

He chuckled, shaking his head, as Catherine warned, "Watch it, or you'll end up in the director's cut."

Still laughing, Cade pulled out his phone. "All right, you two. Before I become some misguided centerfold, let's talk about these plans to get you home."

The aircraft dipped into its descent over Sioux Falls, South Dakota, and Macy clutched Cade's hand with eager anticipation.

"I still can't believe you found such a great deal with only a couple of weeks' notice," she said. "I'm sorry we couldn't make Chicago work this time."

Cade gave her hand a gentle squeeze and smiled. "It's all right. We'll be there soon enough for Christmas. They can't wait to meet you. And it's easy to find deals if you know where to look. Last-minute cancellations pop up all the time. Plus, I had a companion fare on my credit card."

"Well, that's handy!" Macy beamed. "It's about an hour's drive down to Springwater from here, but the foliage is at peak—should be beautiful. Funny, the last time I came home, I was marveling at the spring flowers. Now everything's turning again."

Cade had booked them comfort seats, so they disembarked ahead of the crowd. With only carry-ons, they bypassed baggage claim and ordered an Uber straight to the farm.

As the car pulled away from the airport and into the outskirts of Sioux Falls, Cade gazed out the window. "It's beautiful here."

"It really is," Macy agreed. "I've never really explored the city, but the drive through this area is always pretty. Maybe next time, you and I can tour a bit before heading back to New York?"

He looked at her hopefully. "Does that mean you're on board with me sticking around a while? Maybe making this long-term?"

"I wouldn't have let you start staying with me if I weren't," she said simply.

They watched as the city faded into open highway, then into the gently rolling hills of northwest Iowa. Golden fields stretched toward the horizon, dotted with aging red barns beneath a crisp blue sky. As they neared the Walker farm, the landscape burst into reds and oranges, with purple wildflowers mingling in the tall, sun-bleached grass lining the hedgerows.

It was harvest season in Springwater. Along the dusty roads, massive farm equipment rumbled through the fields, gathering the final crops of the year. The Uber turned down a gravel drive, and Cade took in the faded yellow farmhouse with its wraparound porch.

On the porch, a very pregnant Joy rocked gently in a chair, sipping sweet tea beside Rebecca, who jumped up the moment she saw the car.

"It's so quaint!" Cade said, eyes wide. "That must be your mom and sister-in-law?"

"Yep. Welcome to the country," Macy laughed. "Ever been to a place like this?"

"I can honestly say no. Definitely not in the greater Chicago area. And absolutely *not* near Manhattan."

Before they could open the car doors, Ethan came charging toward them, practically bouncing with excitement. He wasted no time grabbing their bags from the trunk, and as Macy stepped out, he wrapped her in a bone-crushing hug.

"I can't wait to hear everything," he whispered in her ear, just for her.

Rebecca stood on the porch with a gentle arm around Joy's shoulders as Joy made a slow attempt to rise. Macy quickly waved her off.

"Don't get up, Joy! We'll come to you."

Cade followed with Ethan, carrying his own bag toward the house. Rebecca offered Cade a warm smile as he approached, and just as they reached the porch steps, the front door creaked open.

George stood in the doorway, shoulders squared like a man preparing for battle. His eyes flicked between Macy and Cade, and beads of sweat betrayed her nerves. Cade's face paled slightly, and Macy shot her father a pleading look.

The familiar "V" of concern appeared on George's forehead, but when Cade turned to face the other way, he gave Macy a subtle wink.

Cade stepped forward, arm slipping around Macy's waist with quiet reassurance. "It's a pleasure to meet you at last, Mrs. Walker, Mr. Walker. Macy's told me so much about you! This must be the lovely Joy—and Ethan, of course, I just met."

Macy suddenly was self-conscious under the weight of so many eyes, but Cade's steady presence grounded her.

George gave nothing away, staring right back at Cade. "And what exactly has she told you?"

Cade's smile didn't waver. "That you're a close-knit family who looks out for each other. And that Ethan likes to give her a hard time."

Ethan clapped his hands. "Finally, someone who understands my role in life!"

Joy rolled her eyes. "Ignore him. It's nice to meet you, Cade. Please, sit! I'd offer to pour you a tea, but…" She gestured at her belly with a wry smile.

Macy bent to hug Joy, laughing a little. "We've got you covered." She pulled up a few chairs so they could all settle in and enjoy the warm fall afternoon.

Rebecca stepped forward, extending a firm but welcoming handshake. "Welcome. I hope the journey was smooth. We are so thankful that you made this happen for Macy. We haven't seen her in months, now!"

"I couldn't possibly let her miss such an important occasion," Cade replied, his tone gracious. Then he turned to George, offering his hand. "Sir."

George hadn't taken his eyes from Cade since they stepped on the landing. He gripped Cade's hand with just a little too much force, making Macy subtly wince. Cade, to his credit, didn't flinch.

"So, Cade," George said slowly, releasing the handshake, "what are your intentions with my daughter?"

Macy's eyes flew wide as she gaped at George. "Dad!"

But Cade chuckled, unfazed. "Well, sir, I intend to treat her like the queen she is, and make her happy for as long as she'll let me."

George didn't answer right away. He studied Cade, eyes narrowing like he was sizing up cattle at auction. Then, slowly, the "V" in his forehead began to smooth.

"That's the correct answer," he said at last with a nod.

But Rebecca wasn't about to let the moment pass. "Where do you stand on marriage and children?"

Macy groaned and buried her face in her hands. "I think I need something stronger than iced tea. Mom, can you at least let the man set down his duffel bag before you start grilling him like a Whopper?"

Cade, however, put a gentle hand on Macy's, quieting her. "I'm glad you asked, Mrs. Walker. I'm ready to settle down. I've always wanted a family—and I want it sooner rather than later. I'm almost thirty now, so I'm actually beyond ready."

Ethan leaned forward with a smirk. "All right then, my turn. What's the answer on children?"

Cade grinned. "As many as she'll allow."

Macy choked on her tea. She downed the rest of the glass and retreated to the kitchen, muttering as she went, "I need something stronger than iced tea if I'm going to be a part of this conversation!"

As she poured herself a glass of wine, Ethan's unmistakable cackle echoed into the kitchen. Curious, she peeked out the front door. Cade was seated at the table, animatedly telling a story. She couldn't make out which one, but judging by the expressions around him, he had them all eating from the palm of his hand.

Ethan spotted her and waved her back outside. "Your man was just telling us about the time he tried to impress you with Scotch and thought you were about to spit fire across the bar."

Macy leaned against the doorframe, arms crossed. "Did he mention that he failed to warn me it would taste like I was licking a campfire?"

Ethan shook his head in mock disappointment. "Did I teach you nothing in high school?"

Rebecca's eyes widened in horror. "Ethan James Walker!"

"Kidding, Mom!" Ethan said quickly, hands raised in surrender.

Cade laughed along with them, then continued the story. "I was afraid I was about to lose your daughter to the bartender when he handed her the Cosmo she actually ordered. She looked ready to leap over the bar and kiss him."

"At that point in time, I would have tried anything to get that taste out of my mouth," Macy shot back with a grin.

As the afternoon melted into evening, Macy helped Rebecca set the table for dinner. The scent of fried chicken and fresh biscuits filled the air.

"There's nothing better than Mom's fried chicken," she told Cade. "It'll beat anything I could find in the city."

"I look forward to finding out," Cade said, settling into his seat. Then he leaned toward her with a playful smile. "Don't forget your plan, though."

"What plan is this?" Rebecca asked, pulling a pitcher of lemonade from the fridge.

Self-conscious, Macy glanced at Cade. Her voice held the barest hint of a tremble as she explained, "Cade's been helping me get healthier. That's actually how we started falling for each other: We kept running into each other at the gym. He'd lost a lot of weight himself and offered to help train me."

"Well, that's nice," Rebecca said, though her tone carried a hint of caution. "But you know we don't think you need to change anything."

"Thanks, Mom," Macy replied warmly. "But I'm doing this for me. I want to feel stronger. It's not about anyone else."

Joy perked up from her seat. "Wait, how did you two meet in the first place? I don't think I've heard the whole story."

Macy and Cade exchanged a smile.

"He actually came to my rescue at Club Echelon." Macy beamed at him.

Ethan piled his plate with another pair of drumsticks and a heap of fried potatoes. "Oh, now that sounds like a story worth hearing!"

"Shut up, and I'll tell it!" Macy shot at her brother, giving him a playful shove. "Jack decided he had made a mistake in breaking up with me, and knew I was going to be at the club with the girls. He tried to get me to talk to him, and I refused. When I tried to walk away, he grabbed my arm—"

"And that's when I said, 'I believe the lady told you no,'" Cade finished. "After that, we started chatting."

Macy jumped back in, animated. "But he didn't ask for my number, so I figured that was that."

Cade chuckled and patted her hand. "I knew I'd see you again. A couple of weeks later, we were on the same side of town—her for work, me visiting a client—and I spotted her and Catherine heading into Eataly. I staged a little meet-cute, then found her on social media and reached out."

"You never did tell me how we both ended up in the same place that day," Macy said, narrowing her eyes playfully.

"Kismet, baby," Cade said with a grin. "Though I'll admit, I saw you going in and followed."

Macy rolled her eyes affectionately. "Then he finally wore me down and convinced me to go on an actual date. And the rest, as they say, is history."

She turned to gauge her family's reaction. Rebecca smiled, though there was still a flicker of caution in her expression. George, however, looked more concerned than convinced.

"So," he said, the familiar "V" of worry etched into his forehead, "how long have you known each other now?"

Macy hesitated, sensing the shift in his tone. "Well…it was right after I was home last. So, about five months? It was maybe two weeks after I got back that Cade and I ran into each other."

That explanation appeased George, at least for the moment. He nodded slowly. "All right. So, how long have you two been a couple?"

Cade glanced at Macy before answering. "We've been friends for most of the time we've known each other. But we realized it was more about six weeks ago. I know it's fast, Mr. Walker, but I love your daughter. I've never met anyone like her, and I want to give her the world."

Rebecca softened slightly, though her tone remained cautious. "That's very sweet, Cade. But you are right, that's awfully fast. We want to make sure she's not going to be hurt again."

Ethan flashed a devil-may-care grin, playfully punching his fist into the palm of his hand. "And if someone hurts her, he'll answer to me!"

Cade laughed, matching his energy. "I wouldn't risk that wrath! Please don't worry, Mr. and Mrs. Walker. I only want to see her happy."

He turned to Macy with a grin. "And you were right, Mace. This is the best fried chicken I've ever had. No offense to yours."

"None taken," Macy said, winking at her mother. "I'm just Mrs. Walker Junior in the kitchen."

After dinner, Cade helped clear the table and load the dishwasher. Macy walked him down the hall to Ethan's old room, a soft smile playing on her lips.

"We're still an old-fashioned family here," she said, pausing at the doorway. "No matter what you and I get up to in the city."

"That's all right," Cade replied, stepping inside. "It's charming. They worry about their little girl, that's all. But they'll see, you're in very safe hands."

He pulled her gently into his arms, and she burrowed into his chest with a contented sigh.

"Very capable ones, too," she murmured, then slipped away to her room upstairs with a teasing smile before he could respond.

Chapter Fifteen

THE BOND OF SISTERS

By Saturday, the living room had undergone a full transformation. Pastel streamers twisted along the crown molding, pink and blue balloons bobbed in every corner, and a banner reading *Welcome, Baby W!* hung above a gift table already overflowing with onesies, stuffed animals, and enough diapers to survive a Midwestern tornado. A handful of cousins loitered near the punch bowl, and someone had rigged a Bluetooth speaker to play a suspiciously curated playlist of mom-to-be anthems.

Macy stepped through the kitchen archway, balancing a tray of deviled eggs in one hand and a vegetable platter in the other, carefully sidestepping her cousin Jillian's Pomeranian, who had claimed ownership of the living room floor. Macy placed the trays on the banquet table pressed against the wall beneath the picture window, which framed a view of the farmhouse's side yard.

Joy, radiant in a flowing baby blue maternity dress, sat in the rocking chair with a plate of fruit skewers and exactly two minutes of peace. Her soft brown hair, usually pulled back, now swept gently across her shoulders. That peace was shattered when Aunt Erin burst in, brandishing a crocheted baby blanket she'd made "with extra love in every stitch."

Her head on a swivel, Aunt Erin zeroed in on Macy and beelined in her direction. "*Where* is this gentleman you brought with you, and *why* am I always the last to know about these things?"

"Oh, Lord, your mother has me in her tractor beams," Macy muttered to Nina, who had arrived that morning. "Hi, Aunt Erin. He's in with my dad if you want to go chat."

Nina didn't even glance up as her mother walked right past her and into the kitchen, where the men sat. "She's basically given up on hoping I'll have any, so I don't think I exist to her anymore."

Before Macy could ask Nina if she had even seen her parents since her wedding, Ethan strolled in from the back porch and made the fatal error of asking if anyone needed help. Six women immediately handed him empty plates, two offered half-full cups, and Aunt Erin launched into unsolicited instructions. The rest didn't even look up from their conversations.

"He deserves that," Macy said under her breath, smirking as her brother was conscripted into dish duty.

"Hey, Ethan!" she called out. "Don't look so flustered. You're going to need to know how to juggle when this baby gets here. Imagine the bottles, the diapers, the toys, the clothes, and—"

"Okay, Little Red, I got it!" he shot back with a mock glare.

Macy laughed, savoring the rare moment of getting under his skin after years of being on the receiving end.

Joy waved her over. "I swear, if one more person tells me I'm glowing, I might scream."

"You are glowing," Macy said, dodging the playful swat that followed. She set her plate of hors d'oeuvres on the coffee table and sank into the seat beside her. "But if it helps, you're also radiating a very subtle rage."

Joy sighed with theatrical relief. "That's more like it."

Macy smoothed her skirt and scanned the room. Cade was still chatting with her dad, looking surprisingly at ease for a man surrounded by three dozen small-town relatives. All of whom had repeated her parents' interrogation from the day before about his intentions. He caught her eye and winked before turning back to explain the New York subway system to Uncle Raymond, who remained convinced it was just "a lawless rat tunnel."

"Your city man's holding his own," Joy said, popping a grape into her mouth.

"He's trying," Macy replied, exhaling slowly. "It's the first time I've really seen him out of context. Away from the city. Away from...me."

Joy turned to her, frowning slightly. "And?"

"And...It's weird," Macy admitted. "Not bad. Just strange. Like watching your apartment furniture try to make friends with a barn."

Joy burst out laughing. "Well, that's certainly a visual. He doesn't seem to be struggling at all!"

"No, he's doing great," Macy said quickly. "It's uncanny how he's always polished. This world isn't, you know?"

Before Joy could respond, someone shouted, "Time for games!" and the room erupted in motion. Plastic baby bottles were handed out like party grenades. Macy groaned, and Joy nudged her with a grin.

"Welcome to my world."

The next twenty minutes descended into delightful chaos: racing to pin diapers on teddy bears, blindfolded "guess the baby food" competitions, and Joy laughing so hard, she nearly cried.

After the games, Joy carefully worked through a mountain of gifts while Ethan tallied who'd brought what. A cake frosted in powder blue and pink was passed around, and slowly, the crowd began to thin.

With the house finally quiet, Macy collapsed onto the couch beside Cade, breathless and covered in two kinds of mystery puree. Cade broke into a package of wet wipes and handed her one, along with a paper cup of punch, as if he were presenting a medal of valor.

"You were incredible out there," he said solemnly.

Macy dabbed at her sleeve. "I feel like I just returned from a very messy, pureed, diaper-filled war. And it's not even my baby."

He kissed her temple. "I can't wait until it's our turn."

Macy blinked, surprised, but didn't pull away. "I wouldn't let my dad hear that just yet."

Cade chuckled and glanced toward the dining room. "I think Dad and I are good."

"Dad?" Macy coughed as she choked on her punch. "You're calling him Dad now?"

He winked and put a finger on his lips to shush her. "Later."

After bidding her family—and Cade—goodnight, Macy curled into her childhood bed and gazed out the window. The full moon cast a silvery glow over the familiar landscape she'd called home for the first eighteen years of her life. She thought back to her last visit and now this weekend, and couldn't imagine things going any better.

Cade had fit in surprisingly well, despite being so different from her small-town roots. Macy hoped he had left them with the impression that he would take good care of her. She'd spent so long taking care of herself that it was comforting, even a little thrilling, to consider the possibility of letting someone else share that load.

Though the house was quiet and her goodnights had been said, sleep eluded her. She padded softly down to the kitchen to brew a cup of herbal tea. As she reached for the kettle, a soft squeaking sound drifted in from the front porch. Curious, Macy stepped outside.

Joy sat in the porch swing, a mug cradled in her hands, a brown-and-green crocheted Afghan draped over her shoulders. She looked up as the door opened.

"Sorry," Joy said, pausing the swing. "I hope I didn't wake you."

"I think we had the same idea," Macy replied, nodding toward Joy's teacup. "I just started the kettle."

Joy swirled the tea in her mug and hummed thoughtfully. "You won't have to wait long. Come join me after you pour yours."

Macy tiptoed back through the hallway and into the kitchen, and she flicked on the soft stove light. Her mother's cupboard still held a familiar tin of herbal teas. She chose chamomile, the most logical option, and waited until the kettle whistled before pouring herself a mug and returning to the porch.

Joy's mug sat empty in her hands. She rocked the swing gently with restless feet, her gaze lost in the moonlit yard. "We're so happy you came home, Mace. I hope you know how much we appreciate that Cade brought you back."

She turned to Macy and motioned for her to sit. "How are things going, really?"

Macy settled beside her carefully, as if Joy were made of glass. She took a sip of tea, letting the warmth settle her nerves as the swing resumed its slow rhythm.

"It's been a whirlwind," she admitted. "The new job, Cade, coming back here...It's a lot to take in. But mostly good things."

"Mostly?" Joy echoed gently.

"Yeah. The job was exactly what I needed, right when I needed it. My coworkers are great, and we get along really well."

"But?" Joy prompted, her voice soft.

"I had to take a big pay cut," Macy said, her tone quiet. "Things got tight. I honestly didn't think I'd make it home this weekend. I was really worried about Thanksgiving, so I'm relieved Mom and Dad are coming to us. I'll miss you and Ethan, though."

Joy nodded, her hand resting on her belly. "We'll miss you, too. But yeah, traveling with a newborn? Not happening."

They sat in silence for a moment, the swing creaking gently beneath them, the night wrapping around them like a blanket.

"I want to make sure you get to meet him as soon as it's practical. I just have this gut feeling it's a boy. It's hard sometimes, with you living so far away. We really miss you."

"I know," Macy said softly. "I miss you all, too. I'm sure we'll figure something out. It's just tough with work. I lost some vacation time when I switched jobs. I really do like it, though. I don't want to sound like it's all bad because it's not. It's just...not where I thought I'd end up."

Joy tilted her head. "How's your boss?"

"Amara? She's...a lot to get used to. It's hard to get a read on her outside of the job itself. You can almost never tell what she's thinking. I swear, she must play a mean hand of poker. But she's sharp. Demanding, but sharp."

Joy gave her a knowing look. "Speaking of intense...let's talk about this man of yours."

Macy looked down at her teacup, fingers curling around the warmth.

"Don't misunderstand me," Joy said gently. "He clearly cares about you. And as I said, we're grateful he got you here. But he's a lot to take in."

Macy glanced up, her voice tentative. "Do you think he made a good impression this weekend?"

Joy smiled. "Well, your brother likes him. That's a start. Your dad's harder to read. I think we're all just a little guarded. It's happening fast, and we want to make sure you're making choices that are right for you. That he's not running the whole show."

Macy nodded, her thoughts drifting to Catherine's earlier concerns. Their words echoed with unsettling similarity. "He cares. Deeply. It's different, but it's what I wanted. I'm not used to being someone's first pick."

Joy reached out and placed a gentle hand over Macy's. "I can see that he loves you, Mace. Just don't let this become your whole identity."

Macy squeezed her hand in return and took a slow sip of tea. "I hear you. And I appreciate the advice. How did you know things were right with Ethan?"

Joy's gaze drifted toward the horizon, her smile soft and nostalgic. "Something just clicked. It's hard to explain, but when we were together, it felt like he'd always been there. We didn't have to try. Everything just...happened."

"That makes sense," Macy murmured, letting her thoughts wander.

"There's such a different sound to an Iowa night than a Manhattan one," Macy said, her voice low.

Joy chuckled. "I can only imagine. Why don't you go get some rest? It's a long trip back to the city tomorrow."

Macy leaned in and hugged her gently. "Yeah, you're probably right. Good night."

She had just reached the door when Joy called out softly behind her. "Hey, Mace?"

Macy turned back, her hand resting on the doorknob.

"Thank you for being here," Joy said softly.

They shared a warm smile, and Macy slipped inside. Joy followed quietly, gently closing the front door behind her. That night, both sisters finally drifted into a restful sleep.

When Macy woke Sunday morning, she was greeted by the sound of roosters crowing in the yard. The peaceful stillness of the previous evening had given way to the hum of farm equipment tilling the remnants of the harvest. Horses nickered in the field, and through the window, she spotted her dad and Ethan feeding the pigs.

The scent of cinnamon buns greeted her as she landed at the base of the stairs. In the kitchen, Rebecca was sliding a fresh pan into the oven while Joy glazed a batch she'd just pulled out. Cade sat patiently at the table, but his face lit up the moment he saw Macy coming down the hallway. He stood, already holding a mug, and met her halfway.

"I hope you slept well," he said, kissing her forehead. Then, with a playful whisper, he added, "You know, you could've come to see me if you couldn't sleep."

Macy giggled softly, accepting the coffee. "I couldn't. This is my parents' house."

Joy brought the first plate of cinnamon buns to the table, but Cade paused Macy at the threshold between the hallway and kitchen.

"You're an adult now, Mace," he said. His tone was teasing, but his eyes lacked their usual warmth. "Are you afraid Mom and Dad will get mad about you being in a boy's room?"

Macy flinched, surprised. "I just don't want to disrespect them. Please, let's not fight. It's been such a good weekend, and you'll have me all to yourself again soon enough."

His expression softened. He wrapped an arm around her waist and smiled. "No such thing as soon enough," he murmured, smile finally reaching his eyes.

"Secrets don't make friends, you two!" Ethan called out as he entered the kitchen, scrubbing his hands at the sink.

Macy jumped back, nearly spilling her coffee. "We were just talking about the trip home," she said quickly. "We probably need to order the Uber soon."

"I already did, Bella," Cade replied, the gleam gone from his eyes. They walked hand in hand to the table, and he served her a cinnamon bun before helping himself.

Breakfast was lighthearted, filled with laughter and teasing, but tinged with quiet sadness. Macy hadn't felt so at home in this place since she was a child. Now, for the first time, she felt the sting of tears as she thought about leaving. As much as she looked forward to seeing Catherine and returning to her routine in New York, something inside her ached with nostalgia.

After breakfast, Macy and Cade quietly went their separate ways to pack. The final flurry before the Uber arrived was a gentle bustle of rinsed coffee mugs, double-checking airline reservations, and one last cinnamon bun tucked into a napkin for the road. Macy pulled a light blue sweater over her T-shirt and stepped outside, breathing in the crisp, early fall air.

When the Uber pulled into the drive, Cade shook hands with Ethan, then hugged Rebecca and Joy. He thanked them for their hospitality and for the warm welcome, promising he was looking forward to helping Macy host Thanksgiving in the city.

Macy lingered in the hallway, not quite ready to leave. She hugged her mother a little longer than usual.

"I'll call you when we get back to the apartment," she said.

Rebecca smoothed Macy's curls with one hand and kissed her forehead. "Please do. And text me when you land. Tell Catherine hello for us."

"I will," Macy replied, her throat tightening. "I'll let you know when Nina gets in, too."

Rebecca laughed, throwing her head back. "Thank you, Mace. We appreciate it, since Nina won't even tell her own mother she made it home."

Ethan pulled Macy into a bear hug, then passed her gently to Joy. As Joy embraced her, she leaned in and whispered, "Call me."

Macy pulled back, searching for clues to the meaning behind her request, and nodded. Joy smiled, soft and serene as always. "Safe travels."

Outside, George helped Cade load the last of the bags into the car. He extended a hand, firm and steady.

"Thanks for bringing my baby home," he said. "You take good care of her."

There was warmth in his voice, but Macy caught the faintest edge of warning beneath it.

"Always," Cade replied, returning the handshake without hesitation.

George turned to Macy last and pulled her into a tight hug. "We're proud of you, Mace. I want to make sure you know that."

Fighting tears she couldn't quite explain, Macy buried her face in her father's chest. "Thanks, Dad. And thank you for this weekend."

Cade came around and opened the car door for her. Macy slid in, buckled her seat belt, and gazed out the window, waving to her family. Joy stood on the porch, one hand resting on her growing belly, her eyes still fixed on Cade as he climbed into the car.

As the Uber pulled away, Cade reached across the seat and linked his fingers with Macy's. She looked up at him, a ghost of a tear in her eye, but a smile still on her lips.

"What's the matter, Bella?" he asked gently.

"Nothing," she said, her voice soft. "For the first time, it feels like things are locking into place."

But even as she said it, the look in Joy's eyes lingered in her mind—quiet, unreadable, and haunting. It chilled Macy to the bone.

Chapter Sixteen

WALKERS IN NEW YORK

"What time is Romeo getting out tonight?" Catherine asked as she and Macy sat down to breakfast. The Walkers' flight was due in any moment, but she knew they had at least an hour and a half ahead of collecting bags, navigating the terminal, and taking the subway up to Fifth Avenue.

Macy rolled her eyes. "Romeo? Really?"

Catherine shrugged, unapologetic. "Why not?"

"He was hoping to leave early, but it's not looking good," Macy said, reaching for her coffee. "I'm surprised they're not giving him any grace, especially since he already put in his notice."

Catherine glanced around the apartment, hands on the small of her back, as she mentally counted the number of bodies that were soon to be crammed in there. "I wonder if it's too late to ask Brian and Nina to host if we still do the cooking. I don't know how we're going to fit everyone in here."

"Worth asking," Macy said. "My whole family's already there, and your parents would just have a few extra minutes on the train."

At 1:30, Macy got the text: Her family had their bags and were headed to the subway. She had also received a text from Joy.

Shit, she thought to herself. I was supposed to call her. I'll have to do it later.

She sent Joy a text that she would call her later, and by 2:00, was headed out the door with Catherine. Just as they stepped into the hallway, they heard footsteps behind them. Theo was locking his door, takeaway bag in hand.

"There's my favorite redheads!" he called out.

"Happy Thanksgiving, Theo!" Catherine replied. "Where are you off to?"

"Takeout time, of course. Where else would I be going?"

Macy stared at him. "Theo, it's the night before Thanksgiving, and you're getting takeout? Please don't tell me that's your plan for tomorrow, too."

He shrugged. "What else am I gonna do? My parents went back to Puerto Rico, and my brother's working at the ferry terminal. I'm not roasting a turkey for one."

Catherine and Macy exchanged a glance, then nodded in unison.

"You're joining us," Macy declared. "No way you're spending the holiday alone with a box of fried rice."

Theo's face lit up. "Really? I'd love that! What time?"

"We're planning to eat around two," Catherine said. "Come by any time before that."

Theo paused, thoughtful. "You know, you're cramming a lot of people into one tiny space. I don't think one oven is going to cut it. What if we spread out between your place and mine? I can help cook over here if you need a hand."

Catherine cocked her head. "Have you ever actually used your oven for anything besides storing lo mein?"

Theo grinned, dimples on full display. "That hurts a little. But I'm sure I can figure out how to bake rolls and warm up a can of corn."

Macy threw her arms around his neck, catching them both off guard. After a beat, he returned the hug.

"This is great, Theo. Thank you," she said. "I think it's going to be a really good day."

"No, ladies. Thank *you*. It'll be nice to spend the holiday with family."

They walked together toward the subway, sorting out the logistics of their impromptu Thanksgiving plan. Macy would handle the turkey and salad, and Catherine would bake the rolls in Theo's oven. Theo, newly promoted to co-host, would take on the corn and potatoes. They agreed to set a table in each apartment, doors open so guests could move freely between the two spaces.

At the entrance to the tunnel, Theo pulled them both into a hug and kissed their cheeks. "You two are lifesavers," he said, waving them off as they descended the stairs. Then he turned and headed toward his favorite dive bar for a pre-holiday burger.

"Well, that'll be great!" Macy said, her voice lighter now. "I was actually starting to worry about how we were going to pull this off. But this? This is going to be even better."

As the train rolled through Manhattan toward Fifth Avenue, Macy and Catherine continued hashing out details until the conversation drifted to Christmas.

"Shane should be home just in time," Catherine said. "Are you going to go back to your parents'?"

"Cade's talked about heading to Chicago," Macy replied. "We couldn't make it last time we traveled, so it's only fair. This will be his second time meeting my family. I haven't met his yet."

Catherine smirked and nudged Macy in the rib with her elbow. "Ahh. So, you *have* decided you've got it bad."

Blushing, Macy nudged her. "Oh, shut up." But she was smiling.

They walked together, one arm looped through the other, braced against the autumn chill. When they arrived at the Simpsons' penthouse, they were surprised to find the Walkers already there. George and Rebecca greeted their daughter with open arms as the elevator doors slid open. Laughter spilled from the kitchen, and after quick hugs and hellos, Macy and Catherine joined the conversation.

Just as they settled into the living room, the elevator chimed again. Cade stepped out, dressed in a dark wool coat, a bakery box in one hand, and a sheepish grin on his face.

"Sorry, I'm late," he said. "Office wouldn't let me escape."

"Good thing you're cute," Catherine replied dryly, standing to take the dessert box.

Cade glanced at Macy for backup, but she only shrugged with a laugh. "She means it with love. I think."

"If this is love, I'd hate to see her in a bad mood."

"Stick around," Catherine muttered, disappearing into the kitchen.

"Better be cannoli in that box!" George called without turning around.

"They're cannoli," Cade confirmed, earning a subtle nod of approval.

"Smart man," George said, wiping his hands on a towel. "Come on in."

Cade leaned in to kiss Macy hello, his grip around her waist tighter than usual. She chalked it up to travel stress, maybe nerves. With the holiday tomorrow, everyone was a little on edge.

Nina passed around wine glasses while Rebecca stirred the cranberry sauce. The room buzzed with overlapping stories: George recounting how the neighbor's tractor caught fire, Macy launching into a tale about Catherine's teenage obsession with velvet pants.

"Not velvet. Velour," Catherine corrected flatly.

"There's no saving it either way," Macy teased.

"Wait, you were a velour girl?" Cade asked, laughing. "Like Juicy Couture?"

"She had an entire drawer dedicated to rhinestones," Macy said, gesturing toward Catherine. "I genuinely thought she was going to bedazzle her name into her pillowcases. And for the record, she threatened me with sequins when I couldn't pick an outfit for our first date."

"I still might," Catherine muttered, sipping her wine.

Across the table, George turned to Cade. "So, are your folks coming in tomorrow?"

"They're staying in Chicago, doing the usual," Cade replied. "My mom's hosting her sister, and my dad will be parked in front of the football games pretending to help my stepmom."

"Sounds familiar," Rebecca said, nudging her husband.

"Thanksgiving universalism," Cade quipped.

Catherine raised her glass. "To men everywhere pretending to help."

"To velour, rhinestones, and cannoli," Macy added, and they all clinked glasses.

After the meal, Macy, Cade, and Catherine decided to head out so the Walkers could settle in after their long travel day. By the time they were back on the train home, the plan was officially in motion: two apartments, three kitchens, one potluck miracle. It wasn't traditional, but it was theirs. And Catherine and Macy were genuinely excited about it. Macy still needed to brine the turkey for the morning, so while she handled that, Cade helped Catherine set the table for the next day.

"It's still early," Cade said as they settled in for the night. "Do you still have the Switch set up? The one I sent over?"

"I'm going to pass this time," Catherine said, standing. "Shane and I haven't been able to talk in a few days, but he sent me a long email this morning that I need to catch up on."

"Everything okay?" Macy asked.

"All good!" Catherine smiled. "Just the usual business. Good night, you two. See you for Thanksgiving!"

Catherine disappeared into her room, leaving Macy and Cade curled up on the couch with controllers in hand. After three rounds of Mario Kart and two chaotic Mario Party battles, they called it a night.

She hated lying to her best friend. But if Macy knew who she was really about to talk to, and what it was about, she'd be furious. And that was the last thing Catherine wanted. Things between them already felt tense, and she wasn't sure how much more strain their friendship could take.

Sitting alone in her room, Catherine turned on a bit of rock music to mask the conversation. It would still be believable that she was emailing Shane, and if voices were overheard, she could easily say he'd called instead. Usually, Macy was so wrapped up in Cade's web that when they were together, she noticed nothing else.

Cade, on the other hand…Catherine kept her eyes open around him.

She'd meant it at first—nudging Macy toward him gently, thinking he might be a good match. On the surface, he appeared charming, attentive, and stable. But there were things Catherine couldn't ignore in good conscience. It was all happening too fast, and something about Cade made her uneasy. Nina was just as swept up in the romance as Macy, so Catherine knew there was only one person she could talk to and actually be heard.

Carefully, she dialed the number and waited. Relief washed over her when Joy picked up on the second ring.

"Hello?" Joy said.

"Joy, it's Catherine Phelps. I hope it's okay that I'm calling this late."

"Catherine, of course! Yeah, this baby's making it impossible to get comfortable anymore, so I'm wide awake. Guess he or she is just giving me practice for what's coming."

Catherine laughed, a little too nervously. "Yeah, buckle up. If that baby's anything like his father, you're in for a ride."

The line went quiet, the air crackling with cautious tension. Neither spoke first.

Catherine cracked her door open just enough to peek out. Macy and Cade were still on the couch, locked in a serious round of Mario Kart. She quietly closed the door again and took a breath.

"I bet you're wondering why I'm calling," she said. "I'm not one to mince words, so I'll just come out with it. How do you feel about Cade?"

On the other end, Joy sighed—a sound that carried more weight than words. "I had a feeling that's what this was about. Honestly, Catherine, I'm so glad you called. Macy's so under his spell, and I just have a really bad feeling about him. You're closer to them than we are, so we don't see the day-to-day. I kept hoping I was wrong. But it sounds like I'm not."

"Let me ask you," Catherine said gently, "what exactly has your hackles up?"

"It's mostly a gut feeling," Joy admitted. "When they were here at the farm, his behavior was too perfect. Too smooth. Too attentive. I wondered if I was being overprotective. Macy is like a little sister to me, so maybe I was seeing things that weren't there. But then, the morning they left, I overheard him asking her about why she didn't go to his room the night before, and he wouldn't take 'I don't want to disrespect my parents' for an answer."

Catherine's breath caught.

Joy continued, "Now, I wouldn't care if she had gone in there. She's an adult, and I know they're spending nights together back home. But this was her parents' house, and they're not comfortable with that. She told him that, and he looked…mad. I asked her to call me to talk about it, but she hasn't yet. I'm telling you, though, Catherine, it didn't sit right."

"Hmm," Catherine said slowly. "That tracks with what I've seen. She told me that when they went out for dinner the first time, he had her immediately box up half so she wouldn't overeat."

"He what?!" Joy shouted.

"I know. Macy justified it, said she'd asked him to help her lose weight, and he was just supporting her with portion control."

"I don't like it," Joy replied, her voice sharp with defiant anger.

"Me either." Catherine paused, risking another glance into the living room. They'd moved on to Mario Party, still locked in their own little world. "There've been a lot of little things like that. She insists he's not controlling her, but it's a slippery slope from suggestion and 'what's best for her' into full-on control."

"I agree," Joy said. "We have to handle this carefully. If we push too hard, we risk pushing her away."

"That's exactly why I called you," Catherine said. "How's the rest of the family feeling?"

Joy considered. "George is hard to read, but you know he'd do anything to protect her. Ethan likes everyone. He won't be much help unless he sees something firsthand. I think Rebecca's cautious, too. We all want Macy to be happy, and right now, she seems happy. But what happens when she's not?"

"Exactly." Catherine paced the room, then sat at her desk, ready to jot down thoughts if needed. "The more I bring up my concerns, the more upset she gets. She's my best friend. I don't want her to shut me out completely. So, how do we do this?"

"We have to accept that we can't save her from this," Joy said gently. "If we try, we'll lose her. She has to come to the realization herself that what's happening isn't normal. And when she does, she needs to know we're here, ready to help her out. The hard part will be watching it crumble when we can already see the cracks."

Catherine nodded, her voice dropping to a whisper. "We can keep encouraging her to do things with us, without him. That separation might help her see more clearly, especially if he throws a tantrum about it."

"Has he ever hit her?" Joy asked quietly.

"I don't think so," Catherine said. "But Nina told me she felt like she was forced to say she loved him to avoid hurting him. It makes me wonder what else he's pressured her into."

"Oh, God," Joy muttered, her voice laced with fury. "I'll kill him myself if he did."

"I don't think he's going anywhere anytime soon," Catherine said. "But what do we do if things go even further?"

"You mean…if he hits her?"

"That too," Catherine said. "If I ever see a bruise, I'll be calling George myself. But I meant, what if the relationship escalates? He's been getting serious, fast."

Joy was quiet for a moment. "You mean marriage."

"Yeah," Catherine said quietly.

Joy sighed, the kind that came from weighing whether to say something out loud. "I know how worried you are. Believe me, I'm right there with you. If I talked to Rebecca and George, even if they didn't already see what we do, I think we could help them see it. But if he asks and Macy says yes…we can't stop her. All we can do is be supportive. Be there for her if it all goes to hell."

"How am I supposed to stand there and smile," Catherine said, voice tight, "when I'm afraid she's making the biggest mistake of her life?"

"I know, Catherine. Trust me, I do." Joy grunted in pain and muttered a curse. "Sorry. This kid's going to be a soccer player."

Catherine smiled despite herself.

Joy continued after another brief hesitation. "I've seen this happen before. A friend from high school. I tried too hard to get her to open her eyes, and she accused me of being jealous, that I was trying to sabotage the relationship. He convinced her everything was her fault. When he hit her, it was because she'd 'stepped out of line' or broken some imaginary rule. I tried to get her out, but he had her convinced everyone was against them. That he was all she had."

Catherine's stomach turned.

"She eventually blocked my number," Joy continued. "I haven't heard from her since. After that, I went to a counselor. He told me everything I'm telling you now. It doesn't feel right, but all we can do is be her safe space. Catch her if she falls. And pray that one day, she sees what we see."

Catherine twirled her pencil, unsettled but slowly accepting the truth. "We can't let what happened to your friend happen again."

"No, we can't," Joy agreed. "But there's something else."

"Oh, good," Catherine said, exasperated. "There's more?"

"Yeah, and it's important. We have to be here to let Macy vent when things go wrong. Every relationship has issues. But if we keep pressing her about our concerns, she'll start to internalize. She won't tell us anything because she'll be afraid we'll tell her to leave him. We've said our piece. Maybe we're wrong, and things will turn out okay. But if we're right, she'll need us. She needs to know that no matter what, we'll have her back."

Joy's voice softened. "This is going to be hard. But I want you to know you can call me anytime. Vent, cry, scream. Whatever you need."

"Thanks, Joy," Catherine said. "I should go before Macy realizes I'm not actually emailing Shane."

"We're going to get her through this, Catherine. You're not alone. We're in this together."

Catherine ended the call and sank into bed. She set her phone face-down on the nightstand and stared at the ceiling, the soft pulse of music still humming in the background. Her chest ached – not from fear, but from helplessness.

She was glad she'd called Joy. Glad she'd spoken the words out loud. But now, more than ever, she felt the weight of what they couldn't do. Nina wouldn't help. Macy's family was halfway across the country. Shane would be home soon, but until then, Catherine couldn't shake the feeling of being completely alone.

Deep down, she knew Joy was right. They couldn't drag Macy out of this.

They could only hold the door open.

And hope, when Macy needed it most, she'd let them help her walk through.

Chapter Seventeen

THANKSGIVING

Thanksgiving morning arrived with three showers and a flurry of activity. Cade headed home for fresh clothes and his daily medications, while Macy drained and stuffed the turkey, and Catherine peeled potatoes. Theo came over late in the morning, asking what he could do to help. Catherine handed him their extra set of dishes to start setting his table upstairs, and Macy slid the turkey into the oven.

One by one, families began to arrive. Patrick and Kelly Phelps, Catherine's parents, were the first through the door, bearing a large bowl of salad and warm hugs for both girls. Not long after that, Macy's parents arrived with a stack of pies, and Cade followed last, carrying a tub of ice cream. He made his way around the room, introducing himself to Catherine's parents with a polite charm.

From next door, Theo heard the commotion and burst through the door, practically vibrating with excitement. "Are they here? Everybody's here!" he exclaimed, bouncing on his toes. "Okay, so Macy very graciously invited me to join since my family's all in Aguadilla. We were worried about people sitting on top of each other, so we decided to set up the table in my apartment, too. That way, people can move back and forth."

Cade strolled over and draped an exaggerated arm around Macy's shoulders. "I'm Cade, the boyfriend. And you are…? She hasn't mentioned this plan to me before."

"Oh, we just came up with it last night when we bumped into each other," Theo said, extending an enthusiastic hand to shake. "I'm the next-door neighbor, Theo! You brought Macy home once when I was outside drying a painting, but I don't think you saw me."

Cade pursed his lips and nodded at him but said nothing.

Theo turned to George and Rebecca. "You must be Mr. and Mrs. Walker. Macy's parents, I mean." He laughed at himself and kept rambling. "Shame I won't get to meet Mr. and Mrs. Walker, the younger, but I hear you've got your first grandchild arriving any day now?"

As Macy slipped away to check on the turkey, Theo moved on to greet Catherine's parents.

"Uh, Theo?" Catherine interrupted, narrowing her eyes. "Who's watching your stove?"

Theo flashed his dimples. "My Spidey senses?"

Catherine muttered, "Shit," and bolted toward his apartment. "The potatoes are boiling over, Theo!" she called from the doorway.

With another toothy grin, Theo excused himself and dashed after her.

"Well, he seems like quite a character," Kelly said, amused.

"He's a good buddy," Macy replied. "Funny thing is, we've lived next door for five years and barely knew each other until recently. He caught me brooding one day and offered to share his Chinese takeout while we talked it out. We've been pretty good friends ever since."

She glanced at Cade, and through gritted teeth, he muttered, "Hilarious."

The turkey beeped that it had reached its perfect internal temperature. Macy pulled it out and turned to Patrick. "Mr. Phelps, would you care to do the honors?"

As Patrick carved the turkey, George whipped up gravy from the drippings. Rebecca and Kelly headed over to Theo's apartment to help finish the potatoes and vegetables. The open doors between the two apartments blurred the space—voices crossing freely, guests drifting from one apartment to the other as if it were one long room. Finally, everyone sat down to begin their meal.

George opened his laptop at the kitchen island and dialed up Joy and Ethan.

"Coming to you live from the northwestern corner of nowhere, Iowa!" Ethan announced as his face filled the screen. The kitchen behind him had a sleepy glow, quiet and almost somber in its emptiness.

Joy sat nearby in an overstuffed chair, tapping her belly with mild impatience. "Still pregnant!" she declared.

"Any signs of movement?" Catherine asked.

"Only between his or her feet and my rib cage," Joy grunted. "This baby has taken up permanent residence."

Theo swept back into the room to say hello. "You need to evict that little mooch! Hi, I'm the neighbor."

"You know what might work?" Ethan offered. "Big plate of spicy tacos and a drive down a bumpy road."

Joy shot Ethan an irritated look, but Theo only grew more animated. "You two should've come to New York! The one thing I do know how to cook is a good taco. No dirt roads here, but those subways can get pretty bumpy."

Ethan leaned closer to the screen. "You have a big 'Thanksgiving wildcard' energy there, Theo!"

Catherine draped herself playfully across Theo's lap to get into the view of the iPad camera. "We frequently hear swear words in Spanish followed by raucous laughter while he's considering his latest masterpiece."

Ethan grinned. "So, what's the deal? Is it really art you're working on over there? Or is that just your excuse to cover the plot to take over the world?"

Theo thudded a fist against his chest, indignant. "Don't be spoiling all my secrets before dinner is even served!"

The room erupted with laughter.

Theo shrugged, still grinning. "All I know is, she was having a rough day. Everything was going wrong, so I made it weird and offered her Chinese chicken and egg rolls."

Ethan guffawed and raised his glass in salute. "I like this guy. Macy, why did you never bring him home before?"

Macy's stomach dropped, and her skin crawled with the sensation of a bucket of ice being dumped over her head. "Ethan!"

Joy winced and elbowed Ethan, hard, in the ribs. "What?" he said, oblivious. "He's a cool guy! I think we would be friends, that's all!"

Cade's hand shifted possessively onto Macy's knee. His jaw tightened, teeth grinding. His voice boomed at the monitor, sharp and controlled. "Ethan, you realize her boyfriend is sitting right next to her, yes?"

Ethan held up his hands, bewildered. "Jesus, sorry! Didn't know it was a federal crime to ask about your *neighbor*."

"You weren't *asking*," Macy snapped. "You were stirring the pot, like you always do."

Ethan went quiet. The tension crawled across the split screen.

Joy muttered, "Well, this is festive," rubbing her forehead.

Rebecca looked between her children with concern. George busied himself adjusting the laptop angle—and failed.

Theo tried to break the tension. "Well, if this doesn't seem like the perfect time to go check on the stove. Catherine?"

Conversation slowly returned to normal across both apartments. Macy sat in her apartment with Cade, Kelly, and Patrick, while Catherine, Rebecca, George, and Theo gathered next door. During dessert, Macy and Catherine swapped locations, with Cade trailing Macy. As the men settled in to watch football, the women split up the cleanup, each taking a kitchen and half the dishes.

"I'm leaving the putting away to my boyfriend and my neighbor!" Macy called into the living room as she started scrubbing.

Eventually, the last dish was dried, coffee brewed, and the whole group reunited to enjoy the final stretch of the holiday. Theo and George traded easy banter, keeping everyone laughing. Rebecca and Kelly, once neighbors themselves, caught up on changes at the Walker farm and George's plans to retire.

Kelly turned to Macy. "So, how did you and Cade meet?"

"I completely charmed her," Cade said, grinning. He retold the story of their meeting at the club and running into each other at the gym. "Eventually, I wore her down enough to go out with me."

Laughing, Macy nodded. "Yeah, that's about the gist of it."

"And where's your family, Cade?" Kelly asked.

"They're still in Chicago. I moved here for a big job in marketing, but we see each other a couple of times a year. We've got plans for Christmas. Macy, I'm sure they'll love meeting you."

The room fell silent. George and Rebecca exchanged a glance. All eyes turned to Macy.

"Macy," George said gently, "when were you going to tell us you weren't coming home for Christmas?"

Cade looked at her, his gaze steady and hopeful, silently pleading for her to say yes.

Macy's heart thudded in her chest. "We haven't really decided yet," she said quickly. "We still need to talk about it more. But I promise I'll let you know once we've made a decision."

Rebecca reached for her wine glass; her smile tinged with sadness. "You're an adult now, Mace. I know you'll want to spend the holiday with your new beau. Just…don't forget to tell us these things."

The tension hung in the air like steam off the coffee mugs.

Theo jumped in, sensing the shift. "So, Macy, that turkey was phenomenal. That brine made it so juicy! I'm stealing your recipe next time I make one."

Catherine and Macy looked at each other and burst out laughing.

"Theo," Catherine said, shaking her head, "didn't we talk about this last night? You usually use your oven to store your takeout containers when the fridge runs out of space."

"I'm sure, with the help of your lovely bestie, I could nail it just as well as she did!" Theo said, flashing a grin.

Cade placed a hand on Macy's shoulder, firm and possessive. George noticed. Rebecca, seated beside him on the arm of the couch, watched carefully as Theo kept talking. When Macy's hand brushed Theo's arm mid-laugh, Cade's blue eyes darkened for just a beat.

The tension in the room began to mount until Patrick glanced at Kelly, who gave a subtle nod.

"I hate to cut the evening short," Patrick said, rising to his feet, "but it's a long ride back to Elmont. I think we'll head out."

He shook hands with George, Ethan, and Cade, then turned to Theo. "Hope you're keeping a good eye on Catherine and Macy."

"You bet, Mr. Phelps!" Theo replied brightly. Cade's hand tightened on Macy's shoulder.

Patrick hugged the women goodbye, and Kelly followed suit, embracing each guest warmly. Catherine walked them to the door, and Rebecca joined Kelly, linking arms as they stepped into the hallway.

As the others moved down the hall, Rebecca slowed just enough to whisper in Kelly's ear, "You're closer than George, and I am. Can you keep an eye on that one? Let us know she's okay?"

Kelly put her hand on Rebecca's and squeezed it gently. "If we don't, Catherine surely will."

George and Rebecca hugged Theo hard, thanking him for his shared hospitality.

"It was a pleasure, Mr. and Mrs. Walker," Theo said with a respectful nod. He mumbled something about making sure he turned the stove off before turning into his apartment and shutting the door tight behind him.

As Macy closed the door behind her family, a strange unease settled in her chest. Only Catherine, Cade, and she remained.

"We did it!" she said brightly, trying to shake the feeling. "Our first holiday meal—we survived."

"That turkey really was delicious," Catherine said, stretching. "It's been a long two days. I'm calling it a night." She pointed between Macy and Cade. "You two behave."

With a sassy grin, she flounced off to her room.

"Well, that went better than I could have imagined," Macy said to Cade, but his expression was tight.

"What's wrong?"

He rounded on her, fury blazing in his eyes. "Are you kidding me? Do you really have to ask me that right now?"

Macy's mouth formed an "O" of surprise at his sudden temper. "Other than my brother shoving his foot in his mouth up to his knee, I thought that was a good dinner!" Her voice was quiet, timid.

"Yeah. Your brother. What was that?"

Cold again, Macy gasped for breath as she tried to talk. "You can't really be mad at *me* for something *Ethan* said."

Cade pursed his lips. "I sure didn't hear you coming to my defense at all when he was saying you would be better off with Theo."

"He never said that!"

Cade laughed, but the sound had no humor. "He didn't have to. Do you think I didn't see the way he looked at you? He wants what he can't have. And your brother thinks it's funny to call that out in front of me."

"Cade, he knows I'm with you. You know I'm with you. And I really don't care if Ethan thinks otherwise. Isn't that enough?"

"I'm sure I'll get over it eventually," he said, voice low. "I'm going to head home and get some rest. My head isn't a nice place to be right now."

He turned toward the door, Macy trailing him.

"Cade, wait. Don't go."

He paused, then placed his hands gently on her shoulders and kissed the top of her head. She burrowed into his arms, hoping it would change his mind.

"I love you, Macy."

"I love you, too," she whispered, lips puckered into a pout. A single teardrop pooled in the corner of her eye.

He pulled back, squeezed her hand, and walked out the door.

As it clicked shut behind him, Macy dissolved into silent tears. *What just happened?* she thought. Just hours ago, everything felt perfect. He was talking about the future. Was he really about to take it all back over her being friends with the neighbor?

Ethan had crossed a line, but had Theo?

Macy didn't think so. He was a good friend, and she cared about him, but that was all. Still, she replayed her laughter and conversations with Theo, and wondered if that was the moment Cade saw something slipping. Was she really being careless with Cade's heart?

She locked the door behind Cade and leaned against it, wiping tears from her cheeks. The silence wrapped around her like a too-tight sweater.

She replayed the moment he left. The way he kissed the top of her head. The way she'd melted into him, hoping it would change something. Hoping she could change something.

But it didn't.

She'd told herself it was just a misunderstanding. That he was tired. That maybe she had been too casual with Theo. But the more she tried to justify it, the more it felt like she was stacking excuses like bricks, building a wall between herself and the truth.

She thought about the dinner. The way he'd tightened his grip when Theo spoke. The way his laugh hadn't reached his eyes. The way her parents had looked at her when Cade mentioned Christmas plans.

She hadn't told them. Not because she didn't want to, but because she wasn't sure. And that uncertainty was starting to feel less like indecision and more like instinct.

She reached for her phone, thumb hovering over Joy's name. But she didn't press it. Not yet.

Instead, she opened her notes app and typed:

I love him. I think I do. But sometimes, I feel like I'm shrinking around him. And I don't know if that's just the way love is, learning to meet each other's needs, or if I've really done something wrong.

She stared at the words. Then she locked her phone and set it aside.

Tomorrow would come with cleanup and leftovers, and laughter. But tonight, Macy let herself sit in the quiet. Not to solve anything. Just to feel it.

She sat on the edge of her bed, still in the clothes she'd worn for dinner, her fingers curled around the edge of the comforter like she might fall off if she let go. The apartment was quiet now. Catherine's door was closed, the hum of the fridge the only sound. Cade's absence filled the room like fog.

A knock came from the door, and despite the temptation to ignore it, Macy dragged herself back to unlock it. Cade stood there, tear-streaked, one hand raised like he wasn't sure he should've knocked at all.

"I'm sorry," he said softly.

That was all it took. Macy melted into his arms again, like she always did. Like he knew she would.

"Do you still want me to stay?" he asked, already sounding prepared for her to say no. He gently brushed a curl behind her ear.

She opened the door wider for him to step inside.

"Maybe I should start keeping a set of sweats here," he joked.

He smiled. She didn't.

Without another word, Macy led him to her bedroom and quietly closed the door behind them.

He wasn't leaving her again—not tonight.

Chapter Eighteen

THE HOLIDAY RUSH

No sooner had the Thanksgiving dishes been washed and tucked away than New York began to shimmer with holiday magic. Storefronts bloomed with toy trains and cashmere coats, garlands curled around every lamppost, and the city hummed with anticipation.

It was December third when Macy's phone rang, her brother's face lighting up the screen. Her heart raced, anticipating.

"He's here, Macy!" Ethan's voice burst through the line. "You have a nephew!"

Macy sat down on the edge of her bed, trying to contain the flood of emotion. "Congratulations, Ethan! How's Joy feeling?"

"Exhausted. But they're both perfect. He's eight pounds, three ounces of absolute perfection. And get this: He's got green eyes. Just like you, Auntie Macy."

Her voice cracked. "I wish I could be there. Cade and I leave for Chicago on Christmas Eve, and I don't know how I'd swing another flight home."

In the background, Joy called out, "Use our sky miles!"

With that, Macy broke into sobs.

Forty-eight hours later, Macy and Cade were back at the old farmhouse. Outside, the world was a dull gray, swirling with the first winter flurries. But inside, the house was warm and welcoming. Joy lay on the couch, feet propped up, a water jug within reach. A tiny blue bundle rested on her chest, rising and falling with each delicate breath. Her usually perfect ponytail had collapsed into a messy knot, and even Ethan looked sleep-deprived but radiant.

Ethan gazed at Joy with reverence as he gently lifted the baby from her chest. The infant whimpered in protest, but Ethan whispered, "Meet your nephew, Caleb Joseph," and placed him in Macy's waiting arms.

Caleb yawned, barely opening his eyes, and nestled into her embrace.

"Hi, Caleb," Macy whispered. "I'm your favorite aunt."

They sat in peaceful silence, Cade beside her, his hand resting gently on the small of her back. He beamed at her as she beamed at the baby, her heart lurching with the most perfect kind of love. Caleb's tiny fist curled near his lips, searching. At the touch of his hand on his cheek, his mouth opened instinctively like a baby bird waiting for its mother.

"I think he wants you, Mama," Macy said, rising to return him to Joy just as he began to fuss.

"The new never-ending story," Ethan joked, helping Joy off the couch to nurse in privacy. "Feeding an infant."

When they left the room, Macy turned to find Cade watching her, eyes glassy with emotion.

"You were so tender with him," he said softly. "I can't wait until you're holding mine."

Unable to speak, overwhelmed, Macy buried her head in Cade's shoulder and waited for her brother to return.

By the time she was back in the city, her heart still full from meeting her nephew and her suitcase faintly scented with farmhouse cleaning products, New York had fully transformed. Lights twinkled from every window, carolers spilled out of subway stations, and the air buzzed with December energy. Macy barely had time to unpack before Catherine and Nina swept her into their annual Fifth Avenue shopping day.

"Let's go into Dior!" Nina chirped.

"Oh, honey, you know we're on an H&M budget," Catherine replied.

Nina grinned mischievously. "Who said we're spending your money?" She brandished Brian's credit card like a trophy.

"Nina, you are positively evil," Macy said, eyes gleaming.

"You're welcome!" Nina winked. "Speaking of evil, what's going on with Mr. Dark and Mysterious?"

"What do you mean?" Macy asked, feigning innocence.

"You and Cade," Nina said, pushing them through the doors at Saks and heading straight for a wall of shoes that cost more than Macy's entire wardrobe. "You're practically joined at the hip and glowing brighter than a Christmas tree. Spill the tea!"

Macy smiled dreamily. "Things are going well." She shook her head at a pair of stilettos that looked like they'd lost a fight with a Bedazzler. "He's thoughtful, expressive, attentive…"

"Attentive?" Catherine cut in. "Is that what we're calling helicopter boyfriend energy now?"

Macy tossed a wad of tissue paper from a shoe box at her. Catherine swatted it back with ease, hitting Macy square on the nose. The three of them burst into laughter, earning sharp glances from nearby shoppers. A sales associate glared at them over her glasses, hands on her hips in silent warning.

Catherine took a breath, her expression softening. "I like seeing you happy, Mace. I really do. But I'm worried. At first, you were unsure. You said it felt like too much, too fast. And now, before I could say 'Happy Thanksgiving,' you're in lockstep with him. I saw the way he looked at Theo. The way he charmed your dad. I know you love him, but I just want you to ask yourself: Is this relationship unfolding on your terms as much as his?"

Macy paused, thoughtful. They drifted toward the New Year's Eve dresses.

"That's a fair question," she said slowly. "It has been fast. Sometimes, I feel like I blinked, and we went from tentative to serious. But I took what Nina said to heart—I decided to stop overthinking and just feel."

"Okay," Catherine said, her voice careful. She didn't look convinced, but she didn't press. "I don't want to drive a wedge between us. I've got your back, no matter what."

"Me too, you crazy bitch," Nina added. "Now help me spend my husband's hard-earned money!"

Nina selected several winter outfits, complete with matching bags and shoes. She refused to let them leave without picking something for New Year's Eve. Catherine chose a black sheath gown by Mac Duggal; its bodice and sleeves were covered in beads and rhinestones.

"It looks like a glass of champagne," she said, eyes sparkling. "I have to have it."

Macy chose a sea-green chiffon gown, also by Mac Duggal, with a draped front and delicate floral embellishments cascading down the bodice. Nina tried to convince them to spring for matching shoes, but Catherine and Macy refused to let her charge that much to Brian's account. Even the dresses felt a little extravagant, but Nina insisted the party would demand it—especially once she was done with the planning.

"So, Mace," Nina asked as they left the store, "what have you and Cade decided about Christmas?"

Macy hesitated. "Well…you know I took a bit of a pay cut with the new job. Things were tight for a while. I didn't want you to worry, Catherine, so I made sure to set aside my share of the rent. But I didn't know how I was going to afford presents for my family, let alone fly out to meet his."

She fidgeted with the gold cross around her neck, then finally admitted, "So…he gave me five hundred dollars. Just…handed it over. Said he wanted me to enjoy the season without stressing."

Catherine and Nina both stopped in their tracks.

"He did *what* now?" Catherine asked, eyes wide.

"I didn't ask for it," Macy said quickly. "And I didn't plan to keep it. He left it in my purse. It was just such a grand gesture, I didn't know what to say."

She took a breath. "So, when we talked about holiday plans, both of our families have traditions. We did Thanksgiving with mine, so he really wants me to meet his for Christmas. I wanted to go the rest of the way to see my parents, but it's just too much. We're going to do a video call instead."

"I can't imagine Amara being thrilled about that," Catherine said. "Especially after you took all that time off to run around the country."

Nina was still staring at Macy, with stars in her eyes.

Macy let out a dry laugh. "She's tolerating it. But with Christmas landing midweek, it's complicated."

"I'll say," Nina muttered, finally snapping out of her reverie.

Catherine and Macy exchanged a look. "When's the last time you had to worry about work schedules?" Macy teased.

Nina shrugged. "When it means Brian's going to be home all week."

Catherine rolled her eyes. "Do you even realize how good you have it?"

"Never mind," Nina huffed. "Just don't let him get away with any bullshit."

Macy saluted in mock agreement. They reached the Simpsons' apartment building, and Nina hugged them both goodbye. The doorman let her inside, and Catherine and Macy headed off toward the train.By Monday, just days before her trip to Chicago, Macy found herself daydreaming at her desk. Her mind drifted to the night before, curled up at home with Cade.

Shane's deployment was officially ending on Christmas Eve, and he was already *en route* home. Macy had spent the afternoon enduring a grueling workout with Cade at the gym, and after a long, hot shower, they'd collapsed onto the couch with a pizza box between them. It was half-empty, their attention barely on the movie playing in the background. Two mugs of hot chocolate sat forgotten beside the pizza—cooling slowly as the night wrapped around them.

As the movie came to an end, Macy and Cade paused, taking each other in. He was leaving for Chicago the next day, and she'd follow on Christmas Eve.

"I can't believe we're here already," Macy said, her voice warm with excitement. "It's Christmas!"

"I'm hoping we can make it a better one for me this year," Cade replied. "Something always goes wrong for me on Christmases and birthdays."

"Well, this year, you've got me," she teased. "Though I am meeting your family, so maybe I'm the one who should be worried about something going wrong."

He smiled and gently brushed a lock of hair behind her ear. "Nah, they'll love you. And maybe next year, we can start our own traditions. In our home. Would you like that?"

His gaze shifted—serious, almost vulnerable. Macy hadn't seen that look on him before. His voice quivered when he spoke, like he was afraid of her answer.

"Why wouldn't I?" she asked cautiously.

"I just want to be sure," he said, though the worry lingered in his eyes.

"I told you, Cade. I invested myself in this when we decided to be serious. All in. Remember?"

"I do," he said quietly. "I just worry sometimes you'll change your mind."

"I don't do that unless I'm given a reason."

Apparently satisfied with her answer, he settled back into the couch. Macy nuzzled against him, and he sighed her name.

"Macy..."

"Macy..."

"Macy!"

The voice snapped her out of her daydream like a splash of cold water. Amara's voice, sharp and unmistakable, echoed from her office. Macy felt a jolt of panic in her stomach.

Uh oh.

She jumped up and hurried through Amara's door. She let the door glide closed behind her and sat in the chair opposite Amara's desk.

"Sorry, Amara. I must've been really in the zone."

"I'll say," Amara replied, unimpressed. "How's the Westline project coming along?"

"I'm glad you asked," Macy said, recovering quickly. "That's exactly what I was working on. I'm giving it a final run-through, trying to break it. If I can't, it's ready for beta testing."

"Good." Amara leaned back slightly, her tone measured. "You really do have a good eye for detail, Macy. And I'll tell you this: If Westline likes the dashboard, there may be a new opportunity developing for you."

Macy nearly sprang out of her chair. "Really? Amara, thank you. That's incredible!"

A ghost of a smile flickered across Amara's face, then vanished. "It's not yours yet. Keep up the good work. Keep your head out of the clouds. We'll talk."

"Yes, ma'am," Macy said, trying to contain her excitement.

"Now go finish your testing," Amara added. "And I understand you've got a plane to catch tomorrow?"

"Yes," Macy said, smiling. "I'm meeting my boyfriend's parents for the first time. And at Christmas. What a time we picked for that."

"Well, you make sure he brings you back, you hear me?" Amara said, her tone gruff but unmistakably fond.

"Loud and clear, Amara."

"Good. Now go." She handed Macy a small card. "Hope this helps make it a merry Christmas. Open it at home."

"Oh! Okay—thank you. Merry Christmas to you, too!"

Macy's heart fluttered. Just three months ago, she'd been afraid to check her bank balance, bracing for overdraft letters. Now her boss was hinting at a promotion, and a future Macy hadn't dared to imagine. She swallowed the emotion before it could rise to her cheeks.

After signing off for the day, Macy met up with RJ and Sebrina. They rode the elevator down together, gossiping and laughing.

"I knew you were going to win her over," RJ gushed.

"It's not in the bag yet," Macy said. "I still have to impress the client."

"From Amara, that's practically a love letter," Sebrina laughed, clapping her on the back. "You've really taken what RJ and I gave you and run with it."

"And the mysterious envelope you're not allowed to open," RJ added, gesturing dramatically, "that's your Christmas bonus. Not every department does them, but Amara pays them out of her own budget as an 'I'm sorry your boss is a grump' prize."

They all laughed, then made their way to the subway, parting ways with hugs and holiday wishes. Macy could hardly believe how much her life had changed in just three months. All that remained was one night with the reunited Catherine and Shane, then she'd step into the next chapter of her whirlwind romance.

Macy's plane touched down in Chicago just after noon on Christmas Eve. Cade had already arranged a ride from the airport to his father's house, where they'd be spending the holiday. He'd gone ahead to "prepare," though he wouldn't say for what.

The Uber took her north of the city into Winnetka. As they neared the lake, the houses grew larger, more extravagant, until Macy felt completely overwhelmed.

Just who are his parents? she wondered. He said they were comfortable, but this is next level.

They turned into a quiet cul-de-sac, and she caught a glimpse of Lake Michigan shimmering in the near distance. The driver helped her with her bag and walked it to the front porch. Taped to the door was a note.

> My love,
>
> Please come inside and find the map of the house table in the foyer. Your Christmas gift awaits. Bring your bag up to our room, where you'll find your next instructions.
>
> Cade

Macy pushed the door open cautiously. "Hello?" she called out.

The house was breathtaking.

Straight ahead, the foyer gleamed with black tile. Beyond it, a hallway led into a spacious kitchen. To her left, a grand curved staircase spiraled upward. To her right, an immaculate living room glowed with holiday lights. A six-foot pine tree stood proudly beside a marble fireplace, and stockings hung neatly above it, each embroidered with a family member's name.

She gasped when she saw one stitched with hers: Macy, in delicate, intricate lettering.

As promised by the note on the door, a marble table stood in the foyer with another envelope waiting for her. Inside, she found a map of the house.

She unfolded the map and studied the second-floor layout: five bedrooms and four baths. Each room was labeled—"Master, Dad's Office, Sheryl's Office, Library, and finally, Cade's Room (That's us!)".

As Macy climbed the grand staircase, she marveled at the view from the overlook and the ornate artwork lining the walls. A crystal chandelier sparkled above the entryway, suspended beneath a cathedral ceiling crowned by a picture window that framed the winter sky.

At the end of the hall, she found the door that had been labeled Cade's Room on the map. She knocked gently. No answer. Slowly, she pushed the door open.

Inside, the room was warm and inviting. On the four-poster bed sat a box wrapped in a red ribbon. Macy opened it to find a pair of green satin pajamas, soft to the touch, and another note tucked beneath them.

Go find your stocking by the fire.

She scanned the downstairs map again, leading her to the living room—the one dressed in holiday lights, with the glowing fireplace and stockings.

The room welcomed her with plush brown sofas, a flat-screen TV, and a sound system tucked into the corner. She walked to the fireplace and reached into the stocking embroidered with her name.

Inside were a Stephen King novel and another clue.

I'm in the backyard

She passed through a formal dining room, which was already set for Christmas Eve dinner, and entered the kitchen. It was as extravagant as she'd imagined.

A stainless-steel double oven gleamed from the wall. Cobalt blue China sat behind glass cabinet doors. Marble countertops stretched across white cabinetry, and a large island held the stovetop and a cozy breakfast nook.

Beyond the kitchen, through a second living room, was a door leading to the back patio. On it, a swing built for two.

She followed the path and stepped outside.

The back yard was blanketed in snow, fenced in, and glowing with a soft cascade of holiday lights. The display shimmered as if it had been waiting just for her. Near one of the decorations stood a middle-aged blond woman and a dark-haired man, arm in arm, their faces radiant.

"Mr. and Mrs. Laurent?" Macy asked, stepping forward, uncertain.

Howard smiled warmly. "It's a pleasure to meet you, Macy. I believe our son is waiting for you."

He gestured behind her.

Macy turned—and there was Cade, seated on the porch swing. He wore a tailored black suit, his dark hair artfully tousled. The string lights cast a soft glow across his face, and the snow around him sparkled like something out of a dream.

Her feet moved before her thoughts could catch up. Was this a date? A gesture?

And then he stood.

And then he knelt.

And her breath caught in her throat.

She barely heard herself whisper, "What's happening?" over the pounding of her heart.

With a dimpled smile, Cade pulled a small box from his pocket.

"Macy," he said gently, "I came alive the day I met you. Will you marry me?"

Part Five

Whirlwind

Celeste's Office

"Macy, come in!" Celeste greeted me with a warm smile, gesturing toward the familiar space. It was getting easier to walk through that door. I'd been seeing Celeste for three months now, and with every thread we untangled, I felt closer to being free from the dark shadow that had followed me for so long.

I took my usual seat in the corner of the couch while Celeste closed the door and settled into her chair, notepad in hand.

"So, last week we talked about the holiday season," she began gently. "How are you feeling about that discussion?"

I paused, letting the question settle. "It's a lot," I admitted. "But I'm starting to see how he was able to get in. I was incredibly vulnerable after everything I'd been through at my lowest point. I did have feelings for him, or at least I thought I did. I knew I wasn't where he was emotionally, but I didn't want to hurt him. I assumed I'd eventually catch up, so I went with it. He used my empathy to get what he wanted. And now…I'm starting to think maybe I don't have as much to feel guilty about as I thought."

Celeste nodded, her smile reassuring. "How did you feel when he was pressing you to say something you weren't ready to say?"

I let out a quiet laugh. "Pressured is the only word for it. Things had been going so well, and I didn't want to risk the relationship. I knew I wasn't ready, but I said what he wanted to hear to avoid damaging what we were building. And then…he kicked it into higher gear."

Celeste jotted something down, then looked up thoughtfully. "Can you tell me more about what you mean by telling him what he wanted to hear?"

I sighed. "I thought that maybe if I told Cade I loved him, my feelings would eventually catch up to the words. He let me believe it would have broken him if I didn't say it. From the outside, we looked like a couple who'd been together for months. Maybe even years. We were perfectly in sync. After work, if we weren't at the gym, we were at one of our apartments playing video games, talking about books, and watching science programs. We had mutual interests. We both loved the city. We both wanted marriage, kids…So, why not with each other?

"In the beginning, he did all these thoughtful little things, flowers, coffee, even groceries when money was tight. Constant texts checking on me. It was sweet, like he genuinely cared about me and my safety. So, it seemed like I should love him, right?"

I paused, taking a deep breath.

"That's exactly what you were telling me about a few sessions ago, isn't it? The love bombing."

"Yes, Macy!" Celeste said, her voice bright with affirmation. "That's exactly right. Still…when he proposed, you hesitated?"

"Yes," I said slowly. "I think deep down, my gut was screaming whoa, but I wanted so badly to buy what he was selling that I didn't listen. Not to my gut. Not to Catherine. Not to Joy. God, that makes me sound so foolish. But it all happened so fast that I didn't have time to think about whether it was right. I had to just react."

"Sometimes, our judgment gets clouded in the face of our desires," Celeste said gently. "Do you want to talk about your family meeting him at Thanksgiving?"

I laughed. "Well, it was an *event*, for sure.

"Nina and Brian stayed home to have their own dinner, trying to reconnect. We'd just decided to invite Theo, because…well, he's our friend. He shouldn't be alone on a holiday. He won everyone over instantly with his wit and humor. He's just like Ethan. Cade didn't like that at all.

"Well, that, and Ethan's stupid remark on Thanksgiving about bringing Theo."

Celeste looked up from her notepad. "How did you handle the family discourse?"

"My mom started to pick up on it. The control. The jealousy. She didn't say much, but she has this habit of biting her lip when she sees something she doesn't like but doesn't want to talk about."

"And Catherine?" Celeste asked. "She'd been close to you throughout the relationship. How did you feel when she expressed concern?"

"I brushed it off," I admitted. "I justified everything…like the argument over portion control. Cade always needing to have his way. That's when he started planting the idea that she didn't like us together. That she was trying to come between us."

Celeste leaned forward slightly. "You've made a very important point here, Macy. Let's pause and sit with it."

I stopped, thinking. Cade had accused Catherine of being jealous. Of not liking him. Of trying to sabotage us. My jaw fell open as the realization hit.

"He was putting a wedge between the people I loved on purpose and me," I said slowly. "To make it seem like he was the only one I could count on."

Celeste's expression softened into something that looked like pride. I let the thought sink in. He'd done this deliberately. Even before I chose to distance myself from Catherine to protect her.

That bastard.

"Another classic technique of the narcissist," Celeste said, "is to make you need them. To convince you they're the only one who truly understands you. If they isolate you from the people who care about you, who's left to tell you what they see from the outside? And even if someone does…why would you believe them, if he's already made you doubt their intentions?"

"Wow," I muttered.

"My coworkers noticed, too," I added. "That I had my head in the clouds more than usual. I told Cade I didn't want to get in trouble at work for texting too much. Knowing how strict Amara is, he didn't push it. At least…not at first.

"But then, at Thanksgiving, he started dropping hints about his long-term plans. About how I was *the one*."

"Still, you were caught off guard by his proposal." Celeste's voice was calm, but the statement landed with weight. It wasn't a question – it was the truth.

I nodded slowly. "I mean…Cade dropped all the hints. And then he did it in front of his parents, at Christmas, with this huge romantic gesture."

I paused, the memory tightening in my chest.

"Even if I wanted to…how could I say no?"

Chapter Nineteen

THE PARTY

"Speechless, I see?" Cade said, still kneeling, his voice laced with expectation. "Macy?"

Her mind spun. She couldn't seem to catch her breath. Cade's father stood with his arm around his wife's shoulders, both watching quietly. The longer Macy stood frozen, the louder her thoughts became.

Are we ready for this?

But I don't want to hurt him. Not here, in front of his parents.

Even saying "I need more time" would break his heart.

I can't do that to him, not today.

But it's so fast.

But no one's ever loved me like this. No one's ever made such a grand gesture.

It's fast…but we love each other.

Right?

Just say yes. We'll take our time planning. Weddings take time.

It'll be okay.

Right??

"Macy," Cade said, shifting slightly. "My knee's starting to freeze here. Is that train of thought you're on going to pull into a station anytime soon and let me on?"

Her jaw still slack, she managed to find her voice. "Y-yes, Cade. Yes…I'll marry you."

"You will?" His face lit up with joy.

"Yes," she said again, stronger this time.

Howard began clapping, and Sheryl clasped her hands over her mouth, eyes brimming with tears. Cade stood, swept Macy into his arms, and spun her around before kissing her hard.

"Here," he said, breathless. "This is for you."

He pulled the ring from the velvet box and slid it onto her finger. The one-carat, brilliant-cut diamond caught the glow of the holiday lights, sparkling so brightly that it shimmered on its own. Macy stared at it slack-jawed. He had selected a perfect solitaire, with delicate filigree engraved along the band.

"Merry Christmas," Cade said, still watching her with that hopeful, expectant look.

Macy finally met his eyes and gave a small, rueful smile. "Merry Christmas. I don't think my gift is quite so extravagant."

They all laughed.

"Your '*yes*' is the only gift I needed," Cade said. "Come on. There are a couple of people I want you to meet."

"Macy," his father said warmly, stepping forward, "I'm Howard Laurent, but please, call me Dad. And this is my wife, Sheryl."

"It's really a pleasure," Macy said, still trying to catch up with the moment. "I wasn't expecting all of…this. Mrs. Laurent, you—"

"None of that," Sheryl interrupted gently. "You're part of the family now. Please, call me Mom."

Macy smiled, the word catching in her throat. "Mom. Thank you so much for the warm welcome. You have such a beautiful home."

"Well, why don't we go inside and enjoy it?" Cade said, grinning.

Macy followed, her hand tucked in his, as they made their way back into the house toward the dining room. Cade winked at her, and she raised an eyebrow.

"Do we have some kind of secret with that wink?" she asked.

"We had that argument about New York-style pizza versus proper Chicago tavern style," he said smugly. "And you're about to find out just how wrong you've been."

"Seriously?" Macy teased. "We just got engaged, it's Christmas Eve, and the language of love is Chicago-style pizza?"

Cade's lips curled into a mischievous smile, his eyes sparkling. "You'll see. I'm going to change now that this suit's done its job."

"My answer would've been the same if you were in regular clothes, you know."

He leaned in and kissed her hard. "I'm glad to take your word on that." Throwing a wink over his shoulder, he headed upstairs.

Macy turned back toward the kitchen, where Sheryl was already bustling around. "So, Macy!" she said brightly. "Very important question before you officially join our family."

Macy straightened, suddenly serious. "Of course, Sheryl—er, Mom. What is it?"

"Do you drink coffee, and do you play euchre? Okay, that's two questions. But still, how about it?"

"I can't live without coffee," Macy replied with a grin. "And I used to play euchre every day in college. Couples or guys vs. girls?"

"All right!" Sheryl cheered. "This one's mine, Howard. You get your son. Macy, how do you take your coffee?" She poured two mugs and motioned for Macy to sit.

"Black, please. I'm not fussy."

"I've got options! Milk, sugar, flavored cream. Take your pick."

"Just get used to it, Mace," Cade said, reappearing in a burgundy long-sleeved polo and jeans. "Be fussy."

"Okay, maybe just a splash of French vanilla if you have it."

"There you go," Cade said, pouring his own coffee.

Sheryl set down her and Macy's cups, then poured one for Howard. "I've got a deck already separated. This is a long-standing family tradition, but we've had to play cutthroat for ages. It'll be nice to finally have a competent partner!"

Cade shot her a look as he picked up the deck and started dealing jacks to determine who'd go first. "Mom, is tonight really the time to talk about Hannah?"

Sheryl covered her mouth, sheepish. "Sorry, Cade. I'll keep my mouth shut. You know how I feel about that whole situation. I'm just so happy to finally meet you, Macy. Cade's been talking about you non-stop since the day you met."

"It's all right, Mom. Let's just play," Cade said, picking up the deck. "What do you say, Dad? Ready to show the ladies who the euchre champions of Winnetka are?" He wiggled his eyebrows at Macy.

Howard chuckled as he took his seat. "I don't know, son. I want to make a good impression here. Maybe we should go easy on them? Don't want to scare your lady off too soon."

"It'll take more than losing at euchre to scare me away, sir," Macy said, settling in with her coffee and folding her feet beneath her. "You don't know yet who you're tangling with."

"I like this one, Cade!" Howard said. "Let's just hope she can back up that big talk."

"Deal me in, Cade. Game on," Macy said with a confident grin.

An impromptu tournament stretched on for over an hour. The lead bounced back and forth between teams, with Macy suffering through a particularly frustrating hand: a perfect set of Hearts, only for Sheryl to call Clubs. Still, in the end, the women triumphed, winning three games to the men's one.

Sheryl pulled Macy into a warm hug and whispered in her ear, "Let's talk tonight."

Macy helped to tidy up the kitchen and set the table for dinner. When the pizza arrived, coffee mugs were swept away and replaced with wine goblets and a decanter of Chianti. Howard poured with a flourish and offered Macy a glass.

"The wife and I try to visit Italy at least once a year," he said. "We tour a different region each time and usually end up bringing back half a vineyard. Have you ever been?"

"It's on my bucket list," Macy replied, swirling her glass and inhaling. "Excellent nose. Earthy, and I can smell the oak from the barrel."

Howard raised his glass. "The girl knows her wine, too! You'd better keep hold of this one, Cade."

Cade smiled. "I think the ring on her hand speaks for itself. Maybe next time we go, she'll join us."

"How could I say no to that?" Macy said. She turned to Cade with a playful smirk. "Now, tell me: How does your beloved tavern pizza stack up against the source in Italy?"

"The Italians learned pizza from us," Cade said, winking. "I don't care what the history books say."

Macy pursed her lips in mock critique. "I see. So, you know you're wrong, but you're still insisting you're right. Is this a preview of things to come?"

Sheryl chuckled behind her wine glass, but Cade's expression shifted. He snapped his head toward Macy, a sudden fire in his eyes.

"What's that supposed to mean?" he asked, voice tight.

"Whoa. I was kidding," Macy said quickly, raising her hands.

Howard leaned forward, concern etched across his face. "Son, are you all right?"

Cade set down his wine glass and rubbed his eyes with his fingers. "Sorry. You didn't sound teasing, and I jumped to conclusions. It reminded me of something Hannah would've said. I'm sorry, Macy. You didn't deserve that. Forgive me?"

Macy took a long sip of her wine, letting the warmth settle her nerves. "Don't do that again," she said simply.

Cade nodded, subdued.

The moment passed, temporarily forgotten as wine flowed and pizza was served. Macy still wasn't sold on the crust. It was too crispy, and not nearly enough toppings for her New York-trained palate, but it was good enough to go back for seconds.

After lunch, Cade offered to give her a tour of the house. Every room was dressed in Christmas finery, each one more charming than the last. He ended the tour at the guestroom, where they'd be staying for the week. As they stepped inside, Cade circled the foot of the bed and wrapped Macy in a tight embrace, pressing a kiss to her forehead.

"I really am sorry for snapping at you, Mace," he said softly. "That wasn't me. I've been so in my head about getting everything ready today, and I realized I forgot to take my morphine this morning. I'm feeling a little off, and I'm guessing that's what triggered my little faux pas."

He gave her a sheepish smile. "I'm going to get that sorted and lie down for a bit. I should be back to myself in time for the Christmas party tonight. I hope you came prepared for a grand celebration."

"I think I can throw something together," Macy said, returning his smile. "And I get it. You're allowed to be a little grumpier than usual today." She winked, and he chuckled.

"I'll see you in a little while. Why don't you go spend some time with my parents?"

Macy made her way back downstairs and found Howard and Sheryl in the kitchen, tidying up from lunch. Howard spotted her and immediately pulled her into a warm hug.

"I'm so sorry about what happened earlier," he said. "I've never seen him like that before. Is he okay?"

"He's all right now," Macy assured him. "He forgot to take his medication this morning, and it threw him off a bit. He's resting now."

Howard nodded and squeezed her hand, then went back to washing the wine glasses.

Sheryl sat down at the table and motioned for Macy to join her, her eyes soft. "I'm glad you were able to smooth things over. I did want to talk to you now that you're officially joining the family."

Macy's stomach fluttered, face quickly draining of color. She nodded cautiously for her to continue.

"I know things happened fast between you two," Sheryl continued, "but that's just Cade. He feels things deeply. He's passionate, and sometimes overwhelmingly so. That can scare people off, but he's never been one to play games. He wears his heart on his sleeve."

She paused, her gaze steady. "I just want to make sure you're okay. That he didn't put you on the spot so much that you felt like you didn't have a choice in how you answered."

"Oh, no!" Macy said quickly. Too quickly. Her voice pitched higher than she intended. "I'm happy. Really. I've been through a lot before Cade, and I met, and you're right that he's passionate. That's one of the things I love most about him. I never have to guess where I stand. He's fully transparent."

Sheryl smiled warmly. "Good. I think you'll fit right in with us. I know he said you two have been working hard at the gym, but I hope you're ready for the annual Laurent Christmas Eve party. It's not for the faint of heart."

Macy swept back upstairs and into the guestroom to find Cade lying on the bed, eyes closed, though not entirely asleep. One eyelid cracked open as she began rummaging through her duffel bag.

She hadn't been briefed about a party when she packed, but thankfully, she'd brought a dress in anticipation of holiday festivities. The clock read 4:00. She didn't know exactly when the party started, but figured she had enough time to grab a shower.

Cade continued watching her quietly as she pulled out her comb, shampoo, and makeup case. She hadn't packed fancy shoes to match the dress, but stocking feet would do just fine inside the house. As she took off her watch and turned to lay the dress out on the bed, she jumped slightly, catching Cade's gaze still fixed on her.

"Enjoying the view?" she asked, amused.

He snapped his eye shut but smiled. "Always. Towels are in the guest bathroom. Want some company?"

"I thought you were resting," she teased.

"I have strength enough if you want me to follow."

Macy walked over and kissed his forehead. "Maybe after the rest of the house is asleep."

She headed for the door, and Cade called after her, "I hope you know that I hate that you're right!"

Three hours later, Cade was back in his tailored suit, and Macy had transformed. She wore a retro-style black dress with a V-neck, cap sleeves, and a flared skirt that fell just above her knees. Her hair was long and loose, curls tamed with gel, and her makeup playful: pinks and reds with a subtle touch of green on her eyelids.

Cade offered his arm and escorted her down the stairs. Macy took in the sight of the already festive foyer, now bustling with guests flowing in and out of the living room. She spotted Howard and Sheryl mingling with the crowd, and a pit began to form in her stomach.

So many new faces.

"Are you ready to meet my mother?" Cade whispered, nodding toward a woman entering from the living room.

She was short and round, with shoulder-length salt-and-pepper hair pulled into an elegant bun. Her olive complexion glowed under the lights, and she wore black square glasses and a simple red tunic dress.

"Diane! I'm so glad you made it!" Sheryl called out, waving her over.

Discarding her coat, Diane Donovan made her way to Sheryl, and the two women kissed each other's cheeks.

Macy leaned toward Cade. "Okay, this is something you don't see every day. Do they actually get along, or is this just for the holiday?"

Before he could answer, Diane spotted them.

"Cade!" she shouted, bouncing on her toes. "Is this her? I have to meet her. Now!"

Suddenly, Macy felt every eye in the room turn toward her.

"Well," she murmured, "I didn't want to feel invisible anymore. Ready or not, here I go."

Cade squeezed her hand. "You're going to do great."

Diane rushed over and wrapped Macy in a tight hug, kissing both cheeks with theatrical flair.

"Macy, let me look at you!" she exclaimed. "I just knew the first time Cade told me about you that we'd be standing here one day. You are stunning. This is the best Christmas gift I've ever received! I never trusted Hannah, you know. I told Cade—"

"Mom!" Cade cut in, his tone firm but polite. "Can we not? Let Macy breathe, please."

Waving him off, Diane grabbed Macy's hand and began leading her away. "You hush, son. It's my turn now."

Macy glanced back at Cade, who offered a helpless shrug and a smile that said, *I can't stop her either*.

"Macy," Diane continued, barely pausing for breath, "you'll have to let me know when you set a date. I never had a daughter, so I've never had the chance to go wedding dress shopping. I simply can't wait to take you out and help you pick something! With those red curls, you'd look divine in this vintage satin gown I've saved from my grandmother…"

Macy tried to keep up, offering a polite "Uh-huh" and "That sounds lovely" as Diane swept her through the crowd, still talking a mile a minute. Her eyes were scanning the room, looking for Cade, when a slightly taller, blond version of Cade came through the door toting a tray of cookies.

"Sean!" she heard Cade call out from behind. "It's about time. Where's the cannoli?"

"What is it with him and cannoli?" Diane murmured.

Macy chuckled softly, trying to excuse herself to go meet Sean.

Diane, however, tightened her grip on Macy's arm and grabbed a glass of white wine for her and one for Macy. "Oh, don't leave me yet, young lady! We still have so much to talk about."

Macy's stomach dipped. She accepted the wine glass, but barely let the cool liquid touch her lips. "Mmhmm," she said, on instinct.

"Now, listen." Diane had walked Macy through the living room, foyer, and near the kitchen, where conversation buzzed, and glasses tinkled against each other as partygoers made toasts and shared jokes. "I know you know about Hannah."

Macy cringed, once again looking for Cade. "Yes, he told me about her. That had to be so hard."

"Oh, my dear, harder than you can imagine. They were here when it happened, you know. We had no idea when they walked out the door that day...! Well. People always surprise you, I suppose. You wouldn't think it to look at him now, though. Ever since he found you! You wouldn't believe it was only just last spring that she—"

"Macy!" Sheryl called out over the noise. "There you are. Howard is about to launch into one of his toasts, and I think he wants you and Cade so he can officially introduce you to the family. Can you come with me?"

Diane turned to Sheryl, smile tight. "I was in the middle of telling Macy about how far Cade has come since the spring when Hannah..."

Macy's breath hitched. The spring? But we met in the spring. And I thought he said they were visiting her family...

"I'm sure it can wait," Sheryl said pleasantly.

Macy flipped her gaze uneasily between them and took a tentative step toward Sheryl. "Excuse me." She allowed herself to be led back into the kitchen, where Cade and Howard were pouring glasses of chardonnay.

Sheryl's eyes softened. "Are you okay? I know Diane can be a little...overwhelming."

"I am, but..." Macy trailed off. "Something she said about Cade and Hannah. When...?"

Sheryl smiled at Macy and guided her toward the men. "Don't even worry about it. Cade has always lived his life in fast-forward, but he knows what he wants. Settling down and starting a family has always been his goal. Yes, they got engaged quickly, after only about four months, but that's just Cade. Hannah wasn't cut out for that. I don't know why she even said yes, honestly. As soon as she did, it was like she started changing her mind. That's not for Cade. He doesn't hesitate. He chooses, and he expects the world to keep up."

Macy's mind was spinning. She thought she had been learning Cade, piece by piece. But suddenly, she felt like she was stepping into someone else's unfinished story, rather than writing her own.

She wondered how well she truly knew the man she had just agreed to marry.

Chapter Twenty

SHARING THE NEWS

Cade spotted his brother across the room and waved. "Hey, Sean! Get over here with that cookie tray and meet your future sister!"

Sean smiled, and for a moment, he looked like Cade's twin, only lighter-haired and more laid-back. Dressed in khakis and a black polo, he held a tray of Italian cookies.

"I saved the last cannoli just for you, brother," Sean said. "And this must be the infamous Macy. Sorry, I don't dress up. This is as fancy as I get."

Macy laughed nervously and reached out to shake his hand. "That's all right, I won't tell anyone. So, you're Cade's brother."

"Guilty as charged." Sean turned to Cade. "And you'll be interested to know, Talia's on her way. She and Dean called it off tonight. He just texted me that she stormed out."

"Ouch. They broke up on Christmas Eve?" Cade winced. "Poor guy."

Sean placed a hand on Cade's arm. "You should know, I told her about your engagement. That's what sparked the fight. She wanted to know when Dean was going to catch up with you. It didn't go well. Dean got his boxers in a knot because you're engaged again. Congrats, Macy, welcome to the family. But now Talia's pissed he won't even talk about commitment."

Before Macy could ask questions, the front door swung open and slammed shut behind a petite, olive-skinned woman with sleek black hair, wearing a luscious green cocktail dress. Her brown eyes flashed with fury.

"Cade!" she called out, voice sharp.

Cade gave Sean a look of pure exasperation as Talia stormed toward them.

"Talia," he said calmly, "this one's on Dean, not me. I'm not responsible for him being afraid of commitment."

She marched up, barefoot now, strappy black sandals in hand, and Macy wasn't entirely sure she wasn't about to throw them. The room fell silent. Conversations ceased. Macy could feel every eye turn toward the unfolding spectacle.

"Dean and I were together for three years, Cade. Not months. Not weeks. Years." Talia's voice cut through the room like glass. "Now he sees you racing to the altar again and thinks I'm pressuring him to shit or get off the pot."

She paused, finally noticing Macy standing just behind Cade.

"This must be the latest lucky lady," she said, her irritation immediate and unfiltered. "Regards."

Macy flinched and shook her head, then reached out a hand for Talia to shake. "I'm sorry to hear about your breakup. I hope that we can—"

"Yeah, however that sentence was going to end, don't count on it." She sneered at Macy's hand and made no motion to take it.

"Talia, that's enough," Sheryl said sharply, stepping forward with a look that brokered no argument.

Talia huffed and turned away, but not before Sheryl caught her eye with a quieter warning. "I didn't raise you to be so indecent."

Talia's gaze flicked back to Macy. Her tawny eyes held less fury now, more calculation. But whatever she was thinking, she didn't say.

She tossed her purse and sandals into the closet and stormed up the stairs, leaving behind a trail of silence.

"She'll come around," Cade said, though his voice lacked conviction.

From upstairs came the muffled sound of raised voices, followed by the slam of a guestroom door. Cade's phone buzzed. He glanced at the screen and sighed. "Okay, so she won't be cooling off tonight. She wants the guestroom since she's not staying with Dean. I'd better smooth this over. Sean, can you take Macy to meet more of the family?"

Sean nodded and gently steered Macy toward the living room. "Come on, let's introduce you to the less dramatic side of the family."

The evening had become a haze of introductions and inside jokes, and Macy found herself scanning the crowd for a familiar face who might anchor her in the chaos. Relief washed over her when Cade finally reappeared at the foot of the stairs.

She met him halfway. "What's the resolution with Talia?"

Cade exhaled. "Honestly? I think she's jealous we're moving forward, and she's not. It's not personal. She doesn't even know you. But since we're two and she's one, I convinced her to let us keep the guestroom. She's taking the pull-out in the library."

Macy nodded, too tired to unpack the layers of that answer. "Okay. Can we go find that guestroom now? It's been a long day."

He slipped an arm around her shoulders and guided her upstairs. "Sure. But hey, you survived. And we don't have to invite anyone to the wedding if you don't want to. Well, except my parents, of course."

"Of course," she echoed, managing a small smile. "Everyone was nice enough, but I'm just…overwhelmed."

At last, peace appeared in the form of a bedroom door. Macy reached for it like a lifeline. "Please tell me tomorrow won't be so fast-paced."

Cade shut the door gently behind them. "I am happy to confirm. Tomorrow, we sleep in, eat a big breakfast, and binge *A Christmas Story* with cookies and cocoa. Christmas Eve is always the big event here."

"Good," Macy said, slipping into her new pajamas. "I'll want to FaceTime my parents, though. They should know about…" She trailed off, gesturing to the ring on her hand.

"They should," Cade agreed, stepping closer and placing his hands on her hips. He breathed her in, slow and deliberate. "We're alone now, you know."

Macy put a hand on his chest, gazing up at him. "Your sister already hates me, and she's on the other side of that wall."

Grinning at her, mischief sparkling in his eyes, Cade reached for the light switch. "Then keep quiet."

The morning found leftover cousins crashed on the couches in the living room. Sheryl paced the kitchen, wrapped in a powder blue terrycloth robe. She filled glasses of mimosa and piled stacks of French toast onto a plate. Howard stood at the stove, scrambling eggs, bacon sizzling in a cast-iron skillet.

Sean and Talia sat at the table with their mimosas; Sean was peeling an orange, and Talia was nibbling a bagel. Nursing hangovers, the cousins munched on leftover cookies with Tylenol and coffee chasers.

Macy had slipped into her new satin pajamas, and Cade pulled on flannel pants with a white T-shirt. Hand in hand, they joined the rest of the family in the kitchen. "Hey," she whispered to Cade. "Please don't tell me there's going to be a quiz on which cousins are still here?"

Cade laughed and grabbed them each a glass of mimosa. "No worries." He put a hot mug of coffee in front of her and stood behind her, fingertips resting on her shoulder.

"So!" Sean said, brightly. "Sleep well?" He gave Cade a knowing smile and winked at him, earning an eye roll from his brother and Macy burying her face behind her coffee mug.

"Don't worry," Talia said flatly. "I didn't hear *everything*."

"Oh, God," Macy groaned and got up to go help Sheryl with the dishes.

"That's what she said," squealed Sean, and even Talia couldn't help but laugh.

Howard and Sheryl curled up in the impressively tidy living room to watch *A Christmas Story* after gifts had been unwrapped, while Macy and Cade retreated to their room to get dressed. Sheryl had gifted Macy a stack of bridal magazines and style guides, which she flipped through as Cade put his pajamas back into his suitcase. Through the thin wall, Macy could hear Talia's voice, sharp and urgent, on the phone with someone she could only assume was Dean.

Macy paused, listening. The words weren't clear, but the tone was unmistakable: frustration, longing, and something else that Macy couldn't quite name. She turned back to Cade, who was buttoning his shirt. "Do you think she'll ever warm up to me?"

He hesitated. "Eventually. Maybe. She's just…complicated."

Macy nodded, but the question lingered. So did the feeling that this family—warm, chaotic, and full of history—was going to take more than one holiday to understand. She pulled on a pair of simple black leggings, paired with an oversized burgundy sweater dress. After checking her reflection one last time, Macy returned to the kitchen and poured herself another mimosa. Her hand trembled slightly as she lifted the glass. She knew she had to call her family and tell them. The engagement felt surreal, and the timing was definitely fast. But if not now, when? Waiting would only make things worse. Concern could turn into hurt.

Cade set up a phone in Sheryl's office and pulled up a chair beside Macy as she hovered over the "send" button.

"You can do this," he said gently. "It's just your parents."

Macy hesitated. Her finger hovered, frozen. Cade reached over and pressed her fingertip to the screen, initiating the call to Springwater.

It connected on the second ring. Ethan's face appeared first, with Joy swaying in the background, Caleb nestled in her arms.

"Hi, you guys! Merry Christmas!" Ethan grinned.

"Merry Christmas!" Macy replied, hoping the brightness in her voice was convincing enough. "How was everyone's morning?"

"You missed a great one, Mace," Ethan said. "Aunt Erin tried to flip eggs by flicking the pan, but overshot it. Eggs everywhere. Including her."

Joy elbowed him. "Then your dear brother wandered in and told her that having egg on your face isn't supposed to be literal."

"I would've loved to see that," Macy laughed. "Did she stick around?"

"Are you kidding?" Rebecca chimed in, stepping into view. "She probably ran off to spread gossip that someone else did it."

George appeared behind her, drying his hands on a towel. Macy's nerves twisted. It was time. "Mom, Dad. Merry Christmas. I miss you all."

"We miss you, too, Mace," Rebecca said warmly. "Cade, it's nice to see you."

"Nice to see you all as well," Cade replied. "We're glad we caught you together. We wanted to share Macy's gift from me—"

Before he could finish, the office door creaked open. Talia stepped inside, her face twisted back into the same scowl she'd worn the night before. She walked directly into the camera's view.

"Hi. You don't know me, but you should see this."

Macy barely had time to react before Talia grabbed her hand. Realizing what was happening, Macy tried to pull away, but Talia was faster. She thrust Macy's hand toward the camera, holding it up for all to see.

Rebecca gasped, hand flying to her mouth. George leaned in, squinting. Macy yanked her hand back, her heart pounding.

Mission accomplished, Talia turned on her heel. She tossed a cold smile in Macy's direction and threw her perfect black hair over her shoulder. "Bye!" she called, flouncing out the door.

"Talia!" Cade shouted, jumping up. "Excuse me, please."

The door slammed behind him.

On screen, George cleared his throat. "Was that what it looked like on your finger?"

Macy nodded, her mouth twisting into a nervous smile. "This isn't how I envisioned telling you. Cade planned a scavenger hunt with gifts, clues, the whole thing. He was waiting at the end with the ring."

Ethan blinked, stunned. "Does this mean—? You're—?"

"I'm sorry about my sister," Cade said as he returned, locking the door behind him. "So, I guess the diamond's out of the box."

Ethan continued to stammer in the background, clearly still processing.

"Well," George said after a long pause, his tone measured. "That's…unexpected."

"I can see how you might be surprised," Cade replied, steady. "But I love your daughter, sir. And I don't believe in wasting time."

Rebecca tried to recover her composure. Joy looked on the verge of tears. She turned away from the camera and excused herself, saying she needed to put the baby down for a nap.

"Macy," her mother said gently, "this is awful quick."

The worry in her eyes was impossible to miss.

"I know," Macy said simply. She was unsure how to convince them when she was still wrapping her own head around it, and words started tumbling out.

"I met the rest of his family last night. They're all really excited for us. Well…Talia might take a little longer to warm up." She laughed, though it came out brittle. She wasn't sure why. Only that if she didn't laugh, she might cry.

George's lips pressed into a thin line. "Macy, can we speak with you alone for a minute?"

Cade's jaw tensed, just for a moment. But Macy turned to him and gave a small nod. He kissed her temple before stepping out of the room, casting one last glance at the screen before closing the door behind him.

Her father's voice dropped low.

"Mace, this is a lot to process," George began. "You've only known him a few months. Are you sure this is a good idea so fast?"

"Dad…" Macy exhaled, searching for the right words. "I know it's unexpected. But Cade's taken such good care of me. He loves me. He makes me feel like I'm the most important person in his world. I don't want to rush the wedding. I want to savor this and take our time planning."

Joy re-entered the screen, biting her lip. "Macy, can I say something? It's all been so fast already. What makes you think he won't push to close the deal just as quickly? I love you, and I want to see you happy, but I'm just as worried as your parents."

"I know," Macy said, her chest tightening. "I promise I'm taking this seriously. I love him."

George sighed, his expression unreadable. "You're an adult, and this is your choice. We won't stand in your way. But I want you to promise me that if you have any doubts about this, you will talk to us."

Macy's throat tightened with threatening tears. Nodding, she looked up at the screen. "I promise, I will."

When the call ended, Cade returned, scanning her face carefully.

"How'd it go?"

"They're surprised," Macy admitted. "But they'll come around. They just want me to be happy."

He smiled, the tension in his shoulders easing. "I hope so. I want to give you the world. I hope they'll see I'm the one for you, and be happy about it. I thought this would make you happy."

"It does," she said quickly, though her voice faltered.

"You don't sound very sure."

"It's nothing," Macy said, brushing a hand through her curls. "I just need time to let my nerves settle. I didn't know how to expect that call to go, and I'm not sure still how I'm feeling about the way it went."

She hesitated, then added, "And honestly, I don't know what to do about your sister. I was hoping to have a good relationship with her, like I have with Joy. But she hates me. I might have a chance to win Sean over, but Talia feels like a lost cause. There's just…a lot coming at me all at once."

Cade sat down in the chair next to her, crossing his arms across his chest. "I hate to bring up Thanksgiving, but we already know your brother wishes you were with your neighbor instead of me. I'm sure he's been whispering things in your family's ear."

Macy shook her head emphatically. "He didn't mean that, Cade. He likes that he and Theo were able to banter with each other, but that doesn't mean he thinks he would be better for me than you are."

"Doesn't it?" Cade asked, frustration lacing his tone. He raked his hands through his hair and swiveled his chair to face hers. "He's your brother, so I'm going to try to be patient with him. But I have this bad feeling he's going to try to turn the rest of them."

The silence stretched between them. She hung her head, thoughts twisted and confused. She brushed a single tear from her cheek.

From the living room, the TV blared, "You'll shoot your eye out!" and Cade nudged her playfully. "Come on. Let's go watch with them. It'll help you relax."

Macy nodded, but didn't move right away. She watched the snow drift softly outside the window, the last sip of her mimosa warming her throat. Her thoughts wandered back to Joy's worried face and the words she'd spoken after their first visit to the farm together.

They just don't know him the way I do, Macy told herself. That's all. They'll see.

But even as she repeated it, uncertainty fluttered in her chest. Or the quiet ache of wanting everyone to believe in this as much as she did.

Chapter Twenty-One

CADE STAKES HIS CLAIM

Macy and Cade spent the rest of their holiday break enjoying the easy, relaxing pace of the post-holiday rush with the Laurent family. Sheryl and Macy sat together discussing Macy's vision for her wedding gown, and earmarking styles to try. On the morning of the 28th, Macy and Cade were on the flight home to New York.

The hum of the plane was steady, and Lake Erie shimmered below as they cruised at altitude. Macy glanced down at her ring, still marveling at how quickly everything had changed. Cade was her fiancé now. The word was still foreign and exciting, but also a little unreal.

Her bond with Sheryl and Howard was off to a sturdy start, but she hadn't seen Sean or Talia again after breakfast and gifts. Their absence lingered in her thoughts.

Finally, she couldn't hold the question in any longer.

"So…Sean and Talia."

Cade looked up from the window. "Hmm?"

"Did I do something to offend them?"

"No!" he said quickly. "I told you the other day you didn't. Sean just moved out last year. He's still figuring out how to be independent while staying connected to the family. I'm sure you know what that's like, right?" He winked at her.

Macy laughed and looked away. "I have no idea what you're talking about."

Cade flashed his most charming grin. "Exactly."

He shifted in his seat. "As for Talia, it's not about you. It's about her and Dean. He was her first…well, everything. When Hannah and I got engaged, she started nudging Dean to step up. But they were only twenty. He didn't feel ready. She got a little antagonistic toward me after that, and honestly, we haven't been the same since. Sean and I saw the writing on the wall with Dean, but we didn't expect it to blow up on Christmas.

"So really," he continued, "it's not you. She wants what we have, and she thought she'd have it with Dean."

"To be fair, I'm twenty-seven," Macy said.

Cade shook his head. "She doesn't care. Talia wants what she wants, and she wants it now."

Macy nudged him gently. "Sounds familiar, huh?"

He laughed and turned back to the window. "Maybe we clash because we're too much alike."

Macy settled back in her seat, the conversation having run its course. Her thoughts drifted to home. How she'd break the news to her friends, and what it would mean for her and Catherine's living arrangements. Shane had arrived right on schedule while they were in Chicago, and she was sure he and Catherine would appreciate having the place to themselves.

She hesitated, then spoke again. "So…"

Cade turned to her slowly, biting his lip. A quiet huff of a sigh escaped him.

"A lot's changed this week," Macy said. "Shane's home, we're engaged…I still haven't told Catherine. What's the plan for our living situation?"

"I assumed you'd start moving your things in once we get home," Cade said. "I want to start our life together. We should get on with it, shouldn't we?"

Macy tilted her head, thoughtful. "It's a big change, Cade. I want to at least talk to Catherine and Shane before springing it on them that I'm moving out."

His expression shifted. "Are you more worried about hurting their feelings than mine?"

"That's not what I'm saying." She looked down at her hands, folded in her lap.

"Then why can't we just start getting you moved in when we get home?"

Macy took a deep breath, choosing her words carefully. She didn't want to start a fight, just to be understood.

"Catherine's been my best friend since we were kids. When we knew Shane was coming home, we talked about how things would change. But even then, she was focused on making sure I was okay. It's her relationship, and her apartment too, but she made sure I knew my feelings still mattered. I want to give her that same consideration."

Cade pursed his lips, dissatisfied. "I see."

"Are you saying she doesn't deserve that?" Macy asked, her voice tight with the barest hint of anger. But when she saw the stricken look in his eyes, her temper cooled to regret.

"That's not what I'm saying." He ran a hand through his hair and rubbed his eyes. He spoke without looking at her, face still in his hands. "I just waited so long to find you. I don't want to wait anymore. What's so wrong with that?"

"Nothing," Macy said gently. "You know what I've gone through, too. Let me talk with Catherine before you start hauling in boxes, okay? I don't want it to feel abrupt or blindsiding. Isn't that fair?"

He took her hand, toying with her engagement ring. "I can see you're not going to budge on this. I just hope this doesn't become a pattern—Catherine interfering with our plans. Will February appease her?"

Macy smiled and threw her arms around his neck. "Thank you, Cade. Yes—February it is."

She leaned back in her seat, heart quivering with a mix of excitement and unease. February would come fast. But at least she had a little breathing room and some time to get her bearings before the next big step.

She tried to imagine how Catherine would take the news. Nina had been cheering her on every step of the way, but Catherine? She had not been as quiet in voicing her concerns. Macy pushed the doubts down. She was doing what people in love did, and taking the next step. And she was in love.

Right?

They linked hands and rode the rest of the way into JFK in silence. As the plane descended over New York City, Cade slipped an arm around her shoulders and grinned.

"Welcome home, future Mrs. Donovan."

"Walker-Donovan," Macy replied and winked up at him. "I'm a modern woman."

He winced. "Oh no. You're not really going to do that, are you?"

"I've thought about it," she said with a shrug. "It's my name, after all."

"Well, that's kind of my point," Cade said as they grabbed their carry-ons and headed toward the terminal exit. "It's my marriage, too. I thought we'd be united. One family, one name."

"I guess that makes sense," Macy murmured, though her tone lacked conviction.

He led her through the terminal and out to baggage claim. As they waited, he stood behind her, arms wrapped around her waist, watching the endless parade of black and blue luggage roll past. Finally, her green roller bag appeared, and he stepped forward to pull it off the carousel for her.

"Ready?" Cade asked.

"Take me home," Macy replied.

They had a long subway ride ahead, starting on the A train, then transferring to the line that would take them back to the apartment she shared with Catherine. As they settled into their seats, they made themselves as comfortable as the rattling car would allow.

Cade reached for her hand and gently turned her ring between his fingers. "I can't wait to start planning."

"Me too," Macy said, finally allowing herself to be excited. "Your mom wasted no time talking about dress shopping. Honestly, I think that's the part I'm most looking forward to: trying on pretty dresses and getting all fancied up."

"You know she's been waiting for this almost as long as I have," Cade said. "After Hannah and I got engaged, we never really made plans. She kept pushing it off. I don't know if she even wanted to get married or just wanted the security I gave her. So, it's exciting for all of us to finally move forward."

Macy hesitated, then spoke cautiously. "I don't know if this is appropriate to ask, but there's something I've been wondering."

Cade nodded slowly, concern flickering across his face. "Well…why don't you ask me, and we'll find out together."

"I just was wondering, what does Sheryl do for a living to afford that gorgeous house?" She paused, cheeks flushed with embarrassment.

Cade burst into the heartiest laughter she'd heard from him since before the trip. "Is that all?"

"I knew you'd laugh. Forget I asked." Macy angled away, staring down at her feet.

Still chuckling, Cade gently turned her back toward him and tipped her chin up. "I'm sorry for laughing. You caught me off guard, that's all. Of all the things you could've asked, that wasn't on my bingo card."

Macy crossed her arms, pouting, until he finally stopped laughing.

"She has a pretty standard office job. She's a business analyst. But she inherited the house. Her dad was a renowned surgeon. So, no, they're not wealthy, and neither am I, really. But we're comfortable. And since they don't have any debt, that's close enough to rich these days. I hope that's okay."

Macy let her shoulders relax and returned his smile. "It really doesn't matter to me. I was just curious."

She leaned her head on his shoulder, and they rode in silence until it was time to change trains. When they finally reached her stop, she turned to him.

"Do you want to come up with me to share the news, or let us have a ladies' heart-to-heart?"

He walked her to her apartment door before deciding. "As loath as I am to be away from you, I should probably unpack and start making room for your things. But hopefully I'll see you tonight?"

"Why don't you come back around dinner time? We'll celebrate together. All four of us."

"I was thinking you could invite them back to my place. Nina and Brian, too, if they want. The couch pulls out, and there's plenty of room if anyone wants to stay."

Macy set her bags down and reached up to wrap her arms around his neck. "That sounds lovely. I'll bring the wine."

He kissed her full and deep, his hand slipping down to squeeze her bottom.

She squealed and pulled back. "Cade! Someone might see!"

He winked. "How boring if they don't?" Then, without waiting for a reply, he turned and headed back toward the subway tunnel.

Macy watched him go and jumped when she spun and saw Theo approaching from the other direction. "Theo! How was your Christmas?"

"It was good. I went to Aguadilla to visit my parents." He nodded toward the direction Cade had gone. "Someone wants to make sure his territory's marked."

"You saw that, huh?" Macy cringed, and her face turned crimson.

"He made sure of it," Theo said, his tone more serious than teasing.

Macy blinked, surprised. "What are you saying, Theo? He was just being playful. I'll talk to him. He knows I'm not comfortable with that level of PDA."

Theo didn't back down. "Macy, he looked me right in the eye before he did it. That wasn't just playful. That was for my benefit."

"I don't understand," Macy said, shaking her head. "If my stupid brother hadn't made that remark at Thanksgiving..."

Theo hesitated, then gently pulled her into a hug. "Look, don't be mad, okay? I've come to think of you and Catherine as family. That makes me protective of you. I'm not the kind of man who will go after someone who's involved with someone else. And he needs to trust that you would turn down anyone who would. It concerns me that he felt the need to make a public display to prove a point when he should just trust his partner."

Macy took a breath, steadying herself. "I appreciate your concern, Theo. Really. But he and I already talked about it. He knows you're just my friend. I chose him."

She held out her left hand, showing him the ring.

"Ay, Dios mío!" Theo exclaimed. "Wow. Congratulations, Macy. I really am happy for you. As long as you're happy."

"I am," she said softly. "I promise. Now I need to go tell Catherine that she and Shane are going to have the place to themselves pretty soon."

Theo's eyes dimmed with a hint of sadness. He gently squeezed her arm. "I'll miss you around here, Mace. Just promise you won't be a stranger."

She smiled. "That's the easiest promise I can make. I'll see you soon."

She pulled open the door and stepped through. Theo watched her go, his usual playfulness replaced with concern.

Macy ran up the stairs, her heart pounding with anticipation. As she opened the door to her apartment, she called out, "Caaaaatheriiiine!"

A tall, lanky man with spiky blond hair and bright blue eyes stepped out from Catherine's room.

"Macy! Welcome home!" Shane grinned. "It's so good to see you."

Macy gave him a quick hug. "Welcome home, yourself, soldier. I'm so happy you're back!"

Catherine appeared behind him, her smile warm but slightly reserved. "Merry Christmas, Macy. Now let's see that ring."

"How did you know?" Macy asked, glancing down at her gloved hand.

"Come on, Mace. You've been joined at the hip since your first date, and he's been dropping hints like breadcrumbs. Congratulations, honey."

She hugged Macy tightly, but she lacked her usual enthusiasm. In its place, Catherine was uncharacteristically thoughtful. Still, she took hold of Macy's left hand and pulled off the glove. "Tell him I said nice job. It's beautiful."

"You know the promises we made still stand, right?" Macy said. "I'll always be a pain in your ass, and we'll always make time for each other."

"Don't you ever forget it," Catherine said, wagging her finger at Macy.

"That reminds me, actually—"

"Oh, God," Shane groaned melodramatically.

Catherine nudged him with a grin. "Very funny, loser."

"Cade invited us all over to his place tonight to celebrate," Macy said. "Sleepover optional. I think it's a no-brainer."

"I haven't seen the place yet. That'll be fun!" Catherine gushed, her usual enthusiasm flickering back to life. "Shane, go pack us some overnight things. I'm calling Nina!"

Macy headed to her room. "In that case, I'm going to pack a few things to leave over there."

Catherine pulled Shane back into her room. While he started tossing clothes into a bag, she quietly pulled out her phone and sent a text to Joy:

Catherine

*Thank you for the heads-up
about Macy. It's hard to put on
a happy face about this, but
I'm going to do my best to
keep my mouth shut.*

Meanwhile, in Macy's room, she packed her tote with a change of clothes, the bottle of red Cade liked, and her makeup bag, just in case. She knew she'd need to keep most of her things here until the move was official, but she added another bag with work clothes, two pairs of shoes, and a gym outfit. The permanence of the moment left a hollow ache in Macy's chest.

When she returned to the kitchen, Catherine and Shane were waiting.

"Ready?" Shane asked, grabbing Macy's larger bag and insisting on carrying it down to the subway.

The train ride uptown stretched longer than usual. Macy spent most of it staring at her ring under the flickering fluorescent lights. The silence between them was louder than the rumble of the train. Catherine had seemed supportive enough, but Macy sensed resignation more than excitement. Acceptance, not celebration.

By the time they reached Cade's building, snow had started falling again—tiny flakes melting on Macy's coat but clinging to the ends of her curls. Shane slung her bag over his shoulder and gave her a kind smile. As they climbed the stairs, Catherine caught Macy's eye and offered a warm, almost wistful smile. Both of their expressions seemed to hold the same thought: *Everything is about to change.*

When Cade opened the door, the scent of cinnamon and clove wafted from the oven. Nina and Brian were already there, plating spaghetti and meatballs while Brian tossed the salad.

"Dang, you put them straight to work, didn't you?" Catherine joked.

Nina dropped her serving fork and rushed over, sweeping Macy into a bone-crushing hug. "Let me see it!" she squealed.

"It's nice to meet everybody. I'm Shane," he said, still holding Macy's bag.

Brian shook his hand and took the bag from him. "Here, let me get you a beer. Welcome, and welcome home."

Cade popped the cork on a fresh bottle of wine and poured six glasses. He handed one to Brian. "No, Brian. A soldier deserves a proper celebration. It's great to finally meet you." He shook his hand and thanked him for helping Macy with her things.

Then he turned to Macy and pulled her close with one arm, raising his glass with the other. "You look beautiful," he said. "Now all we need is to set a wedding date."

"No pressure or anything," Catherine said, her snark returning right on cue. When Cade turned to face Macy, Catherine's eyes rolled skyward.

Macy laughed until she saw Cade's face. He wasn't joking. His stare was intense, focused. He meant it.

"Um, well," Macy said quickly, "we need time to organize things. Reception halls, photographers—they book out pretty far in advance. We could start there and work our way in. But I'm sure we could pull something together by the end of next year. Wouldn't a winter wedding in the city be gorgeous?"

Cade snorted. "I'm not waiting that long to marry you. We're getting married in the spring."

"Do I get a say in this?" Macy asked. She was laughing, but she wasn't joking.

Neither was he.

"Of course," Cade said, his tone light but firm. "But I told you earlier, I don't want to drag this out. Let's just start our life together and be done with it. Don't you want that, too?"

A cold pit settled in Macy's stomach. Her mouth opened, but no sound came out at first. "I—I do. But spring is just a couple of months away. I need more time than that."

Catherine glanced at Shane and Nina. "Why don't we give them a minute to talk this over?"

Cade raised a hand, his eyes still locked on Macy. "No, don't go. I want witnesses for this. We're celebrating tonight. Let's get this resolved and pop another bottle. How about it, Mace? Spring in the gardens? Maybe the High Line? Let's not drag this out."

Macy's breath caught. "Cade, I—"

"You love me, don't you?"

"Of course," she whispered.

"Then what are you waiting for?"

She smiled, but more from nerves than joy. She should be thrilled. This was everything she'd wanted. So, why was something inside her nagging to throw on the brakes?

Why did it suddenly feel as if something would break if she didn't say yes right now?

"This just isn't how I envisioned my wedding," she said carefully. "I don't want to throw something together just to get it done. I plan on doing this only once, so I want to do it right."

Cade's expression fell. He turned from her, avoiding her eyes. "I mean, if some elaborate party means more to you than being married to me, then…all right. We'll do it your way."

He turned toward the kitchen and gathered plates for the table. Macy thought she saw him swipe at his eye—quick, discreet.

Dammit, she thought. Why do I ruin everything?

Chapter Twenty-Two

STRENGTH WITHIN

The mood at Cade's had officially soured. Even with another bottle of wine passed around the room, the tension lingered thicker than smoke. Conversation grew sparse, and laughter became increasingly forced. Nina and Brian excused themselves shortly after cutting into the apple pie Cade had baked.

As Nina hugged Macy goodbye, she whispered, "It's going to be okay."

Cade pulled out the sofa bed for Catherine and Shane, then disappeared into his bedroom. When Macy went in to join him, he lay down facing away from her and went straight to sleep without a word.

The next morning, breakfast was quiet. Cade gave Macy a brief kiss on the cheek before she left with Catherine and Shane. They did not make plans to see each other that evening. The air between them was still heavy with unanswered questions and bruised feelings.

Back at the apartment, Macy closed the door behind them and turned to her friends.

"Am I being selfish?" she asked.

Shane raised his hands in mock surrender. "Don't look at me! This sounds like straight-up girl talk."

Macy reached out and placed a hand on his arm. "No, please stay. I want a man's opinion. And not Ethan's or my dad's. I want someone unbiased. You just met Cade last night, so your perspective is fresh. I'll make coffee. Don't go."

Shane nodded and sat at the table with Catherine while Macy moved to the kitchen. As she brewed the coffee, her thoughts churned.

"I know I hurt his feelings last night," she said, her voice carrying from the counter. "I didn't mean to. I just wanted to have that conversation in private, so we could actually talk, not perform. But…a girl dreams of this day from the time she first knows what a wedding is. I don't want some quick, thrown-together courthouse affair. Why should I have to settle when it's something this important?"

Plus, things are happening way too fast, and I need time to breathe.

She poured three mugs and joined them at the table.

Catherine spoke first. "I don't know if you want to hear this, but I'm going to say it anyway. Your relationship has moved faster than anyone can keep up with. And I'm not the only one who's worried it's been too fast. You know I've raised concerns before about how Cade seems to need things his way. But I'm proud of you for standing your ground last night. You're facing one of the biggest decisions of your life, and you're not wrong for wanting time to process it."

Shane took a thoughtful sip of his coffee. "Cade's reaction did seem a little…extra. But my impression is that he's deeply passionate about you and about being married to you. That said, it was my first time meeting him, so I could be off. A lot of people want the frilly white wedding, and that's totally fine. A lot of people don't. And that's fine too. But when one person's in each camp, you've got to meet in the middle. You'll have to work together to find a solution that works for both of you."

Catherine beamed at him. "Wow. That was incredibly insightful."

Shane smirked. "Such a tone of surprise."

Macy smiled, letting their words settle. "You're both right. This is something Cade and I have to figure out together. The inertia of everything lately has left me dizzy—like we're plunging from one step to the next without ever savoring the moment we're in. But this is our wedding, not just his. It's the start of our life together, and it needs to be our decision."

She looked at them both with gratitude. "Thank you. That gives me a lot to think about."

They finished their coffee in relative silence, Macy quietly reflecting on the day before. When the coffee pot was empty, Macy excused herself to her room to unpack from her week in Chicago. And to think.

While breaking down her suitcase, she caught a glimpse of herself in the mirror: hair mussed, arms full of laundry, leftover Christmas gifts that hadn't yet found a home spilling open across the bed. The chaos of the room mirrored the chaos inside her. Eight months ago, she'd been crying in an airport bathroom, wondering where her life was going. Now she was planning a wedding, her career was finally on a steady path, and she was preparing to leave the first place that had ever embraced her as she was.

It was bittersweet.

She sat on the edge of the bed, utterly drained. She hadn't slept well, her mind spinning with worry about what the morning would be like with Cade.

What to do about Cade?

No date had been chosen. No colors, no venues. Macy *was* stalling. Not just because she wanted time to plan a proper wedding, but because she needed time to breathe.

He wanted to marry her. Quickly. It was flattering, but she didn't like being put on a deadline. And the pressure was all on her.

Cade wasn't happy with her, and she knew it. It hurt to know he was hurting. But right now, it was a relief to have a quiet hour alone with her thoughts. She thumbed miserably through her bridal magazine, looking but not seeing, to keep her hands busy.

A soft knock pulled her out of her reverie. She turned toward the door just as a hand appeared, holding a steaming mug.

"Yes, please," Macy said, tossing her magazine aside and opening the door to find Catherine attached to the mug. She settled beside her on the bed.

"I sent Shane to pick up groceries," Catherine said. "You okay?"

Macy twisted the cross charm on her necklace, tugging it gently. "I think so. Just…processing."

"I'm glad," Catherine said. After a beat, she added, "I just want to say again, I'm proud of you for standing up for yourself. I know that couldn't have been easy."

Macy inhaled the warm aroma of the coffee. She caught a hint of cinnamon and let the heat from the mug seep into her hands.

"You know," she said, "sometimes, a hot mug of coffee really warms you down to the soul." She took a sip. "I sure didn't feel brave last night. He was so upset, he turned away from me in bed without saying a word."

"He pushes hard, Mace. I'm glad you didn't fold just to appease him."

Macy looked down at her mug, still conflicted. But she was grateful to feel like she and Catherine were truly okay.

"I love him, Cath. I do. But it feels like everything is happening around me, and I'm just clinging on by my fingertips. Like I'm a passenger in my own story."

Catherine nudged her shoulder. "You don't have to figure it all out today. Just take it one day at a time. Shane and I have your back. You know Theo does, too. And your family. Even Nina. I think," she added with a playful grin.

Macy finally laughed. "Her party's coming up, isn't it? God, I sprang out of reverse straight into fast-forward. Where's the pause button?"

Catherine offered a warm, understanding smile. "Take today as your pause. Don't see him. Just talk on the phone, and if he asks, tell him you have a headache. Today is yours. Unwind, relax, and later, we'll kick Shane out again and watch a trashy rom-com. Tomorrow's problems can wait until tomorrow."

Feeling encouraged and more relaxed, Macy returned Catherine's smile. "Thanks, Cath. That sounds perfect. And then tomorrow, we kiss the year goodbye."

New Year's Eve night, Macy studied her reflection in the mirror as she adjusted her gown. The draped back was open, and she spun to catch a glimpse of her exposed skin.

"Why do I keep doing these things to myself?" she murmured. Though she'd lost thirteen pounds, she was still self-conscious about her body.

"Stop fidgeting," Catherine said, entering the room in a dress that shimmered with every movement. "That dress is perfection."

She swept Macy's hair into an elegant bun with some carefully placed tendrils. Macy kept her makeup simple with mascara, a soft pink blush, and a swipe of lipstick.

As she added the final touches, a knock came at the door.

"Are you ladies decent?" Shane called. "The car's here!"

"We're ready," Catherine replied. "Let's go party."

Macy stopped short when she saw Cade waiting at the front door, dressed in his tailored suit. When they'd spoken the night before, he hadn't been sure he'd come.

"This suit's gotten more use in the last month than in all the years since I bought it," he said, offering her a single stargazer lily. "Peace offering?"

Macy smiled warmly and placed the flower in water. "You know those are my favorites. Thank you."

"Of course I do." He extended his elbow. "Shall we?"

They'd decided to arrive in style, skipping the subway in favor of a car. The drive through Manhattan traffic was long, but they finally arrived just after eight. The elevator opened onto the Simpson penthouse, revealing a breathtaking scene.

Black and gold decorations covered the ceiling. Servers in tuxedos circulated with trays of champagne. Guests mingled in glittering gowns and sharp suits, laughter and music filling the air.

"Well, well, well," came a voice from across the room.

Nina strolled through the crowd like a blond Jessica Rabbit. Her strapless red gown hugged every curve, her hair swinging freely as she tossed a lock over her shoulder and joined Brian.

"Didn't know if we were still going to see you tonight," she said, eyes flicking between Macy and Cade.

Macy cringed, remembering the tension at Cade's house. She chose her words carefully. "We thought we'd start the year off with a bang."

Nina stared at her a moment, unmoving, then smirked. She grabbed a glass of champagne from a passing tray and downed it in one go. "Let's see if you can keep up."

Cade said nothing, but watched the women with a distant expression. Brian approached, sensing the mood.

"You feeling any better?" he asked quietly.

"Not really," Cade admitted. "I went down this road before—with my late fiancée. She kept putting off setting a date, and I found out she was about to end things when she died. I thought things would be different this time with Macy. But now…it feels like she's starting down the same path. And we've barely even announced the engagement."

Cade plucked a champagne flute from a passing server and scanned the room. "Nina seems like she's in her element tonight."

"Yeah," Brian said flatly. "Give the woman champagne, and suddenly, everyone's her best friend. I can't figure her out sometimes. It feels impossible to make her happy."

He paused, watching Nina laugh with a group near the bar.

"She came to New York to get on stage and struggled. I didn't want her to feel like she settled for me, but I thought we were in love. I never stopped her from auditioning—she just…gave up. She never wanted the 'domestic life.' I think she resents me because I'm here. I'm convenient. A scapegoat for everything she's unhappy about."

Brian shook his head. "Anyway, this is a party. I think I've bitched enough. Let's go mingle."

Cade approached Macy from behind and whispered in her ear, voice low and smooth. "Have I told you how beautiful you look tonight?"

Macy blushed, glancing shyly at the floor. "Thank you."

He reached out and gently tugged at the stray curls left loose from her updo. "I prefer these down, though."

"I know. But keeping them tame is a lot of work!"

He leaned in and nibbled her ear. "But isn't it worth it, knowing your man's turned on by it?"

She laughed, swatting at his hand. "Cade, stop it! Later."

He winked, still grinning, but the moment was short-lived.

Nina rejoined them, slipping away from the circle of Brian's coworkers' wives. "So," she asked, eyes bright, "any decision about a date?"

Macy shot daggers at Nina for bringing it up. Cade's smile vanished. "Bit of a sore subject for us at the moment, isn't it, Macy?"

Macy stiffened, her gaze dropping. "Cade, this isn't the time or the place."

"But why not?" he pressed. "I love you. I know what I want. I don't believe in dragging out engagements. People lose interest, things fall apart. I won't let that happen to us."

"It won't," Macy said, her voice tight. "Actually, the more I think about a winter wedding, the more I like the idea. Imagine New York at Christmas—lights, snow, everything sparkling. Wouldn't that be beautiful?"

"But I don't need all that," he said. "I just want to be married to you. Isn't that what you want, too?"

She hesitated. "Do you really think I'll lose interest just because we wait until winter?"

The room had gone quiet. Conversations faded, and the weight of every set of eyes in the room pressed down on her.

"Can we finish this later?" she asked, voice low. "In private?"

Cade's expression hardened. "Right. Maybe you can get your brother's opinion while you're making up your mind."

Her eyes narrowed. "What's that supposed to mean? You're making a scene…"

He scoffed. "Nothing. Never mind. I forgot, the wedding matters more to you than the marriage."

"Cade…" Macy's voice cracked, pleading.

The penthouse went silent enough to hear the catching of every breath as they waited for the conversation to continue. No one spoke.

Her thoughts spiraled. What will my family think? But I'm an adult. Why should it matter? But what about what I want? I want a real wedding, not a trip to the courthouse.

He stared at her, unblinking. "I just don't know what to think right now, Mace. I thought we were on the same page. I thought you wanted to marry me."

"I do, Cade!"

"Do you?" His voice was sharp now. "You didn't just want a status symbol and a pretty ring?"

Macy's eyes welled with tears. "Can we please talk about this in private? Everybody's staring."

"So what?" Cade said. "Maybe the truth comes out when people are watching. Why did you say yes—in front of my parents, no less—if you didn't mean it?"

"Why can't you just let me have time to think?" Her voice trembled. "Just because I want to take this part slowly doesn't mean I don't want to marry you."

"But if you really wanted this, what's the big deal about just doing it?" His tone was rising. "I know what I want. I'd marry you today. If the roles were reversed, I wouldn't be stringing you along like this."

"Cade…" Macy sobbed, feeling cornered. "Can we at least go talk in the guestroom?"

He crossed his arms, his face set as hard as stone.

Is he right? she wondered. I want this, but I want a real wedding. But if I keep pushing for my wants, will it push him away? Are my wants more important than his feelings? He's so mad…what if he breaks up with me over this? I can't lose him. Everyone around me is already married or getting married. I don't want to wait too much longer to start having kids. Maybe I should just agree.

No. Not today. Stand your ground.

"Cade, I can't do this right now," she said, voice trembling. "If you're mad at me, we'll deal with that later. But this is a conversation I'm not prepared to have in front of all these people."

He pursed his lips, nodding curtly. "If that's how you feel. I'll leave you alone. I told you the holidays are always cursed for me."

Tears spilled down her cheek, leaving streaks of black from her mascara. "Cade, wait!"

"You just said you don't care if I'm mad at you," he snapped. "That tells me everything. Maybe you were never really in this. Maybe I was just a convenient source of attention. I'll go away."

He turned and strode toward the elevator, shoulders rigid, leaving Macy frozen in place. Her breath caught in her chest. The pit in her stomach dropped out, and nausea surged.

Mascara streaked down her cheeks as the tears finally broke through. Nina and Catherine rushed to her side. Brian and Shane stood nearby, stunned into silence.

"It's okay, Mace," Nina said gently, wrapping an arm around her. "We're going to fix this."

But Macy couldn't be soothed. She was the center of attention again, but for all the wrong reasons. Every pair of eyes in the penthouse was on her, and she couldn't bear the mix of sympathy and curiosity in their stares.

"I'm sorry, Nina. I have to go home."

Catherine stepped in, firm and protective. "I'll take her," she said, guiding Macy toward the coat closet.

"Me too," Shane added, shaking Brian's hand to say goodnight.

Brian pulled Macy into a hug. "I'm so sorry, Mace. Do you want me to talk to him?"

"If you want," she murmured. Her voice was flat. She felt completely numb.

Catherine held Macy's right side, Shane her left, as they walked her to the waiting car outside the building.

When she got upstairs, Macy didn't bother to wash off her makeup or change out of her dress. She curled into bed, mascara staining the pillowcase, and stared at the ceiling, wondering if she had just made the biggest mistake of her life.

Chapter Twenty-Three

LOVE AND LOSS

By Monday morning, Macy had no choice but to pick herself up and return to work.

She hadn't heard from Cade all weekend. Her texts went unanswered. Her calls went straight to voicemail. She stood in front of her dresser, staring at her engagement ring. *Do I even wear it? Are we still engaged? Or was it over before it really began?*

Catherine had gently offered to swing by Cade's apartment with Shane to collect Macy's things, but Macy couldn't bring herself to accept. Not yet. Not without a conversation. She still hoped Cade would cool off and reach out. That they could talk, smooth things over, and find their way back.

But that hope was beginning to wither. Her phone remained silent.

Dragging herself from bed, she washed her face. Makeup felt pointless. Her hair went into a loose, effortless bun. She pulled on the most comfortable professional outfit she could find: black leggings, a long lilac button-down dress, and her worn black ballet flats.

One last glance at her phone. Still nothing.

She dropped it into her purse and shuffled into the kitchen. Her eyes clung to the floor, her shoulders heavy. A pot of coffee waited for her, travel mug cleaned and ready.

Bless you, Catherine.

The subway ride was a blur. Just before her stop, Macy pulled out her phone and typed one last message:

Macy

I don't know where we stand right now, and I really wish you would respond so we could talk this out. Or call Brian, even. I'm sorry I hurt you, and I want to fix this if you'll just give me the chance. I love you.

She hit send as she climbed the stairs out of the station and made her way toward the OptiHealth building. Her stomach churned. *What am I going to tell the team? They'll all want to know.*

"Well," she imagined herself saying, "he proposed at Christmas, but he was so excited to set the date that he probably called it off when I wanted to slow things down."

The tears threatened again, but the elevator doors opened before she could fall apart. She weaved through the departments and reached her desk beside Amara.

Before she could even power on her computer, RJ's head popped over the cubicle wall.

"So? How was it?"

Macy slipped off her coat and gloves, revealing the diamond ring still on her finger.

RJ gasped. "Are you two nuts?!"

"What?!" Sebrina stood up, eyes wide. "I knew it. Amara! Come look. Macy came home with a ball and chain!"

RJ and Sebrina burst into her cubicle laughing, RJ bouncing with excitement. "We want to hear everything!" he said.

Macy blinked, overwhelmed by the rush of attention. Her throat tightened. She fought to keep the tears at bay. Then came the familiar clicking of heels. Amara emerged from her office, arms crossed, lips twitching with restrained amusement.

"Well," she said, surveying the scene and the sparkle on Macy's hand, "either a miracle happened, or Macy finally realized Cade's a total catch."

Macy's heart thudded. *I can't tell them what happened. Not yet. I have to keep it together until I know where things stand.*

She pasted on a smile, swallowing the ache in her chest.

"Both might be true."

"You're not wrong," Sebrina said, leaning in to examine the ring. "This is serious bling, girl. Have you set a date? Or is it too soon for that?"

Macy hesitated, suddenly self-conscious. "Well…not exactly. Cade really wanted to lock something down, but I want to take our time and make sure it's the right date."

"Girl, you know he just wants to lock you down," RJ teased, waggling his eyebrows.

Everyone laughed, and Macy leaned back in her chair, letting herself enjoy the moment for just a beat longer. Then Amara clapped her hands.

"Okay, okay—celebrations later. Macy, come to my office. I have something I need to talk to you about."

The mood shifted instantly. RJ and Sebrina exchanged wide-eyed glances. Macy's face drained of color. Her fingers instinctively twisted around the gold chain at her neck.

This can't be happening. Not again. I don't even know where I stand with Cade. Please don't let me lose my job, too.

Amara gave what passed for her version of a laugh and waved off the dramatics. "I've got feedback from the client on her dashboard. You two can get the rest of your gossip at lunch. Macy?"

Macy followed Amara into her office, trying to keep her tears in check.

"Breathe," Amara said, settling into her chair. "You look like a dog about to have its bone snatched."

Without preamble, she continued. "The client loved your dashboard. They specifically mentioned how intuitive and clean your layout was. And your data hierarchy? Perfect. They've already requested a secondary version with extended metrics."

Relief flooded Macy's chest, and for the first time since New Year's Eve, she smiled. "Really? That's amazing!"

"Yes," Amara said, nodding. "Which is why, as of next week, you'll officially be our data solutions lead. It comes with a nice salary bump and a full-time analyst to support you."

Macy blinked. "I—yes—you, I mean—thank—yes! Wait—"

Amara barked out a rare, genuine laugh. "We'll get you some practice in presenting."

She leaned forward. "I knew you were wasted in an assistant role the moment Brett handed me your résumé. I promised him it would only be temporary until I could secure you a better offer. You've earned this. I'll get your contract and official offer letter to you by lunch. You'll move to the empty cubicle on the other side of Sebrina."

Macy giggled, barely containing her excitement. "Thank you, Amara. For believing in me. I won't let you down."

"I know you won't. I've short-listed candidates for your support analyst. After lunch, review their portfolios and start arranging final interviews. Ready or not, you're about to be a manager. The final decision is yours."

Amara gestured toward the door. "And if you want to knock to get RJ and Sebrina off the other side of that, go ahead. I'm sure they've already overheard everything."

Sure enough, the door swung open, and RJ stood there, sheepish, holding a coffee. "Another coffee, Amara?"

She rolled her eyes. "Page 57 of the survival guide, RJ."

He ducked and retreated, and Macy followed him out, laughing. For the first time in days, she really believed she was going to be okay. She quickly texted her mother: *Big news to share tonight. No, I'm not pregnant.* Then, a group message to Nina and Catherine about the promotion. And finally, one last message to Cade.

She stepped into Sebrina's cubicle, where RJ was already waiting.

Sebrina looked up and gasped. "You got it, didn't you?!"

Macy nodded. "I got it."

The small crowd erupted into cheers, sweeping her into a whirlwind of hugs and high-fives.

Her phone lit up with messages.

Mom
We look forward to hearing all abcut it tonight!

Catherine and Nina
Hel! yeah!!

But still, nothing from Cade.

Still buzzing from her conversation with Amara, Macy packed up her personal items and moved into her new cubicle beside Sebrina. She swapped laptops, organized her desk, and tried to settle into the new rhythm. Though her official duties as data solutions lead hadn't begun, Amara wasted no time assigning her fresh projects.

That afternoon, Macy began skimming through the analyst candidate files Amara had handed her. Two stood out: Brielle Chapman and Steve Puttnam. Steve was scheduled for Wednesday morning, and Brielle for that afternoon. Both had already survived interviews with Amara and endured RJ and Sebrina's informal vetting. They were holding back their opinions until Macy had hers.

By the end of the day, Macy packed up to leave with her coworkers, only to freeze when she saw Cade waiting at the door. A single tear rolled down his cheek. In his hands was a stunning bouquet of red and white stargazer lilies.

Macy's heart raced. She reached out tentatively and accepted the bouquet. Cade swiped at his eyes, trying to compose himself.

Before she could speak, RJ and Sebrina spotted him and rushed forward.

RJ sighed dramatically. "We heard she got a title upgrade over the holidays. She was too busy for us today, so we need the full scoop!"

Sebrina grinned and extended a hand. "You locking her down before some Wall Street exec poaches her?"

Cade chuckled as they all stepped into the elevator. "Funny you mention that. I'm on this side of town handling onboarding paperwork for my new job down the street. Thought I'd stop in and see her."

Sebrina pressed the button for the lobby as they all turned to look at Cade. "What's with the tears?"

"I'm just…proud of her." He reached for Macy's hand and laced his fingers through hers. "I think we have a lot to talk about on the train ride home. You still want to be commute buddies?"

Sebrina swooned. "Okay, that's adorable."

RJ made a sour face. "I don't know, man. You two together on the train every day and married? Sounds like a sitcom waiting to happen."

Everyone laughed, and Macy smiled too, because she was expected to. But inside, her thoughts ran rampant.

Why is he here instead of meeting me at home? Or even outside the building?

Are we going to talk about what happened? Or is this his way of pretending it didn't?

He curled their joined hands to his lips and kissed the back of her knuckles. Macy held on like he was the eye of the storm swirling around her.

They stepped out into the winter evening, the city still glowing with the remnants of the holidays. RJ and Sebrina buzzed with questions about the proposal, the ring, and where they were registered, despite them not being registered anywhere yet. Macy headed toward her usual entrance to catch the 4 train while RJ and Sebrina peeled off in the opposite direction.

Finally, she and Cade were alone.

"Where are you going?" he asked, still holding her hand.

"My train…?" Macy replied, uncertain.

He pressed her hand to his chest, over his heart. "Please come home with me. You don't know how much I've missed you."

She hesitated. Part of her wanted to run to him, let the tension of the last few days melt away. But another part feared the conversation would pick up right where it left off: sharp, unresolved, and raw.

"I need to call my parents," she said. "They don't know about the promotion yet, and I promised I'd call tonight."

"You have a cell phone," he said gently. "Call them from my place. Please, just come with me. You've got clothes there. You know I want it to be your place, too. I'll make dinner, and we'll figure this out. Please?"

At last, she caved, stepping into the warmth of his chest. "You still want it to be my place, too?"

He wrapped her in his arms, resting his cheek against her head and breathing her in. "If it's what you want."

"I want you to fight for me, Cade," she whispered. "Don't just walk away when we disagree. I've had no idea where we stood these past few days, or if we were even still together."

"Of course we are," he said, as if New Year's Eve had never happened. "I'm in this for the long haul, Macy. I just need to know that you are, too."

"Why do you think I was blowing up your phone?" she asked, a faint smile tugging at her lips.

He began guiding her toward the A train tunnel, and she let herself be led.

"I don't even want to wait until we get home to settle this," he said. "If you feel that strongly about December…then December it is."

Macy gasped and threw her arms around him. "Thank you, Cade! You'll see, a winter wedding in New York will be perfect."

He smiled, his face finally relaxed. "Whatever you want, Mace."

"I just had a thought," she said. "I'll swing by home and grab another bag of stuff. That way, I can tell Catherine in person. You go start cooking something to wine and dine me with, and I'll meet you there."

Cade hesitated. "Are you sure that's a good idea? She already hates me. Won't this just add fuel to the fire?"

"I don't see how it would," Macy replied. "She was there on New Year's Eve. She witnessed the fight. She'll want to know we've worked it out. And that she doesn't need to wait up for me tonight."

Cade laughed to himself. "I suppose you're probably right. Don't be late."

Then, for the first time since before their fight, he kissed her. It wasn't a casual, see-you-later kiss; it was a kiss that meant business. Macy melted into it, surprised by the heat, the certainty.

"I'll put these in water for you," he said, taking the bouquet and releasing her hand as she turned toward the subway entrance.

On the train ride home, Macy let her thoughts race. At least for now, they were back on track. But the knot in her stomach hadn't fully unraveled. She still didn't feel completely settled about what had happened. And she doubted she would until they actually talked about it. Still, the kiss had meant something. And that had to count.

She stepped through the door to her apartment and was instantly met with confetti poppers and champagne corks. Catherine and Nina were cheering. Theo and Shane stood nearby, holding a banner that read, "Congratulations, Macy!"

She laughed, touched despite everything, and hugged each of them tightly. "You guys didn't have to do this."

"Of course we did," Catherine said. "You got promoted, boss lady!"

Macy smiled and accepted a glass of champagne, but still, the hairs on the back of her neck stood at attention. Her friends were all hesitant, as if they were all waiting to see which version of her had walked through the door. The room, for all its cheer, didn't quite crackle with the excitement she'd expected.

"I have to tell you," Macy said, raising her voice over the music, "Cade and I made up. He's come around to my idea of December for the wedding."

The response was more subdued than she'd anticipated. Catherine lifted her glass but didn't speak. Nina took a long sip of champagne, eyes darting back and forth between Macy and Catherine. Theo glanced at Shane, then back at Macy.

"That's...something," Catherine finally said. "I'm glad he's willing to meet you halfway."

"I just hope it stays that way," Theo added quietly.

Macy paused, her smile faltering. "I thought...I thought you'd all be a little happier that he came around to my idea."

Catherine stepped forward, her voice softer now. "We are, Mace. We just...love you. And we saw how upset you were. It's not that we aren't happy for you, it's that we want to make sure you're happy. And not just pushing ahead because it's easier than pulling back."

The knot in Macy's stomach loosened slightly. "I get that. I do. I'm still figuring everything out. But we're talking, and we're trying. That has to count for something, right?"

"Of course it does," Shane said. "We've got your back, no matter what."

Macy nodded, the disappointment easing as she recognized what was really behind their hesitation: care. "Thank you. That means a lot."

She glanced at the time. "I still need to call my parents and pack a few more things."

"Go," Catherine said with a warm smile. "We'll be here when you're ready."

She disappeared into her bedroom with her laptop, at last alone with her thoughts.

They saw that look on his face. The pain in his eyes. The way his voice cracked when he asked why I said yes, if I meant it. I don't know what made him finally come around, but he did.

Macy took a deep breath and opened her phone, hovering over the FaceTime icon. Her family had been waiting. She pressed "Send."

The call connected almost instantly.

Rebecca's face lit up. "Hi, Mace! Dad's on his way in, but we couldn't wait to hear what you have to say. Should we wait for Ethan and Joy?"

"Hi, Mom! If they come in, they're welcome to stay, but it's okay if you want to fill them in later."

George entered the frame and sat beside Rebecca. "I think they're at a doctor's appointment for the baby. Just routine."

"Well, I won't hold up the news. As I said in the text, I have some big news." She grinned. "Amara told me today that the client loved my dashboard. And…I've been promoted to data solutions lead!"

Rebecca's eyes widened. "Macy, that's incredible!"

George's expression softened into a proud smile. "They finally realized what they've got, huh?"

"That's not all—I'm getting my own analyst. I'm officially someone's boss!"

Just then, Catherine popped her head into the room. "Wait, you didn't tell me that part! Hi, Mr. and Mrs. Walker!"

Rebecca waved. "Good to see you, Catherine!"

Macy ushered her back out with a laugh, but not before Catherine added, "Did you tell them the other thing?"

Macy groaned, covering her face. "Not yet, Catherine. I was working up to that. Thanks for the segue!"

Catherine winked. "My work here is done. Bye, Mr. and Mrs. Walker!"

George and Rebecca chuckled at the exchange.

"I'm so glad things are working out for you two," Rebecca said. "How did she take the news about you and Cade getting married?"

"Well, Mom, funny you should ask…"

Macy smiled nervously. "The other thing is, Cade and I have set a general timeline for the wedding."

George's breath hitched slightly. "And?"

"We're targeting December."

George nodded slowly. Rebecca's posture loosened. "We're happy to hear you're taking it slow. You've had a lot come at you recently, and taking a year to plan is smart."

Macy's heart warmed. "Thanks, Dad."

"And don't even think about going dress shopping without me," Rebecca added. "Can you imagine it, George? Dress shopping in New York City!"

Macy laughed. "We'd be thrilled to host if you came in for a weekend. Make sure Joy's home for that one, too!"

"You got it, baby girl," Rebecca said. "We'll let you go, but we're only a call away if you need us."

She arrived at Cade's just in time for dinner. The apartment was warm with the scent of garlic and rosemary, something bubbling gently on the stove. Smooth jazz floated in from a Bluetooth speaker tucked somewhere in the bedroom. Cade stood at the counter wearing an apron that read "Kiss the Cook."

"Wow," Macy said, smiling. "You went all out, didn't you?"

He didn't look up, but focused on stirring the pot. "I'm proud of you. Hope the conversation with your parents went well?"

"It did," she said, stepping closer. "Do you want to tell me what changed your mind?"

"About the wedding?" He leaned his head back, finally meeting her eyes. "I thought about what you said. About wanting to savor things, not just rush through them. I guess I realized…maybe I've been running so fast toward the future that I haven't stopped to enjoy the present."

Macy studied his face, searching for something beneath the words. "That means a lot, Cade. Thank you."

He kissed her knuckles and set their plates on the table, eyes dropping quickly from her face back to the task at hand.

"It feels like something's still bothering you," Macy said gently.

He looked up at her and smiled. "Of course not. I just started feeling a little off earlier. I'm downsizing the morphine again, so it's probably just my body adjusting. I took one of my emergency pills to take the edge off. I'll be fine."

He reached for her bun and tugged it loose, letting her curls fall around her shoulders. "You know I prefer it when you doll yourself up and wear your hair down."

"Yeah, I know," she said quietly. "It's been a stressful few days."

A beat passed.

"You know," he said, voice casual, "if December starts to feel too far away…we can always adjust."

Her stomach tensed. She smiled anyway.

"We'll see," she said, keeping her tone light.

He leaned in, voice low. "Now, we just fought and made up. Want to go finish making up properly?"

Macy recoiled at his words. Her body didn't respond with warmth or longing, only a soft shudder. The idea of being intimate right now, of folding herself into him as if nothing had happened, made her skin crawl. She didn't want closeness as a shortcut to resolution. She wanted clarity. Safety. Space to breathe.

She forced a smile, nodding toward the table. "Let's eat first. I'm starving."

Cade grinned and turned back to the stove, seemingly satisfied.

Macy sat down, her heart thudding. *One step at a time,* she reminded herself. *But not that step. Not tonight.*

Part Six

Raising the Stakes

Celeste's Office

"It's hard to say when things started to shift, really," I said, my voice low but steady. "The only way to really explain it is—I was the frog on the hotplate, and he was the sadistic freak turning the dial."

Coming to Celeste's office was starting to feel natural. Familiar. Safe. Five months had passed since I arrived in Boston, and I hadn't heard a whisper from Cade. I wouldn't let my guard down—not yet. But here, in this softly lit room with candles flickering and the quiet hum of the city outside, I could breathe.

"It was the little things at first," I continued. "After the love bombing, he used my feelings to get me to say 'I love you' before I even knew if I meant it. Catherine was right—he manipulated me into letting him stay over that first night. But it didn't feel like pressure. He applied it so deliberately, so gently, I didn't even notice."

I paused. My fingers twisted in my lap, giving my gold chain a break.

Celeste looked up from her notes, her expression as composed as ever. "That analogy makes a lot of sense. It's a common dynamic in coercive relationships. Manipulation, guilt, gaslighting—these are tools used to erode someone's sense of self over time."

"I wonder sometimes if he ever really loved me," I said quietly. "Or if I was just a means to an end. Something he could mold into what he wanted."

"That's a painful question, and a fair one," Celeste said. "But love, for someone with those traits, often looks very different than what we think of as love. It tends to revolve around control, not connection."

I swallowed hard. "Am I…co-dependent?" The words barely made it out.

Celeste placed a gentle hand over mine. "Codependency isn't who you are. It's a pattern. Usually learned. And often, people who are empathic, nurturing, and attuned to others' needs fall into these dynamics. That speaks more to your kindness than any flaw."

"I do tend to wear my heart on my sleeve," I murmured. "So, it really wasn't anything I did wrong, was it? He took advantage of me."

The thought echoed louder each time it passed through my mind. My face hardened. My hands balled into fists, and my body tensed.

Celeste tilted her head gently. "You look like you're feeling something right now."

"I'm angry!" It burst out of me, sudden and sharp. The rage I should have felt years ago—buried under fear, sadness, guilt—finally broke through. I stood up from the couch and began pacing, unsure what to do with the heat rising in my chest. "I was vulnerable, and he knew it. He used it. And then he made me believe I was the problem. How dare he!"

Celeste's voice was calm but firm. "This is an important moment. Let yourself feel that anger. It's been waiting to be heard for a long time."

Feeling strangely proud of my anger, tension I didn't realize I had been carrying drained from my shoulders. I was starting to see it clearly now: things hadn't been perfect, not like he wanted me to believe. But he made it feel like the imperfections were mine. That I was the one holding us back. That's how he got me to agree to move the wedding up."

I paused, letting the memory settle.

"So, Cade had agreed to wait for the wedding, but it wasn't really over. Not for him. I'm realizing now, he wasn't giving in. He was waiting. It was another manipulation. A peace offering, just long enough to regroup. He was recalibrating his angle. Waiting for a new opening."

I met Celeste's eyes. "And the worst part? I think a piece of me was relieved. That I didn't have to keep fighting. That maybe if I gave him what he wanted, things would go back to easy. But of course, they didn't."

Celeste nodded once, gently. "What happened after that?"

I sank back into the couch, my voice steadier now. "The weeks that followed…they were weirdly quiet. Like the calm after a storm, before you realize you're in the eye of it. Cade was on his best behavior again. Sweet. He kept saying how happy he was that we were back on track."

I twisted the chain around my fingers again. "Work got busier. Amara promoted me to lead, and I started building out my team. We brought on a new analyst, Brielle Chapman. She came from a cybersecurity background and walked in with the kind of confidence I used to envy. There was another candidate, too, Steve. Nice guy, but too timid. Just not the right fit."

Celeste tilted her head. "That sounds like a big transition."

"It was. And Cade had just started his new job near my building, so looking in from the outside, everything was lining up. I was juggling more at work, we were settling into a routine at his place, and I kept telling myself: this is what normal looks like."

I paused, thinking about how tightly I'd clung to that idea.

"I was supposed to be fully moved out of Catherine's by the end of January. It didn't happen until almost March. I told myself it was logistics. But honestly…I think I was stalling. Like once I moved all the way in, there wouldn't be any excuse to hit pause if I needed to."

Celeste stayed quiet, giving me space.

"That's when he started turning the heat up again," I said softly.

Chapter Twenty-Four

NO TURNING BACK

Cade stood watching as Shane and the women moved boxes out of Macy's apartment. He would help get them inside, but it wouldn't do for him to strain his back just yet. The last thing he needs is to give her one more reason to stall on moving in.

That was how it happened, wasn't it? People had dreams—bright, golden dreams—and then when they start getting them, they get scared and withdraw. They'll use any excuse: Responsibility. Distractions. Doubt. That's what had happened to Hannah. She got overwhelmed and withdrew. But him? He had to hold it all together. Start over.

Was Macy starting to do it, too?

He could already see the pattern: hesitation about her feelings. Her job, pulling her away. Theo, hovering too close. Then her damn brother made it clear he prefers the neighbor for her. A month to move in became three. She was still insisting they "take her time" planning the wedding. But he'd seen this movie before, and wasn't interested in a sequel. "Taking time" became "needing space," which became "growing apart." Which became Hannah.

No. He wasn't going to let another woman slip through his hands just because she got spooked by real life.

He wasn't the villain here. He was the one fighting for their marriage.

Macy had been through hell, but so had he. That was why he was trying so hard. But her friends and her brother didn't see it. Catherine especially. She wore that faux-concern like a virtue badge, always skeptical, always watching. Joy had looked at him like she expected a confession. And Ethan, pretending his remark was harmless. But Cade saw the way that neighbor looked at Macy. It wasn't innocent.

They didn't get it. He needed to protect what was his.

Macy was someone worth anchoring to. She was soft where he was sharp, hopeful in a way he'd forgotten how to be. She just needed help staying the course. It was easy to get distracted in this city. Easy to listen to people who thought they knew better. She'd come to him broken. He would be damned if someone was going to sweep her off her feet now that he had made her whole.

He was the good guy. He just had to remind everyone of that. Because in the end, it was about holding on and finally getting what he deserved.

Tears pooled in the corners of Catherine's eyes. "I think that's the last of your things, other than your bedroom furniture."

"You might as well keep that," Macy said, brushing a hand over the doorframe. "I've got no need for it at the new place, even if we had the room. Plus, it'll give you a ready-made space for when Shane steps out of line and needs to sleep in the doghouse."

"Heard that!" Shane called from the hallway, hauling the last box of Macy's cookware out the door.

"Who says I didn't mean for you to hear it?" Macy shot back.

Catherine laughed, wiping her eyes. Cade had rented a pickup truck to haul the final load to his place. While he was out of earshot, Catherine leaned in and said quietly, "It's here for you, too, if you ever need it."

"Thanks, Cath. I know things will be different, but you'll still see a lot of me."

"I hope so," Catherine said, squeezing her hand.

Macy picked up her last duffel bag and scanned the apartment one more time. "Oh, the Switch! Think I can talk Cade into a game night before we head to the other side of the park?"

"Yes! And we'll order pizza."

Macy dashed outside to catch Cade's attention. She tossed the duffel into the back of the truck and relayed the plan to him and Shane. Cade looked down at her with a tenderness she hadn't seen since before Christmas. Her heart stuttered as she relayed the plan.

"Pizza and gaming, huh?"

She bounced on her toes and grabbed his hand. "Can we?"

"How could I say no to that face?"

Shane headed back upstairs, and Macy led the way to their favorite pizza shop around the corner. Twenty minutes later, they returned, boxes in hand. As they were about to turn the key in the apartment door, Theo poked his head out of his own door.

"Theo! Is it takeout time?"

He gave her his warmest smile and wrapped her in a hug. "You know me well, Mace." He extended a hand toward Cade, who took it, slowly, but Macy noticed the way Cade's jaw tightened. His eyes never left Theo's face.

The door to Macy's apartment swung open, and Catherine stepped out to greet them. "Theo! Where have you been, stranger? Cade, Macy, come in! Theo, if you're not too full of Chinese chicken later, please come back."

Theo flashed his dimples, though his eyes held a trace of sadness. "I might do that, thank you, Catherine. I haven't caught up with Shane yet. I'm sure he's got stories. But I wonder if I could talk to Macy alone for a minute."

Catherine nodded and headed back inside. "Of course. You know where to find us."

Macy barely had time to respond before Cade grabbed her by the arms and kissed her hard. He never took his eyes off Theo. "Don't be long."

As the door closed behind him, Theo shook his head. "I wanted to tell you how sorry I am for the last time we met, Macy. You and Catherine have become my best friends these past few months, and I don't want there to be any bad blood."

Macy waved him off, relieved that this was what he wanted to talk about. "Don't even worry about it, Theo. You're just looking out for me. I didn't have much of that from anyone but my family until I came here, and I appreciate you."

"Good. I'm glad. I know you're moving out today, so I really hope this isn't goodbye."

She placed a gentle hand on his arm. "Of course it's not goodbye. Catherine's still here, so I'll be popping in and out all the time. And we have these crazy little devices called 'cell phones.' I know you know how to use them…occasionally, they can be used for something other than takeout." She winked.

Theo grinned, his full megawatt smile returning. "Perfect. Okay, I'll let you go. I know he's probably seething." He winced, realizing what he'd said. "Sorry!"

Macy rolled her eyes at him, but smiled. "I hope we'll see you later, Theo."

She gave him a lingering hug before opening the door to her apartment to rejoin her other friends. They had set the table, and Cade was plating slices of pizza while Catherine poured red wine into a decanter. As soon as he saw her, Cade's eyes flicked toward Macy, darkening with suspicion.

"What was that all about?" he asked.

"It was nothing," Macy said quickly, grabbing a wine glass and sliding into a seat. She hadn't told him about her last conversation with Theo. It didn't feel right to keep things from him, but she also knew the truth would only stir up more tension. "He knew I was getting the last of my things tonight and wanted to make sure it was a 'see you later,' not a 'goodbye.'"

Cade didn't look convinced. "Why's he so worried about that? And why can't he ask it in front of me?"

A chill ran through Macy's chest. Her heart picked up speed. *Not tonight. Not in front of Catherine.* She kept her voice calm. "He's seen a lot of people come and go in this building. He said I was one of the few who felt like family. He didn't want to lose another friend. That's all."

Cade narrowed his eyes, but said nothing more.

Dinner passed in relative calm, and soon, the gaming system was fired up.

"Don't forget I'm Peach!" Shane announced.

Catherine laughed and swatted at him. "You can be Peach as long as I'm Bowser."

"You're both nuts," Macy said. "Everyone knows Toad is the best."

"Unless you're facing Yoshi," Cade added.

They gathered around the TV, each grabbing a controller. One game turned into three, then five. Laughter filled the room, and for a while, the tension faded.

Until the door opened, and Theo stepped inside.

Macy looked up and made a quick decision. Better to leave on a high note.

"Well, Cade," she said brightly, "we should probably get that truck unloaded before someone starts rifling through it. And I think Theo's going to need a controller."

"You've already got one of those, Macy," Theo muttered under his breath. He hugged her tightly, promising to stay in touch, and shook Cade's hand.

Catherine walked Macy to the door, where she held out her key.

"I don't want that," Catherine said, waving it away.

"But…"

"No," she said firmly. "That stays with you. The door is always open."

They hugged tightly, tears slipping down their cheeks as they shared a quiet, tear-soaked smile.

"I'm just on the other side of the park," Macy whispered.

Still, walking down those stairs was different in its finality. Life was about to change. Now, there was no going back.

Cade waited in the truck. Once Macy buckled herself in, she took one last, lingering look up at her old bedroom window. It disappeared behind them as Cade pulled away. He reached over and took her hand. "I should take care of my lady when we get home."

They rode the rest of the way in silence. When they reached the apartment, Cade followed her inside and said, "Go get into your bathrobe. Ten minutes."

She looked up, puzzled. "Why?"

"You'll see."

Rather than question it, Macy did as he asked. She kicked off her shoes, wiped the makeup from her face, and slipped out of her clothes, wrapping herself in her bathrobe. From the hallway, she could hear water running and smell the soft, soothing warmth of vanilla.

"Mmm," she murmured under her breath.

She padded into the bathroom and found Cade crouched near the tub, lighting a candle. The room glowed in golden flickers. A fresh towel hung neatly on the rack. A mug of hot chocolate steamed on the edge of the tub.

"You read my mind," she said quietly. "Though I don't know how, because I didn't even realize this was what I needed."

"A hot bath always helps me unwind," he said. "You've been working hard. I figured you could use an hour just for yourself. I'll empty the truck while you relax."

He stepped toward her, slowly easing the bathrobe from her shoulders. He kissed her collarbone, his hand grazing the small of her back.

"Don't feel obligated to get dressed when you're done."

She giggled softly, shy but grateful, and sank into the warm water. Cade closed the door gently behind him, leaving her alone with the flickering candlelight and her hot chocolate.

This right here, she thought. He knows me better than I know myself sometimes. This is what I needed. He really gets me. It's nice to feel seen.

She woke up the following morning to an empty bed. Boxes and suitcases lined the bedroom, waiting to be processed. From the kitchen, she heard the clanging of pots and pans and the comforting crackle of a percolating coffee pot. She groaned slightly as she stretched and rubbed the rest of the sleep out of her eyes, not ready to get up and face the day just yet.

The bedroom door swung open, and Cade swept in with a pair of mugs in hand. He set her mug on her nightstand and pulled her up into a lingering kiss. "Good morning, beautiful."

Macy blushed and reached for her coffee. "Thank you. Why don't you join me?"

Cade sat on one of the boxes next to her side of the bed, blowing the steam away before taking a tentative sip. After a long pause, trying to sound casual, he asked, "So…when are you going to try on dresses?"

Macy hesitated for half a beat. "Oh, I'm not in a hurry. December is long enough away. I've earmarked a few in the magazine Sheryl gave me, though I'll never be able to afford them." She shrugged casually. "Why do you ask?"

He exhaled sharply through his nose, a sound that carried more disappointment than he probably intended.

"It's just…" He climbed up into the bed next to her, putting an arm around her shoulders. "I've been thinking. December's still so far off. I don't want this part of our life to feel like we're in a holding pattern."

"It's not a holding pattern," she said gently. "We're planning. Things are moving forward. Maybe not quickly, but we've looked at a few venues, and once we find one with a date we like, things will come together from there."

"I know," he said. "But think about it, Macy. Spring in New York is gorgeous, too. We've already started planning. Why wait nine more months?"

Macy set her coffee down and turned to face him. "Because it's what we agreed on."

His gaze didn't waver. "Plans can change. They do all the time. I just think we're ready. I'm ready. Aren't you?"

"I am," she said slowly. "But I also want a wedding I can breathe during. One I'm not racing toward. We already talked about this."

"I know," he said again—too quickly.

He paused, then added, "It's just…I hate dragging this out. I don't like long engagements. Something bad always happens before…before the big day."

He stumbled over the words, like he'd meant to say something else.

Macy's breath caught as her chest tightened. She wondered what he'd meant to say, but decided not to press. But in her heart, she knew the conversation about the date wasn't over, by a long shot.

He smiled affectionately and leaned in to kiss her temple. "We'll talk more later," he said. "No pressure. I just want you to be my wife. I don't want anything standing in our way."

But the way he said no pressure felt an awful lot like pressure.

Chapter Twenty-Five

MACY BENDS

March passed in a blur as the weeks folded into each other. On Friday afternoon in the last week of the month, Amara poked her head into Macy's cubicle. "Hey, Macy? Got a minute?"

Startled, Macy jumped slightly in her chair. "Yes, of course."

She followed Amara into her office and closed the door behind them. "Is everything okay?"

"Yes, Macy. Nothing urgent. But there's something I need to talk to you about. And I'm not the only one who's noticed."

Macy's eyes flickered wide, and the familiar chill of anxiety bloomed across her body. "Okay. I'm listening."

"Your work's been top-tier, so that's not the issue. But your phone…" Amara paused, choosing her words. "I know you're planning a wedding, you've got a new nephew, and a lot on your plate even outside of work. But your phone's been going off more than usual these past few weeks."

Macy's heart climbed into her throat. She usually only answered texts during breaks, but sometimes, those breaks happened at her desk. She knew how that must look. Her breathing quickened.

Amara held up a hand. "Before you spiral into a full-blown panic attack, let me be clear. You're not in trouble. Your work is solid, and I trust your judgment. But I need whoever it is to dial it down a notch before it *becomes* a problem. Let's keep it to emergencies or break time, okay?"

Macy nodded quickly, voice an octave higher than normal as she replied, "It's mostly Cade. He just gets a little…eager sometimes. Wedding stuff, job stuff. But I'll talk to him. I'll make sure it doesn't become a thing."

"I trust you will. How's Brielle working out?"

"She's brilliant," Macy said, grateful for the change of subject. Her heart rate began to settle. "We're working on the new health information management system. She's poking at the security, looking for holes. Her cyber-hacking skills are top-notch. She's already flagged a few things we've patched. Cade and I both considered cybersecurity for a while, but the field's so saturated. Brielle's got instincts I wouldn't have thought to follow."

"I'm glad to hear it," Amara said with a smile. "All right, back to it."

Back at Macy's desk, Brielle popped her head in. "I hope I didn't get you in trouble. Amara asked if we heard your text alert as often as she did. I told her you never answer it until break."

Macy stretched her neck and settled back into her chair. "It's fine. I just need to tell Cade to cool it a bit. He's just…overzealous."

Brielle giggled, the sound light and effervescent. "But the way he looks at you? It makes me swoon, and I'm just a bystander. Who wouldn't want that?"

"Heh, yeah. It's something I never thought I'd find, that's for sure."

She pulled out her phone and typed him a message.

Macy

Hey, I just got pulled into Amara's office for a chat. Everything's fine, but she asked if we could cut our

> *texting to breaks and emergencies. The alert going off all day is getting attention.*

Cade replied almost instantly:

> **Cade**
> *What did you tell her?*

> **Macy**
> *That it wasn't a problem. I'll turn off my ringer and only check my phone on breaks, away from my desk.*

> **Cade**
> *Is that more important than talking to your future husband?*

Macy stared at the screen.

> **Macy**
> *You know, Cade, sometimes I can't tell if you're joking about these things. You know how Amara is, and I have to be professional while I'm on the job.*

A pause.

Cade
I see.

She frowned at the screen, a sick feeling in her stomach, knowing his answer meant he was unhappy.

At lunch, Macy excused herself from her coworkers and stepped outside to call him.

"Cade, what's up with your text message?"

"What do you mean, what's up with it?" His voice was calm, but clipped. "I thought it was pretty clear. You're the most important thing in my universe, Macy. Am I not the same to you?"

Macy put her face in her free hand and sat at the break room table, rubbing her temple. "Of course you are, Cade. But my job matters, too. Who's going to cover my share of the bills if I lose it? When I'm here, work has to be my priority. That doesn't make you less important."

"Doesn't it, though?" he said, an edge of impatience creeping into his voice. "You just said your job is your priority. How does that not mean I'm second?"

Macy ran a hand through her hair, frustration rising. She stood and began pacing the break area, careful to keep her voice low. The last thing she needed was an argument with her whole team in earshot.

"Because, Cade, keeping this job is part of building our life together. If I lose it, I can't contribute. I need to be present here, for us."

She paused, trying to make her words land the way they made sense in her head. "Is something else bothering you? Did you drop your morphine dosage again?"

She heard a long sigh on the other end. "You're right. I'm a little off today. We did drop the dosage again. Trying to be off everything by the wedding. You're right, I'll shut up."

"I don't need you to shut up," she said gently. "Just…keep it to a minimum while I'm working. Unless it's an emergency."

His answering tone was slightly less edgy. "10-4, boss lady. Go eat something. I'll see you tonight."

Macy ended the call and turned to find Sebrina standing behind her.

"Everything all right?" Sebrina asked softly. "That sounded intense."

"We're okay. He's under a lot of pressure with his new job, and they're working on tapering down the meds again. He's just a little extra sharp right now. But I think I got through."

Sebrina studied her face, searching for the truth beneath the words. "Do you need a hug?"

"Please," Macy said, letting herself be pulled into a warm, office-mom embrace.

"Medication withdrawals can be brutal," Sebrina murmured. "I went through it with my brother. We were all navigating a minefield around him."

She smoothed Macy's hair and held her at arm's length. "And getting used to living together? That's a whole adjustment on its own. You've got a perfect storm going. But you love each other. You'll get through it. I hope you know, you can confide in me if you need to."

"Thanks, Sebrina," Macy said, wiping away a tear that had crept into the corner of her eye. "I saw this side of him once before, right after we got engaged. We had a huge fight about the wedding timeline. I honestly thought we were done before we even started."

"I've seen the way he looks at you. We all have. No matter how mad he gets, I think he'll always want to fix it."

Macy let her shoulders relax, the tension slowly draining from her spine. "Yeah. You're probably right."

She poured herself another coffee and, at the end of lunch, returned to her desk to finish patching the information system they were developing.

Just when her eyes were about to cross, Brielle popped into her cubicle with the latest test results. Her dark curls escaped a messy ponytail, oversized glasses sliding down her nose as she leaned over the partition. "This is looking much better. You're a computer person, so you know nothing's ever bug-free, but I think we're ready for testing."

"You're a marvel, Brielle. I just finished the patches. I'll get them loaded so you can find another twenty-three bugs tomorrow."

Brielle laughed and lifted Macy's mood instantly. "It's just about time we got out of here. Is your man going to be waiting at the elevator again?"

"Maybe!" Macy grinned. "Either that or lurking by the subway tunnel."

She stood and peeked over the wall into Sebrina's cubicle. "You two ready?"

Sebrina was powering down her computer, gathering her things. RJ rounded the corner with his coat in hand. Brielle and Macy joined them, calling out a cheerful "Goodnight!" to Amara as they headed out together.

The elevator entry to their floor was quiet, save for the receptionist shutting down for the night. Macy scanned the space, trying not to show her disappointment. Cade wasn't there.

Maybe he'd left the office late and was still on his way up. But she wasn't counting on it. She stepped into the waiting elevator and rode down to the lobby.

Now that she was taking the A train home to the apartment she shared with Cade, she walked in the same direction as RJ. Sebrina and Brielle both took the R to Brooklyn, so they said their goodnights and headed off in opposite directions.

"So, how are wedding plans going?" RJ asked.

"Well, we're still trying to figure out a venue before we can lock in a date, so it's moving slowly." Seeing Cade standing in the subway tunnel, waiting for her, she quickly pivoted on RJ. "Hey, are you bringing a date to the wedding?"

RJ laughed. "Nice try, Mace."

"Oh, come on!" she groaned.

He winked. "Your groom awaits. I'll see you in the morning."

RJ gave Cade a nod and called out, "Enjoy your night, kids!"

Cade turned his full attention to Macy. Unsure where they stood after the tension earlier, she kept her eyes down at his feet, suddenly shy.

"Sorry, I didn't make it up to the office," he said. "Didn't want to risk leaving before five and getting in trouble, so I figured I'd meet you here. I would've texted, but I didn't want to get you in trouble."

The hint of disdain in his tone made Macy flinch. "Please don't be like that."

"Like what?" he asked, feigning innocence. "I get it. Your job's important. I just didn't expect to feel like a nuisance for missing you."

Macy lowered her head and started walking toward the tunnel. "I thought we were past this. You know why I said what I did."

They rode in silence from the tunnel, through the train ride, and all the way home. Macy couldn't find the words that wouldn't make things worse.

When they reached the apartment, Cade unlocked the door and gestured her inside. He took off his coat and shoes and placed them neatly in the closet. Macy did the same, hanging up her purse.

Without a word, she headed into the kitchen and began prepping tacos. It wasn't the silent treatment, not exactly. But she didn't trust herself to speak without triggering another argument. As Sebrina said, it was like navigating a minefield.

"I mean it, Mace," Cade said, his voice softer now. "I'm sorry for how I acted. But I need to get something off my chest. It's the meds, yeah. But it's more than that."

Macy looked up from the counter, fear flickering in her eyes. "What is it?"

He hesitated, then stepped closer. "I just…I never thought I'd get a second chance like this. I lost Hannah before we ever got to say, 'I do.' And now, with you, I feel like I'm losing again. Like I'm always the one who wants more."

He poured himself a glass of Pinot Grigio and sat at the table, facing the kitchen.

"I'm trying not to take everything personally, Macy. I really am. But it's hard not to feel like maybe you're not as sure about this as I am."

"Is this about the wedding date?" she asked quietly.

"That's part of it." He took a sip of wine. "But it's more than that. It's how everything else seems to come first: your job, your friends, even the planning itself. It really stung today when you said your job is your priority. I understand the logic, but I want to be your priority the way you are mine."

He looked at her, eyes heavy with emotion. "I'd walk out of my job tomorrow if you asked me to. Because you matter more. I'm not trying to pressure you, but I'm starting to feel like I'm always the last thing on your list. And that's hard, Macy. I don't want to beg to be your priority.

"I mean, you were more concerned about hurting Catherine's feelings when you moved out than about how delaying would make me feel," Cade said, voice rising. "Aren't I your future? She doesn't even like me! She's trying to interfere with our marriage before it's even started, and you still call her your best friend. Or your goddamn neighbor, Theo! You let him flirt with you right in front of me and don't even think about how that makes me feel!"

The longer he spoke, the louder he got. He couldn't sit still. Macy gasped, sputtering in disbelief. They'd already had this conversation. She thought it was resolved.

"Catherine has never tried to come between us," she said, her voice rising to match his. "She's protective of me, that's all. And we've talked about Theo! He knows I'm with you, and he's not the kind of guy to pursue someone who's already involved with someone else. I would *never* flirt with someone else, especially not in front of you. And giving Catherine notice was just a courtesy. You agreed with me!"

"I agreed because you didn't give me much choice!" Cade snapped. "But you dragged out moving, just like you're dragging out the wedding date. It's been over two months, and we still don't have a date or a venue."

He paused to sip his wine. When he spoke again, his voice was quieter, but heavy with sorrow. "I just don't understand it, Macy. I'd marry you tomorrow. I'm all in. I thought I'd shown that from the start. But every time I think we're moving forward, you pull back. And I get it, you've been hurt. But dammit, so have I. Why does everything have to be on your timeline? If you can't see all of that, maybe I'm the only one truly fighting for us."

He walked out of the kitchen, placed his glass on the coffee table, and sank into the couch with his head in his hands.

Macy stood frozen, as if she'd been punched in the gut. *Am I really the problem?*

He spoke again, filling the silence she couldn't yet break. "Maybe I messed this up by wanting it too much. I made you feel pressured, and now you're pulling away. You don't have to worry. I won't bring it up again."

Her mind spiraled. How can I make this right? How do I show him I'm just as committed?

There was really only one way.

But what would everyone think?

Isn't that the problem? I'm more worried about what other people think than about what's right for us. What if I just say yes?

She stepped into the living room and turned on the light. "Cade?"

He didn't look up.

"Cade, look at me."

He wiped his face and lifted his eyes to hers—dark blue, still wet with tears.

"What if we compromise?" she said softly. Her heart thundered in her ears. "What if we don't wait until December?"

"What do you mean?"

Her hands trembled at her sides. This was the moment. Once she said it, it couldn't be unsaid.

"The fall," she whispered. "What if we move it to, like, September?"

For a second, he just stared at her, like he was afraid to trust what he'd heard.

"Why not summer?"

She swallowed. Every instinct in her body screamed that this was too fast. Too reactive. But his face held so much hope. So much need.

"Okay," she said.

The relief was immediate and overwhelming.

He surged to his feet and swept her into his arms, spinning her as if the weight that had crushed him moments before had vanished. When he set her down, he cupped her face and kissed her with an urgency that stole her breath.

"I love you, Macy," he whispered. "Thank you."

"I love you, too," she said. And she meant it, even as a quiet tremor of uncertainty rippled through her.

"We should tell everyone," he said, energized now. "Now. Before we lose momentum. And you should order one of those dresses, now!"

Her stomach fluttered. "I'll…I'll tell my family. You should probably call your parents, too."

He nodded, already reaching for his phone. "They're going to be thrilled."

Chapter Twenty-Six

ON THE LINE

Macy retreated into the bedroom, her steps slow despite the rush in her veins. She sat against the pillows, phone heavy in her hands. She leaned into the stillness of the room to steady her nerves.

Her fingers hovered over Nina's contact. This one, at least, should be easy. She pressed the FaceTime icon, and Nina answered on the second ring.

"Hey, cousin! What's up? Did he finally lock down the guest list or something?"

Macy let out a nervous breath. "We moved the wedding up."

Nina's smile froze. "Up…how far up?"

"Summer."

For a split second, Nina's expression flickered from surprise to calculation before the performer snapped back into place.

"Summer?" she shrieked. "Shut up. No, don't shut up. Tell me everything. Are we doing early summer florals? Rooftop? Garden? Oh, my God, I need to start a Pinterest board immediately—"

Macy laughed weakly, sinking back against the pillows. "You're…you're okay with this?"

"Okay with it?" Nina scoffed. "Mace, I live for chaos. And mad, passionate love. And dramatic timelines. This is on brand for you right now."

That should've comforted her more than it did.

Nina studied her face through the screen. "Hey. You good? Like…actually good?"

Macy hesitated. Just half a second too long.

"I think so," she said carefully. "I'm more than a little scared to tell Cath and my parents."

Nina's expression softened. "They're scared because they love you. That doesn't mean you're wrong. It just means this is big."

"Yeah," Macy whispered.

Nina nodded. "Whatever happens, I've got you. Now, do I get to wear something scandalous, or are we going classy?"

That finally pulled a real smile out of her.

After Nina's call, the silence of the room weighed more heavily than it had before, like all the noise had drained out of it. Macy stared at the wall for a long moment before opening Catherine's contact.

She almost hoped it would go to voicemail.

It didn't.

"I hope I'm not interrupting anything," Macy said automatically.

There was a pause. "Do you think I would've answered if you were?" Catherine said lightly.

Macy swallowed. "Well, I might as well rip off the Band-Aid. We moved the wedding."

Another pause. This one is longer.

"Let's have it."

"Summer."

The line stayed silent long enough that Macy pulled the phone slightly away from her ear, thinking it had disconnected. Finally, Catherine said, very quietly, "So, the emergency brake is officially disabled."

Macy's stomach tightened. "Cath, it's not like that. Things changed. He's right, there's no reason to wait."

Catherine exhaled slowly. "Does it feel right…or does it feel inevitable?"

The question landed hard.

"I wouldn't do this if I didn't want it," Macy said, but even she could hear the defensive edge.

"I know," Catherine said. "And I'm not trying to be the villain in your love story. I just…I watched you fight so hard to slow things down. To protect yourself. And now, suddenly, you're letting him sprint again."

There was movement on Catherine's end—footsteps, a quiet door shutting.

"I'm scared for you," she said honestly. "That doesn't mean I won't support you. Just, I wish you had stood your ground."

Macy closed her eyes. "I don't want to lose you."

"You won't," Catherine replied immediately. "But you don't get to outrun my worry just because you love him."

A long silence stretched between them.

Then Catherine sighed. "Okay. If you're doing this…then we do it right. We've got three months and change to pull off a miracle."

Macy let out a shaky laugh. "That's the Catherine I know."

"I'm still terrified," Catherine added. "I'm just choosing not to turn it into a war."

Tears slipped down Macy's cheeks. "Thank you."

The bedroom door opened quietly as she ended the call.

Macy wiped at her face and looked up to find Cade leaning against the frame, watching her with soft eyes, a glass of water in his hand.

"What happened?" he asked.

She hesitated. "I've only gotten to call Nina and Catherine so far. I haven't gathered up the nerve to try my parents yet."

He nodded slowly and set the glass on the dresser, crossing the room to the bed, where she sat. Sitting beside her, he took her hands between his palms and pressed a kiss to her knuckles.

He leaned in closer. "My family is thrilled. I'm sure yours will come around. But what matters is that *you* chose this. You chose *us*."

A quiet pressure settled in her chest as she dialed her parents.

Rebecca's face appeared, smiling instantly. A queasy sensation washed over Macy, dreading the conversation to come.

"Hi, sweetheart, Cade, I'll go get your dad!" Rebecca said, disappearing from the screen. They returned a beat later. "I told Ethan and Joy to dial in, too. They should be on soon!"

"Wait, are you not all in the house?"

"No," George said, pride sparkling in his eyes. "Mom and I moved into the guesthouse so the new family can get adjusted."

"That's exciting!" Macy said. "Well, I might as well get to it. I've got something to tell you."

Rebecca leaned in. "What's going on?"

"We've decided to move up the wedding," Macy said quickly. Cade nestled beside her and put an arm across her shoulders, rubbing gently with his fingertips.

Rebecca flinched, expression unreadable. "How much are we talking?"

"Summer."

A beat of silence.

"That's…sooner than December," George said.

"I know," Macy replied. "But after everything we've been through, Cade and I realized we were so caught up in planning the perfect wedding that we forgot the point: We already know we want to be together. We don't need more months of being almost there. We're ready to say yes."

George and Rebecca looked at each other with a silence that stretched so far that Macy started to squirm. George opened his mouth to finally speak when Ethan and Joy logged in to the call.

"Did we miss something?" Ethan asked. "You look like someone's dying. Is someone dying?"

"No," Macy said. She tried to laugh, but it came out shaky. "We've moved the wedding up. It's going to be in the summer."

Joy's face fell, and Ethan scratched his head, eyes falling to avoid the screen.

"Macy, I've got something to say," George broke the silence at last.

"Cade, can you give us a moment?" Macy asked.

"No, I think it's time he hears this," George said, holding up his hand. "I've held my tongue because you're an adult, and this is your life. But I can't do that anymore. I can't condone this decision. The last time we talked, you said you wanted to take this part slowly. You two haven't even known each other for a year. What changed?"

Macy opened her mouth to explain, but Cade jumped in before she could start. "We've done a lot of talking about this. She wants this, too!"

"Does she?" Joy asked. Her voice sounded sharp, but in her eyes, a shine of tears betrayed her sadness. "Macy, you're a sister to me, and I want to support you, but your dad is right."

Tears pooled in the corner of Macy's eyes. "I hoped you guys would be happy for me."

Rebecca reached across the desk for a tissue. "I'll be honest, Macy, this was the last thing I expected you to say tonight. Obviously, we can't stop you if your mind is made up, but I agree with your father."

Cade patted Macy's hand and turned the computer toward himself as tears spilled from her eyes. "Dad, I know you're upset, but I promised I would take good care of your daughter. The only thing that's changed is we're going to make it legally official."

George's normally warm brown eyes flashed, his forehead instantly sinking into an angry "V." "I never asked you to call me Dad."

Cade's face reddened, and his hands clenched into fists that he dropped to his sides.

Macy looked pleadingly at Ethan, hoping for just one of her family to back her up. He started pacing the floor. "I'm not very good at this kind of thing, Macy. I'm sorry. You know we love you no matter what, but I need some time to wrap my head around this."

Cade pointed at the screen and got off the bed. "What did I tell you, Macy? I told you after that remark at Thanksgiving, he is going to try to come between us."

George shook his head, straining to control his temper. "And that's the last straw with you. I can't stop you from seeing my daughter, but I will not have such blatant disrespect toward this family. Ethan has always been welcoming toward you, and there is no excuse for that accusation.

"I'm sorry, Macy, but if you insist on letting him have his way with this wedding, we will not be there. I can't smile and pretend I'm okay with giving you away to...this."

Joy wiped her eyes and nodded her agreement.

Ethan sank onto the edge of the guest bed behind him. "I'm sorry, Mace." He pointed at Cade through the screen. "And as for you. I apologized for my remark, and I told you that it had nothing to do with you. But maybe my gut reaction was right."

Cade balled his fists and raised his hand to fire back, but Macy put a hand on his to stop him.

"Please don't do this," Macy begged at the screen. "You're my family, and I need you. I'm trying so hard to make everybody happy. I'm trying to meet everybody halfway. But I can't. Please don't make me choose."

George gave one final, gentle shake of his head. "I'm sorry, sweetheart. If you ever want us to help you get out, we will be there in a minute. But we can't be there for this."

After a sorrowful look, the screen went dark.

A hollow thud landed in her chest as the silence expanded. She replayed the conversation in her mind, confused, wondering when her life became one never-ending battle. Cade exhaled slowly beside her, too slowly, too measured.

"Bella..." he said gently, almost mournfully. "I hate that they're doing this to you."

Her fingers tightened on the comforter.

"To us," he corrected softly. "I just—" He swallowed hard, voice trembling in a way that felt both fragile and pointed. "I need to know you're not going to let them make you choose."

Macy blinked, shaking her head. "How am I supposed to choose?"

"I'm not asking you to," he whispered. "I would never ask you to. But they just did." He brushed a thumb down her arm, tender, pleading. "And I need to know you're still with me. That you won't let them push you away from what we're building."

"I *am* with you. But they're my parents! I can't erase them because we disagree." She twisted her gold cross furiously in her fingers until the gold bit into her skin.

"I see. So, you're going to let them break your heart, and then turn around and break mine? When I'm the one who's never done anything but stand by your side."

Macy dropped her hands into her lap and gazed miserably out the bedroom window. Cade sat beside her and pressed the water glass into her hands. She held it without drinking, fingers loose around the rim.

"Maybe this is for the best."

Her eyes flicked toward him, then away. "How could this be for the best?"

The heat in her face didn't match the cold that rushed through her limbs. Her ears buzzed faintly, like the hum of fluorescent lights.

Cade cupped her cheek, guiding her to look at him. "You don't need them to approve us," he murmured. "Families panic. They judge. They don't understand what we have."

His thumb stroked her cheekbone, grounding her. But her brain slipped free again, drifting.

"You have me," he said softly. "You'll always have me. That's enough."

She heard the words as if through water. Her mouth opened, but no sound came out. Time stretched and unhooked—seconds stretching, collapsing, reforming. Something inside her floated just above her body, watching this scene from a distance.

"Macy," Cade whispered, kissing her forehead. "They don't want to let their little girl be married – at least, not to someone they didn't choose. Let them stay home if they want. We don't need them. You and I…we're the family now. Why don't we go ahead and order you a dress, now?"

His arms wrapped around her. She didn't hug back, but her body folded into him without really thinking. Her mind hovered somewhere just over her shoulder, watching the two of them on the bed.

Watching herself disappear a little more.

Chapter Twenty-Seven

WEATHERING THE STORMS

"Girl, you are *crazy!*" RJ said over lunch the following Monday. "We never know what you're going to do next!"

"What?" Macy replied, half-defensive. "People move up wedding dates all the time!"

"Of course they do," Sebrina chimed in. "But usually, the word *shotgun* is involved. There's not something else you're forgetting to tell us, is there, Macy?"

Sebrina very deliberately looked down at Macy's belly. RJ and Brielle burst into laughter as Macy's cheeks flushed pink. "No, I'm not pregnant!"

"But do you *know* you're not pregnant?" RJ teased.

"I should never have said anything," Macy muttered, gathering her things to move to another table.

Sebrina reached out and gently touched her arm. "No, don't go, Mace. We're only teasing. We're happy for you. Really."

On the surface, Macy knew they were joking. But underneath, a familiar doubt crept in. *Is this what everyone's going to think? That I'm rushing because I have to?*

I thought I wasn't caring what people think anymore. Just what Cade and I want.

She bared her teeth in a mock snarl, then forced herself to laugh with the rest of them. But her heart wasn't in it.

"I wonder how Amara took the news," RJ said.

"She regaled me with song and dance and the greatest fanfare you could imagine," Macy deadpanned, rolling her eyes. "How do you really think she reacted?" she asked, pausing mid-salad.

Brielle grinned. "Edge of her mouth barely teased a curve upward, and she said, 'Yay. What are you working on today'?"

After confirming Amara wasn't nearby, the table erupted in laughter.

"Brielle, you've figured her out fast," Sebrina said, shaking her head.

"So, do you have an official date now?" asked Sebrina.

"Yeah, Cade wasted no time there," Macy said, her answering smile shaky. "He called a wedding planner Saturday, and they had an opening at Central Park on June 20th. They're taking care of all of the details, so we only have to show up. I picked out a dress from a secondhand seller, and that should be coming this week."

"Wow," Brielle said, eyes wide. "He is not playing! Must feel good to have someone that dedicated."

Macy nodded, though her eyes brimmed with silent tears. Knowing her family wouldn't be there made the plans feel empty and incomplete. But she didn't see how she would be able to bridge the wedge that Cade's fight with her family had made.

At the end of the day, Macy and Brielle walked to the elevator, chatting about the finer details of the health information management system they were designing. With the back-end stable and handed off to QA for security testing, they could finally focus on the user interface.

Cade was waiting in the lobby, seated near reception. The receptionist smiled and winked as Macy approached.

"There's my beautiful bride," he said, sweeping her into his arms.

Brielle looked away, awkward but smiling. "Guess I'll see you tomorrow, Mace!"

She waited for the next elevator, giving them space.

Cade and Macy held hands as they exited the building and made their way to the train for their meeting with the wedding planner.

"I talked to Sheryl during lunch," Cade said, practically glowing.

"What did she say?"

"She's thrilled, obviously." He took her hand between his and turned serious. "She wants to throw you a bridal shower. Not just you, but Catherine and Nina. She wants to host everyone at their house. A big celebration. For you."

"And you," Macy said, smiling. "When?"

"You let Sheryl figure that out. But it'll be soon, obviously."

He tucked her under his arm, and she rested her head against his shoulder as the train bumped and squealed along the tracks. Her mind raced as they rattled towards home, wondering again about patching up her relationship with her family.

They stepped off the train and climbed out of the subway tunnel, sunlight greeting them with the promise of Spring. Still, the city air held a heaviness that wasn't there before. The sky was a hazy blue, clouds drifting lazily above the buildings. Everything felt unreal, like the line between a dream and real life had blurred.

Cade pulled her close and kissed her temple. "One day closer."

They arrived home hand in hand. In their mailbox was a bright pink slip with Macy's name on it. She gasped, then started jumping up and down. "It's here! I can't believe it's already here! My wedding dress!"

Cade stole a quick kiss and headed upstairs, giving her space to collect the package. Macy dashed to the residents' office and returned with a long cardboard box. She rode the elevator up, ran past Cade in the kitchen, and into their bedroom, slamming the door behind her. There wasn't a moment to lose. She had to make sure it was perfect.

From the kitchen, Cade heard her laughing as he started prepping tacos for dinner. Then everything changed.

She screamed.

He dropped the knife and ran to the bedroom door. "Macy! Bella, what's wrong?"

Inside, he could hear sobbing. "No, don't come in! You can't see!"

"But you screamed! Are you okay?"

He heard the rustle of fabric, the zip of a garment bag being closed, and then silence.

"Mace?"

She opened the door, tears streaming down her face. "It's too small!"

"But you picked the right size, didn't you?"

"It should have been. But it doesn't zip! The zipper won't go up any higher with about three inches to go from the top! What am I going to do?"

Macy stepped out of the bedroom and curled into Cade's waiting arms.

"We've been a little lax at the gym," he said gently. "We can ramp things up again. Revisit your nutrition. The wedding's still seven weeks away. We've got time to figure this out. You can lose some inches by then."

She wiped her eyes, her voice low. "Cade, we've been at this for ten months. I've only lost fifteen pounds. What makes you so sure I can make that kind of progress now?"

"If we dial things back in, I know you can do it. We've got this."

Macy nodded, drying her eyes, though her mind was already spinning. *How am I going to do this? Should I just send the dress back and find something else?* She'd worked hard, and the lack of results stung. Still, she knew she could do better. She had to do better – not just for the dress, but for herself.

She flipped open her laptop and started scrolling through social media, searching for a trustworthy seamstress, just in case.

As she scrolled, Cade prepared dinner. He called her to the table and placed a single taco in front of her.

"Just one?" she asked, eyes growing wide, jaw slightly open.

"You want to lose the weight, right? You have to trust me."

She ate slowly, stomach still grumbling in protest when she licked the last drop of the spicy salsa from her thumb. "What else can I have?"

He handed her a bottle of water. "Fruit and vegetables, love. Your body's going to feel uncomfortable at first, but we've got to get those portions down. No more lunches out at work, no more McDonald's stops, and those chips you love? They've got to go."

Macy lowered her head in quiet resignation. "Okay. I trust you."

The words came out automatically. Trust was safer than arguing. Trust was quieter.

The next afternoon, Macy sat at lunch, pushing her salad around the plate with a downcast gaze. *I can do this. I just have to fit into the dress. Then I can stop eating like a rabbit.*

Sebrina slid into the seat beside her, setting down a steaming plate of Chinese chicken and broccoli with rice. Macy's mouth watered instantly.

"Honey," Sebrina said, eyeing her salad, "you're stabbing that Caesar so hard, it's about to ask you, *'Et tu, Brute?'* What's going on?"

Macy gave her a morose look, trying to rein in her thoughts. "My dress came in yesterday. It's at least a size too small. I've got seven weeks to lose an inch and a half."

"Oh, honey!" Sebrina said. "That's so scary! But let me let you in on a little secret. After I had my youngest, I had this stubborn pooch that just wouldn't quit. Then I started this workout that changed my life. Ever heard of *The Inferno*?"

Macy blinked. "Well, yeah, I've read *The Divine Comedy*. But…how is that going to help me?"

Sebrina laughed at Macy's confused expression. "*The Inferno* is the name of the workout. It'll challenge you like nothing else, but if you stick with it, you'll see results. Want to borrow my DVDs?"

Without a second thought, Macy launched herself into a hug. "You're a lifesaver."

Sebrina patted her arm, grinning. "I'll bring them tomorrow. Buckle up. You're going to experience some things. The best thing I did was join a Facebook support group for people doing the program. No sales pitches, just women encouraging each other. Want in?"

"Is the pope Catholic?"

They laughed and returned to their lunch, Macy feeling optimistic for the first time in days.

Saturday morning, Macy sat cross-legged on the bedroom floor in her gym gear, laptop open. She'd told Cade she wasn't going to the gym today. Through the wall, he heard the computer shout, "Let's burn it *uuuuppppp*!"

He peeked in. "What's going on in here?"

"Sebrina loaned me these DVDs," Macy said, breathless with anticipation. "She said it's the hardest workout she's ever done, but it changed her life. So, I'm giving it a try. If there's ever a time for something called *The Inferno*, it's now."

Cade sat on the edge of the bed, watching. Fifteen minutes in, Macy paused for water, drenched and gasping.

"Well," Cade said, swinging his feet up to lie down on his side, "that definitely looked straight from the fires of hell."

"Are you kidding?" Macy panted. "That was just the warm-up."

Forty minutes, a lot of sweat, and some swear words later, she peeled herself off the floor and crawled into the shower. Cade headed to the kitchen and made her a sandwich with fruit salad on the side, plus a chocolate protein shake.

Her hands were still trembling when she emerged, but she steadied herself and dressed for the bridal show they'd planned that afternoon. Though the planner had most things covered, Macy had begged to go just to explore vendors and soak in the experience.

She chose a coral skirt that flared playfully above her knees, paired with a crisp white button-down. Her curls dried naturally, scrunched into soft waves.

Cade was making his own lunch when she walked into the kitchen and sat down.

"What are you all dressed up for?" he asked, sliding into the seat beside her.

"Don't you remember? We're going to the bridal show today."

Cade frowned, disappointment flickering across his face. "I forgot. How insistent are you on going?"

"I was really looking forward to it," Macy said, trying to keep her tone light. "It'll be fun. We haven't been up to this part of the city in ages. Feels like all we do is work and settle in since I moved. It'll be nice to get out."

"I don't really see the point of the show," he muttered. "But if it makes you happy…"

"We still need to order your wedding ring," Macy reminded him.

Cade had been unusually quiet all morning. Macy kept trying to draw him out, but he offered only short answers before retreating into silence again.

They rode the train into Times Square, Macy increasingly aware of Cade's sour mood. Still, she was determined to enjoy the afternoon.

She'd given up a lot to make this wedding timeline work. Going to a bridal show was one thing she refused to skip.

The Marriott Marquis conference rooms were packed with vendors, brides, and a few disgruntled grooms trailing them. Macy bounded into the main room, vibrating with excitement.

"Look at all these people. Do we really have to do this? We've got everything set through the planner," Cade added quickly, teetering on the edge of a whine.

"Wedding ring!" Macy reminded him with a playful jab to the ribs. "Besides, this is a bride's rite of passage."

He groaned and rolled his eyes, but stayed at her side. They wandered through the vendor tables, sampling hors d'oeuvres and cake slices, entering raffles and giveaways. Eventually, they reached a jeweler's booth with a sleek selection of bands for men and women. Cade chose a simple white gold ring, and they placed the order.

Cade, growing restless, leaned in and asked quietly, "Can we go now? We got what we came for."

"You're really not enjoying this?" Macy asked, frowning.

"To be honest, my knees and back are killing me, and this crowd is giving me anxiety. There's a reason I avoid Times Square. I just want to go home."

Macy took a last longing glance around the vendor space. Her shoulders hunched as she followed him out of the room, tossing her sticker marked "Bride" in a garbage bin on the way out.

They rode the train back to their apartment in silence. As soon as they walked in, Cade headed straight to the bathroom and took extra pills from his emergency stash. He added an anxiety pill and lay down in their bed, curling into himself.

The silence in the apartment weighed more heavily on her than the crowd had. Macy placed her purse on the counter and waited for him to come out, but he didn't.

She drifted from room to room, picking up cups that didn't need washing, folding blankets that were already neat. The apartment was spotless. It always was. Cade liked things tidy. It gave her nothing to focus on. Nothing to fix.

After twenty minutes of pretending to be busy, she hovered at the bedroom door. The light was off, the door mostly shut. She pushed it open gently.

Cade was curled on his side, shaking, arms covering his head.

She stepped inside. "Cade?"

He turned toward her, eyes red and wet, cheeks blotchy. "I'm sorry," he said, voice cracked and raw. "I know how much you wanted today to be special, and I ruined it. I'm so broken, Macy. You deserve better than this."

Her breath caught. "Cade, no. You told me about your injuries, your limits. I knew."

He shook his head. "You didn't know this. I can't even walk around a bridal expo without screwing it up. I'm no good for you." He pulled his knees in tighter. "You should move back in with Catherine and Shane. Or Nina and Brian. At least they wouldn't drag you down the way I do."

Macy knelt beside the bed, heart hammering. She reached out but didn't touch him. Not yet. His words hit like a trap disguised as mercy.

He'd pushed for this wedding. For the date. For all of it. So, why did it feel like he was trying to sabotage it now? Why the guilt when things were finally moving forward?

She sat back on her heels, watching him. "You just took some pretty hefty medicine," she said quietly. "Maybe you just need to sleep this off."

He didn't respond. Just rolled to face the wall, shoulders still trembling. She went back to the living room quietly so he could rest and flipped helplessly through the options on Netflix.

When he emerged around five, his smile was bright and easy, like nothing had happened.

"Hey," he said, crossing to the kitchen. "Want to get Thai for dinner?"

Macy followed him to the couch, her stomach still tight with everything she hadn't said. She still wasn't sure she should. Part of her wanted to talk about the meltdown, the things he'd said. But instead, she nodded at the takeout menu in his hand.

"Thai sounds perfect."

As he scrolled through the menu, he called over his shoulder, "We should probably skip your soup tonight, though. That coconut milk is loaded with fat."

The storm had passed. The air felt calm again. And that, somehow, frightened her more than the breakdown had.

Chapter Twenty-Eight

THE BRIDAL SHOWER

The plane wheels screeched against the tarmac just before noon, jostling Macy back to reality. It was Friday with four weeks to go, and she was already running on fumes. She hadn't slept more than a few hours the night before, her mind spinning with checklists and calorie counts. By 7 a.m., she was in sneakers, breath fogging the living room window as she powered through her daily *Inferno* workout. Three weeks in, and it still kicked her ass. But now she needed only two pauses instead of five.

The ride to the airport was a blur of caffeine, flight check-ins, and Catherine insisting she'd triple-checked the seating arrangement to keep everyone "strategically" placed. Which, of course, meant Cade got his own row just ahead of them, buffered from the girl talk and safely out of Macy's elbow range.

Sheryl had gone full Midwest hostess when they pulled up to the house in Winnetka. She sat in a rocking chair on the porch like something out of a Norman Rockwell painting, a pitcher of lemonade gleaming in the spring sun.

"We're so glad you're all here!" Sheryl said, sweeping open the screen door. "Less than a month to go. Are you excited?"

"Couldn't be more excited if we tried," Cade said smoothly, snatching Macy's suitcase before she could. "No lemonade for Macy. Water. She's off sugar."

Catherine's face froze. She caught Macy's eye, and Macy gave her the faintest shake of her head. Barely perceptible, but enough. *Don't.*

Sheryl nudged Macy and winked. "How's about a coffee instead?"

"Sounds great," Macy said, smiling gratefully as she followed Sheryl inside. She let Cade play the front-porch fiancé and took the chance to escape the spotlight.

"Wait for me!" Catherine called, hurrying after her. Once they were out of earshot, she tugged Macy's arm. "What was that?"

Macy sighed, already dreading the conversation. "My wedding dress doesn't fit. I've got to do whatever he says for three more weeks, get the damn thing zipped, and then we can relax."

Catherine eyed her skeptically, searching for any sign to keep probing. "You know, if he ever hurts you, I'll rip off his—"

Macy clamped a hand over Catherine's mouth before she could finish. But Catherine's feisty protectiveness brought a laugh to Macy's lips.

"It's nothing like that," Macy said. "I think the pressure of a quick wedding is just taking its toll."

"You know your room's always there if you need a night to think," Catherine said gently. "And you don't have to go through with anything if you're having doubts."

When Macy and Catherine returned to the porch with their mugs, they found Cade and Sean entertaining the group with childhood stories. Cade was mid-recount of the time they tried to build a fort in the woods, and Sean broke his leg when the floor collapsed.

A shiny black Land Rover pulled into the driveway as he finished his story. Howard and Talia stepped out. Talia sneered at the porch gathering and headed inside without a word.

"Great to see you, little sister!" Cade called after her, voice dripping with sarcasm.

A pretty brown head popped back out the door. "Guestroom is mine." She gave Sheryl a barely-there wave and shut the door behind her.

Sheryl sighed and sipped her lemonade. "I don't know what I'm going to do with her."

"It's all right, Mom," Sean said. "We're not all going to rain on Cade and Macy's parade."

Howard greeted Macy with a warm hug and shook Cade's hand. "This other redhead must be Catherine, which makes you Nina," he said, scanning the patio. "Welcome, we're happy to have you both."

Howard put a hand on each of his sons' shoulders. "Let's let the ladies bond. Time for our bachelor party."

Macy turned to look at Cade. "Bachelor party?"

Cade smiled and kissed her hand. "Nothing wild. What kind of trouble can I get into with my dad?"

Sean gave Cade a look that reminded Macy of her own brother: playful, mischievous, with a glint in his eye. "With our dad? Plenty."

Dawn crept into the basement in hazy streaks of blue-gray. Macy had slipped out of the sofa-bed in the library, careful not to wake Cade. Talia had won the argument with Sheryl the night before to claim the guestroom, on the condition that Talia had to let Nina and Catherine share it with her. With a dry remark about hosting a slumber party, she'd begrudgingly agreed.

Macy tiptoed down to the basement and laced up her sneakers. Her Facebook fitness group was already buzzing with sweaty selfies. Day 22 of *The Inferno*. She clicked play, let the warm-up cue, and surrendered to DeMarcus Martinson's voice for forty punishing minutes of sweat, burn, and shallow breaths. When she emerged, she showered and twisted her curls into a low bun, ready to face the day. Sort of.

The kitchen smelled like coffee and toast. Sheryl handed her a mug and leaned against the counter like they were old friends.

Talia stalked in from the living room and poured her coffee like it had personally offended her.

"Hi, Talia!" Macy said, offering a smile. "I was glad to hear you and Dean were doing better."

Talia didn't blink. "Hmm. I'm sure you were." Her voice snapped like a frozen branch. "You'll figure it out. One day. That you and Cade are a little too codependent for your own good."

Macy blinked. "I'm…sorry?"

"You're crazy to be getting married. But I'm sure you'll 'see' soon enough."

And just like that, Talia vanished down the hallway.

Sean bounded down the stairs, earbuds around his neck, smirk already in place. "Ignore her. I always do."

"Sean," Sheryl said, more weary than stern.

He kissed her cheek. "Sorry, Mom." Then to Macy, grinning, "Don't worry. I brought your hubby home in one piece last night."

Before Macy could respond, Cade entered, unsteady. His shoulder grazed the wall as he walked, one hand dragging along the kitchen table for support. He moved like his legs were filled with gravel.

"Remember," he muttered, slurring slightly as he kissed her cheek, "what happens at the bachelor party stays at the bachelor party."

The coffee pot hissed behind him.

"My back is killing me," he groaned. "One day, I swear it's going to lock up on me."

Nina and Catherine swept into the room, whispering like they shared a secret. They were already dressed for the day, Catherine in a blue chiffon sundress, her bob clipped back off her face. Nina's golden waves swung loosely down her back, and she wore a pastel peach pantsuit cinched with a wide black belt. She scooped up a coffee mug and gestured at Cade, who sat with his head in his hands, steam rising from his untouched drink.

"Party too hearty last night?" she teased.

Cade groaned. "All we did was play poker. I shouldn't feel like I've been hit by a truck."

"It's true," Sean added. "No alcohol. No strippers. Just cards and complaints."

Sheryl gave him a look. "Why don't you make yourself useful and start hanging decorations for the party?"

"Is there anything I can do to help?" Macy asked.

"Yes," Sheryl said, smiling. "Go get dressed!"

She placed her coffee mug in the dishwasher and went back up to her room for the weekend. She had brought a blue-and-white dress with wide straps and a square neckline. The abstract swirled pattern danced across the fabric, and the skirt landed just above her knees. She'd planned to leave her hair down for Cade, but today was her day, and she was already warm. So, she swept her curls into a waterfall twist down each side of her head, draping the tail over her right shoulder.

When Macy came down the stairs, the living room resembled the cover of a bridal magazine. It smelled of buttercream and vanilla. A banner reading, "Congratulations, Macy and Cade" hung over the picture window—the same one that had framed the Christmas tree during her last visit to the Laurent house. Pink and ivory streamers cascaded from the hallway chandelier, and a long table was draped in delicate lace, with a two-tier cake standing proudly at its center. To the left was a pile of wrapped gifts. To the right, another stack was reserved for party games.

She had barely reached the bottom step when Diane swept in.

"Macy, my darling, let me look at you!" Diane spun her, Macy's blue-and-white skirt flaring at her knees. She gave her a once-over, eyes sparkling with appraisal. "You look a vision. Are you ready?"

"Ready as I'm going to be!"

The doorbell rang, and Diane dashed off to answer it, leaving Macy momentarily overwhelmed before the party had even begun. Sheryl placed a gentle hand on Macy's shoulder.

"I'm really sorry about the problems with your family. Have you talked to them at all since?"

Macy shook her head, smile faltering. "Not a lot. They wanted to make clear they're still my family, and they still love me, but Cade...How much did he tell you about the phone call?"

Sheryl sighed and pressed her lips together. "Honestly, not a lot, only that you were trying to have a reasonable conversation with your parents about why you changed the timeline, and they didn't want to hear it. He admitted he might have been out of line speaking out against your brother in front of him, but still, their reaction sounded a bit extreme to me. At any rate, Howard and I are happy to stand in for you as our daughter. Because you are now."

A single tear escaped as Macy forced her smile back on for the good of the guests. "Thank you, Sheryl."

"Mom," she reminded her, smiling warmly and squeezing her shoulders.

Sheryl turned to address the house full of party guests with a tap of a butter knife against her glass.

"Everyone! Let's give a quick toast before Macy opens her gifts. We're so proud of you, and thrilled for this next chapter."

Glasses lifted. Macy gave a small curtsy. "Thank you. I feel so loved today. I'm overwhelmed and so grateful to Diane and Sheryl for going out of their way to celebrate Cade and me."

"Oh, sweetheart, I always love on the bride," Diane said, reaching to tuck a stray curl behind Macy's ear. "It's the marriage that's hard."

A pause settled over the room. Sheryl quickly handed Macy a wrapped box. "I think it's time for gifts!"

"You all right?" Nina's voice was soft behind her.

"Just overwhelmed. Mostly in a good way."

Nina stepped closer. "Are you sure?"

Macy nodded too quickly. "It's just a lot. Ever since that fight with the family, everything feels wrong. They should be here."

Nina gave Macy's arm a gentle squeeze. "You know they still love you, sweetie. And I'm sure they'll all make amends when they've had some time to cool off."

Diane passed by, sipping her third glass of white wine. "You know, Macy, I still can't help feeling a little disappointed we didn't go dress shopping. We talked all about it when we met at Christmas."

Macy's expression faltered. "Diane, I'm sorry it didn't work out. With the change in the timeline, I had to just pick something and hope for the best."

"But I'm Cade's mother, and he's my only child," Diane said, her tone sharp beneath the smile. "I won't get another chance. You could have come here to shop in person in Chicago. And after all, Sheryl and I are the ones who are still sticking by you two. Where is your family today?"

Before Macy could respond to the biting remark, Talia swept in and distracted Diane with news that Dean was finally considering "the next step," so maybe she'd need a shower of her own soon. Macy gave Talia a surprised, grateful smile. Talia gave her a subtle nod in return.

As the crowd began to disperse, Macy lingered by the dessert table with Catherine.

"Was it everything you imagined?" Catherine asked.

"Yeah," Macy said. "Except being accosted by my future mother-in-law."

Nina snickered. "If you want to run off to a Vegas chapel, I'll distract everyone so you can make your escape."

"I'll keep that in my back pocket."

Across the room, Diane was pointing out her handiwork to Sheryl. Nina leaned in next to Macy.

"Don't let them rattle you," she whispered. "Talia and Diane are just jealous. You and Cade, you've got the real thing. They don't have that."

Macy smiled, but her eyes drifted toward the window. Cade had returned with Sean, and they paraded into the foyer to applause from the remaining guests, who were still sipping mimosas and nibbling cake. His arrival signaled the party's end. Nina and Catherine helped pack up the gifts while Sheryl and Diane ushered guests out the door. Diane left shortly after for her shift at the nursing home.

"Uh, Cade?" Macy said, suddenly realizing the logistical nightmare. "How are we going to get all of this back to New York?"

Before he could answer, Sheryl turned. "Howard and I will drive whatever doesn't fit in your suitcases when we come in for the wedding."

Macy sank into a chair, head spinning. Lately, every decision felt made for her. She was tired. Tired of smiling, nodding, pretending everything was perfect. And tired of feeling like the wedding was something that was happening to her rather than what she was choosing.

When the last streamer was torn down and the final guest had gone, Macy turned to Cade with pleading eyes.

"Is it time for a nap?"

He laughed and took her hands. "You did great today."

Her head throbbed. The day had been long, and tomorrow would be longer with the journey home, the return to routine, the weight of everything still unresolved.

For now, all she wanted was quiet.

Macy woke Sunday morning to birds tittering outside her window like they hadn't gotten the memo that she was still tired. She stretched, rubbing her neck, which was stiff from the sofa bed and, she was sure, the weight of the day before. The last thing she wanted was to hear DeMarcus Martinson shouting "Light it up!" at her, but she was nearly halfway through the program and hadn't missed a day yet. Today wouldn't be the exception.

Rolling over, she noticed the other half of the bed was empty. Cade had been there when she had lain down. She'd even nudged him in the middle of the night to stop snoring. She dressed in her sports bra and shorts, grabbed her laptop, and headed for the basement.

It was early, just after 7:00, and the house was still quiet. As she crept toward the basement door, a voice startled her from the kitchen.

"Forget your T-shirt?"

Macy nearly dropped her laptop. "Cade! You scared me half to death."

He didn't smile. "Did you forget your T-shirt?" he asked again.

"It's hot in here. I usually wear this at home. What's the problem?"

"We're not at home," he said. "You're walking around half-naked in a house where my dad lives. My brother could walk in any second."

"Cade, I'm not showing anything people wouldn't see if I were wearing a swimsuit."

"I'll get you a shirt," he said, voice clipped, signaling the conversation was over.

He stepped toward her, pain carved across his face. His hands shot to his lower back, and then his knees buckled. He collapsed forward, kneecaps hitting the linoleum with a sickening thud.

"Cade!" Macy screamed, dropping her laptop as she rushed to him.

He stayed on his hands and knees, silent. Macy tried to loop his arm over her shoulder, but he pulled away. "No. Let me do it."

He crawled back toward the kitchen table and used the chair to haul himself upright. His head dropped into his hands. "Go get a damn shirt, please."

Whatever motivation Macy had for working out evaporated. "I might just swap in a rest day," she said quietly. "Or maybe I'll do it tonight when we get home. Do you need ice? Tylenol?"

He shook his head, still hunched over, breathing heavily. "I just need you to put on some clothes and not embarrass me by droning on about this. Please."

Macy picked up her laptop and headed back upstairs. On the way, she flipped the lid open to check for damage. To her relief, it whirred to life.

It was only 7:15, and the day already stretched behind her.

She tucked her workout clothes back into her suitcase and changed into her travel outfit: black leggings and a royal blue swing top. She pulled out her ponytail, ran her fingers through her curls, and caught her reflection in the closet mirror.

She barely recognized the woman looking back at her.

Her body had changed—toned shoulders, a thinner waistline, a more defined jaw. But her eyes looked gaunt, puffy. Aged.

With her bags already packed and nothing left to do, Macy decided to text Cade and ask if he wanted some company. While waiting for his reply, she folded the bed back into the sofa. Her phone dinged.

Cade
You didn't even ask me if I was okay when you saw me in the kitchen, or why I was up so early. I don't feel good, but it seemed like you were so preoccupied with working out that you didn't care to ask.

Macy stared at the screen, her fingers tightening around the phone. Her thumbs flew over the letters.

Macy

You didn't even give me the chance to. Before I realized you were sitting there, you were accusing me of trying to tempt your family with my perfectly normal workout gear.

His reply came quickly.

Cade

You're right, I'm the bad guy, aren't I? Isn't it strange that I don't want other men looking at my fucking fiancée in barely more than her underwear? I'm so unreasonable.

Macy

Cade, please. We're a month away from our wedding. We both have new jobs. Things are still not right with my family. It's been a long weekend, and we're stressed. Let's not take it out on each other, please?

Cade

You're not even going to say you're sorry for your behavior? Dressing like that in front of other men is inappropriate.

Macy

Okay, I'm sorry! I dress like that all the time at home, so I didn't think anything of it!

Cade

That's exactly it, Macy. You didn't think.

Macy

I'm sorry, Cade. Please forgive me.

Cade

Why do you always insist on making me the enemy? All I've ever done is try to take care of you.

Her heart sank, and heat crept up her neck. Why did I do that? she thought. How would it look if I came up from the basement in a sports bra and shorts, and Sean was sitting at the table? Or worse—Dean and Talia?

The icy feeling in her chest wouldn't go away. She found herself pacing the library to burn off the anxious energy. Everyone else was still asleep; it was too early to knock on Catherine and Nina's door without risking waking them. The quiet made her thoughts too loud.

Having run out of tasks, Macy decided to be helpful and pack some of Cade's things. She laid out an outfit for the day and folded what he'd worn the night before. On the dresser sat his toiletry bag, half-zipped, faint orange labels peeking out from inside.

Macy hesitated. He'd told her before that he tried to keep everything organized and color-coded so he didn't accidentally double-dose. Her mind flashed to him hitting the floor in the kitchen.

Did he forget his medicines again? Maybe I should check?

Her hand drifted toward the bag.

Before she could think further, the door opened.

Cade stood in the doorway, expression blank and unreadable. His bathrobe hung loosely and untied over black sweatpants and a T-shirt. Macy's breath caught, her hand jerking back from the counter.

She quickly stammered, "I was just trying to help get things packed so it's easier for you."

He glanced at the bag, then at her. "It's fine. You can't mess it up."

He crossed the room, zipped the toiletry bag closed, and tucked it straight into his suitcase. The movement was almost too casual. Almost.

"I had a rough night," he finally said, voice low. "Kept waking up feeling…wrong. Tight chest. Jitters. I got up at five and took an anxiety pill, but it didn't help. I sat at the table and waited. Nothing."

He sank into the armchair opposite her, elbows on his knees, eyes distant.

"I'm not in pain, not exactly," he said. "I just don't feel right."

Macy's voice trembled. "Are we going to talk about it?"

Cade pursed his lips. "There's not much to talk about. I'm a broken man, Macy. You saw it downstairs. First, my reaction to your workout, then my back seizing. I'm just bringing you down."

"Why do you say that? You're not bringing me down!"

"Look how stressed you are because of this wedding. The fight with your family. I did that. You should just leave me here and go home with your girlfriends."

Macy's heart pounded. "Cade, why are you doing this? We're so close to the finish line. If you want to postpone, we can. Would that help?"

Her voice was rising, panic creeping in. She forced herself to breathe, remembering the rest of the house was still asleep. She couldn't let them hear this.

"You deserve so much better than this." Cade's voice broke as he leaned over the arm of the chair, hiding his face. Tears spilled freely, and he shook his head at her. "I don't want to lose you, Macy. But I'm so afraid one day you'll wake up and realize what you gave up your family for."

Macy knelt beside him, gently reaching for his hand. "I didn't give them up. We just have some things to work out. I'm in this with you for the long haul. Remember?"

His eyes met hers, red-rimmed and vulnerable. "Do you promise?"

"That's the plan," she said softly. "On June 20th."

The tension between them finally eased. Cade leaned in and kissed her—chaste, but full of quiet urgency.

With the storm seemingly having passed, she led the way downstairs in search of breakfast. Cade offered her fruit salad and yogurt while she brewed a pot of coffee. As the aroma filled the air, Catherine appeared at the foot of the stairs.

"That coffee smells heavenly," she said, sliding onto a stool at the breakfast bar. "Please tell me that coffee is for sharing."

"Always," Macy said, filling mugs.

"How's everybody feeling?" she asked, eyeing Macy a little too closely. "Recovering from yesterday's parade of strangers?"

Macy forced a smile. "Just tired. It's been a long trip."

Catherine's gaze lingered for a beat, as if she wanted to ask more, then it slid away. "Well, at least the shower looked gorgeous. Sheryl really went all out."

"She did," Macy agreed. "I wish my family could've seen it in person."

The words slipped out before she could catch them. The room went quiet for a breath.

Nina slinked into the room and gave Macy a quick squeeze from behind. "They should've been there. That's on them, not you."

Macy nodded, blinking fast. "We should probably finish packing. Howard will be here soon."

"I'll get the bags," Cade offered, squeezing her hand before retreating back upstairs.

As he returned with their luggage, Howard pulled into the drive. They loaded the truck, and Sheryl walked with them to the porch.

"We're so glad you came," she said, pulling Macy into one more hug. "I know it's complicated with your family. I hope you still felt celebrated."

"I did," Macy said, meaning it and not meaning it, all at once. "Thank you for everything."

"We're all family now," Sheryl said, hugging a little tighter, as if that might make it true sooner.

Chapter Twenty-Nine

BACHELORETTES

After claiming their bags, Macy, Cade, Nina, and Catherine boarded the subway that would take them home. The A train that carried them through the neighborhoods of Brooklyn and into Manhattan rattled and shook beneath them, none of them uttering a sound.

Macy hugged Catherine and Nina both in turn as they said their goodbyes and got up to change trains. She and Cade continued riding home in uneasy silence. Cade had slept on most of the flight home, with Nina and Catherine plotting with Macy for her bachelorette party.

Cade was less than impressed with the idea.

"Can we talk about the bachelorette party?" Macy asked tentatively as the train clattered through the Theater District.

"What's to talk about?" Cade said. He turned to look at her, crossing his arms. "Didn't you just have your party?"

"Well, no," Macy said, twisting the chain around her neck. "That was my bridal shower. The girls want to take me out. Like you got to go out with your dad and brother."

He pursed his lips. "No."

This was one battle she wasn't willing to lose. "You've got to have a bachelor party. Why can't I go out with the girls?"

His arms crossed, and his face hardened into a mask of jealousy. "Right. So, some better-looking guy can bump and grind on you one last time before you run out of chances?"

"It's not like that," Macy said, trying to stay calm. "They want to take me back to the club where you and I met. To celebrate how far we've come."

"Then why can't I come, too?"

"Because it's ladies only," she said, jabbing his chest for emphasis. "I promise no shenanigans and no strippers. I won't even drink that much. I just want one night out with my girls."

He squeezed his eyes shut and shook his head. "Alright. Here's the terms: You're not wearing one of those sashes that tells everybody you're the bride. That's just asking for trouble. Second, you're not drinking. I'm not taking any chances with your safety. Clear?"

Relief flooded through her chest. "That's fair! Totally fair. Thank you, Cade!" She looped her arm through his elbow and rested her head on his shoulder.

He placed a warm hand over hers and kissed the top of her head. "I'm sorry, Macy."

She tipped her head up to look at him. "Hmm?"

He took a deep breath, shoulders sagging. "I haven't been much of a picnic to be around lately, and I—I'm sorry. I think the stress of everything is finally getting to me, and when I'm scared, I self-sabotage. You don't deserve that. You deserve a night with your girls to unwind. Spend the night if you want."

Her face brightened. "Yeah?"

He smiled at her and kissed the top of her head. "Yes."

The train screeched at last to their stop, and Macy, still staring in disbelief at Cade, squeezed his arm before releasing it and grabbing her bags. "I appreciate that, Cade, more than you know." She laughed and started leading the way off the train. "I don't think even I realized how much I needed to hear that."

Cade threw his duffel bag over his shoulder and dragged her rolling suitcase behind, leaving her with only her backpack to carry, so he could take her hand to lead her home.

Macy sat cross-legged on her old bed, heart thudding harder than it should, trying to convince herself to push the send button on her phone. She told herself she was waiting to make this call until this night, the night of her bachelorette party, so she could have some privacy in the apartment she used to share with Catherine. But the truth was, she was afraid.

"Come on, Mace," she whispered under her breath. "It's just your mother."

She pressed the FaceTime button, and on the second ring, Rebecca's face filled the screen, forehead knotted with worry. "Macy, hi! Is everything okay?"

Macy's smile was thin, but genuine. "Yes, things are going smooth here. Smoother than they have in a while, actually!"

Rebecca's expression immediately softened, tension easing. "I'm so glad, sweetheart. Your dad is going over the books with Ethan. Do you want me to get him?"

"No, it's okay," Macy said. She crossed her legs underneath herself and allowed herself to sink into the back of the couch. "I know we haven't talked very much since…everything happened. I wanted to make sure that we're all okay."

Tears welled in Rebecca's eyes. "There's nothing you could do to make us not be, Macy. I hope you know that our decision that night had everything to do with Cade and nothing to do with you. We'll never stop worrying about you until we know that you're okay."

Macy's pulse slowed. "Honestly, Mom, ever since we went to Chicago for the bridal shower, Cade has been like a new man.

"I don't know what finally did it, but something finally scared him straight. He's been just like the way he used to be: kind, thoughtful, patient. I told him I was going to try to call tonight, and he wants me even to tell you all that he's sorry, and he hopes one day we can all move past it."

Rebecca nodded slowly and pursed her lips, turning Macy's words over in her mind. "I appreciate his apology. Whether we can move past it or not is going to come down to his behavior from here on in. I don't want to speak for your father and brother, but I believe they would agree."

"That's fair," Macy said.

"So," Rebecca said, "Two weeks to go until the big day. How are you feeling?"

"Well," Macy laughed, "it's my bachelorette party tonight. I came over to the old apartment to get ready with Catherine and Nina, and decided there was no better time to get in touch. You know, just in case you didn't want to see Cade."

Rebecca smiled brightly. "Bachelorette party? That sounds like just what you need right now."

"It is!" Macy smiled warmly in return. In the background, she could see George walking into the room. Her breath caught. He stared at the monitor, "V" of concern instantly appearing on his careworn forehead.

"She's okay," Rebecca said, turning to look at George. "Everything is okay."

George let out a slow breath. "Macy, we're sorry. We—"

"Dad, it's alright. You don't have to."

He nodded, relief softening his features. "So, did I hear you tell your mother you're going out with Catherine tonight?"

Without warning, Macy's door flew open, and Catherine appeared behind her. "That's right, Mr. Walker. She's mine and Nina's tonight!"

Macy rolled her eyes, but laughed as Catherine left just as quickly. "Yes, we're going back to the place where Cade and I met. We're not planning on getting too crazy, just the three of us and some dancing like we used to do."

Catherine swung the door open again. "Yeah, like we did before she became *boring!*"

Macy spun around to look at Catherine. "Don't you have anything better to do than listen at my door?"

Catherine gave her a wicked grin. "Nope."

George and Rebecca laughed heartily. "We are so glad you're together tonight," Rebecca said.

Macy threw a pillow at Catherine, which she dodged, cackling.

"It looks just like old times between you two!" Rebecca said, continuing to laugh. "I'll let you go get ready for your night out, but I'm so glad you called."

"Me too. Love you." Macy smiled, content, as she disconnected the call.

Catherine scooped up the pillow Macy had thrown and tossed it back in her direction. "Come on, Nina will be here any minute!"

"Alright," Macy said as she started towards the door. "You go pour your drink; I'll start getting dressed."

"I can't believe you agreed to no alcohol tonight, Mace." Catherine went into the kitchen, pulled a pair of glasses from the cabinet, and a bottle of Pinot Grigio from the fridge. "It's your bachelorette party! You have to at least have *one!*"

"I don't, though!" Macy said. She sat down at the kitchen table. "I've worked so hard to lose this weight to squeeze into that dress. I can't blow it now!"

Catherine sipped from her glass and poured a second one for Nina. "Are you sure that's the only reason?"

"Yes, Catherine," Macy said, voice sharp. She shook her head, looking down at the floor. "Sorry."

Catherine eyed her suspiciously, tapping her upper lip. "You look tense. Maybe a little cocktail would calm you down."

Their eyes locked, mouths twisted into scowls, and after a beat, they burst out laughing. The buzzer alerted to Nina's arrival, and Macy rose from the table to let her in.

Nina burst through the door in a sleek red minidress and black stilettos, blond hair flying loose and wavy to the middle of her back. She set her black clutch purse on the table and grabbed the wine bottle from the counter.

"Nice to see you too, Nina!" Macy said. "The glass here was for you."

"No, it's not," Nina answered, taking a swig from the bottle. "It's yours."

"I can't!" Macy said, eyes wide. "My dress!"

Nina rolled her eyes. "Oh, live a little. One glass isn't going to make or break if your dress fits or not."

"But—" Macy started, with Nina cutting her off by waving a finger in her face.

"Tonight is about *you*. Not his wishes disguised as your self-doubt," Catherine said, taking Macy's hands. "Let's get you dressed and see if you change your mind."

Macy groaned and followed behind Catherine into her and Shane's room. The green strap of fabric that had doubled as a dress the year before had hung in Catherine's closet; Macy had insisted she would never wear it again. Catherine pulled it from the closet and held it out to her.

"You've got to be kidding me," Macy said.

"Have we met before? No! I'm not kidding."

Macy snatched the hanger from Catherine and pointed her finger in her face. "I don't know when, I don't know how. But I will get you for this."

Nina giggled from the kitchen as Macy returned to her old room to slip into the dress. It fits Macy very differently now. Though looser, it hugged her body in a new, sultry way. She hesitated, wondering if it was too on-the-nose to wear the same dress to the same club, just weeks before marrying the same man she'd met there. But at the same point in time, it was a moment of coming full circle.

She checked her reflection in the mirror, the sparkling green dress catching the leftover sunlight. "Well, if tonight's about me," she told the lady in the mirror, "this hair is going *up*."

She swept her copper ringlets into a loose, messy bun with stray tendrils framing her face. Nina leaned on the door frame.

"No need for makeup tonight, babe," Nina said. "You look flawless."

"You know what?" Macy answered, spinning in the mirror. "I would never have believed this seven weeks ago, but I really like strong me."

"That's my girl," Nina said.

"Oh, screw it," Macy said, storming out of the bedroom and into the kitchen. She seized the wine glass that still waited on the table and held it up before taking a sip. "Here's to *us*, ladies."

"*Yes!*" Nina exclaimed. "Now it's a party!"

From her old room, Macy could hear the buzz of a new text message arriving. She started back to the room to check it, but before she could, Nina scooped it up off the bed. When Macy lunged for the phone, Nina tossed it over her head to Catherine's waiting hands.

"Ah, ah!" Catherine teased. "Not tonight. You are off duty!"

"What if it's an emergency?"

Catherine peered at the lock screen with the preview of Cade's message. "Yes, it's urgent. Asking if you left yet. What do you think, Nina? Should we tell her she's getting Theo's opinion about her dress?"

Nina laughed into the wine bottle. "Don't be cruel!"

"Come on," Macy said, reaching for the phone. "Give it to me. Please let me just answer him?"

"I got it!" Nina said, putting down her wine bottle and fishing her phone out of her clutch. She spoke as she typed, "*No need to worry. We're leaving the apartment now, will deliver your bride safe and sound in the morning.*"

Macy squinted at her. "You guys text?"

Nina tucked her phone back into her purse. "Problem with that?"

"No! Just didn't know you had traded numbers." Macy took a long swig off her glass, continuing to study Nina's expression.

"Oh, stop looking at me like that!" Nina hollered. "How do you think he got your ring size?"

Blushing, Macy finally looked away. She chugged the last of her wine and put the glass into the sink. "Who else is ready for a party, then?"

Catherine drained the rest of her glass. "Thought you two would never stop bickering. Let's go!"

Nina laughed and opened the door first. "We weren't bickering! You'll know when we're bickering."

Macy slipped into a pair of black, flat sandals and grabbed her purse. "Yeah! If I want to pick a fight with Nina, I'll just do this." Creeping up behind her, Macy grabbed the bottle of Pinot out of Nina's hand and tucked it under her arm.

"Hey!" Nina shouted. "Fine, you need it more than I do."

Catherine closed the door behind them and locked up. They took turns passing the bottle back and forth between them as they stepped down the winding staircase until they were out in the early evening air.

For a moment, Macy allowed herself to feel the anticipation of the things to come. She was with her favorite girlfriends, and her wedding was two weeks away. And finally, she and Cade were back on track.

Since the trip to Chicago, he had been the model fiancé. Every morning, he brewed the coffee and packed their lunches. He cheered her on while she was exercising. It was as though a dark cloud had lifted from over their relationship, and they felt new again. She had gone into the evening after they had spent most of the day in bed, enjoying each other, leaving only for bathroom or food breaks.

A limo waited outside the Brownstone, courtesy of Brian, where they shared another bottle of champagne. Catherine pulled her phone out of her purse and started shooting pictures as they rode to the club. It buzzed in her hand before she realized she had taken out Macy's phone instead of hers, and stuck her tongue out at it when she saw it was, once again, Cade.

"Nina, are you sure you texted the right Cade? He's texted her three times already."

"Yep!" Nina said. "He answered, too. Said, 'okay'!"

"Make that four," Catherine said, looking at the phone again and lowering it back into her purse. As they pulled up to the club, the phone rang, and she once again pulled it out. "Bloody Hell, Cade! Don't you have any friends to bother? Macy is with *us* tonight."

Before he could reply, and before Macy could react, Catherine ended the call and buried the phone back into her purse. The limo pulled up in front of Club Echelon. Macy tried to snatch Catherine's purse to get her phone back, but Catherine pulled it just out of reach before she could get it. "You are just Macy tonight!"

Macy whined but followed, contemplating stealing Nina's phone instead later in the night.

The bass inside Club Echelon thundered, making the floor under Macy's feet vibrate. The lights cast colorful ribbons of light through the dark room as bodies bumped and swayed with the music. Between the pulsing nightclub and the wine that she'd already had, Macy's head began to spin.

She closed her eyes against it, allowing her body to be moved by Nina onto the dance floor. "Don't think, tonight," Nina said in her ear. "Just dance."

Catherine joined from the bar, the first round of drinks in hand. Her auburn bob swayed in her face, drink held over her head, as she spun and wove back to the rest of their party. She held out a glass for Nina, which she eagerly took, and offered the other to Macy.

Macy shook her head, determined not to break her promise any more than she already had. Catherine waved the glass in her face, insistent. "I already bought it. You gotta drink it. Girl code of alcohol honor!"

"That's not a thing," Macy said, but she snatched the cocktail out of Catherine's hand anyway.

"It is now!" Nina said, words already starting to slur.

Macy sipped tentatively at her drink and swayed with the music. She closed her eyes, leaning in to the rhythm, and didn't realize she had danced away from the girls until she felt an unfamiliar pair of hands on her hips.

Her eyes flashed open to find a man with a short black ponytail behind her, smiling as he danced. Macy laughed awkwardly as she shook her head and stepped back towards her friends.

"Relax!" Catherine said, throwing an arm around Macy's shoulders. "It's only dancing. He seems harmless!"

Macy shook her head again, tension racing up her neck. In her mind's eye, she was trying to imagine Cade's reaction if he had seen, even if it was *harmless*.

They danced more songs together before easing off the dance floor towards the bar for water. Macy reached for her purse out of reflex, then stared expectantly at Catherine.

"Not gonna happen," Catherine said, clamping a protective hand over her purse. "And if you try to sneak it out when I'm not looking, I'm putting it in the freezer."

Nina shrieked with laughter. "Do it!"

"Cath, let me check it! I just want to make sure he's not freaking out."

"Let him freak!" Catherine said, taking her water glass. "Tonight is *your* night."

Even as she said it, her purse continued to buzz. "Damn, he sure is insistent, though."

"Just let me tell him I'll be home late tonight."

"Let her have one, Cath," Nina countered. "But after you've had some fun. You deserve this!"

Macy growled at them, but relented. She drank her water, and they went back to the dance floor. She let herself be pulled back through the crush of bodies. This time, she didn't fight the beat; she let her hair fall loose from the bun, curls springing wild in the strobe lights.

They danced until sweat made Macy's curls cling to her cheekbones, until she was breathless and lightheaded. When they finally spilled back toward the bar for another round of drinks, Macy leaned against the cool metal and closed her eyes. "Alright, phone time!" Macy said, insistent. At last, Catherine fished it out of her purse and handed it over.

Macy had four missed calls, all with voicemails, and nine text messages. Each message had an increasing urgency, asking her to call him.

Her insides immediately went cold, and she regretted checking her phone. She kept the message simple:

Macy:
I'm sorry I haven't answered. Catherine took my phone so I would be able to just be present. I just got it back from her. I'll call you in the morning. Love you.

She hit send just as the bartender set down a round of three Cosmos. Catherine took the phone back from her just as Macy tried to argue that they hadn't ordered the drinks.

"Compliments of the gentleman on the other end of the bar," the bartender said.

Macy looked and saw the same black-haired man who had danced with her waving at them, and holding his own glass up in cheers.

"I have to put a stop to this," Macy said.

"I got it," Nina said, syrupy smile spreading across her cheeks. She slunk away towards the man, drink in hand, and sat up on the barstool next to him.

Catherine raised her eyebrows at Macy and took up both glasses, handing one to Macy, before Nina swept back over to them.

"Boring. The guy said it was a peace offering in case he made you uncomfortable with the dance," Nina said. "Now let's go get out there."

Macy took her glass and followed her back onto the floor. She didn't see her phone light back up. She didn't feel the vibration of the text messages multiplying.

Instead, she fought desperately to reclaim that lightness she walked into the club with, instead of the shattered cold that tried to reclaim her.

Tonight was for her. Tomorrow, the consequences would be whatever they were.

Tonight, she was free.

Chapter Thirty

FALLOUT

Macy woke early the next morning, head throbbing in time with the choices she'd made the night before. Too much alcohol, not enough food or water. Too much bass, and not enough sleep.

Worse than the physical hangover was the emotional one: the dread lingering in her stomach like a stone.

The moment she opened her eyes, the memory of Cade's unanswered texts slammed into her chest. She hadn't dared to call back or answer, knowing how much she'd drunk.

She lay still, heart stuttering, trying to summon the courage to reach for her phone. She wasn't ready for the consequences. Not ready for him.

A low groan escaped her when she sat up. She stretched, immediately regretting it, and pressed her hands to her temples. She knew she had to call Cade and apologize. The cold ribbon of fear slid down her spine as she questioned her choices from the night before. Knowing she shouldn't have had the drinks. She couldn't do anything about the phone, but she didn't have to break her promise about alcohol.

She finally willed herself to turn over her phone. There were five missed calls and eight texts. Her stomach dropped as though she was falling through the mattress and each floor below her.

Shit.

Her fingers twisted into her gold chain, pulling on the cross until the chain started biting into the back of her neck. The bedroom door swung open, and Catherine stepped inside, carrying a glass of orange juice and a pair of Tylenol. Her powder-blue bathrobe hung loose around her shoulders, her normally immaculate bob in disarray from sleep.

"Morning, Sunshine!" Her voice was tipped with affectionate sarcasm.

Macy tried to muster some humor but could barely manage a crooked smile. "Thanks, Cath."

Catherine's eyes narrowed. "You alright? I didn't think you'd gotten *that* lit last night."

Macy smiled thinly. "I'm out of practice."

She paused, gesturing towards her phone. "I haven't read the messages yet, but I know he's pissed. I should probably get home sooner rather than later and try to fix this."

Catherine's mouth pressed into a thin line. "You should hydrate first and have some breakfast. You look like someone through you down a flight of stairs."

Macy laughed, but it was a brittle sound. "Feels like it, too."

"I'm going to make some scrambled eggs," Catherine said. "Why don't you have something to eat, and then we'll figure this out?"

Macy nodded, slowly, but whimpered when pain ricocheted behind her eyes. Her heart was beating too fast, too shallow. Instinctual fear, knowing how angry he must be, coiled in her gut.

She closed her eyes, bracing herself, contemplating what to say to him. Before she could read through all of the messages, the door buzzer rang out in the kitchen, sending a stab of ice through Macy's heart.

She flinched so hard her glass sloshed. *Not yet, I'm not ready!*

She raced to the mirror, trying to smooth her hair. Her curls were limp and frizzy from sweating the night before. Her eyes were a swollen and red-rimmed mess. There was no fixing that.

She looked like someone who had done something wrong.

Why did I let them talk me into drinking?

"Ready or not," she whispered. "Here we go."

Tentatively, she stepped into the kitchen. Catherine stood at the stove, swirling eggs in a hot pan. She had hastily dressed into jeans and a loose t-shirt, hair smoothed but still missing its usual polish. Coffee percolated on the counter, filling the apartment with the aroma of warm French vanilla. It did nothing to ease the tide of dread rising in her throat.

Shane stood by the door and put a comforting hand on Macy's shoulder as she walked past.

"It's going to be okay," he murmured.

His voice didn't reach her. She nodded mechanically, and her body started to shake. She sat down in her usual spot at the table just as footsteps outside the door signaled Cade's arrival.

Catherine plated the eggs, but Macy put a weak hand up. "Thanks, Cath, but I don't think my stomach can take them right now."

Catherine nodded, putting a warm hand on Macy's as the door swung open, revealing a disheveled Cade.

"We'll give you some privacy," Catherine said, taking the plate and following Shane to their room.

Cade closed the door behind him, eyes locked on Macy. She met his gaze and saw the bloodshot in his eyes matched hers. His black curls fell haphazardly across his forehead. He didn't speak, but fixed her with an electric stare, waiting for her to explain.

Her breath caught in her throat as she frantically searched for words. This was the version of him she feared most. The one she'd seen before. Only now she knew what she'd done wrong, and her body remembered the fear. She reached instinctively for her gold chain but forced her hand back down into her lap.

"I'm sorry," she blurted.

"Sorry?" he barked. "Sorry! Do you know how frantic I was when I didn't hear from you last night?"

"You knew I was with Catherine and Nina. You knew where we were going! And Nina texted you that we were safe."

He pursed his lips and nodded. "I can see I'm already the bad guy."

She recoiled.

He crossed his arms in front of himself. "There was a reason I wanted to talk to you, which you would have known if you had cared enough to ask."

"I told you already she took my phone!" Macy said, voice thin and brittle.

"How many drinks did you have last night, Macy?" His voice was low. Controlled. It scared her more than if he had yelled.

"I—" she stammered.

"I already know you drank, so don't bother trying to lie."

Panic bubbled in her chest. "How…?"

He held up his phone and showed her a picture of herself with Catherine at the bar, Cosmos in hand, laughing without a care.

Her stomach lurched. She could barely whisper. "Were you…?"

"There? Yeah. I was there. They wouldn't let anyone else in. But I got a very interesting text message from a friend of mine. He recognized you and went to say 'hello'."

"Nobody came—"

"Arlo, Macy."

"What?" She squinted at him, mind racing, searching for a memory. He held up his phone again and showed her a picture of himself, smiling, next to a man with a black ponytail.

The man who bought them drinks. The man who escorted them to the rooftop dinner during their second date.

"You sent him to spy on me?" The clouds of confusion gave way to betrayal as the floor seemed to tilt under her feet.

"I didn't have to. He saw you and said you were making a spectacle."

A shiver raced up her spine, her skin crawling as she remembered his hands on her hips as she danced with a drink in her hand. She gasped for breath, but none came.

His voice changed, suddenly soft and wounded.

"You didn't even ask what was so important that I felt the need to interrupt your night out. The night out, if you remember, that I said from the beginning was a bad idea." He continued to stare, unblinking, while the weight of his words settled over her.

"I talked to Talia last night," he continued. "She's not coming to the wedding. While you were out getting drunk with your girlfriends, conveniently out of reach, dancing with whoever came over to you, I was having my heart ripped out by my own sister. Only to have Arlo rip it open when he told me you broke your promise not to drink, and not to flirt with other guys."

Macy's eyes snapped up. "Did he forget to tell you that as soon as I felt his hands on me, I shook my head and walked away from him?"

"But it didn't stop you from accepting the drink he bought you."

She froze, mouth open. There was no justification she could conceive of for accepting the drink, especially when she promised she wouldn't have any.

He shook his head, letting his forehead come to rest in his hands. "I don't know how to stand in front of a priest in two weeks and vow to honor you when you dishonored me so badly last night."

Her mouth opened, but no sound came. Her pulse roared in her ears, skin prickling with cold. But buried somewhere beneath the guilt and the panic, something whispered, *is this what you want for the rest of your life?*

"Cade, what are you saying?" Her breathing quickened, tears pooling in the corner of her eyes.

He didn't sit, but instead hovered near her, pacing a slow and furious line, breath shallow and clipped.

"Macy, you couldn't even keep a promise for one night to not drink. How am I supposed to trust you to make a promise to last for the rest of our lives? How can I believe you're ready for marriage if you can't control yourself for one night?"

Her fingers curled into fists, and her heartbeat thundered so hard she could feel it in her ears. The shame was real, but deeper; another emotion was fighting to free itself.

She was angry.

Her voice was thin, but controlled. "Cade, you knew where I was and who I was with. I danced. Yes, I had a couple of drinks. And yes, I accepted a drink from Arlo. And then Nina went to make it clear that I *am not available.* I explained why I didn't contact you, and it *is* the truth. I didn't betray you."

"So, I *am* the villain," he said, putting a hand to his chest. "Is that what you're saying?"

She gave her head a rapid shake, but even as she did it, she rounded her shoulders, dropping her head into her hands.

"You ignored me, Macy. Even after you got your phone back, you didn't call me? You never followed up? Do you know what that did? I didn't sleep, Macy! They made me leave the damn club, and I couldn't stop pacing the floors until I heard from Arlo that you had left, with only the girls."

"Maybe this is a sign, Cade."

He blinked and froze as if she had slapped him. His voice was a dangerous whisper. "What did you say?"

Macy swallowed hard, forcing herself to stand and face him. She was breathing so fast and so hard that she was afraid she might faint. Still, she steeled her nerve and faced him. "Between my fight with my parents, the dress not fitting, now Talia, maybe it's a sign we need to slow down."

His expression clouded with anger and hurt. "She got into your head anyway, didn't she?"

Her voice cracked. "What? Who?"

"Fucking *Catherine*." He shouted it loud enough so Catherine was sure to hear. "She's been trying to turn you against me from the beginning. That's why she stole your phone last night, isn't it?"

He turned to stomp towards her room, and Macy surged forward, blocking him.

"Don't you dare! This is between you and me."

She pressed her fingers to her temples, nausea rising again. "We've been in such a hurry that we've never stopped to think about what we're doing. We pretend it's all perfect because we're scared of what it'll mean if we don't."

Cade froze. "Macy, what are *you* saying?"

Her chest squeezed, making her breath painful. They stood staring at each other, Macy trying to form the words she knew she needed to say, but didn't know if she could.

"I think we should take some time to think about this. Maybe go back to the original plan for December."

Cade stared at her, anger finally leaving his face, leaving shock and heartbreak behind. "And there it is. You've been waiting for the opportunity to find a way out of this, haven't you?"

Her voice shook, but gained momentum as she spoke. "That's not what I meant, Cade."

His eyes shimmered with unshed tears, but a new darkness sharpened at the edges. "So that's it then? You're delaying our wedding because I didn't want you to go out and get drunk?"

"No," Macy whispered, tears finally spilling. "I'm saying we need to see our problems clearly before we do something we can't take back. I'll stay here for a while so we can think. I'll send Nina over to pick me up some clothes. I'm sorry, Cade, but I need you to leave now."

Her voice trailed off as she ran into her room and closed the door. She collapsed on the bed, finally letting the tears spill free, and when she heard the apartment door open and close again, she allowed herself to grieve a little louder.

A tentative knock came to the apartment door. Macy didn't have it in her to look who it was, but instead, barricaded herself further under her pillow. The door creaked open, and Catherine spoke with someone in quiet tones. The responding voice was warm, familiar, and welcome.

Theo.

Macy considered coming out of her hiding spot, but one look at herself in the mirror had her immediately changing her mind: swollen eyes, blotchy cheeks, hair a nest of frizzy curls. She looked like a woman who'd fought a storm and lost.

The apartment door swung closed again, and a gentle knock followed at her bedroom door.

"Mace?" Catherine called, gently. "Do you want some company?"

There was nothing in the world she wanted less, but she knew she didn't have to hide from Catherine. She inched herself off the bed and pulled the door open slowly, in case Catherine wasn't alone.

She was.

"Theo was just here. He heard you two arguing and wanted to make sure you're okay. He said he'll give you space but wanted me to remind you, General Tso is the cure for everything."

A weak laugh escaped her. "Yeah, he would say that."

She pushed the door open a little further and let Catherine inside. They sat next to each other on the edge of Macy's bed, silent, no words to say but knowing none were needed.

"So, I'm sure you probably heard it all anyway. These walls are paper-thin," Macy eventually said. She laughed uncomfortably, playing with the duvet and absently straightening the edges.

"I heard enough. You don't have to tell me anything you don't want to relive. But you should know I'm proud of you. I know that wasn't easy."

Macy nodded, numb. "I don't even know where to start unpacking everything. It just hit me when he was talking about being up all night pacing the floors, and trying to get into the club, and over Talia not coming. We can't get married like this."

"Do you think he'd go to counseling?" Catherine asked.

Macy shrugged. "I've never mentioned it, but who knows?"

Her phone heralded a text from Nina, brisk and practical: What do you need? Clothes? Toiletries? Laptop? I'm grabbing food too. Tell me what you want, or I'll choose.

Macy typed out a quick list. Nina pinged back: *Be there in fifteen.*

Macy snorted absently at the idea of food. "It's ironic, isn't it?" she said to Catherine. "I've been starving myself for weeks to fit into that damn dress. Now who knows if there's even going to be a wedding, and I don't think I could eat a cracker if my life depended on it."

Catherine smiled and put a gentle hand on Macy's back. "You're not going through this alone. We'll just take it one breath at a time."

A single stray tear rolled down Macy's cheek, and she marveled that she had any left. "How am I going to decide what to do?"

Catherine grabbed the tissue box from Macy's nightstand and gave it to her. "You'll know. Just like you did today."

Macy swiped absently at the tear on her cheek, skin starting to turn raw.

"Shane can make himself scarce, too, if you need him to," Catherine continued. "Whatever you need."

"No," Macy said, waving her off and managing a feeble laugh. "I'm not *so* fragile that I have to kick your man out of his home. Except maybe just for tonight."

"Consider it done," Catherine said. She floated out of the room and back towards her own.

Macy wrapped the duvet around herself and considered braving the living room. Her phone still sat untouched on the nightstand, though it had been buzzing most of the day. She did have one message from her mother, asking how the bachelorette party was. The rest were all from Cade.

Cade

*Macy, Bella, please don't do
this.*

Cade

*I'm so sorry I lost my temper
with you. It wasn't fair. Please
talk to me.*

Cade

I'll do anything to fix this.

Cade

*Nina just left with your things.
So, I guess it's really
happening.*

Before she had the chance to start to type a reply, a new message arrived
from Sheryl.

Sheryl

*Macy, Cade just told his dad
what happened. Can you call
me, please? We need to figure
this out.*

"We?" Macy said to her phone. "I really can't handle talking to Sheryl
right now, too."

"Then don't," Catherine said, appearing back in the doorway. "You
don't owe her any explanation tonight.

"Shane is going to bunk with Brian, and Nina is going to stay here. The circumstances are shitty, but we're going to have some ice cream, watch some trash TV, and forget all about this for a few hours. The rest can wait until tomorrow."

Duvet still around her shoulders, Macy finally ventured into the living room when Nina arrived, and Shane left. The phone remained in her room, where she could pretend that if she didn't hear it buzz, he wasn't still waiting for her to answer.

Chapter Thirty-One

THE HEART'S COMPASS

Sleep had become a commodity. It was a luxury often denied to Macy in the days after her fight with Cade, coming in blocks of an hour or two at a time. But never enough to be restorative.

Her mind ran a constant treadmill, recalling the year since she met Cade Donovan. Where, exactly, did they make the wrong turn when it started out so right?

By mid-week, she felt like she was moving through fog. Her body was present, but her thoughts lagged several steps behind, drifting and colliding with themselves. She ignored most buzzing notifications, answering only the people who didn't know what had happened. Anyone else felt like a live wire she couldn't touch. When she arrived at her desk on Wednesday morning, she froze. A massive vase with red and white roses waited at her desk. They were so voluminous that they nearly blocked her view of her monitor. A card leaned against the glass.

Her heart jumped into her throat.

She didn't need to open the note to know who it was from, and her fingers trembled as she pulled it open.

"If it's space you need, I will let you have it. Please don't give up on me. On us. I'll do anything. -C"

Her throat tightened painfully as she fought more tears away.

She stuffed the card into her purse just as Brielle appeared in her cubicle. "Ugh, you two are so nauseatingly cute."

Macy forced a thin smile that didn't quite land. "Yeah, he isn't stingy with attention."

Before Brielle could press, RJ swooped past, whistling. "Damn, girl! What did he do?"

Macy's laugh came out thin and shrill; unconvincing even to her own ears. Sebrina promptly elbowed him in the ribs. "Leave her alone! She's into the final countdown, here. Last thing she needs right now is you two vultures swirling around looking for drama."

Macy looked up at Sebrina and mouthed *thank you*, earning a wink from Sebrina. Anything more, and Macy might have cracked open right in front of them all.

She kept her head down the rest of the day, buried in spreadsheets. Ten minutes before shutdown, she knocked on Amara's door and asked if she could head out early. It wasn't a lie to say her head hurt—a dull, throbbing ache that hadn't left her since Saturday morning, her eyes looking bruised. Amara took one glance and didn't question it.

Macy grabbed her purse and scurried out of the building before Cade would have a chance to catch her at the exit.

By the time she arrived at the brownstone, she felt like a raw nerve ending.

"Hey," Catherine said. "Nina's coming over tonight. I hope that's okay."

"Sure," Macy said, voice flat and eyes vacant. She tossed her purse and shoes into her room and sank into a chair at the kitchen table, head in her hands.

"Rough day?" Catherine asked.

"More so than usual, you mean?" Macy said, a dry smirk tugging at her lips. "He delivered two dozen roses and a card to work, and I just…I can't talk about it with them. I don't want to damage their view of him if we manage to work things out. I can't talk to my parents, either, because they already hate him. I can't risk rocking either boat until I know which way I'm going."

Catherine cocked her head, contemplative. "That makes sense. You don't owe anyone an explanation. But that's why you have us. You don't have to make this decision alone."

"Don't I, though? I'm the one who will be walking down that aisle, or not, and I can't keep stalling on it. I owe him some kind of answer, and soon."

The door buzzer startled her so violently that her knee hit the underside of the table. Catherine moved toward the intercom.

"That'll be Nina," she said.

Footsteps climbed the stairs, followed by laughter, one voice unmistakably masculine.

Macy stiffened, and her breath hitched. "Oh God…what if it's him? Catherine, please, can you check before he storms in here?"

"I got you!" Catherine promised. "But, do you really think he'd willingly walk into my line of fire right now?"

Slightly reassured, Macy willed her heart rate to slow down. The footsteps finally came to rest at the door, and Catherine opened it to find Nina with two white bags of takeout and Theo at her side.

"I don't have to stay," Theo said quickly, warmth in his voice and his smile. "I just ran into this one coming in and thought I'd say hello. It's probably dumb to ask, but how are you?"

Macy returned his smile, and it was the first one that felt genuine since her party. Nina strutted past her to the table, and Macy let Theo fold her into a warm hug. "It's nice to see a friendly face," she said.

They settled in at the table. Nina unpacking sushi and hibachi, while Catherine pulled a bottle of Chardonnay from the fridge.

"Don't take this the wrong way," Macy said, getting up to pour a glass of water, "but I've had enough alcohol for a while."

Catherine chuckled quietly. "That's fair."

They ate in a heavy and unsettled quiet, the only sound being chopsticks tapping on plates. Macy's eyes darted around the room uncomfortably, looking for an excuse to break the silence.

Nina finally broke it. "So! Someone has to address the elephant in the room. Have you decided what you're going to do yet, Mace?"

Macy choked on a piece of shrimp. "Nothing like going straight for the throat."

Nina popped a tuna roll into her mouth and stared at her expectantly. A piece of rice clung to her lip, which she brushed at absently, giving Macy a smile that seemed almost predatory.

"I don't believe in wasting time."

"Yeah," Macy said, sipping on her water. "That's what Cade said, and look where that got us."

"I'm just saying," Nina said, stabbing a carrot with her chopstick a little too forcefully. "He screwed up. But let's face it, so did you."

"Now wait, just a minute here!" Macy's sushi roll dropped onto her plate, soy sauce splattering the table. "You were the one practically pouring those drinks down my throat."

"You know it's deeper than that, Mace!" Nina continued. "All he wants is to be with you. People would kill for that kind of adoration from a partner. That kid of fire. Don't you think there have been times you've been stringing him along a little?"

"What? No!" Macy shouted.

"Nina, passion doesn't give a guy a pass to guilt-trip her to get his way," Theo said. "You didn't see the look he gave me after he thought I was after his girl. I feel very protective of you, Macy, but I hope you realize I would never want to pose any kind of threat." He trailed off, looking at Macy, forehead scrunched, eyes wide.

Macy shook her head. "Of course, Theo. You're a good friend. I've made that clear to him that that's all."

Nina waved her hand dismissively. "Look, Mace. What you two have…that's magic. Most people never get that level of passion from their partner. You guys burn hot, and sometimes fire gets messy. But that doesn't mean it's not worth keeping."

Catherine sighed and rolled her eyes, pouring another Chardonnay. "Here we go."

Nina ignored her and scooted her chair closer to Macy. "He screws up because he cares so much. He's terrified of losing you."

Catherine slammed her fist onto the table. "Passion doesn't excuse controlling her, which he's been doing from the beginning."

Macy put her head in her hands while Catherine and Nina continued to argue. Their voices volleyed around her like a storm, and she sat, perfectly still in the middle, wishing she could sink into the floor.

"Alright, enough," she finally said. She lifted her head and put her hands at her sides, calm and resolved. "I love you both. You know that. But this isn't about either of you, and *you* arguing about what *I* should do isn't helping."

She took a shaky breath, all eyes on her. "This is between Cade and me, so it will be resolved between Cade and me. On Saturday, I am going to go talk to him. I'm going to tell him exactly what I'm feeling. After that, whatever happens, happens."

Nina stared at her expectantly. "And you're going to tell him…?"

She picked up her chopsticks and stared right back. She answered, "My decision." Smiling curtly, she went back to her food.

Theo brushed his hand against her arm. "You good?" he whispered.

"Better than I've been all week," she said, smiling again, and this time, she meant it.

Macy stood at the door of the apartment she had shared with Cade, resolve wavering. She had texted him on Thursday and told him that she would have a decision on Saturday. He immediately called, but she sent it to voicemail. She wasn't ready to tip her hand. Not yet.

Catherine respected her decision and didn't press. Nina had been asked to leave when she continued to plead her case.

Macy knew what she wanted to do, and she wasn't going to let anyone change her mind. Too many decisions from the last year had been made for her, and this one would be hers. When the deed was done, she would handle telling her family and her friends that the wedding was on hold.

But now, standing at the door, her heart was thundering like a bird's. He deserved the truth, even if it hurt. She couldn't get married like this. Yet, after having practiced her words for days, they scattered as she tried to picture saying them out loud.

Just knock, Mace. He's expecting you.

She raised her fist and tapped it twice. The door swung open almost instantly, as though Cade had been waiting behind it.

He stood unshaven, hair an untamed mass of curls, exhausted bags under his eyes. Something inside her came undone at the sight of him, but she straightened her spine and held her neutral expression.

He stepped to the side, allowing her in. "I've had a pot of coffee keeping warm for you, hoping you would come."

She walked into the familiar living room. The normally tidy home looked as disarrayed as he did—coffee mugs littered every surface. Blankets and laundry were kicked into piles on the couch as well as the floor. Dirty dishes sat in the sink.

Cade shut the door behind her. "I'm so glad you're here. I've been a wreck since last week."

Macy took a deep breath, squaring her shoulders. "We need to talk."

His breath caught. He nodded slowly. "You're calling it off."

Her palms were slick. Her pulse hammered. But for once, she didn't let herself sit down, didn't let herself fold. Her fingers intertwined with her gold chain, tugging painfully on the cross. "Not exactly, but…"

His shoulders sagged with relief. "Thank God. I've been losing my mind. I know I messed up, and I'm ready to do counseling. I'll do whatever it takes."

Her chest tightened. It would've been so easy to nod, to step right back into his arms and what was familiar. To erase the last week. But she couldn't.

Don't back down, Mace, she said to herself.

"Cade, I'm not here to fix this today." Her voice came out smaller than intended, but steady. "I love you, but we're not okay. We can't get married until we are."

His face crumpled. "Macy—"

"No," she said gently but firmly. "I just need you to listen."

He closed his mouth and collapsed into the chair behind him.

Macy took a deep, anchoring breath. "What happened last weekend wasn't a one-off incident. It showed me all the cracks we've been pretending for months weren't there. I'm not calling it off, but we need to put it on hold, at least until we—"

A buzz at the door stopped Macy in her tracks.

"Are you expecting someone?" she said, voice wavering.

Cade shook his head. He walked to the intercom and pressed the button to talk. "Yes?"

"Surprise!"

Macy froze, tears threatening, as she immediately recognized the voices on the other end of the intercom.

They were here.

Her parents.

Chapter Thirty-Two

FOR BETTER OR WORSE

Nina passed around a pitcher of lemonade to Joy. She was holding a glass for herself as well as for Ethan, who was on the floor changing a fussy Caleb. Nina wasn't used to having a baby in her penthouse and wouldn't know what to do with one if it were handed to her. But this was for Macy.

She loved her cousin, but the girl had become her own worst enemy. Macy was about to throw away the kind of love Nina wished she'd held out for, and she wasn't about to sit by and let her do that. Macy might be mad if she knew the truth, but it was the best thing for her, in the long run.

After their dinner Wednesday night, Macy had been frustratingly evasive, refusing to tell either of them what her decision was about Cade. All she knew was that Macy was going, today, to tell him her decision. Nina had a feeling Macy would choose love. So what if she had called to make sure her parents were there to seal the deal?

Nina didn't see it as meddling, exactly. Her mother was the meddler and the gossip. This was an intervention. Macy always needed a nudge in the right direction. Catherine sure wasn't going to do it, so if she didn't, who would?

Joy swirled her glass and sipped at the lemonade, the tangy sweetness light on her tongue. "Rebecca was so glad you called, Nina, but I can't help but wonder why you did?"

Nina shrugged, nonchalant. "Macy's been pushed to her limits lately with the promotion at work, and trying to make everything fit together for the wedding at the last minute. After that fight you all got into, I was really worried about her. It just about pushed her to the edge."

Ethan poked his head up within sight of the table, holding Caleb from rolling off his changing mat. "She did call last weekend and told them how much better things were going. It seemed like she was feeling pretty good!"

"And she was!" Nina said, pouring her own lemonade. "But I knew how much she needed you all here. It sounded to me like the bridge had been built, and someone needed to be the one to invite one of you to cross. Macy was afraid that if she did, you guys would say no. So, I took it upon myself."

Leaning in and putting a hand on Joy's arm, Nina dropped her voice so only they could hear. "Don't tell her I told you that, though. She would be so embarrassed, and not in the 'she wore too many sequins in high school' kind of way."

Ethan smiled, eyes crinkling. "I know the kind. I think that's just the number the bullies did on her when we were kids. She was always determined to keep a stiff upper lip. She didn't want anyone to know how much she was hurting and let them exploit it."

"Exactly," Nina said, meeting his smile with one of her own. "And that's why I sent your parents right over. She's been hurting more than she would ever admit, and she needs them, right now."

It was true that Macy needed her parents, but she also knew that she needed her parents *there* to stop her from making the biggest mistake of her life. Macy would throw herself on the blade before she'd ever see break the heart of someone she loved.

One day, she was sure, Macy would thank her for this.

Macy frantically scooped coffee mugs into the sink and threw Cade's dirty laundry into the bedroom. She slammed the door closed just as Cade opened the door for George and Rebecca.

"We couldn't stay away any longer," Rebecca said. "Can we…?"

His eyes remained slightly hooded, but Cade opened the door further to allow them entry. Macy reappeared behind him, eyes wide, stomach twisting into knots.

"Did we interrupt something?" George asked, taking in Cade's haggard appearance and the untidy apartment. "We should have called first, Beck."

"No, it's alright," Cade said quickly. He ran his fingers through his hair, smoothing it, and flipped his expression: eyes bright, smile wide, and exhaustion turned to surprise. "Macy and I were just enjoying a lazy morning and debating how we want to spend the day now that we're a week away from the ceremony. Isn't that right, Bella?"

Macy's breathing quickened as Cade slipped easily from the broken man she met at the door and the version of himself her parents wanted him to be. She watched it happen like an out-of-body moment, drowning helplessly in his relief but losing her own.

He turned to look at her, continuing to smile, but underneath the smile was a pointed glare that held desperate and unfiltered hope. It screamed, *not in front of them.*

"We weren't sure what we were going to do until a couple of days ago, really," Rebecca said. "After Macy called and told us how well things were going, we wondered if we might have misjudged you, Cade. So, we're here to support our daughter and see this through."

Cade stood next to Macy and put an arm around her waist. It was the first physical contact they'd had since their fight, and her body reacted before her mind could. Almost against her will, she melted into his side. Her knees went weak, trembling with the weight of expectation.

Macy felt the walls start to close in on her. Their approval, the pride in her mother's eyes, pressed on her chest like a weight she couldn't lift.

"It means the world to us that you're here, Mr. and Mrs. Walker," Cade beamed.

George and Rebecca looked at each other and back at him. "I don't think we're ready for you to call us Mom and Dad," George said. "But you might as well at least call us George and Rebecca."

Cade gestured for them to sit at the table and pulled the last set of clean coffee mugs from the cupboard. "Now, Mace?" he said gently. "Weren't you saying something before they knocked?"

Her mouth went dry, and her legs continued to shake. Her rehearsed speech, the one she'd repeated in the mirror and whispered on the train, vanished from her lips as if it had never existed. Her parents were smiling at her, encouragement in their eyes. Cade watched her like she was his lifeline. The clock raced forward towards the wedding she had just tried to delay.

And the final bedrock of her resolve crumbled under the weight of their stares.

"I…" Her voice was small and strangled. She swallowed painfully and tried again. "I was just saying how overwhelming this week was. That's all."

As Cade beamed and poured the coffee, Macy felt an invisible door slam shut.

Chapter Thirty-Three

I DO?

Cade prepared lunch for the four of them—sandwiches and chips for himself and Macy's parents, and a salad with chicken and hard-boiled eggs for Macy—as he gushed over how excited they were to have Rebecca and George with them for the rest of the week. When they explained that Ethan and Joy waited with Caleb at Nina and Brian's penthouse, Cade fell over himself to make plans to make things right with Ethan.

Macy held her silence, her smile too wide, the idea of her voice betraying her stunning her in place. *We can still make this work,* she told herself. *It was a bad fight, but he does always make up for losing his temper. It's going to be okay.*

She had come back to the apartment empty-handed, except for her purse, and would need to make arrangements to get her things back from Catherine's. Knowing Catherine also would need an explanation, she pulled out her phone.

Macy:
Everything is okay. I'll swing by tomorrow to get my things. We're a go for launch here.

Her fingers hovered over the keys, typing and deleting a long explanation of what had happened. Finally, she sent the message just as it was, and after dropping her coffee mug and salad plate in the sink, she hid her phone in her purse so she couldn't hear when Catherine inevitably texted back with her feelings on the matter.

Rebecca and George excused themselves to settle in with Nina and Brian, and Macy choked down the urge to beg them not to go. As she embraced her mother at the door, Rebecca whispered in her ear, "I'm so relieved to see you happy."

The door closed behind them, and the words left unspoken between Macy and Cade echoed in the silence. He took a tentative step towards her, hand cupped and outstretched for her cheek.

"Is this okay?" he said, softly.

She nodded and let her face rest against his hand. He let a sharp breath out and hastily wrapped his free arm around her back, pulling her close. He buried his face in her hair.

"God, Mace. You smell like heaven right now. I missed you so much."

Macy hesitated before raising her hands to wrap them around his back. *Maybe Catherine did influence me too much. He really does love me. I'm going to give him the chance to fix this.*

"I'm so sorry," he continued, barely pausing to take a breath. "I know I scared you. When Arlo told me he saw you at that club, I just panicked. I know it's not an excuse, but I just…I can't lose you because I turned into the worst version of myself."

Macy allowed her head to come to a rest on his chest. He kissed the top of her head. "Please say something."

She pulled back enough to look up into his eyes. Deep, blue, and tormented. *I did that,* she thought to herself. The wall of ice she had so carefully constructed began to thaw.

"We need to go to counseling if we're going to go forward with this wedding next weekend."

He nodded with such force that it shook both of their bodies. "I'll make the call on Monday and see when they can get us in."

The stiffness in her shoulders eased the smallest amount, and her breathing slowly returned to normal. "I have to get my things back from Catherine's."

"Of course," he said, releasing her but taking her hand. "We can head over now, if you want."

"No," Macy said, squeezing his hand. "I should go alone. She's going to want to talk; to know that I'm really okay."

"Well, I'll go with you and just wait outside. After this past week, I don't want to let you out of my sight again any time soon."

Relenting, she picked up her purse, and they left hand in hand.

"It's probably just as fast to walk as to take the train. We can cut through the park." He pushed the door open for her, still keeping one hand tightly in his.

"I can't wait to tell my dad and Sheryl the good news. They've been almost as distraught as me," he said. He continued to talk as they walked across Central Park, but Macy wasn't hearing the words. "But I swear nothing like this will happen again."

He was still making promises when they arrived at her old brownstone. She turned the key in the lock, but he held tight to her hand and pulled her into a searing kiss. He backed her up against the door and cupped the back of her head with his free hand. After a moment of resistance, she returned the kiss, wrapping her arm behind his back. When he released her, he was breathing hard, face flushed.

"Don't be too long in there," he growled, releasing her.

Slightly dizzy, and more than a little embarrassed by the very public display, she turned inside and ran quickly up the stairs. Turning the key in the lock of her old apartment, she found Catherine inside, folding laundry at the table.

Catherine looked up when the door burst open. She studied Macy's face a little too closely: her red cheeks, slightly mussed hair, just a hint of gloss smudged from her lip.

"You caved," Catherine said.

Macy's eyes darted around the room, twisting her engagement ring around on her finger. She shrank against the wall, head tipped toward the floor. A lock of curls fell across her ever-warming forehead.

"I'm not judging you," Catherine said, then paused and retreated. "Okay, maybe I am a little. Is this what you chose? Or were you backed into it?"

"I chose it," Macy said, flat. "I want this to work."

"I know you do, sweetie. But how can you know this won't happen again?"

"He promised to go to therapy," Macy said, risking a glance upward. "I think this is really a new start for us."

Catherine nodded as she folded a towel and stacked it on the table, reaching for her glass of iced tea. "I'll support you no matter what. You know that. I just hope you know what you're doing."

"My parents are here," Macy said.

Catherine's head immediately snapped to attention. "You didn't lead with that because…?"

Macy laughed, guard slowly releasing. "As usual, you didn't give me the chance! They're staying with Nina and Brian. Ethan and Joy are here, too, but I haven't seen them yet. I swear it feels like things are back on track now, Cath."

Catherine flinched imperceptibly at the mention that her family was staying with Nina. But she tucked the information away; a conversation to be had with Nina later about how and why Macy's family came to be here.

Friday night, Macy lay in one of the spare bedrooms at Nina and Brian's penthouse, staring up at the faint shimmer of city lights reflecting off the ceiling. The house hummed with quiet, but her nerves refused to settle.

The week since her family's arrival had blurred in strange and disjointed pieces. Cade had been perfect. Every apology was gentle, every request a question. Every morning, she woke to coffee waiting for her, just the way she liked it, and every night, he encouraged her with *Inferno* and made sure she felt satisfied after dinner. A protein shake was always waiting for her when she finished.

It was a velvet curtain.

The fight was barely mentioned. When Macy tried to circle back on it, he kissed her forehead and told her, "We will talk about it in counseling. I promise!"

Each day, she smiled wider and leaned "all in" until she believed the worst of it was behind them. Her coworkers showered her with attention, hanging on her every word about the final details of the big day ahead. Ethan and Cade had shaken hands, and in an attempt to smooth things the rest of the way over, Cade invited Ethan and George to play poker with him, Brian, and Arlo at the apartment while the women tried Macy's gown for the final time.

"Alright, girl," Nina crowed as they surrounded Macy, beaded gown in hand. "Moment of truth."

Rebecca and Joy took Macy's hands as she stepped into the gown. Catherine gently pulled it up so the spaghetti straps rested on Macy's shoulders. They all held their breath as Nina eased the zipper up.

It was a perfect fit.

Tears in Macy's eyes and her mother's, Macy beamed as she looked into the mirror. "I'm so happy," she said with a muffled sob. A mild ache developed as the bodice squeezed across her chest, and she wondered if it was the tightness of the dress or something else she didn't dare to name.

Now in the dim quiet of the Simpsons' spare room, the truth bubbled to the surface.

I'm scared.

She rolled onto her side and pulled the quilt to her chin. The city outside continued to pulse, and matched the buzzing of her cell phone on the dresser.

Cade

Can't wait to make you my
wife tomorrow!

Queasy, she squirmed and rolled over in the bed.

She wanted to be the girl she used to be; the one who danced with him on a rooftop and believed they had the world at their feet. She wanted the version of him she had dated and glimpsed again in the weeks after Chicago.

It could stay this time. Couldn't it?

Her eyes stung as she whispered into the dark, "Please let this be the right choice."

Sleep finally found her, but it was thin and restless, with dreams she would forget by morning.

Macy awoke to the sounds of her nephew calling for breakfast from the next room. *Today is my wedding day. We're here.*

She rubbed the sleep from her eyes and stretched, checking her watch. She was getting married this afternoon, but that didn't mean skipping her morning date with DeMarcus Martinson. Even during her and Cade's pause, the daily burn had become a ritual, a grounding force. Rest days made her antsy and anxious.

Catherine, hearing the thuds and grunts from the next room, burst in with a coffee mug in hand.

"What! The hell! Is that?" she asked, eyes wide.

"*Inferno*," Macy panted.

"I can't believe you're really doing that right now."

Through labored breathing, Macy grunted, "Can't...stop...now."

She paused for water, then dove back in.

When the workout was finally over, and the sweat washed away in the hottest shower of her life, Macy's nerves began to settle. Her muscles ached, but her mind was clear.

The penthouse buzzed with movement—curling irons, camera flashes, perfume, and floral arrangements. Joy laid Caleb down for a nap and handed Macy a box with white satin ballet flats.

"For after the photos," she said. "We'll keep them nearby until you're ready."

"God bless you," Macy whispered.

She didn't know what waited beyond today. They weren't taking a honeymoon until they could save a little money. But this—this was what they'd been building toward. And she couldn't let the circles under her eyes show up in the wedding photos.

Nina stood behind her, sweeping Macy's hair into an elegant twist, leaving soft tendrils loose around her face. Catherine dusted her cheeks with a simple, feminine coat of makeup. Macy stepped first into her blue pumps, then into her dress, holding her breath as Catherine reached for the zipper.

Catherine gasped and clapped her hands. "Way to go, girl. You did it!"

"I worked hard for this. Seven weeks of *Inferno*, and every bead of sweat was worth it. Cade's portion control helped, too. It wasn't easy adjusting to smaller meals, but my stomach's learning to live with less."

Her mother stepped into the room, unable to hide the sob that escaped her. She handed Macy a red velvet box that held a pair of sapphire earrings and a matching necklace, providing a contrast to Catherine's rich blue tea-length gown.

Nina took Macy in with a smile. "Let's see. Something old—your dress, passed down from another bride. Something new—your veil. Blue—your jewelry. You just need something borrowed."

She dashed into her closet and returned with a blue silk handkerchief. "Tuck this into your bouquet," she said. "Now you're perfect."

Macy turned to the mirror and barely recognized the woman staring back. Her face was slimmer, her shoulders more defined, her belly flatter. But beneath the makeup, she could still see the weariness in her eyes. She looked like the perfect bride. But inside, cold nerves curled tightly around her ribs.

"Are you ready, Mace? It's just about time." Catherine gathered up Macy's train as they shuffled one by one into the elevator.

They needed two trips to get everyone downstairs. The lobby erupted in cheers as Macy passed through, her dress catching the light, her smile practiced but pale.

The first day of summer was drenched in sunshine, with the first hint of humidity in the air. They rode together in the limo—everyone laughing, talking. Everyone except Macy. She stared out the window, remembering the nights she and Cade had spent in the city, how seamless it had once been. *What comes after today?*

It was a short drive from Fifth Avenue to Central Park. George gently helped Macy out of the limo and into the preparation room, where the photographer waited. The wedding planner greeted her with bouquets and whispered, "Your groom's arrived. He looks heartbreakingly handsome."

The terrace smelled of fresh-cut roses and dewy moss. Sunlight streamed through breaks in the elm canopy, casting golden lace across the stone path. A soft breeze lifted Macy's veil, as if nudging her forward. Piano music drifted through the trees. Birds chirped overhead. The sky was bright and clear, clouds swept back like a painted promise.

Roses framed a beautiful archway where the officiant stood beside Cade and his brother, Sean. Macy stepped forward. Cade reached for her hand, his fingers trembling slightly. She caught the scent of his cologne—woodsy and clean—and noticed a faint line of sweat at his hairline. He looked stunning in his tailored suit, blue eyes shining in the afternoon light.

George placed Macy's hand in Cade's, officially giving her away. A single tear shimmered in her father's eye as he lifted her veil and kissed her cheek before joining Rebecca.

For a half second, Macy wanted to grab his hand and not let go. Not because she didn't love Cade—God help her, she did—but because she missed the version of herself who used to feel safe. Her father's trembling smile carved a hollow in her chest. He thought he was giving her away to a man who would treasure her.

Macy didn't doubt Cade's love for her, but rather than secure, his love made her feel exposed.

Macy scanned the faces of her most beloved. Theo gave her a subtle wink from beside Shane. Nina and Brian stood behind them. Cade's family watched from the other side—Sheryl dabbing her eyes, his father stoic and proud. Diane stood nearby. Talia's absence echoed briefly, but didn't linger.

Everyone smiled back at her as if they all knew a secret she didn't. As if this were the happiest day of her life. Their joy pressed against her, warm and suffocating at the same time.

The officiant smiled warmly. "We are gathered here today in this beautiful place to celebrate the joining of two lives, two hearts, in love."

Macy blinked, trying to focus. The words washed over her like soft rain—pretty, ceremonial, utterly unreal. Deep inside, her doubts from the night before echoed louder than the officiant's words. But surrounded by love, expectation, and sunlight, the doubts felt traitorous. She swallowed them down.

Macy turned back to the officiant just in time to repeat, "I do."

Catherine's eyes caught hers: steady, gentle, and searching. Macy tried to draw strength from that look, but her carefully crafted facade wavered. She shivered like a child stepping off a ledge because everyone told her she had wings.

With the exchange of rings, the officiant declared, "You may now kiss the bride."

Cade didn't wait. He cradled her face and kissed her like no one was watching. The crowd erupted with applause. Macy smiled because the cameras clicked and her family cheered. And because she did believe she loved this man, even when she feared him.

When they finally broke apart, Catherine and Nina surprised them with a toss of birdseed, and the crowd erupted in applause. Macy's body responded—smiling, kissing her brand-new husband, playing the role of the blushing bride.

Cade turned his eyes down to her and stared so he could burn a hole through her. His arms coiled tight around her waist, and he whispered so only she could hear, "*Mine*."

And Macy's world narrowed. The word wrapped around her finger tighter than the ring. It wasn't warm and tender, but possessive. A demand.

Her pulse tripped, a cold thread weaving through her spine. Everyone else saw a romantic whisper. Macy heard a lock clicking shut.

With a sudden gasp, the zipper from her carefully fastened gown burst open, leaving her body as exposed as her soul. Deep inside her, something fragile cracked open. For the first time since Macy Walker met Cade Donovan, she wanted to run and not look back.

What have I done?

Macy's Journey Continues...

If you enjoyed this novel, please consider leaving a review.

Macy's story is far from over…in fact, it is just beginning. Here is a sneak peek of the first chapter of what lies ahead in…

Bound by Vows

SOME PROMISES ARE SACRED. OTHERS ARE SENTENCES. MACY IS ABOUT TO LEARN THE DIFFERENCE.

Chapter One

THE AFTERMATH

They rode in the back of the limo to Brian and Nina Simpson's penthouse on Fifth Avenue. Macy Walker, the newly minted Mrs. Cade Donovan, sat tucked against her new husband and tried to let the morning catch up to her. The beaded skirt of her dress spread carefully across her knees, sunlight glinting off the delicate filigree through the open sunroof. The faintest brush of air against her spine made her instinctively slide her fingers along the zipper, reassuring herself that it still held.

In barely a year, Macy and Cade had met, danced through the briefest of courtships, and eloped in Central Park. On the surface, Macy appeared composed, every inch the blushing bride. Inside, her first flash of *What have I just done?* still echoed, sharp and unsettling. But as the limo turned uptown, she replayed the tenderness of those first months—his charm, his persistence, the way he showered her with love—and at last some of the tension drained from her shoulders. A dull ache remained, traveling from the base of her neck.

Her copper ringlets, swept into an elegant knot at the back of her head, caught the summer light. She allowed a ghost of a smile to curve her lips as she glanced sideways at her new husband.

Her husband.

After wondering if they would make it to this day—and almost pushing it off—it was here. The vows had been spoken, rings exchanged, and now they were on their way to celebrate with family and friends.

This is the fun part, she thought to herself, a slow curve stretching across her lips. We made it through the hard part, and now we can go back to normal.

Across the limo, Catherine Phelps caught Macy's gaze, mischief blazing in her blue eyes. Her auburn bob swung forward as she lunged for the champagne. The royal-blue maid of honor dress she'd chosen echoed Macy's gown but with her own modern twist—tea length, square neckline, and just enough attitude to make it hers.

She pulled the bottle of champagne from the ice bucket and waved it. "I think we've waited long enough for this!"

The cork popped with a satisfying bang, ricocheting off the ceiling. Golden fizz spilled over the neck and splattered the carpet.

"Hey, watch it!" Sean Laurent leaned across the newlyweds to snag the bottle, all swagger and no filter. He tilted it and wiggled his eyebrows, running his tongue theatrically along the neck.

Cade shoved him back, snatching the bottle. "What's the matter with you? Nobody wants to watch you deep-throat champagne. Especially not my bride!"

"Alcohol abuse, brother!" Sean answered cheerfully. "Can't let good bubbly end up making the floor stickier than it already is."

Catherine dissolved into giggles and plucked the bottle away. "Gross, I don't even want to think about that. Just grab some cups before this turns into an X-rated toast. Hey—!"

Macy leaned forward and seized the bottle, fizz tickling her wrist as it ran down her arm. "Who needs cups?" she said, pressing the bottle to her lips.

"Your dress!" Cade barked, louder than the moment called for, and snatched it back. "Let's not get out of hand with the champagne, okay?"

Macy shrank back into the seat, eyes cast down at her shoes. Heat crept up her neck as she shifted her skirt around. She hadn't needed to grab at the bottle. *Why did I do that?*

Sean snickered, clearly entertained, and dug three cups out of the bar. "Relax, big brother." He handed a glass to Macy, another to Catherine, and the third to Cade. He kept the bottle for himself until three sets of eyes pinned him. Rolling his eyes, he emptied the bottle into a fourth cup and raised it.

"To the Donovans," Sean toasted.

Macy raised her glass. Cade's arm settled over her shoulder, warm and heavy. His smile was dazzling, all dimples and easy charm.

"So, am I doing my best man speech here or waiting until we get to the penthouse?" Sean asked as he drained his glass.

"It depends," Catherine said, kicking off her silver stilettos and tucking her feet beneath her skirt. "Just how much will we make our bride and groom blush in front of the rest of the guests?"

Sean's grin sharpened. "How much do you want me to?"

Cade groaned and dropped his head back against the seat. "I don't need a speech, I don't need this dinner. I just want to take my wife home!"

"So impatient!" Catherine exclaimed. "What's the matter, Cade? The schedule not going the way you rehearsed?"

Sean covered his mouth to keep from spraying them with champagne. The driver glanced at them in the rearview mirror and gave a disapproving shake of his head. Catherine clinked her glass against Macy's before sipping, eyes twinkling.

Cade's scowl stiffened into a smile, but Macy felt his arm tighten on her shoulder. "Don't know how I ever got by without your humor, Catherine."

Sean raised his glass in Catherine's direction. "I'm glad to see someone is keeping him on his toes. You had big shoes to fill, but you are a proper heckler."

Cade rounded on Sean, but his voice held a lightness that wasn't there before. "Careful, or I'll tell them about the time you came home so drunk you mistook Sheryl's hair-removing cream for shampoo."

Laughter filled the limo, bright and careless. Macy leaned into Cade, wishing the moment would last. With the vows behind them and Cade getting what he wanted, Macy hoped he could slow down and let her breathe.

Please, she thought. Please let him stay like this.

The limo pulled up in front of the Simpsons' penthouse, and Macy's stomach lurched. Sean tumbled out first, Cade right behind him. Macy pressed a hand to her belly and blew out a deep breath, closing her eyes to steady herself.

"Need another glass?" Catherine asked.

Macy smiled, eyes still closed, and nodded slightly.

"What's wrong?" Cade asked, brow furrowed as he turned back to her.

"I'm okay!" Macy flashed her brightest smile. "Probably just a little car sick from the heat and champagne. I don't want to sour the mood."

Catherine placed a gentle hand on her back. "Why don't you and Sean go ahead? I'll do my maid-of-honorly duty and deliver the bride at her brightest."

"Your job as maid of honor ended at the park," Cade shot back. Macy shrank back into her seat. "I'm her husband now, I will take care of her."

"It's fine," Macy said quickly. "I'll be right up. Just need a minute to collect myself." She smiled again, trying to reassure him.

Cade crouched by the door. "Let me help you."

Sean leaned back in, clapping his brother on the shoulder. "Come on, let her have a moment! If she was going to make a quick getaway, she would've done it already, right?"

He laughed at his own joke. Cade didn't. His mouth twisted into a scowl. "I'm loving the comedy stylings of Catherine and Sean. Maybe you missed your match, here, Catherine," he said without humor.

Catherine handed Macy a glass of water. Some color returned to her cheeks, and she smiled a little more easily. "I'll be up in five minutes, promise."

Cade gave her an uneasy look but nodded and left with Sean.

Catherine slammed the limo door shut. "Okay. What's going on? Don't tell me 'nothing.' I saw your face turn whiter than your dress."

Macy sipped her water and shook her head gently. "Well, I felt queasy thinking about going up to this party, but this is supposed to be the fun part, right? So why do I feel sick to my stomach?"

Catherine tilted her head. "You know how you're fine while you're spinning, but the second you stop—that's when you get dizzy?"

Macy nodded, twisting her fingers into her necklace.

"You've been spinning since that first date last year. Charging straight for this day. And now you've stopped. The ceremony is over, and reality is setting in. You're married. And it's making you dizzy."

They sat in silence, Macy turning the words and twisting her gold chain.

"That makes sense," Macy admitted, though her insides still churned. "This all happened so fast, I haven't had time to breathe. I keep hoping that maybe he can be a little more relaxed, and be the man I fell in love with in the first place."

Catherine squeezed her hand. "I hope you're right, Mace." Her grin turned sly. "We could always 'lose' the marriage license, you know. Make a break for it."

That finally earned a chuckle from Macy. "I'm okay now. Let's go have some cake."

Catherine drained the last of her champagne. "Had to try," she muttered under her breath. She grabbed their bouquets, swept the limo for stray phones and wallets, and followed Macy out.

The doorman stood waiting in his black suit, holding the glass door open. He nodded as they stepped through. "Congratulations," he said as they passed into the marble lobby toward the elevator.

When the doors opened on the penthouse, Macy froze, taking in the scene.

She had seen Brian and Nina's penthouse many times before, but tonight it was unrecognizable. The pale and airy space had become a space fit for royalty. White orchids spilled from mirrored pedestals. A champagne tower gleamed near the picture window, next to an extravagant three-tier cake decorated with impossible precision.

"This..." she whispered, turning to Catherine. "When did she do all of this?"

Her parents rushed forward, hand in hand. "She's here!" George called, his grin stretching wide. He hugged Macy carefully, pressing a kiss to her temple. "You look beautiful, sweetheart. I'm almost afraid to touch you after..."

Macy laughed and looked down at her dress. "It's okay, Dad. Catherine did a good job putting me back together."

Rebecca lingered, her eyes shining as she took her daughter in. "You are radiant," she said softly.

Catherine smiled at their reunion and caught Shane's eye from across the room. "I'll let you all have a moment," she said. She slipped an arm around Shane's waist. He kissed her temple and guided her toward the hors d'oevres.

Nina flounced out from the kitchen with a glass of champagne, flawless in a black sheath dress, loose platinum waves hanging down to her waist. "I put the crew to work as soon as we left earlier. Surprise!"

Cade followed close at Nina's heels and raced to Macy's side, slipping her hand through his arm. "Better now?"

"I think I was just overwhelmed. I'm good now," she said, forcing a warm smile. She turned to Nina. "This is way too much, you didn't need to do all of this for just us."

Nina waved her hand, brushing away the sentiment. "Nonsense. A love like yours deserves a proper flourish." Her smile was cool, eyes darting between them before resting on Cade. "You don't find passion like this every day. Come, take a glass from that pyramid before it gets knocked over!"

Macy squeezed Cade's arm and smiled at him. "Why don't you get us some champagne while I say hello to the rest of our guests?"

"Do you really need another one?" he asked with a grimace. "Wasn't that what caused your episode in the car?"

For a moment, Macy faltered. Alcohol had almost cost her everything two weeks before. She had promised to be more careful. She had to be better. Embarrassment flashed hot in her cheeks as she replayed the bachelorette party, the argument, the look in his eyes when he said she'd humiliated him. Maybe she had pushed too far.

She forced the thought away.

"It's our wedding!" she said, puckering her lower lip and blinking fake tears, making him finally laugh.

"Alright, fine, I can't tell you no to anything today. Just don't use that to your advantage!" He pointed at her and gave her a playful smile before kissing her and setting off for the champagne table.

Ethan slid in almost immediately. He had already ditched his suit coat and tie, shirt unbuttoned almost to the bottom, with a farm-stained white tank top underneath.

"Welcome to the married club, little sister," he said, winking at her. "You clean up almost as good as I do!"

Joy followed behind him, baby Caleb on her hip in a onesie that resembled a tuxedo.

She rolled her eyes at him and reached out to wrap Macy in a hug. "Don't listen to him. You

know I rarely do, and that's why our marriage has lasted!"

Macy threw her head back with laughter, clinging to the brightness of the moment, and reached for the baby. "I see someone here wanted to give me competition for best dressed! And may have just edged me out."

He cooed and wiggled as Joy handed him gently over. George and Rebecca beamed at their grandson, who smiled brightly up at Macy. He put a warm and soft hand on her cheek. Macy's throat tightened unexpectedly. The uncomplicated simplicity of her nephew's love and trust brought a threat of tears to her eyes.

Across the room, Sean elbowed Cade in the ribs. "Hey, you might have some competition over there, brother! And not from the neighbor guy!"

Laughter rippled, but Cade's jaw tightened perceptibly, and he threw back his glass of champagne. He grabbed another for himself and one for Macy and raced back to her. "Your dress, Mace!"

"It's fine," Macy reassured him, shaking her head. "It's already champagne colored, how much worse could it get?"

"But the beads, he could pull those right off. Or what if he spits up?" he warned. He handed her the glass as Sheryl swept in and took the baby.

"I still haven't met this little guy yet!" she said brightly and kissed his cheek. "And now I have another daughter. We couldn't be more thrilled!"

Howard Laurent followed close behind Sheryl and put an arm gently on her waist. "You did great today, son. We couldn't be prouder. And we're so thrilled to welcome you to the family, Macy. You must be the Walkers!"

Macy's arms, still curved from holding the baby, ached from the sudden emptiness.

She laughed lightly. "I think I can handle a little spit-up."

Cade's smile barely faltered. "It's not about that. I don't want anything ruining today."

Macy's stomach dropped. *Ruining.*

She glanced down at her nephew, nestled in Sheryl's arms as she talked to Macy's parents, noticing a faint champagne spot near the hem of her gown. *Maybe he's right. It wouldn't take much for things to spiral. Wasn't once enough of me letting that happen?*

"I'll be more careful," she said softly.

He bent over and kissed the top of her head. "Good girl."

"Central Park, was it? Very... interesting." Diane Donovan announced her presence, rounding the corner with a fresh glass of champagne in her hand. Pearls gleamed at her throat. She wore a navy blue suit with a knee-length skirt. The jacket was double-breasted with gold buttons and appeared to be mismatched by one.

"It was exactly us," Cade said simply.

"It's a beautiful park, and I love the water," Macy added, careful and measured.

"If you say so," Diane answered. "Not that I would know."

"Mom, this isn't the time or the place," Cade said, nostrils flaring. "Don't you think you've had enough of those?" He gestured at the champagne flute.

"One glass won't kill me, will it?" Though the way her eyes glazed, it was clear she hadn't stopped at only one glass. "You're one to talk, though. Aren't there all kinds of warnings about drinking alcohol with all of those medicines you're on?"

Macy's eyes went wide, and she quickly tucked her face behind Cade's shoulder. Conversations quieted by the slightest degree as several eyes tried not to turn their direction.

Cade's body went rigid, and his grip tightened on his flute, threatening to shatter the glass. "What are you accusing me of?"

From across the room, Nina caught the exchange through her conversation with Theo Martinez. She continued her conversation, laughing like he'd just told the best joke she'd ever heard.

Brian quickly put a gentle hand on Diane's shoulder and guided her back toward the kitchen. "Let's keep the attention today on the happy couple, shall we? You know, I think we have some great sparkling cider to go with the cake. Do you want to help me pour it?"

Diane allowed herself to be led, but not before throwing a last look over her shoulder. "Yes, so happy, especially after the bride almost sabo–"

"*Mother!* Not today!*" Cade snapped, cutting her off.

The word rang in Macy's ears. *Sabotage?*

Cade turned back to her, perfect smile already pasted back in place. "She's had too many," he muttered. "She lashes out when she feels ignored, and she feels left out of all the wedding planning."

Macy nodded automatically, mind reeling. "So. First dance?"

"You know I can't dance," Cade shook his head, cheeks still flushed from the exchange with Diane. "We'll just be doing that swaying with each other thing kids do at the high school dances. It's hardly worth stealing everyone's attention for that."

"Aw, but you know how much I love to dance," Macy said, pouting. Then she smirked at him and dragged her fingers up his arm in a playful walk. "Maybe with another champagne I could get you out there?"

"You do want a wedding night, don't you?" he said, wincing.

"My virgin ears!" Sean screamed, suddenly appearing behind their parents. "Nobody wants to hear about that."

"Says the man who was suggestively licking the champagne bottle not even an hour ago!" Catherine called out from the bar.

Laughter carried across the room, and Macy relaxed into Cade's side. She sipped at her champagne as Sean and Cade continued to banter. Sheryl smiled warmly at her and took her hand.

"Can I steal her for a minute?" she asked Cade, who smiled and nodded, giving Macy a gentle squeeze before releasing her to his step-mom.

"I was hoping we could talk about what happened," Sheryl said as she guided Macy away from the louder conversations.

Macy flushed. "Sheryl, I really don't think it's appropriate–"

Sheryl gave her a firm, maternal look. "I know my son isn't always the easiest to get along with. He was heartbroken, thinking history was about to repeat itself again."

A cold pit formed in Macy's stomach. Her breathing grew more rapid as the thought came faster than she could push it away. In the crowded room, on the first day of summer, a chill raced down Macy's spine.

"Sheryl," Macy blinked. "Exactly what do you mean by 'again'?"

Sheryl hesitated, smile faltering before she recovered it. She smoothed Macy's hair and gave her a practiced smile. "Well, you know how many ups and downs he had with Hannah. Every time they almost called it off, of course." Her eyes darted around the room, settling on the cake. "But you're back on track. He's finally happy. That's what matters."

But the words had lodged in Macy's chest. The phrase hung in her mind like a warning bell.

Questions threatened at the back of her throat, insistent, fighting for release. "But..."

Sheryl waved her off before she could formulate her question. "Don't borrow trouble on your wedding day. Let's see if your husband wants to cut that cake, and I bet we can figure out how to get him dancing. What do you say?"

Macy forced a smile and let herself be led towards the cake table. Her pulse beat hot in her throat, and her mind continued to spin. Cade started towards them, smiling at Macy as though she were the meal.

Frantic thoughts continued to swirl in Macy's head as they cut the first piece of cake and fed it to each other.

He fed her gently. Not playfully, no smashing the cake.

A flashbulb popped.

Cade's thumb brushed a crumb from her lip, and for a moment his eyes held hers too long—blue, bright, intent.

The room cheered. Someone clapped. Someone shouted for another kiss.

Macy laughed with them. She smiled like she meant it. She made herself taste the sweetness and let it convince her. Things could be different this time.

Acknowledgments

I started writing my first novel when I was eleven years old. It was set aside for reasons that no longer matter, and life got in the way of it ever finding its way back to me. My world turned upside down in a single moment. I started blogging about the journey to recovery, equal parts to share updates, to organize my thoughts, and because some things, no matter how difficult, should never be forgotten. With a lot of encouragement from my readers, the idea of creative work began to stir again; quiet but persistent.

I knew that if I was going to do this, it would start with Macy. Those who know me well will know why it had to be her. Still, it took a good deal of coaxing from many people to get me from initial character development to making that eleven-year-old girl's dream a reality.

First and foremost, thank you to my husband and best friend, Jon, and our beautiful daughters. This journey came with many late nights and moments of self-doubt, but you never stopped believing in me. (And thank you for the reminder that Mr. King never quit, so neither should I, or he might get angry and appear in my dreams with attack bears.)

One of my closest and most trusted friends became my alpha reader before I even knew what that meant. Thank you to my real-life Catherine for always being there for me, for calling me out when my ideas went way off the rails, and for always giving me the honest truth. Especially when it wasn't what I wanted to hear. You have helped shape this series in more ways than one.

To my friend who was also my first-round editor, thank you for the countless hours spent reviewing my early ramblings to help this story truly shine. Your insights made a world of difference.

My wonderful family, where would I be without you? My parents, my in-laws who embraced me as one of their own from day one, my sister/siblings-in-law, niece, and nephews. I love you all. Thank you doesn't begin to cover it.

There are more people than I could name individually along the way who encouraged me to do this, and who continued cheering me on. You are seen, you are appreciated, and I thank you!

Thank you to Mikael and the team at Warrington Publishing for taking a chance on me and on this series. I am deeply grateful for the opportunity to bring Macy's journey to life.

Finally, thank you to every reader. Everybody knows someone who's walked the same road as Macy. Maybe you've walked it yourself. You deserve to be heard! If reading this book helps even one reader feel like they aren't alone, I will consider Macy's story successful. Her story isn't over yet, and neither is yours. Better days are coming, just never stop moving forward.

About the Author

Kate grew up surrounded by books and often occupied herself with reading. Most summer breaks, she and her sister would enter contests at the library to see who read the most books. They were always each other's strongest competition!

After years of technical documents, maintaining a personal blog, and a lot of encouragement from her peers, she took the leap back into the creative world. Kate always knew if she decided to tell someone's story, it would be Macy's. She enjoys understanding how and why things work, and what makes people tick. That's what is most fascinating about stories such as the ones in The Deception Series.

Kate lives in New York with her husband, daughters, and pets. Her third love, after family and books, is traveling. She and her husband take at least one vacation a year, usually to someplace different, as they are both determined to experience as much of the world through another lens as they can. When she is not working or traveling, Kate enjoys the martial arts, playing hockey, running, and watching Doctor Who.